THE OPPOSITION

A Novel

GUERNICA WORLD EDITIONS 49

THE OPPOSITION

A Novel

Todd Gitlin

GUERNICA
World
EDITIONS
TORONTO—CHICAGO—BUFFALO—LANCASTER (U.K.)
2022

Guernica Founder: Antonio D'Alfonso

Michael Mirolla, general editor
Scott Walker, editor
Interior design: Jill Ronsley, suneditwrite.com
Cover design: Allen Jomoc Jr.

Guernica Editions Inc.
287 Templemead Drive, Hamilton (ON), Canada L8W 2W4
2250 Military Road, Tonawanda, N.Y. 14150-6000 U.S.A.
www.guernicaeditions.com

Distributors:
Independent Publishers Group (IPG)
600 North Pulaski Road, Chicago IL 60624
University of Toronto Press Distribution (UTP)
5201 Dufferin Street, Toronto (ON), Canada M3H 5T8
Gazelle Book Services, White Cross Mills
High Town, Lancaster LA1 4XS U.K.

First edition.

Legal Deposit—First Quarter
Library of Congress Catalog Card Number: 2021951192
Library and Archives Canada Cataloguing in Publication
Title: The opposition / Todd Gitlin.
Names: Gitlin, Todd, author.
Series: Guernica world editions ; 49.
Description: Series statement: Guernica world editions ; 49
Identifiers: Canadiana (print) 20210380446 | Canadiana (ebook)
20210380489 | ISBN 9781771837361 (softcover) | ISBN 9781771837378
(EPUB)
Classification: LCC PS3607.I85 O67 2022 | DDC 813/.6—dc23

"… those times when everything becomes possible again contain all of life as well as death and destruction."
—**Anna Seghers,** *The Seventh Cross*

To Paul Auster

Contents

Prologue

THE PAST IS VAPOR—No sooner have you caught sight of it than it blurs—You're not sure you saw what you saw—But it's still streaming—with a soundtrack—You have to know where to look—under the outfits—under the hairdos—under the oldies—We breathe the residues—They coat us—Sometimes encrust us—thicken our minds—clog us—What memory thinks it remembers is a memory being rewritten as it disbands—Each crust of what we call the past dissolves as more past builds up on top of it—The past is buried—crumbles—decomposes—degenerates into soil—regenerates—does not go to waste—

Beneath the chords of our music, the music we play and that plays us, sounds the continuo—the bass note that doesn't pause—the rumble that's always on the verge of slipping away—never quite gone—lost—found—both—

Our younger selves existed on ground as confusing and solid as our own—just as treacherous, just as uncertain—Our kids say it's worse now—I see why they say that—

As the glacier of time gouged through the limestone—valleys emerged—gullies—cataracts—We thought we were newly hatched but we were latecomers—Our world emerged from water—and from the elders, who were still alive—or still dead—who were themselves latecomers—Everyone, in the end, is a latecomer—

We saw rivers plunging ahead but they changed course—went underground—broke through the surface—We collected instants—We were deep wells of anguish and hope, we were streaks of desire—We longed—met—kissed—loved—said farewell—We were smudges of fear half overcome—straining to make out the music of America the indecipherable—one nation undermined—cruel, unpolished, unfinished—

Straining to start up the music again, to add an nth movement, in a different key—

We flamed up together—in a nation on fire—despite the nation—because of the nation—willful together—confused together—smart together—stupid together—

One of the problems smart people have is they don't know when they're not being smart—

We gambled desire against fear—We improvised—thought ourselves over—rethought—stopped thinking—hallucinated—went for broke—broke—There was never enough time—

So, by fits and starts, we felt, thought, mattered, charged, tumbled and tore apart—We had energy, mass, dimension, momentum, temperature—We were companions—we rejoiced—we collided—waded to the shores of great oceans of pain—imagined a future where we would be young—

The past is over, but nevertheless it moves—

Ann Arbor, Michigan,
June 11, 1963

T HE PRESIDENT'S FACE—EARNEST, EYELIDS drooping, brow lightly furrowed—hovered on-screen. A curled-up American flag stood erect to his right. *As at a school assembly*, thought Terry McKay, who was a little breathless, having just rushed into his house after a meeting nearby.

Valerie Parr lay down her paperback, James Baldwin's *The Fire Next Time*. She was enthralled by Baldwin's statement: "We, the black and the white, deeply need each other here if we are to become a nation." As blonde as a Fifties starlet, she had been smoking French cigarettes all day after emerging from Terry's bedroom.

The TV picture was scratchy and rolled vertically. Terry, half bemused, half irritated, stood up, adjusted the rabbit-ears on top of the set and smacked the cabinet for good measure. The picture stopped rolling. Terry wore chinos and his shoulders were hunched. The picture started rolling again. Terry chuckled and shrugged.

The president sounded somber and determined: "This Nation was founded by men of many nations and backgrounds. It was founded on the principle that all men are created equal, and that the rights of every man are diminished when the rights of one man are threatened."

Valerie watched, transfixed. She had never heard such words from a president of the United States—certainly not from the previous one, Dwight Eisenhower, who had a general's posture and bore the first name of her mother's father.

Kennedy's words also burned straight into Sally Barnes's heart. The words "all men are created equal" were as close to gospel as she knew, having been raised Unitarian-Universalist. "Dear God," the joke went, "if there is a God, please save my soul, if I have one." Inspired by Rita Moreno in *West Side Story*, she wore gold hoop earrings and bright red lipstick.

"Amen," Terry told the room.

The president spoke about "a worldwide struggle to promote and protect the rights of all who wish to be free. And when Americans are sent to Viet-Nam or West Berlin, we do not ask for whites only."

"Well, that's for sure," Melissa Howard said, sitting on a large green cushion, leaning against the wall. She was willowy, soft-spoken, with a touch of the South in her voice. Her skin glistened in a near-darkness illuminated only by the spooky blue glow of the TV.

"How about we get some liquid in here?" Sally Barnes said, standing up. Pointy little commas of dark hair curled behind her ears. Kurt Barsky stared at her form appreciatively. Terry considered her chubby.

"Sorry," Terry said.

"Be right back," said Valerie, tall, lithe, green-eyed, freckled. Her dirty-blonde hair, under a white headband, culminated in an artful flip. She wore a bright green ring bisected by an irregular platinum design on her right middle finger.

"Difficulties over segregation and discrimination exist in every city, in every State of the Union," Kennedy said, "producing in many cities a rising tide of discontent that threatens the public safety."

"Rising!" Melissa echoed.

"Difficulties!" Matt Stackhouse, Jr., said, giggling mirthlessly from the floor, on his back, leaning on his elbows. Furrows traveled across his brow. Deep parentheses curved down around his mouth. He was almost gaunt, like a medieval monk, and starting to lose his hair.

Holding a jug of Red Mountain wine by its glass ring, Valerie returned from the kitchen. Sally accompanied her carrying a tray of four wineglasses, no two alike, but eying the smudges, she turned and quietly walked back into the kitchen. The sound of running water was heard over Kennedy's words: "We are confronted primarily with a moral issue. It is as old as the scriptures and is as clear as the American Constitution. The heart of the question is whether all Americans are to be afforded equal rights and equal opportunities, whether we are going to treat our fellow Americans as we want to be treated."

"Mmm," Melissa said, "talking to white people, which is fine, but is there something you want to tell *me*?"

Sally stared, struck. *There's something I hadn't thought about before.*

"One hundred years of delay have passed since President Lincoln freed the slaves, yet their heirs, their grandsons, are not fully free ... bonds of injustice ... social and economic oppression ..."

"Granddaughters also," Melissa said. Her parents' grandparents were slaves. Her mother's father, born in Anniston, Alabama, moved to Detroit in 1915, got a job tending a machine at Ford River Rouge, and worked himself up to tool-and-die making. Anniston is where a mob firebombed an integrated Greyhound bus in 1961, just before Melissa moved to Ann Arbor.

"I mean really, can we give the guy a chance?" Valerie said plaintively, though her voice remained rich in timbre. "He's the president of the whole country. He's got all these prejudiced white people holding him back. He can't just—"

"Is it too much to ask that the president do the right thing simply because it's right?" Matt asked. "Whatever objections the scum of the earth may have? What's the point of being president?"

Looks of approval crossed the room. Murmurs accelerated as Kennedy went on: "Redress is sought in the streets ... protests which create tensions and threaten violence and threaten lives."

"*Who* threatens lives?" Melissa wanted to know. "We face, therefore, a moral crisis ..."

"Thank you," said Terry.

Unbidden, the Apostles' Creed came into Matt's mind. He was a lapsed Baptist. His father was a minister. Young Matt knew it was pretentious to think of civil rights workers as Apostles, but his free association was what it was, free.

"It cannot be met by repressive police action," Kennedy said.

"Not bad," said Terry.

"It cannot be left to increased demonstrations in the streets."

"Can't have that!" said Matt.

"Streets is how we got here," said Melissa.

"It is not enough to pin the blame on others, to say this is a problem of one section of the country or another.... A great change is at hand, and our task, our obligation, is to make that revolution, that change, peaceful and constructive for all."

"Sounds good to me," said Matt.

Valerie sipped Red Mountain and said softly that it must be terribly hard to be president of the United States.

"Lots of people have hard lives," Kurt said.

Valerie insisted that Kennedy's coolness under fire was admirable. After all, he decided not to blow up the world when Khrushchev moved missiles into Cuba last year. Yesterday, Kennedy said he wanted to halt the arms race, said he was starting talks on a test ban treaty, said the United States would stop exploding nuclear bombs in the atmosphere.

For several hours this afternoon, Valerie, sprawled on a beanbag chair, and Terry's roommate Kurt, in a butterfly canvas chair, had listened to Bob Dylan's new song, "A Hard Rain's a-Gonna Fall," trying to puzzle out the lyrics, convinced they must have something to do with the missile crisis. To Valerie, math-major Kurt seemed like an odd and interesting choice of roommate for Terry. Having walked Woolworth's picket lines in support of the Southern sit-ins, Kurt had broken out of his mathematical cage and enrolled in a political philosophy course taught by a German émigré who spoke with a gravitas apparently born of personal acquaintance with evil. There Kurt met Terry McKay, the leader of the Ann Arbor chapter of Friends of SNCC—SNCC being the Student Nonviolent Coordinating Committee—who needed a new roommate to share his two-story, chalky-grey clapboard house near campus. It was sort of a clubhouse for "zealots," Terry's word of praise for people who wanted to change the world. Terry admired Kurt's mind even if he didn't understand why Kurt was taken with game theory or Nietzsche. Kurt, who disliked dorm life and its tedious late-night poker games, moved in.

Valerie idly wondered whether she would catch Kurt's eye—she was charmed by his Jewish intensity—but tonight he seemed more interested in Sally, his eyes grazing down her body. *I wonder if she notices*, Valerie thought.

Matt said that the president gave the impression of a man who needed to be dragged into doing what he knew was the right thing.

"Vote for me, I can be dragged," said Kurt.

Sally was surprised by his moment of harshness. "Come on, Kurt, keep an open mind. People can learn," Sally said. "If they don't, we're sunk. Because there aren't enough of us."

"We're on our way," Terry said.

"Something else you do well, Mr. McKay," said Valerie to Terry in bed afterwards.

"Thank you," Terry said, examining her ring.

"Thank you. It was a gift." She paused. "Not from a man."

"Uh-huh," Terry said, inspecting the ceiling.

"Jade," she added. "Can I ask you a question?"

"You just did." He chuckled, straight-faced.

"Ha-ha. No, seriously."

"Seriously."

"Do you ever just lie back and *feel*?"

"You mean like this?" He cupped her breast.

"I don't mean *cop* a feel. I mean feel."

"Oh, you'd be surprised."

She waited. "I have another question."

"Shoot."

"Am I one of your adventures?"

Terry McKay widened his eyes and inspected the ceiling. "Do you want to be?"

"One of your *little* adventures?" Her fingers played a little riff on the back of her hand.

"Sure."

He turned his pale blue eyes to her, that portable sky he carried around with him. "Are you sure? The important thing is not what you want to want, but what you really want."

"I like this line from a Roethke poem," she said, and quoted: "I learn by going where I have to go."

The next morning smashed into them with two sharp knocks at the bedroom door, and Melissa—shoeless, in a plain pink terrycloth bathrobe—charged in. "Y'all decent?"

"Yah," said Terry, yanked awake. "What—?"

"Medgar Evers." The name came out a scream. *Evers, ever, forever. Deadgar.*

The radio in the next room was now faintly audible—the letters N-double-A-C-P and the word Mississippi. "Oh no," Valerie said. "*Stop!*"

Melissa's face was a smudge of tears. "They killed him!"

Terry sprang out of bed in his underpants and pulled on his chinos, spitting out the word "Mississippi" as if it were a whole sentence complete with a subject and verb.

"Beautiful Medgar Evers?" Valerie disbelieved but believed.

"In front of his kids! His *kids* watched him bleed to death!"

Mississippi was where Melissa intended to spend the summer working with hard-charging SNCC. At a Friends of SNCC conference in February, she strode up to Julian Bond—the elegant, creamy-skinned, high-cheekboned, dimpled young man in charge of SNCC's communications—and volunteered for summer work, anything useful. You could have knocked her over when he said right back in his mellifluous baritone, "Why, Melissa, we *always* need fresh eyes," and she wondered what else he saw in her eyes besides freshness, but never mind, she was beyond thrilled that *Julian Bond* said that her eyes were the right kind of fresh for SNCC.

They arranged over the phone that she would stop off in the notorious town of Greenwood, in the Mississippi Delta, where she'd scout out the scene, get a sense of life on the front lines, and then spend July and August working in the Atlanta office. Julian and his colleague, a white girl named Mary King, a minister's daughter, would show her the ropes—take calls from the far-flung field secretaries, call up reporters, compile statements and eyewitness reports of demonstrations, arrests and beatings, write press releases and reports that SNCC would circulate to college newspapers throughout the North.

To qualify for the pittance that she would earn, Melissa had to be vetted by a friendly psychologist on campus, making sure she was level-headed enough to keep steady while all hell was breaking loose around her, because civil rights workers and plain folks who worked with them—not to mention plain folks thought to be uppity by some white thug with a gun—went around with bull's-eyes painted on their backs, just about. She had to gather recommendations from friendly professors, show how down-to-earth she was, brag about how she kept the books for Friends of SNCC in Ann Arbor.

Melissa told her mother a white lie—funny phrase!—that she was going to work in the library at Morehouse College in Atlanta, a paying job in "the city too busy to hate," as the white Establishment called it, although it was not clear that Negroes thought of it that way. Her librarian mother persuaded her high school history teacher father that spending the summer at Morehouse would be educational.

Greenwood, Mississippi, 1963

THREE WEEKS LATER IN Greenwood, a tall, dark-complected, long-jawed young man with oversized black horn-rimmed glasses and an alert look walked up as Melissa stepped carefully down from the back of the bus, the last passenger out. In bygone days, her mother taught her to tell herself that Jesus loves her. Well, she'd made it to Mississippi intact. Jesus must have liked her at least.

I know some serious people up north, she thought, *but this fellow looks like one of Camus's plague survivors,* to speak of the paperback she had been reading during most of her two-hour ride from Memphis. *I'm in Mississippi now.*

"Miss Howard?"

The young man wore a crisply ironed, short-sleeved white shirt, and his eyes worried. He blinked and donated an ungainly smile, then another one, as if unsure that the first one had registered.

"That's me. Melissa will do fine. You must be James Turnbull." His handshake was formal and firm, his smile more a shadow than a forecast. His glasses brought out his cheekbones and the narrowness of his jaw. Up close she saw the sweat stains at his armpits.

"James Turnbull, yes. Welcome to Greenwood."

Greenwood, the sinister legend, looked like a plain town in the Delta, dry as doom, one hundred miles north of Jackson. Greenwood, where Medgar Evers was shot in the back three weeks ago.

James took her suitcase and led her into the Mississippi furnace, which smacked her upside the head and scorched her all up and down her lungs. In the overwhelming light, the shadows were sharp as daggers. She rummaged in her purse for her sunglasses. Even behind the glasses she had to squint.

"I'm not gonna lie to you and tell you you'll get used to it. I've lived around here all my life and I ain't got used to it. Tell you, July goin' to be a burner." He brightened, like the joke was on both of them, reminding her, with his dialect, of her lawyer uncle, her mother's older brother, though her uncle didn't talk countrified anymore.

Across the baking street, a gaunt white man with a leathery face, wearing a straw hat and suspenders—arms crossed, shoulders sloped—squinted at them and drew a bead with his bullet eyes. When Melissa couldn't help glancing his way again, she felt the blast of the full-blown flame in his stare. It was as if hatred were the man's sixth sense.

"James," she said, when they had turned and started down the sidewalk, "you see that man over there, staring at us?"

"Oh yes," James chuckled. "Surely do."

"Do you know him?"

"I cain't say as I do, but I can guess. He's one o' them guys who thinks that God wanted the white man to have everything. He's having trouble getting used to that not being true."

Her thin cotton dress was already drenched. Unforgiving sunlight poured over her. The pavement radiated heat that merged with the heat from on high. Their steps down the sidewalk kicked up little puffs of dust. Even the dust smelled burnt. Nobody had told her about the dust.

"I know that the headquarters of the White Citizens' Council is here," Melissa said, eager to show she had done her homework.

"That's so, but—" his smile was wry "—that guy is more the Klan type."

"Oh."

"Yeah, white trash. You know, here folks say the law of the Klan is the law of the land."

They walked silently.

"I don't know if I should be tellin' you this," James went on, "but you'll find out soon enough. We're countin' on you to remind Julian and them in Atlanta what's goin' on here. I mean, they know, but they're overloaded, they got staff callin' in from all over the state about this, that, and the other, so they have a tendency to forget about us."

The clouds were like pools of white smoke. A lyric came to her mind: "We are not afraid." Melissa's mouth felt like paper. She cleared her throat. "I've read about Greenwood."

Oh my, had she read about Greenwood. She knew it was the county seat of Leflore County, where two out of three people were Black, but Black people made up only 1.2 percent of the registered voters. She'd given talks about the place though she'd never set foot there till now. For so long she had been gobbling up the bulletins that Julian Bond mailed from Atlanta, and then relaying stories of the Delta at Friends of SNCC meetings, it was almost as if she had actually been there before, though goodness knows, one thing she never heard about was the feeling of being dumped into boiling air.

She knew that when SNCC opened its office last summer—it was the night after James Turnbull convinced four Black folks to brave their way into the registrar's office—he got a call from a man who, declaring that he was from the Citizens' Council, said: "If you take anybody else up to register you'll never leave Greenwood alive." She knew that James Turnbull went back the next day with two more folks; and that the registrar called the police; and that, some days later, three white men jumped James and beat him. SNCC sent two more organizers. The police sent dogs.

She knew that James held mass meetings in the First Christian Church, where people stood up to testify and commenced to sing freedom songs and rejoiced that they were on their way to freedom land, and people asked for more meetings so they could get together and sing some more.

She knew that James and the others opened an office and taught classes to train folks, though most of the folks who said they would register didn't, they had second thoughts, and one night a police car drove up in front of the office—James and the others watching from the second-floor window—and just sat there, and when it drove off, another car showed up, bunch of white men piled out, eight of them, and took their sweet time milling around on the street, out front, showing off their chains, ropes, pipes, bricks, rifles, shotguns—folks couldn't agree afterward just what-all they were carrying—until when they were good and ready they charged upstairs, and the organizers did not stick around to converse about what exactly these white men had in mind, but jumped out the bathroom window, crawled onto an adjacent roof, looked down and saw more armed white men arriving, whereupon the organizers leaped to another roof and scrambled down a TV antenna to get away, after which the whites ransacked the office.

She knew those stories backwards and forwards, but she had also told audiences not to dwell on the scary things but look how much energy had been ignited, how the organizers had cracked the fear, broken its back, and how folks were, for the first time in their lives, showing up at the courthouse to register come hell, high water, or the Klan.

She knew that the white power structure had not taken this impertinence lying down. She knew that last winter, the County Board of Supervisors cut off their food—cut them off, thousands of them, from surplus milk and such. Melissa had never been hungry but she now heard a lot about hunger—American hunger! They had no wood, though winter in the Delta was cold enough to freeze your pardon-my-French off.

She knew that the movement was not defenseless, so when a call went out to Friends of SNCC, they collected tons of food and clothes and medicines and headed south, one result being that when a couple of students drove a truck from Michigan State during Christmas week to one Delta town, they got arrested for possession of narcotics, which were nothing but aspirin and vitamins, all confiscated, and the students were sent to jail for eleven days, whereupon Harry Belafonte headlined a fund-raiser at Carnegie Hall, and Dick Gregory chartered a plane to bring down seven tons of food, and the food kept coming, even if some of the local clergymen were afraid to let the organizers passing it out come into their churches.

She knew that Medgar Evers came up from Jackson to support SNCC's campaign and join in the singing.

She knew that when whites showed up at the courthouse to register, they were asked to copy and interpret a section of the Mississippi Constitution that read: "All elections by the people shall be by ballot," whereas Blacks might be asked to interpret a section that consisted of two hundred fifty-six words. For months she had carried around in her purse the text of Article 7, Section 182, typed out on a slip of paper, and read it aloud:

> *The power to tax corporations and their property shall never be surrendered or abridged by any contract or grant to which the state or any political subdivision thereof may be a party, except that the Legislature may grant exemption from taxation in the encouragement of manufactures and other new enterprises of public utility extending for a period of not exceeding ten (10) years on each such enterprise hereafter constructed, and may grant exemptions not exceeding ten (10) years on each addition thereto or expansion thereof, and may grant exemptions not exceeding ten (10) years on future additions to or expansions of existing manufactures and other enterprises of public utility.*

She knew that SNCC had been teaching Negroes about the Constitution of the State of Mississippi, which is a whole lot more civics education than white folks got.

James Turnbull wiped sweat away from his eyes with a handkerchief and shifted Melissa's suitcase to his left hand. They crossed the tracks, and the lawns gave way to scrub and bare patches of dirt. "This is why they call it the wrong side of the tracks," he said.

Melissa stifled a giggle, not knowing whether it was proper to laugh more fully. She patted her brow with her handkerchief, and noted the stain.

In front of a red brick funeral home, James paused and said evenly: "You know, right down here is where the body of Emmett Till lay when they brought him in, his face all mashed up."

"I remember the pictures." *We are not afraid. Oh yes, we are.* "I'm still trying to forget them."

"I'm not tryin' a scare you. Just want to make sure you see all the tourist attractions. Land o' cotton, you know."

"Dixie" flooded into her mind, all those stupid words she had refused to sing during junior high school assemblies. "I wish I was in the land of cotton/Old times there are not forgotten—" Not forgotten, right. She figured that what the song meant by *Look away* is: *Mind your own business.*

She glanced at James but his smile, if any, had vanished. "Actually, things is better than they used to be."

The line that poured into her mind came not from the Old Confederacy but from the current struggle: "*We'll never turn back.*" Could she learn to mean it when she sang it? "I'm really glad to hear that," Melissa said, permitting herself a laugh.

"No, really. Folks register now. Nobody's shot at us for months— Well, hi there, little Victoria!" James waved at two Black girls, maybe eight years old, barefoot, who had hopped around the corner. "Hi, Becky!"

"Hi, Mr. James," said Becky.

"This here's Melissa," James said. "She come to work with us."

"Thank you, Miss—Miss Me-liss-a," said Victoria.

"Cute," Melissa said when the girls had hopped on by.

"Just one thing," James resumed. "Look out for cars that ain't got no license plates. It's like a phone call where nobody's at the other end of the line. Hang up." They trudged along, sweating. "There's been progress," he said drily. "See, there was a time when they weren't afraid to *show* their license plates and the hell with it if anybody saw 'em. Now they have to hide."

She wondered if phlegmatic strength could be learned. On this side of the tracks, there were not many cars, but the ones there were did carry license plates.

"I'm guessing you're wondering what you're doing here," James said. "If I were you, I'd wonder. But I was born and raised up right nearby."

"No, I'm fine, I know why I'm here. My people came from Alabama."

"And we're very glad to have you."

Now the automobiles were fewer, rustier, more bruised, and the sidewalks had given out, as if they plain surrendered. The electrical wires overhead thinned out and they passed into streets of unfinished-looking wood-frame houses, longer than wide, some barely painted gray, or a grayish white. Many had tin roofs. Propped up on little concrete stanchions, they appeared all the more tentative, as if only a shove away from collapse. Even with porches they looked unfinished. Dogs pattered by. All the faces were black: girls jumping rope, boys tossing balls, women pinning clean wash on clotheslines.

Kicking up dust clouds, little twisters, the two of them walked a couple more blocks. James pointed out the red brick white-trimmed church, solid and modest, where the food and clothes and medicines had been passed out last winter. Another station of the cross. Abandoned washing machines and freezers stood by like ruins. James pointed down an alley, said that's where the bootlegger lives—good man to know, an organizer, like the neighborhood mayor, knows everybody. On the next block, he nodded at a tarpaper shack, said that's where Mrs. Decatur lives, she reads and writes folks' mail for them, which makes her, too, an organizer. He pointed out two boarded-up windows, told her that the man who lived in that house, name of Simmons, got home one night from a mass meeting and the next thing he knew, a shotgun blast shattered his downstairs window and another one blew apart the window of his niece's bedroom upstairs.

Melissa had never seen such hurt looking houses.

"'Case you're wonderin', that's not why they call these shotgun houses," James said. "That's 'cause they just go straight back, so if somebody *did* shoot through the parlor, the shot would go all the way straight through. But now—" chuckling at what he knew was a lame joke he'd told too many times before "—they have another reason to call it that." He paused. "'Course now, next mass meeting after that, Mr. Simmons was up all night in front of the church with a shotgun in his lap. Keepin' things nonviolent."

So that's the way it is, Melissa thought. *And why not?*

They headed toward a house coated with peeling off-white paint. James led Melissa up three rickety wooden steps onto a porch where ladder-back chairs stood on either side of the door and a straw broom leaned against the wall—*like a shotgun,* she thought. Melissa patted more sweat off her face, for the salt had started to sting her eyes.

"This one here is where you'll be stayin'," James said and knocked on the door. "Ida Mae's a beautician. Keep you beautiful. Not that you need any help. Anyway, she'll take good care of you."

A fleshy dark mountain of a wide-eyed woman in a shapeless polka-dotted house dress, wearing flip-flops and showing ankles as thick as young cypresses, opened the door and gushed: "You must be Miss Melissa. Now, don't just stand there starin', girl. Come on in for a hug. You come a long way." Her cheeks were big and round. Her smile was a lamp. She enveloped Melissa in an all-around embrace.

"I am so glad to see you. We all are. You make yourself at home." She led Melissa to the kitchen where, across from a wood-burning iron stove, a rickety-looking wood table stood, with four arthritic chairs. A small fan on the floor. On the wall, white Jesus with long blond hair. "You must be hungry."

That was what Melissa's Aunt Dovie always told her as soon as Melissa crossed her threshold. Ida Mae was heavier set, and both women lumbered. "Well, I *could* use a bite."

"And thirsty, too, if I'm not mistaken. Y'all sit down right here." Ida Mae lugged herself to the stove, where on one back burner stood a saucepan of greens, on the other a frying pan full of sliced, browned potatoes. From the oven, she drew a loaf of corn bread. She rested it on the potatoes and carried the whole meal to the table. Melissa sat carefully, so as not to disturb her chair. Ida Mae went to the sink, which had a single faucet, and brought back two small glasses of water. There was a pleasant smell that Melissa couldn't identify—maybe the corn bread.

"James?"

"I'll trouble you for a glass of water, too, Ida Mae, but as for anything to eat, I've got to move on. Tomorrow's a big day. So I'm gonna leave you here, Melissa, in good hands. I'll be back in the mornin'. You rest up."

Melissa scraped her plate clean and polished off three glasses of water. Ida Mae turned her sparkling black eyes on her: "Are you ready for some more greens and corn bread? Some beans? No? How 'bout some sweet potato pie? Fresh." Ida Mae did not look like the kind of woman who skimped on corn bread or beans or sweet potato pie. Melissa said no thanks, she was just fine as she was. She was still fascinated by Ida Mae's resemblance to her aunt—her favorite aunt, as it happened—but her aunt would never have greeted a guest in flip-flops, and her house dresses were more form-fitting.

"You know who that young man *is*?" asked Ida Mae when James was well gone. "He is a blessing, let me tell you, a blessing. You know, he set up that office all by hisself?"

"I didn't know."

"Yeah, well, lot of times folks is slow to step up. Takes a seriously brave man, you know, to pump up a less brave man to be braver the next time, you know what I'm sayin'? So pretty soon the night riders set a fire right by the office, which it did burn down the garage next door, and the dry cleaner, and the café, and the club, but they missed the office, don't know how they did, but they did. You sure you had enough to eat?"

"Thank you, Ida Mae, I'm fine." *This woman wants to be everyone's mama. Maybe she is.* "But please go on."

"Well, so there was a mass meeting that night, people was *angry*, oh my, you coulda started the *next* fire with all that anger, and James got up to speak, and he just flat called it 'arson,' and the *po*-lice came and arrested him for 'issuin' statements calculated to breach the peace,' can you believe it? He was already arrested six times in Greenwood for he'pin' the people and this was number seven, and if that wasn't enough, the sheriff, he spat in James's face."

"Oh Lord." *Dovie would never have sounded so angry and militant. Not in Melissa's hearing, anyway.*

"Yes he did. Straight next to his right eye, and spit jes' drippin' down his cheek. James jes' stood there. Jes' stood there. Really, he turned the other cheek! Well, let me tell you. They put him on trial, and we all showed up at City Hall, nobody ever saw anythin' like it, all packed in the hallway, like bolls o' cotton, and some folks was even drinkin' from the white water fountain, like to give the guards heart attacks. Oh my."

Actual Christians. Christians like *Christ's* Christians. Melissa could hardly breathe.

"So James was sentenced to six months in jail and a five hundred dollar fine, and the judge said he'd suspend the sentence and cut the fine in half if James would stop all this business of reddish the voters, and agree to leave Mississippi for good. And you know what James said?"

Melissa knew from SNCC mailings that "reddish" was how the local folks said "register." "What did he say, Ida Mae?"

"He said, 'Judge, I ain't gonna do that.' That's jes' what he said. So the NAACP put up his bond—that was Medgar Evers' doin'— and that night came another mass meetin', and a whole lot of singin' like you never heard singin' before, it jes' about blew the roof off, and the next day, *more than two hundred folks* went to the courthouse. To reddish. Oh, Lord."

"You folks are so brave," Melissa said, feeling dumb. There's another shade of brave to grow up Negro in Detroit, but it's a pale shade.

"It's one step after another, that's all. You knock on doors. You knock on more doors. You avoid the back roads, you don't go around alone, and you look real close when a car passes by." Her face brightened. "And I have to tell you, Melissa, you come at a good time. Tomorrow we're gonna have us a concert!"

"Oh, that's nice."

"It's special, all right, we're all goin' out to Silas McGhee's farm in the mornin' and we're gonna have us a hootenanny, they call it, sing all day long—"

"That sounds wonderful!"

"—and that ain't all, that fella from up North's gonna be here, the one with the banjo, skinny white fella, what's his name—"

"You don't mean—"

"—Pete Seeger, that's it, Pete Seeger's gonna be here in the morning, and a bunch of 'em!"

Melissa slept poorly in the lumpy bed, with only a single sheet over her and none below. She woke up sticky. She could see and hear swarms of mosquitoes jammed up against the closed window right next to the bed. Worst of all, much worse, a buzzing, whining noise came up like a storm, loud as a call to the Day of Judgment, a screech, uninterrupted, for half a minute, a minute, tailing off, coming back—must be a billion freaky insects droning out there, and there's nothing to do but wait them out. A pallid light was already up when sleep won the day.

But not for long. About eight in the morning, James pulled up in a white car that featured, on the front door, the SNCC emblem: a black hand shaking a white hand. *You might just as well put up a sign that says, "String us up,"* Melissa thought. *But that's how you crack the fear, I guess.* Melissa went out to greet him.

James leaned out the window, said it was going to be even more blistering hot today, crazy hot, people were going to fall over if the concert started in the morning, which was the plan, so the organizers decided to wait till twilight, which seemed sensible to Melissa, and she spent the day listening to Ida Mae, in her housedress, tell stories—oh, how this woman loved to tell stories—and baking more corn bread and sweeping up. She would not let Melissa help.

"Oh Lord, these are the *good* days, you may not believe it, but it's true, 'cause they're scared of us now. Yeah, we're scared of them, but they're scared of us too. Let me tell you. So it was back in Febr'ary, two of the SNCC boys and this Randolph Blackwell fellow, he's a college professor workin' with them, you know, and he went there and parked outside the office, and he saw a car without license plates parked in front of the café, a big ol' white Buick, three white men inside, just settin' there, one o'clock in the afternoon. Every hour he kept lookin'. Two o'clock in the afternoon, those three men was still there in the car, settin'. Four, five, six. Still there. Around six, sun was settin', they switched on their lights, but they was still settin' there at seven, eight, nine. Now Blackwell, he went downstairs and got into his car, and the Buick came back around behind him. So he drove back to the office and told the folks to close up for the night and be careful. He got back in his car with Bob Moses and Jimmy Travis, two other SNCC workers, you know. Jimmy a live wire kind of boy and Bob so quiet and serious, you always want to hush up and listen to him, and they went to a gas station and put gas in the car and sat and ate sandwiches. The white Buick come circlin' around. They headed out on the main highway toward Greenville, to the freedom house, where they were stayin', with the Buick behind 'em. They was all three in the front seat, Jimmy drivin', Bob next to him, Blackwell by the window. And when the traffic thinned out, the Buick pulled up alongside and opened fire, got off thirteen rounds, hit Jimmy, one shot nicked his shoulder but another one went right into his neck—" Ida Mae pointed—"and Jimmy fell over, but Bob, who was settin' next to him, he wasn't hit, nor Blackwell neither, Bob scrunched over and grabbed the wheel and stopped the car by the side of the road while the Buick peeled out, you know, and took off. Bob found somebody who told him there was a hospital not too far away, where they'd be willing to treat a civil rights worker, 'cause quite a few wouldn't, so he rushed Jimmy over there, where they found a bullet behind his spine, and they dug it out."

Ida Mae had gone into a kind of trance. "A miracle, you know. They say they is no miracles but I know different and I bet you do too. The Lord watches over Jimmy Travis and Bob Moses—you think he's called Moses by accident? Ain't no accident, no ma'am. Don' you believe it."

Melissa didn't know what to believe.

"And you know what the mayor said? He said that SNCC shoots at its own workers to get into the papers. Can you believe that?"

Later Melissa told herself that nobody would live here if they hadn't been dragged here in chains, unless they were the ones dragging the other folks in chains.

Came late afternoon and James returned in a beat-up pickup truck with a rumbling muffler, Melissa realizing that SNCC didn't have a whole lot of money to make repairs, so if the cracked muffler sent the police a message that civil rights workers were coming along, well, what choice was there? Ida Mae under a big straw hat shook like a jelly mountain climbing into the passenger seat. She carried another straw hat for Melissa. They stopped to pick up three more folks here, four more there, farm hands, but also some ladies in Sunday dresses, heading out to the McGhee farm, out by the cotton. The insects took to shrieking again, but it was just mood music now.

A few dozen Negroes were waiting in the field, some of them standing, some sitting under umbrellas, sometimes two sharing, women in flowered dresses, the only flowers in sight. In the farmhouse yard some folks dangled their feet from the side of a flatbed truck. Three microphones were planted in the dirt in front of the truck, which carried a generator, and a young white fellow took pictures and later a car of white folks with TV cameras showed up, and *Oh my God*, Melissa said to herself, *may I die and go to heaven right here and right now,* there was *Pete Seeger,* in laced-up boots, all uplifted and banjo-ready, keeper of the faith, with his reedy hallelujah voice, leading them in "Keep Your Eyes on the Prize" and "Oh Freedom." Pete Seeger whose records sounded the way her soul wanted to sound on a good day. Pete putting his whole weight—not that there was much of that—into his guitar strum and once more, "We Shall Overcome." She was so excited that the names of the other singers didn't register with her: the short, stout Negro about Melissa's size from a group called the Freedom Singers who came from Atlanta, and a skinny white kid in a blue work shirt, who smoked a lot. Pete who roused whole auditoriums to sing along by the thousands and take the overcoming out onto the street, hoisted everyone onto their feet, even old folks with canes pushing themselves up to sing, "We'll walk hand in hand …"—Pete Seeger, the man of the big strumming heartbeat and elation under pressure, here in a cotton field on the outskirts of Greenwood, Mississippi.

Pete Seeger was joined by another white fellow about his age, beefier, with a friendly round face, maybe Jewish, and Melissa heard the gospel lyrics well up, as if from the bottom of her mind:

> *Paul and Silas bound in jail*
> *ain't no money for to go their bail*
> *Keep your eyes on the prize, hold on*

She was singing along as the sun dragged down.

Pete introduced the skinny kid in the work shirt, who had a lot of dark curly hair and also wore boots and jeans and looked nervous, Bob something, she didn't catch his last name, and his voice came from way back in his nose, how *strange,* he started singing a song about *Medgar Evers,* how he was killed by "a bullet from the back of a bush," but the man who fired it was not to blame because "he's only a pawn in their game." Melissa was not convinced that the killer was only a pawn in the politicians' game, that he was only "a dog on a chain," but it was a noble thought even if overblown. Ida Mae told her later that the man charged with killing Medgar Evers was from Greenwood, he was a salesman, not exactly a poor man, just a bitter, hateful murderer, like the glowering man across the street from the bus station, who was not too busy to hate, because hate *was* his business.

The skinny kid hung a funny metal contraption around his neck, which held a harmonica, and he was howling and ripping along through a bunch of songs in an accent that sounded like nowhere or everywhere. Maybe he was from Missouri or someplace like that, with a twang, he looked like he might be Jewish, but he was not from New Yawk, like some of the kids she'd gotten to know in Friends of SNCC. It was wonderful the way so many Jewish people stepped up and returned the favor to Black people who, after all, identified with Moses and the slaves God escorted out of Pharaoh's Egypt. It was a beautiful thing. Applause rippled across the yard and way down across the cotton field under the gasping sun.

Later the SNCC workers were hanging around in front of the SNCC office with Pete and Bob and the Freedom Singers, sitting on the steps, drinking Coke and beer, eating some fine ribs, feeling *accomplished,* and Melissa could see Bob regard her out of the corner of his eye. He looked sweet, maybe a bit sly, a bit playful—hard to tell—and he held up a cigarette as an offering and approached her. Now that Greenwood had crashed in on her, and a bad night, and the insects, and all the running around to prepare for the concert, she felt depleted but gave him a big smile, meaning it, and saying she really liked the song about Medgar Evers, and she was so impressed that he wrote it so fast, Medgar Evers being dead less than a month, but no thanks, she didn't smoke.

She thought he looked a little hurt, surveying her up and down. Maybe he didn't understand how shy she was. A flush came over her, was she blushing, she looked down, and he watched her for a long time, and picked out some notes on his guitar, and said, "You know, I think I might write a song about you," and she said,

"Really?" and he said, "Of course, I'd have to spend some actual time with you, get to know you."

"Uh-huh" came out of her mouth, long and drawn-out.

He said, "I don't even know your name."

"Melissa. Melissa Howard."

"That's a pretty name. Melissa."

"Thank you."

"Thank you, *Bob*."

"No, *you're* Bob."

"That's true. I am. You're a funny girl."

"Thank you, I try to be. How long you going to be here in Greenwood, Bob?"

"Mmm, I got to fly back to New York in the morning," he said. "It's a sad thing. But that leaves tonight."

"Yes, it does."

He was very sweet but somehow a little *imposing*, and she was very, very tired.

When James came up and said he was ready to take her back to Ida Mae's if she was ready to go, she felt some complicated kind of relief, and as she walked off with James she looked back and saw that Bob had turned to a blonde girl wearing a checked blouse and a bright blue headband—so pretty she looked like a goddess—and was offering her a cigarette.

Ann Arbor, Summer 1963

MELISSA WROTE TO SALLY Barnes that night, and then again every few days, Sally back in Ann Arbor saving up for the coming year by waitressing, acutely aware of the hundreds of miles that separated her from Greenwood, but needing to know what life felt like down there. It strengthened Melissa's resolve to put down on paper what she experienced. Descriptions were less fearsome than wordless terrors. *We are not afraid.* To feel useful, and with Melissa's enthusiastic approval, Sally typed out her letters onto mimeograph stencils and circulated them to the local Friends of SNCC, which made Sally feel less ashamed for staying North, even though she knew perfectly well that her reason was financial need, not cowardice.

On Saturday mornings, Sally and Valerie audited a summer school class called "Poetry by Women." First up, Emily Dickinson, the fearless and shrewd angel of paradox. It was comforting to witness Emily somehow creating her astonishing voice, not having been born knowing how to make her days strange and marvelous. Dowdy Professor Korn, her straight black hair parted, bun in back, like a nineteenth-century schoolmarm, wore a white smock with big sewn-on pockets (like Emily, she explained, who scribbled down scraps during her daily rounds and pocketed them for later use), and clumped back and forth in her plain black shoes in front of the blackboard dashing off Emily's elusive lines by heart and instructing the students to take heart from their bafflement.

From St. Emily they whiplashed over to the high-spirited melancholy romantic Edna St. Vincent Millay, whose poems struck most of the students as way too pretty, and then veered over to Sylvia Plath, who cast a surprising spell on sunny Valerie but unnerved Sally, who found her altogether too puritan and self-punitive, wondering why a blonde Californian wearing a no-doubt pricey ring would seek refuge in New England harshness. Speaking of self-punitive, when Professor Korn migrated over to Anne Sexton, Sally was repelled by Sexton's preening, her sharp-edged poems outdoing Plath's in their capacity to scrape nerves, squeaking like chalk held at the wrong angle. How come Sexton didn't realize that she felt lonely because she scared everyone away? And yet the sensitive girls were all reading Sexton—"all the rage," said Professor Korn without cracking a smile—who was half in love with her too-splendid darkness.

Chatting after class one day, Professor Korn suggested that the girls look into two new books, Betty Friedan's *Feminine Mystique* and Doris Lessing's *Golden Notebook*.

Kurt Barsky took a summer school course on Recent Topics in Analytic Geometry, though it didn't stir his blood like civil rights or the previous year's political philosophy course—taught by a German émigré named Hartmann, who Terry said had once been Thomas Mann's secretary. Hartmann was equally scathing toward modern society and toward everyone who thought there was much to do about it. Intellectuals should keep their heads because no one else will, he liked to say. Kurt liked the precision with which Hartmann chose his words and wondered if he'd ever translated Mann, who like a dancing bear was as delicate as he was clumsy. Like Hartmann, Kurt had a soft spot for Nietzsche, whom he had adopted as his bad boy in high school.

Terry McKay made his presence known in Hartmann's class. Kurt knew other articulate students—sought them out, in fact—but Terry was different in an unusual way: when he composed his rounded sentences, he gave off little smile-flashes, like a leprechaun, testing you to see if he could set off any sparks. After one class when Kurt echoed Hartmann in approving of Nietzsche's harsh view of nineteenth century idiocy, Terry remarked to Kurt that Nietzsche was more than a brilliant wise guy—he went deep, all the way back to the Greeks. No illusions—was it possible to live that way full-time? From Terry's pixie expression, Kurt could tell that Terry knew a towering mind when he encountered one.

When Kurt ran into Sally Barnes one July day, and she asked him what he was up to, and he mentioned that higher mathematics was beginning to bore him, she recited Walt Whitman's poem, "When I heard the learn'd astronomer," which ends:

> *I wander'd off by myself,*
> *In the mystical moist night-air, and from time to time,*
> *Look'd up in perfect silence at the stars.*

"That's me," he said.

"Aha. A romantic under the skin. I'll keep your secret, sir."

Interesting, Kurt thought. *What's this "sir"? She's a tough cookie. Knows her Whitman. Could be she understands something about me that I don't understand myself. She's substantial. Dark voice. Mystical, moist. Surely, I like the look of her—rounded, not delicate. So why don't I make a move? But she probably wants somebody more exciting than me.*

This summer, Kurt often had the house to himself, as Terry was in and out of town visiting other zealots, promoting Friends of SNCC, recruiting for the upcoming March on Washington, even stopping off during a southern swing for a day in Greenwood, Mississippi, which pleased Melissa, though James Turnbull considered Terry a distraction—too talkative.

Kurt contemplated graduate school in philosophy even as he doubted that philosophy, which was built on language—the hot subject—was capable of moving the world toward justice. Language was too frail to carry the weight of morality. When he read Melissa's letters from Greenwood, he was troubled, of course, but he thought words were too frail to carry the weight of the world. Language was what you lied with. Wittgenstein tried to convince him that language was not a matter of logic but the revelation of a "form of life"—whatever exactly that meant. Maybe it meant, for example, the way Terry barreled through his days from meeting to typewriter to meeting, always *underway*, barely pausing to say hello. Kurt was awed by his energy and surefootedness, but wished he would slow down sometimes, talk philosophy, pay attention to him. Kurt liked to be near the action but didn't want to go up in flames.

Terry was all flame. Kurt was longing. Longing and doubt.

Valerie and Sally grew close.

Valerie was immersed in *The Golden Notebook,* which paid tribute to "free women"—women who helped one another withstand the carelessness and stupidity of men. The two women cooked for each other and compared notes on the ways in which their mothers had surrendered to their respective husbands, so that even after Valerie's father ran off with his secretary (how banal!), and her mother proceeded to tie the knot with his best friend, she ended up with a slightly more stolid replica, whereas Sally was ashamed of her mother for refusing to stand up for her when she went home to Mt. Harmony, Michigan, at Thanksgiving, wearing a SNCC button, and incurred the wrath of her father. Valerie said it was tremendous the way Doris Lessing observed people so closely, the cooking and cleaning, the small longings, the little surrenders, this was what women's lives were like, you could always feel good at the stove and laugh at yourself at the kitchen table. Valerie said she assumed Terry was having "little adventures," which was OK with her as long as he kept them out of town. "I like detours myself," she said. She was thinking about changing her major to art history, and enrolling in a course in Mexico next summer to study the muralists.

Matt Stackhouse, Sr., came down with pneumonia. Matt, Jr., responded to his mother's request to head home to Chicago and help her out for a few weeks. With plenty to read, he didn't mind. His subject was the Apostles. For him it was not a new topic.

This fascination he owed to his father, in fact. Every Sunday after church, Matthew Stackhouse, Sr., would hang his jacket on the hook next to the rear seat and then, in the acoustic intimacy of their shiny black 1954 Plymouth Savoy (young Matt so proud of its whitewall tires), they sang morning hymns, of which "Woke Up This Morning" was one of his favorites. Sundays were blessed—dreamy and unbounded, sunlit days, crowned by the moment when his father strode up to the pulpit, as if stepping up to the plate from the on-deck circle—but with an awkward gait, having lost half his right leg during the Battle of the Bulge—and sobered the congregation by declaring, in his booming baritone without needing to consult a text, what he knew for sure—the words that each week sounded like a revelation never spoken before: "I believe in God the Father Almighty ..."

Those were, young Matt came to learn, the opening words of the Apostles' Creed. A creed was what people believed but more so. A creed made the Church happen. Young Matt's heart always soared when he got to the part about "the communion of saints." As soon as his father went into his cavernous rumble, Matt felt the inner lights of the congregation switch on. Long after he ceased to believe in God the Father Almighty, Matt stayed fascinated by the Apostles, who arose vividly in his mind when he started picketing Woolworth's in support of the Southern protests. During his junior year, he took a course on early Christianity. On a trip home to visit his parents, he bought reproductions of the Apostles at the museum shop in the Chicago Art Institute. One depicted a limestone head that French Revolutionaries had knocked off one of the figures from a doorway of the Cathedral of Notre Dame in Paris. The head featured the apostle's beautifully carved hair and beard, and blank, staring eyes that were, if anything, more compelling because the nose had been smashed. Matt was stirred by the French revolutionaries though the Jacobins' bloodthirstiness gave him pause.

His father even in his fifties looked the part of the former army chaplain. He was pleased that Matt had brought with him a book bag full of library books about the Apostles. He knew enough not to ask Matt whether he went to church, but about the Apostles they could talk.

When, at age fourteen, Matt got up the nerve to tell his father that he would rather not attend church anymore—that was how he put it: "rather not"—he was relieved when his father said, "It's up to you, son, just like it was up to me to serve my country. You're old enough to know your own mind. Here's something of which you can be certain: The church will be here for you when you decide to return."

Matt, Jr., had learned that the Apostles were unreliable historians of their exploits; that they wrote their Gospels with axes to grind, to elevate their reputations and undermine their rivals, telling themselves legends to help them keep their faith and withstand the Roman onslaughts. But he did not need to rub his father's face in historical fact.

Young Matt read about those fishermen and tax collectors and wondered again, as he did when he was a child, why they were chosen over all others, what was so special about them? Were there others who applied and were rejected? How did Jesus size these men up? How did he know what was in their hearts? If he could tell who was sincere and who was not, how could he have so badly misread the mind of Judas Iscariot? Or did he read him accurately? Did he recruit Judas deliberately, setting him up to play the role somebody had to play for the Passion to work? If that was the truth, was it fair to Judas?

Finally, as always, his father would say evenly, "This is the Mystery." It was as if the Mystery were like Jesus—part God, part man, both at once. Which made no sense. Jesus was a Mystery and the Son of God, so you expected strange and marvelous things from him. The Apostles, on the other hand, were human. They were not distinguished for their characters or their lineage. They were meek and unremarkable. When they traveled with Jesus, they fumbled, they lost courage, they had eyes that saw not and ears that heard not, so that Jesus had to chastise them for daring to rebuke him, for slipping up, for being "of little faith," for making course corrections.

Was it possible that, when it came to designate Apostles to carry the Word, Jesus chose these men at random, precisely to prove that anyone could do extraordinary things in the name of the Lord, even down to casting out devils?

At times, Matt yielded to the temptation of showing off, posing junior-year questions for which he knew his father had no answers. Then, he stood with his hands behind his back, like a soldier at ease, awaiting punishment.

On September 16, 1963, the day after a bomb blew up four little Negro girls at Sunday school in Birmingham, Alabama, the Ann Arbor city council debated a fair housing ordinance, to decide whether landlords could legally discriminate against renters of various sorts, and if so, under what conditions. There had already been picket lines, a sit-in, and arrests. The date for the vote had been set weeks earlier, but to Friends of SNCC it didn't seem coincidental that this debate would take place directly after the Birmingham bombing. John Lewis, the chairman of SNCC, would come to speak later in the week.

On the streets near the campus, people raked maple leaves tinged by premature red and yellow. Mail got delivered. Robins hopped around. Students sipped coffee and ate ice cream, and studied, and basked in the feints that summer made as it expired.

On the Diag, Terry McKay's clear voice caromed. He stood on a low wall, wearing a thin black tie on a red shirt and a black armband. He jabbed his index finger and declared, "The question today is whether the four little girls and all the wounded in Birmingham are expendable. That's the test for our whole generation." He jabbed his left finger again, as if Klansmen were burning crosses *right over there* and waiting to find out what students at the University of Michigan were going to do about it.

"Terror is nothing new," he preached. "Lynching is nothing new. What's new is a generation climbing out from under fear and complacency. What's new is so much courage, which we can all see for ourselves on the streets. So it's *about time* that the country is shocked and enraged. Listen to this headline from today's paper." He pulled it out of his pocket and read the headline: "'Such Malice Inconceivable,' Says Shocked Mayor." Terry's voice soared to judgment.

"Inconceivable? Mayor, you're not paying attention! Tune up your imagination!"

Valerie Parr marveled at the rapt faces surrounding her. So did an olive-skinned young man in a suede jacket, who was walking around with a camera, getting different angles on Terry, documenting this thing they were doing. *Yes, this cries out to be documented,* Valerie thought. The intense man with the camera was a few years older than most of the students. He smiled faintly, as if he were the director who had summoned the actors.

Valerie was astonished to see how unselfconscious Terry was as he passed from one expression to another—mockery, disbelief, disappointment, fury. He had nicely tanned skin that ought to have made him look handsome but didn't. His eyes were small, bright, and restless. His hands rested, almost clenched, on his belt. The crowd grew by twos and threes. They stood rapt, even resolute, even devotional—not to him personally, but to the force he incarnated. He transformed a crowd into a congregation.

She saw Matt Stackhouse in the crowd, stepped up to him and whispered: "Isn't it great the way he connects us? He makes people bolder. People like me, who aren't bold."

Terry, his eyes hungry, collected the energy of the crowd and proclaimed: "The Southern movement is breathing new life into the whole country."

Someone shouted, "Yes!"

"Right here in Ann Arbor," Terry said, "south of the *Canadian* border"—a couple of chuckles—"right here, I tell you, this afternoon, the city council is going to decide whether *we're* ready for equal rights. Can you believe that a century after the Emancipation Proclamation we're waiting to see if they think a Negro has a right *to rent an apartment?*"

The crowd broke into applause, soaking up Terry's energy even as he himself looked, for the moment, depleted. Matt thought about Apostles converging. Kurt Barsky thought this was the biggest rally he'd ever seen except for the "We want pants!" crowd outside a girls' dorm last spring, which he and Terry had happened upon, trying and failing to get them to chant "Freedom Now" instead. Melissa Howard thought about Greenwood. *The in-gathering*, thought Sally Barnes. The autumn air was crystalline, the sky an innocent blue.

Sally was stirred. It was one thing—a wonderful thing—to feel what St. Emily said a poem makes you feel: as if the top of your head was taken off. That was rare, but it was solitary. You quivered along with Emily Dickinson in all her singularity. What Sally felt right now was something else—communion, the flesh-and-blood joy of decent people rising above themselves.

Even as the crowd disbanded into individuals with their sober expressions, their eagerness, shame, and perplexity, their resolve, their eyeglasses, pompadours, ponytails, a live torrent of thought and feeling poured itself into the world. They were not at the end of the past: they stood at the beginning of the future.

The City Council met three hours later in the newly dedicated City Hall, a Bauhaus-inspired no-frills creation that featured white horizontals across the exterior—a tribute to the clean geometry of reason itself.

In the auditorium, deadly fluorescence cast an unearthly glow. Friends of SNCC passed out black cloth armbands. A gavel hammered the meeting to order, as in a courtroom movie. The councilmen sat at a long, slightly curved desk, a simple sign of authority in Danish modern style, as if to say, *We are prudent adults*. A snarling Dylan line passed through Valerie's mind: "I want you to know I can see through your masks."

Having passed out all their armbands, Valerie and Melissa entered and sat together, but Melissa got up to sit next to another Negro student—a stocky, stylishly dressed girl who was in the first row, as if she wanted to stare the councilmen straight in the eyes, let them see that they didn't live in an all-white world. Valerie had been feeling that, since Mississippi, Melissa had grown distant from her, or preoccupied at least. Now she was sure it was more than distance. It was estrangement.

In the back row, three young Black men glowered. They were older than the students. One of them Melissa recognized from the fringes of Friends of SNCC meetings: a big, broad-shouldered, sometimes-irascible fellow in his late-twenties named Travis Frye, who was said to have enlisted in the Army at 14, then discharged in Korea when they found out his actual age. The crowd was otherwise almost entirely white.

The councilman who had introduced the bill said that given the bombing in Birmingham the day before, open housing was the very least they could do in Ann Arbor, but since they lived in a free so-ciety, it was reasonable to exclude landlords who owned fewer than four apartments. Another said that if they were serious about open housing there could be no exceptions. A pudgy man in a bright white suit said, "We're all against discrimination—it's un-Ameri-can, but it's also un-American to send the Gestapo to force you to rent out a property you own, which could be the apartment right downstairs, to some bunch of people you may not like or get along with." He went on indignantly: "'Cause *all* Americans have rights, and if a Negro property-owner has three units and doesn't want to rent to me, for whatever reason, or no reason at all, well, that's his right too."

Terry McKay, sitting with Matt a few rows back, peered around like a general inspecting his troops, a slightly mirthful look tick-ling his lips. He spotted Travis Frye, who looked restive. One of the councilmen was talking about "the fundamental virtue of pri-vate property." Matt leaned toward Terry and whispered: "This guy thinks the Declaration of Independence guarantees 'life, liberty, and property.'"

"I know." Terry bit the nail on his left pinky. He was wound tight as an armature.

The open housing bill, covering only dwellings with four or more units, passed by a vote of eight to three.

Melissa and the Negro student sitting next to her jumped up and shouted, "For shame!" Others joined in. Matt loosed a grimace, like a spitball, in the direction of the councilman in the white suit. Terry leaped up, shouting, "This is a travesty!" and others chanted along, "Travesty!" and "Shame on you!" before trailing off. The chairman, annoyed, picked up his gavel, glared around the room for someone to personify the disorder that challenged his mastery and spotted Melissa and her friend, who had joined the "Travesty!" chorus, but he wasn't going to single out *Negroes*, so he fastened on Matt, possibly because he shouted louder than Terry, and smacked his gavel down. Matt shouted, "You're un-American!" The chairman's eyes were frozen, now, as a line of sheriff's deputies posted themselves between the demonstrators and the council table.

If the crowd did not cease and desist this moment, an officer announced, they would be subject to arrest for an offense called "disorderly loitering." Terry launched into a rousing, almost on-key rendition of "We Shall Overcome" as the chairman pounded his gavel and the demonstrators, fifty or more, joined hands, rocking left and right, stressing the *some* in "We shall overcome *some* day," leading to an emphatic "We are not afraid *to*-day-ay-ay-ay-ay." Melissa thought of Pete Seeger, and Terry jabbed his fist in the air and watched from the corner of his eye as a deputy jumped forward and grabbed his outstretched fist and forced it down, and Terry, eyes sparking, flopped down on the floor and "went limp," as it was called, whereupon two deputies yanked him into the aisle and lifted him, not gently, as two more grabbed his shoulders, and all four deputies hoisted him, legs dangling, as he bellowed "Freedom now!" and hauled him out of the chamber as the room pumped up the volume on "We shall overcome," other protesters rising from their seats seemingly at random—no one having primed them on what to do—before sinking onto the chilly parquet floor, so that it took a good while to extract them two or three at a time, and they availed themselves of the opportunity to sing "This Little Light of Mine" and "We Shall Not Be Moved" as the blasé deputies carried them out one by one, wearing that look of men absorbed in strenuous but necessary labor. Travis Frye and his friends declined to be carried.

Inside the jail, the protesters were fingerprinted. Frye, asked for his ID, said his name was Travis Brass—"that's brass for my balls," he told the deputy, who shrugged. The boys were relieved of their shoelaces and belts—"They think we're going to hang ourselves!" said one boy, amazed and amused. Sally, wearing a wide vinyl belt and laced-low boots, noted that the girls weren't considered capable of suicidal protest. Their belongings got stuffed into manila envelopes. They were jammed into holding cells with cinder-block walls. They stretched out on stone floors and cold metal benches. Sleepless, they did not complain. They sang and told feeble knock-knock jokes. The steel toilets lacked seats.

In the morning, young lawyers in suits and ties showed up, having arranged that the students would plead not guilty and be released on their own recognizance—O.R., this was called, the court being confident that they would not skip out to avoid a trial on "disorderly loitering."

"Hell with that," boomed Travis Frye. "None of this recognizance. I ain't no student anyhow. 'Jail, no bail' is what they say in the South. I say we stay in. We're a focus for the community."

"He's right," Terry said. "It works in the South. You jam up the works. It's a big nuisance to them if they have to feed us. If they won't let all of us out on O.R., we all stay." Arguments flew back and forth. Some students didn't want to miss classes. Terry convinced one of the lawyers to come up with bail for Travis Frye and his friends.

Terry told Valerie, pillow to pillow, that Friends of SNCC would hold a "retreat" the following weekend at a university-run camp near town. She asked, "What does *that* mean?"

"Actually it's not a retreat," Terry said, swiveling slightly toward the ceiling as was his wont. "It's an advance."

They spent Friday afternoon in "workshops"—a funny term, she thought, for bull sessions, where they sprawled on the lawn smoking, chewing blades of grass, sizing each other up—talking about "where we're at" (a funny way to put it, in Valerie's estimation) and the future of civil rights in the North and urban poverty. How could they mobilize the poor to create decent jobs and housing? Should they run candidates for the City Council? Organize more militant sit-ins? They started sentences with "I think the question is" or "I think we need to realize that" (it came out more like "*Uh-think*"). Some spoke between long-drawn-out pauses, as if they were thinking their way, rock after rock, across a stream. Was Travis Frye right about "Jail, no bail"? Who was going to take them seriously if they ducked right out? Would it get them more votes for fair housing? Melissa, on the strength of her experience in Greenwood, said it was true that unless there was totally fair housing there was *unfair* housing, but said you had to be strategic about militancy, you had to set up a support system. It does no good to molder in jail collecting merit badges when nothing results. The movement in the Deep South needed Friends of SNCC to raise money, do publicity, expose the racists in Congress, deliver food for the coming winter.

Friday night, they sang freedom songs and danced and drank beer. One of the SDS leaders, Rennie Davis, played a wicked banjo. To the tune of the traditional song, "Go Tell Aunt Rhody"—"Go tell Aunt Rhody the old gray goose is dead....She died in the mill pond standing on her head"—he concocted different lyrics:

> *Marx is like Hegel*
> *Marx is like Hegel*
> *Marx is like Hegel*
> *Standing on his head.*

Valerie turned to Sally and asked, "What's he talking about?"
"Beats me," Sally said, "but he looks sweet."
The unattached surveyed their prospects of becoming attached. It was harvest time, renewal time, hunker-down-for-the-winter

time. As breezes shifted direction, the air was thick with the tang of marijuana, apples, and lust.

Saturday morning just past ten, they gathered on the softball field. Terry McKay, his eyes glowing, stood rigidly at home plate, elevated on a wooden crate that featured a label depicting an orange rising like a stylized rising sun, rays and all. He waited for the murmur to die down, lowered his head, consulted a sheet of lined yellow paper in his right hand, surveyed the crowd, tucked the paper into his back pocket, jabbed his left index finger forward and proclaimed: "We don't seem to be the silent generation anymore!" Which brought forth a boisterous cheer.

Sweaterless in the golden light of late morning, he wore a short-sleeved black-and-white striped shirt (sleeves neatly rolled up, with a toothbrush poking up out of his pocket, brush side showing), squinted into the sun, and paid tribute to how *disciplined* they had been when they sat-in—they should have been charged with *orderly* loitering—and then, as laughter caromed around the ball field, he lopped off his grin and looked *stricken*, as if the treatment of Negroes in America was not only a disgrace but a personal insult. Led by the courageous Negroes in places like Greenwood, he said, "the movement" was building, and it was not only going to destroy Jim Crow, it was aiming at "major social change," because the country was too wealthy to afford poverty, and students wouldn't be satisfied any longer with middle-class emptiness.

Sally didn't exactly understand what "major social change" would look like, but she liked the way that phrase, "the movement," rolled off Terry's lips. It was warm, like "mama" or "murmur" or other words with two syllables both starting with "m"—even sexy. Movement was what they were about, all right.

Now Terry opened his hands and lifted them upward and outward, as if bestowing grace. This work would require massive endurance, and sacrifice, and vigilance, and commitment, he said. He said that when you make bacon and eggs, the chickens make contributions, all right, but the pig shows *commitment*. This line drew chortles and whoops from the crowd.

Valerie, wearing Terry's baggy charcoal sweater, was aglow.

Nothing would come easy. It would take a lot more than overnight stays in jail. Terry quoted Frederick Douglass: "Power yields nothing without a demand." He shook his fist and added, "It never has, and it never will." President Kennedy was moving the right way, he said, but only because the movement dragged him onto his soapbox kicking and screaming. Now the movement was going to have to do a whole lot more than *speak truth to power*, even more than *put our bodies on the line*, it had to *see the world differently*, to see through the *disguises* of *power*. Cheers from the crowd, more raised fists.

Sally greatly admired the feeling, though she doubted she was committed enough.

Terry went on, his voice supercharging, saying that the system was an insult to humanity, so grotesque and entrenched that even to see through the masks of power would not be enough. The masks had to be *ripped off* (he made a ripping gesture)—and in fact not only the masks of *the power elite*, the top politicians and the big bankers who lent money to Alabama and Mississippi, and the corporate boards, all the self-selected hypocrites who lorded it over a society seduced into thinking that it was democratic, but—this might even be harder—our *own* masks, which we got used to because we feel entitled to comfortable lives, and why not, we feel like we've earned them, getting nice grades so we can get our nice jobs so we can tuck ourselves into our nice armchairs in our nice split-level living rooms and put our feet up and drink our nice Martinis.

God, Valerie thought, *he is on fire.*

We are going to have to be *uneasy*, Terry said, *take chances*, live *difficult* lives, *go beyond* having *opinions* and making *analyses*. We are going to have to get *serious* the way the Southern movement is *serious*, and we are going to have to get *disorderly*, because the alternative to *disciplined* disorder is to turn into *good Germans* like the sheriff's deputies, those robots who arrested them, with their sick, scared eyes and their dead souls (Terry had taken a course on Russian literature), just ordinary people who love their children and follow orders, and we all knew where that led—it led to carting away the Jews like so much garbage. He laughed knowingly as he spoke about traveling with the Negroes on "their great trek through the wilderness of the centuries."

The crowd pulsated as Terry set out the truth of their own emotions. Matt Stackhouse, leaning back against the third base fence, arms folded, stared at Terry and beamed. Terry built up his exhortations and slammed into his consonants like drumbeats. He cast his eyes upwards, as if to a summit rising *right over there* past the tree-line.

For all that Sally knew she could not rise to his standard, she thought this was the most powerful speech she'd ever heard, even if he was too nasal for her taste, and some of his phrases were forced—like "cowards in white shirts" (why does the color of their shirts matter?) and "America is a broken home" and "the caste system is terror in slow motion"—and though she thought he was going on too long, she could see where he was going.

Even as he denounced the crimes of the Southern racists, Terry filled the air with intimations of great things to come. *What will you give?* he was wordlessly asking.

People jumped to their feet and cheered, as if their favorite had just crossed the finish line.

Swept up into a state of grace, Sally teared up.

Melissa could see that Travis Frey was well muscled—his tight polo shirt put his biceps on display—and he was certainly nice looking, even sweet and soft-spoken, but the way he tried to maneuver her toward his bed was rather obvious. She sat down on the foot of the bed but kept her feet on the floor. On the table was a well-worn paperback of a book called *Negroes with Guns* by somebody named Robert F. Williams. Pictured on the cover was a statue of an American Revolutionist of indeterminate race wearing a tri-corner hat and holding a flintlock rifle. "Who's Williams?" Melissa asked.

"Was head of an N Double A chapter in North Carolina. Ex-Marine. Founded a rifle club to defend civil rights folks from the Klan. FBI ran him out of the state. Had to go into exile in Cuba."

"Oh yeah? Good book?"

"He lays it out there."

She let the words float in the air between them. "I've seen Negroes up all night in Mississippi, with rifles in their laps, keepin' the church safe. I'm not for any civil right to suicide. But—"

Travis looked impressed. "Well, there you are."

"But I don't know. It's easy to say, pick up guns. We gonna fight it out with the white guys in Michigan? They outnumber us."

"Lot of Negroes be comin' home from the military," Travis said. "Like Williams, like me, like Medgar Evers. Know how to shoot."

Melissa had heard the rumor that Travis came home with a metal plate in his head. In her mind, this conversation had been dubious from the start, but now it zipped itself closed.

"I been meanin' to ask you what's a matter?" Travis said too quietly. "You only like white boys?"

"I'm going out with you, aren't I?" said Melissa.

"Well, you don't act like you like me."

Bludgeoned by those words, she took her leave soon thereafter.

Ann Arbor, November 1963

IN THE DAYS AFTER Lee Harvey Oswald aimed through the scope of his mail-order rifle, fired three shots, and blew John Fitzgerald Kennedy's brains out, many peculiar things took place. Schizophrenics spoke in tongues. Frogs crawled out of ponds. Beavers abandoned their dams. A Christian minister in Cincinnati declared from the pulpit that Kennedy was the Antichrist and that Armageddon was nigh. Malcolm X allowed as how unspecified chickens had come home to roost. In Nashville, a man in a bar who cheered upon hearing that Kennedy was dead was dragged off his stool and pummeled within an inch of his life. Young Trotskyites and wizened segregationists wept.

A fine dust of grief and incomprehension settled everywhere. Millions turned to each other, to passersby, neighbors, anyone, pleading for information. Who was this Oswald? Terry and Matt, accompanied by large pizzas and gallons of Red Mountain, hosted conversations. Was Oswald what he said he was, "a patsy"? Wasn't he seen standing in front of the Texas School Book Depository at exactly the time the shots were fired? Wasn't there a gunman on the grassy knoll? Was Oswald a Stalinist agent trying to bring down Khrushchev, who, after all, had struck bargains with Kennedy, so that killing Kennedy was, for him, a fancy carom billiard shot? No, Oswald was a racist, a fascist, *anti*-Castro. He was a cut-out. He was an above-average marksman. No, he was much better than above-average. No, he was a poor shot. No, that was only a rumor. Out of a haze of ignorance came intricate whorls of speculation. Tales and surmises circulated as if through an enormous switchboard of rumor, overheard and repeated—with variations—as in an endless but ragged feedback loop of distortion.

If Kennedy could be murdered, all bets were off. The dial of history had been jerked. And when the mobbed-up nightclub owner Jack Ruby murdered Oswald *on live TV, right in front of the Dallas police,* the crazy stories went into overdrive. Young people who had never fired a rifle carried on heated discussions of how Oswald could have gotten off so many shots so fast. Kurt and Matt drew diagrams of a place, Dealey Plaza, and a building, the Texas School Book Depository, that they had never heard of before. Terry, who had never studied Latin, asked, "Cui bono?" and Kurt answered, "Lyndon Johnson."

"Well," Melissa said, "at least Oswald isn't Black."

"But Jack Ruby is Jewish," said the tall, olive-skinned man whom Valerie had seen shooting pictures of the rally before the sit-in, and whose name turned out to be Ronnie Silverberg. "The petty capitalists are always Jewish. They front for the bourgeoisie. Marx wrote about it." His bushy eyebrows lowered, eyes slivering. He reached into the pocket of his Levi's jacket, extricated a pack of Winstons, shook out a single cigarette, brought it to his lips, reached back into the pocket for a book of matches, lit the cigarette, inhaled, exhaled a narrow stream, and then said in a slow, mellifluous baritone: "I can't help but think of the Reichstag fire." Ronnie's father had a long memory, which he had implanted in his son. He had been a Communist who pleaded the Fifth before an investigating committee and lost his job teaching high school chemistry. At the rally, Ronnie had held out hope for the protesters. *They're naïve,* he had thought. *But grant them this: They're not flat. They have dimensions. They'll develop.* Now he looked around the room at these young people suddenly looking much younger than him and suspected that there wasn't enough time for them to develop.

Everyone else looked puzzled, as if they were thinking, *What was this Reichstag fire?*

"You know," Ronnie said didactically, "Hitler had the building torched so he could blame the Communists."

"Am I the only one here who thinks that nobody's making sense?" Valerie said.

"This is a horror show," said Sally.

"No," Ronnie said. "In a horror show, you see the monster. This isn't a horror show, it's a blob."

"There has to be a way to think this through," said Terry. "But it's beyond me."

Terry went dark. He awakened in darkness, returned to darkness, was suspended in darkness. Most of his life—bone fractures, break-ups, even his father's death from lung cancer—darkness had barely brushed him. He had read about despair (Dostoyevsky, Sartre, St. John of the Cross) as one might read about the initiation rituals of an Amazonian tribe. Not this time.

"I'm not used to seeing you like this," Valerie said. She stopped herself from reminding him that he had not been all so enamored of the murdered president.

"I'm not used to feeling like this," he said, surveying the ceiling.

But it wearied her. Too often he went blank when he spoke to her. She had seen enough of this kind of darkness, this eye-dead-ness, take over her life.

He felt her retreat like a slap. All that was clear to him was that the very ground he walked on had collapsed and he was in free fall. She tried to get him to see what was happening as a different sort of adventure, the way she had put her life back together after Kathryn was gone, but did she have the fortitude to do it again? Who was Terry to her really?

For as long as Terry could remember, the emptiness of the heavens had been an unexpected gift. He held no nostalgia for an overhanging God.

For some years he collected quotations, typed them out on in-dex cards and Scotch-taped them over his desk. Now he gravitated to one from Pascal, to whom Kurt had introduced him: "Man is a reed, the weakest of nature, but he is a thinking reed." But what does a thinking reed think? Terry consulted Kurt, who recommended further reading. He went to the library, looked up Pascal's *Pensées*, and found the lines:

A vapor, a drop of water suffices to kill him. But if the universe were to crush him, man would still be more noble than that which killed him, because he knows that he dies … The universe knows nothing of this. All our dignity consists, then, in thought.

He knows that he dies. This was the big thing to know. Nobility came from staring down the truth that could not be stared down. The aim of thought was not certainty but dignity. Kennedy, whatever you thought of his policies, however disappointing in so many ways, carried himself with that kind of dignity. In one late-night argument with Ronnie, Terry scoffed that nobody owned the future. The assassination proved that. Ronnie thought Kennedy the weakest of reeds, but even Ronnie seemed to know his hand-me-down socialist hopes were stale. Look at his father.

Terry was not naïve about the torments of history. History had an appointment with disappointment. Of his own capacity for reason he had an understandably high opinion, and until now, he had been adept at finding people to think with. Now he felt stranded. It was not just Kurt getting cold feet but Valerie and Matt pulling into themselves. He had gotten used to thinking one step ahead of his crowd, but now they were equally, and separately, lost.

Terry needed new facts.

Searching for historical wisdom, he consulted his old professor Hartmann, the German refugee. Hartmann reminded him calmly and politely that everything changed. He recommended Heraclitus. There would always be those who anticipated that old orders were doomed and history had a destination, but they were not to be trusted. They were opportunists—scavengers scheming to profit by selling souvenirs carved out of the rubble. Face to face with the juggernaut of history, Hartmann said, the right attitude was stoical resolve. He complimented Franklin Roosevelt. From catastrophe might come improvement. Think about the Great Depression—the disaster that broke the back of predatory capitalism.

Hartmann drew smoke deep into his lungs.

Terry thought Hartmann had earned two rights: (1) the right to suffer, and (2) the right to hope modestly. Terry could glimpse his own political trajectory from a new angle. Since the student movement erupted, every injury led to a reawakening. The jailing of the sit-in students led to the founding of SNCC. The sit-ins and the Freedom Rides, and all the brutality meted out to the movement, turned Kennedy toward new civil rights laws. Medgar Evers, the Birmingham girls—all the martyrdoms were clarion calls. Terrible suffering gave rise to rededication. Perhaps history had a logic, however perverse. Happy endings were not predestined, but starts were possible. However incomprehensibly, apparent endings were middles.

Lyndon Johnson, in his State of the Union address, declared "all-out war on human poverty and unemployment in these United States."

Terry looked bemused, Valerie thought. Or was it bedazzled?

"Human poverty?" Ronnie Silverberg snorted. "Why stop there? All *animal* poverty!"

"Vegetable! Mineral!" Matt chortled.

"And a partridge in a fuckin' pear tree," Ronnie said.

Valerie cringed inwardly. She had not come to the movement for cynicism.

Johnson's words grew creamier: "…unconditional war…in city slums and small towns, in sharecropper shacks or in migrant worker camps, on Indian Reservations, among whites as well as Negroes, among the young as well as the aged, in the boom towns and in the depressed areas—"

"He's painting by the numbers," drawled Matt. It surprised Valerie that Matt, too, fell into derision.

"Our aim is not only to relieve the symptoms of poverty but to cure it and, above all, to prevent it," Johnson declared.

Terry had heard recordings of FDR's calls to arms. By contrast, Johnson's phrases thudded down. But as the camera zoomed closer to the president's great stone block of a face, you had to admit he sounded sincere as he rumbled into a tribute to Kennedy and a commitment to "a nation that is free from want and a world that is free from hate—a world of peace and justice, and freedom and abundance, for our time and for all time to come." With a forced, avuncular smile that ignited on the word "abundance," Johnson staked out his faith.

"Christ," Ronnie said, "what a steaming pile of horseshit."

"Doesn't matter," Terry said, his verve back in tune. "The key thing is that the politics are going to be different now. The Dixiecrats are on the skids. The Solid South is melting."

"What happened to McKay the realist?" said Ronnie.

For once, Sally agreed with Ronnie, the sardonic prince.

"This *is* realism," Terry said. "Don't think Johnson's a hick just because he sounds like a hick." He crossed one leg over the other and shook it madly, then clamped down on his foot to brake it. He seemed to have figured things out. "He's a corporate liberal but he wants to be liberal, not just corporate. He has this huge wave of positive feeling going for him now. He can do anything he fucking pleases."

"And what's that?" Ronnie said.

"He started his career as FDR's fair-haired boy. This is his big chance to take charge of the New Deal, make it his own. This is where we come in. This is the moment for large-scale reform. Watch."

Valerie watched with relief and awe, and wondered how long Terry's new mood would last. Springing out of his darkness, he talked with people from Students for a Democratic Society, SDS, the national radical organization. They were reading the same political signals he read. Whether you loved Johnson was irrelevant. Think of him not as a man but as a force, a vector at work in the great field of action and inertia that makes up the world. The movement could push, goad, shame him—*ally* with him (selectively, to be sure); keep the ball rolling. Hell, if need be, they could dedicate themselves to the promise of the half-hearted Kennedy.

This would be the year of the organizer. SDS decided to promote what they called "the interracial movement of the poor." They would fan out into impoverished northern communities, find local leaders, train them, create organizations of the unemployed and badly housed and welfare-dependent, organize rent strikes, campaign for jobs, protests demanding a livable income. With legal segregation on the ropes in the South, SNCC liked the idea. Automation was coming. Mass unemployment was coming. It would be possible now to cross race lines and to galvanize liberals to support a class-based movement. Working backwards from the New Deal, Terry pored through books about late nineteenth century populism. America actually once had an interracial movement of the poor!

SDS was recruiting students for summer community organizing projects next summer: Newark, Cleveland, Chicago, Philadelphia, Chester, PA, Baltimore, Boston, Louisville, Oakland. Terry wanted to work with them, but outside their structure, not get hung up in their organizational complications.

Bob Dylan released a new album called "The Times They Are a-Changin.'"

Melissa, who loved the album and was bemused by her recollection of Dylan's appearance in Greenwood, was in a quandary. She approved of the new direction percolating out of Ann Arbor. This was not, to her, an abstraction or a pious wish. Greenwood was with her always. But if she returned to Mississippi, where she could do the most good, her mother would strangle her. She'd better graduate first.

Terry, though restored to exuberance, had less time for Valerie, who had thrown herself into art history classes and didn't seem to mind the dwindling of her little adventure. She noticed he was staying late at SDS meetings. Meanwhile, one of the SDS women, named

Marcia, started coming around to the meetings at Terry's house. "I'm liaison," she would explain in a contralto voice that bristled with confidence. She wore dark silk blouses, affected bow-shaped black glasses, and talked fast in a not-quite-English, not-quite-Southern accent. (Baltimore, it turned out.) At meetings, Marcia leaned Terry's way on an adjacent pillow.

Kurt took Matt aside after one meeting and said caustically, "Terry is going off half-cocked. What are we, supermen? We're going to parachute into Newark, Chicago, Cleveland, and then what? What do we do there? Waltz into some bar in a neighborhood we've never seen before, jump up onto a table and howl: *Arise, workers, we're here to lead you—or follow you—or anyway accompany you to the promised land?*" He called the SDS community organizers "Ghetto-jumpers." *Do-gooders of the world, unite!*

Matt was coming around to Terry's position: that Kurt lacked the makings of an organizer. And yet Kurt made sense. Matt echoed Kurt's objections to Terry more mildly. Terry looked hurt and argued back that risk-takers were always accused of recklessness. King said so about SNCC—said that the Southern sit-ins were getting ahead of themselves, that the kids were hotheads, that they lacked discipline and community support, and that they had no strategy for dealing with jail. King was as surprised as anyone when the sit-ins took off. As for Kurt, Terry thought, he would miss the next phase of the grand adventure. So be it.

Still, Kurt kept coming to meetings, which, after all, took place in his own house. He watched the theoretical trial balloons bump around and lose their lift—so it seemed to him. What did they know about poor whites anyway? Collaboration with SNCC was a sweet idea for college students, but Terry's populist alliance of white and Black farmers was tenuous in the first place and expired decades ago. Terry told Matt point-blank that Kurt didn't truly connect to the movement. Intellectuals were like that, he said; they only want to witness; they want good seats to watch the action; they think everything to a standstill. Kurt could read Terry's disappointment all over his face. Terry demoted him.

It was no surprise when Kurt decided he would go to graduate school, though in philosophy, not math. Sally told him, "You're a Whitman guy, Kurt. You're large, you contain multitudes."

"You mean I have a split personality." As if to prove the point, he transformed his grin into a frown. He thought, *She's got my number.*

Sally felt unsettled. Her old gang was moving on, and soon. This was for her a turning point. It wasn't just that Kennedy was dead and they had entered a new political phase. It was that Terry was right all along about the pig and commitment. This organizing venture sounded tempting, like pie in the sky—not the sky she wanted to live beneath. Abstract pie—tasteless. But neither was she tempted by "the life of the mind," a phrase that sounded unironically right in Kurt's mouth but not in her own. Kurt had math and philosophy, Valerie talked about art history—what would it be for her?

Not an academic career, which sounded to Sally like a spinning of off-center wheels, but a practical life of service. Teaching. She wanted to help actual, not hypothetical kids. She was good at asking questions and helping the kids get unstuck. She visited an adviser, who sent her to sit in on ed school classes, which made sense to her. One lesson at a time, one kid at a time.

During the spring, the gang held together for good times even as they sensed that their sands were running out. More was ending than commencing. They felt a kind of nostalgia for the present. As if summoned by the ghost of John F. Kennedy, the Beatles arrived, *yeah, yeah, yeah,* rollicking across the AM dial in the effervescence of just-invented love. If the Ann Arbor group couldn't agree on a direction for the movement, they could at least have some fun. After meetings, Terry, Matt, Ronnie and Kurt played at entertaining the others as a late-night quartet called "The Ghetto-Jumpers," strumming broomsticks, letting their hair grow, crooning falsetto: *She loves you, yeah, yeah, yeah.* Divine hysteria. Elders and doubters sounded pathetic. The Beatles were look-what-we-can-do. Dylan was look-what-we-must-do. The movement was we-can-do.

There must have been times, Matt thought, *when the Apostles got cold feet, although back then, graduate school wasn't an option.*

As the weeks flew by, Ronnie Silverberg dropped still more pellets of scorn into more conversations about the new organizing projects. As a kid, he had learned from a hundred dinner table conversations among battle-scarred old militants that the Working Class—in capital letters—was the key to the future. *Ah*, Ronnie came to think, *the old folks are harking back to their glory days when the working class acted the way the Working Class was supposed to act.* People like his father had paid the price for their faith—even if, as Ronnie well knew but was not eager to advertise, his father had pulled himself together after losing his teaching job, abandoned the lost cause, patented some refinements for making poker chips and translucent jewelry out of plastic, sold them to a big chemical company, and made a fortune.

What was Ronnie doing at Terry's meetings anyway? He had nothing to offer as an alternative to the wispy notion of an inter-racial movement of the poor. "The IMP," he dubbed it. Let the innocents march off, full of themselves! Ronnie was too shrewd to enlist in any fool's errand. He made up his mind to go to law school and bore himself silly. From his family history he had extracted the lesson that you need to get a good education, acquire skills and re-nown, make a name for yourself which you could then put to work in good causes. The movement would need lots of lawyers.

As Ronnie disputed the prospects for an IMP, Terry rolled his eyes.

But why should Ronnie care? How much did Terry know anyway?

"Sometimes he mystifies me," he told Valerie. Had he noticed that Terry's hold over her had loosened?

"Sometimes?" But Valerie cautioned him not to dismiss Ronnie's argument out of hand. Matt understood that she came from old money. At times, in fact, Matt thought of her as a self-indulgent rich kid. In fact, it was her air of floating an inch above the ground that attracted him. But still, he valued her judgment. Possibly be-cause her world was exalted.

The question of where to organize was the subject of many meetings. Terry brought up Newark, New Jersey, where SDS was setting up an organizing project in the black ghetto—Tom Hayden himself, the legendary SDS leader who was promoting "an interracial movement of the poor," had resettled there. With Melissa holding herself in reserve for a return to the South, the Ann Arbor organizing group, face it, would be all white. Matt wanted to get serious about the interracial part. But Terry had a point: Instead of tearing their hair, why not try the IMP and see what happened? Possibilities boiled down to Baltimore, Cleveland, Cincinnati and Chicago. Terry liked Chicago but Matt ruled it out for himself—there, he would always feel under the scrutiny of his father; he would always be Matt Stackhouse, *Jr.*

Feeling like a pioneer, Matt went to the library reference room. All signs pointed toward Cleveland. It had a big population of poor whites, factories shutting down, mothers on welfare. Many had migrated from the mountain hollows of West Virginia, eastern Kentucky and Tennessee, western Virginia, and northwest Georgia. They were culturally distinctive, excluded, so (in theory) they would have an easier time seeing themselves as an opposition, as outsiders, rather than failures who had no one to blame for their poverty but their fucked-up selves. In their collective not-so-distant past, their fathers had gone up against the bosses to organize the coal mines. Maybe the children had inherited their spirit.

Maybe: an Apostle's favorite five-letter word next to Jesus.

Matt loved the way research could open portals into a better future. *They* might have power, but *we* have research.

"Cleveland," Valerie mused. "Sure, why not Cleveland?" Matt hadn't even asked her.

Cleveland, 1964

M ATT AND VALERIE MADE a sortie to inspect Cleveland's Near West Side, and found a low-rise, quiet, modest village nestled inside a city itself without presumption. The neighborhood was a sprawl of little wood-frame, single-family houses, one- and two-story, dotted with bars, tiny groceries, and churches (some in storefronts), a Goodwill thrift shop, along with some grander residences, once posh by the look of them—some fronted by columns, even—before the upper class felt their enclaves crumbling around them and left for the suburbs, surrendering their old homes, high ceilings and all, after some rounds of selling and buying, to be chopped into single-room cubicles equipped with cold-water sinks, bathrooms down the hall. Most of the buildings were painted in pastels or varieties of gray, dirtied by run-off from rooftops and clogged gutters. A lot of paint was peeling. Not exactly ramshackle, but if you looked closer, you saw broken windows and front doors that didn't exactly fit. The Near West Side held onto its honest-to-God picket fences, its free-standing garages out back, fronting on alleys, where rows of garbage cans were lined up like shooting-range targets.

Trees were abundant. Shriveled maple leaves dangled like arthritic fingers. To what degree this was a sign of disease, Matt didn't know.

"It's OK, Matt," Valerie said, chucking him under the chin, "you don't have to know everything."

He liked the way she teased him; there was generosity in it.

By the time she, Matt and Terry made their move, the SDS group—Marcia Stein among them—had settled what they called a "staff house," emulating SNCC. It had eaves; three bedrooms; yellowed linoleum that rippled across the kitchen floor and peeled away from the edges; radiators that clanked too often; and a storage closet big enough to hold a mimeograph machine and reams of paper. Outside was parked a late-Fifties Chevrolet Impala bearing battered West Virginia plates, pale green except for a blue fender, its antenna ripped off leaving a stub. Down the block was a late-model Ford Falcon (with North Carolina plates: "First in Flight"), hood up, as a cluster of young men blew on their fingers and one of them sprayed something aromatic onto the engine while the driver turned the key and got the engine to turn over. For a long time it failed to catch.

Matt and Valerie left Terry the first floor and took the upstairs for their own. The bedroom was a bit dank and moldy, but Valerie declared crisply that it was "improvable."

This woman has pioneer spirit, Matt thought. Their bed was a double-size mattress that cost twenty dollars at Goodwill. Their window overlooked the alley, which collected shriveled maple and oak leaves along with cigarette butts and the detritus of windy days. They shared a card table and a low bookcase which tilted slightly until Matt stuck a matchbook under the short side. Valerie put up flowered curtains and potted four little cactuses for the windowsill. Matt tacked up his picture postcards of the Apostles and—for color, he said—added a print of Salvador Dali's melting watches set in a cartoonishly desolate landscape. The room was small enough to collect smoke easily, though the ceiling was high, so Valerie cut down to a half pack a day.

Everyone got along seamlessly. Valerie never talked about what had happened with her and Terry, nor did Matt inquire. Terry had paired off with Marcia, though for reasons no one explained and about which no one asked, the two of them kept their separate quarters.

Valerie liked to watch the changes flicker across Matt's face—the brooding, the puppy-dog gratitude, the sudden grins, the lowered eyes. He did not consult the ceiling when they talked together. Matt liked kissing the little bump on Valerie's nose. He was thrilled by the soft skin of her thighs, so lean that he could half-encircle them in his hands.

Marcia Stein and Caroline Caldwell had already gotten to work on a welfare task force. Caroline was tall, blue-eyed, from south Texas, with a delicate accent. A narrow gap between her slightly prominent two front teeth compounded her charm. The idea was to head for the welfare office downtown and pass out mimeographed fliers on gold-colored paper (goldenrod, they called it) announcing that they were the CAMPAIGN FOR WELFARE RIGHTS and they were there to work with recipients. "Checks slashed? Caseworkers searching your closets? Hot water dried up? Hall lights missing? Boilers busted? WE CAN HELP."

Marcia, bouncy and articulate, sounded like an old pro, though she had been in Cleveland for less than a month. "Get names and addresses," she told Valerie. "Get phone numbers, if they have them, but most of them won't. Never mind, we'll get in touch with them."

"Right. A whole lot of people is strong," said Caroline, grinning broadly. It was a slogan, but she at least half-believed it.

The first time Valerie went downtown with the welfare group was uneventful—unless it qualified as an event that a spirited middle-aged woman read the flier, stared at Valerie, ducked her head in what might qualify as a nod, folded the paper in quarters and stuffed it into her outer pocket. But the second day, a cheerful young woman—thick-legged, with a cold sore on her thin lips, gripping a wrapped-up baby—came bustling up, glanced at a flier, and then, in a voice like treble guitar strings, twanged:

"Glory, I could use some help, let me tell you. They cut my check, which hit's already so skinny hit's about to faint, and I go in, I ask for an explanation, and they say, 'Policy. It's policy.' And I say,

'What's that mean, *policy?*' And this ol' four-eyes blue-haired bitch, you pardon my language, says, 'Will you calm down or do I have to call security?' And I said right back to her, 'Will *you* calm down?' Lord, I want to get shut o' these people, I swear I do!"

Her name was Charlotte. She came from a mining town south of Charleston, West Virginia, moved to Cleveland with an older daughter and a husband who abandoned her, and was now settled down with a man named Carlos. He was Cuban, of few words, while she talked a mile a minute.

Over the next days, Valerie babysat while Charlotte went out knocking on doors with Caroline and Marcia. Effervescent Charlotte led off: "Hi, we're from the community and we're looking for women who've got problems with the welfare ..." The response Charlotte received often was something along the lines of "Problems! Well, you come to the right place!" Within days a welfare mothers' group was meeting in her living room to share grievances about "this here welfare," which Charlotte called "nothing but slavery." She added, "We got to show these pasty-faced bastards downtown that we're not mops. They can't push us around."

Marcia took Valerie aside at one point and effused: "This woman's a born organizer."

So this is what it means to organize, Valerie thought. *It's fun.*

After two weeks, the trio of outsiders was outnumbered by Charlotte's contacts—"Charlotte's web," Valerie called them— who included (to mention only the ones who spoke up): Sherry, a trim woman from eastern Kentucky who had eleven kids and looked to be no more than thirty-five; Eveline, a huge woman from north Georgia whose arms were the diameters of some people's legs, and who spoke very slowly; Coretta, who had just given birth to a stillborn baby and blamed her misfortune on pitiful welfare payments; Betty, an old Jewish woman who once ran a newsstand and sprinkled her comments with references to "the working class"; and Mary, whose kids were grown and who thought "the colored" had the right idea—the way to make changes was to shake things up.

On Charlotte's couch, you had to sit carefully to avoid a broken spring. At the other end of the room stood a TV set with a hole punched in the speaker, standing in front of a wall that was missing some plaster and exposing the laths. When the other women arrived, their own babies in tow, Charlotte's oldest, Darlene—a girl of fourteen or fifteen, wearing overalls—kept watch over the young ones. Charlotte's baby, Mary-Alice, wandered through, gnawing on a peanut butter and jelly sandwich on white bread. Darlene, vigilant, brought a washcloth from the kitchen and wiped the little girl's mouth. An older girl with ruffled sleeves, holding a can of Pepsi, sat on the floor, watching a game show.

To take some pressure off Charlotte, the group decided to meet at Sherry's apartment the next time, but the stench of urine was too intense there, and the stare of the hydrocephalic boy sharing the sheetless mattress with a box of Tide was unnerving. *How can people live this way?* Valerie asked herself silently. She knew they had been oppressed their whole lives. She knew they suffered from bad nutrition and not enough of it. She knew pity was no help to anyone. She knew the right question to ask was: *How can they find strength in themselves?* But she couldn't stop herself from asking, *How can people live this way?*

The web moved back to Charlotte's. Since Darlene was working late that day at her waitress job, Charlotte's janitor boyfriend Carlos agreed to lend a hand with the kids (five of them now). He was a rotund, soft-spoken, square-faced man, with broad shoulders and thick arms and a pleasant smile. Marcia sat on a wobbly wooden chair, eyes on the kids even as she took part in the meeting.

Soon enough, the mothers' group put together a march on the welfare office. Bundled-up kids carried signs declaring that THIS IS AMERICA and that twenty-two cents per meal was not a decent allotment. They received a few inches of friendly attention in the *Plain Dealer*, with a photo on an inside page. The women were euphoric.

Matt, Terry, and the SDS guys found the going rougher. They read Saul Alinsky's book, *Reveille for Radicals,* and argued—on the basis of no experience—about how to "find community leaders" and "rub raw the wounds of resentment" (Alinsky's phrase). Leafleting at the unemployment office garnered a few dozen sign-ups, but no direction emerged from their unruly discussions. Aside from being unemployed, these men had little in common but alcohol. They lived scattered across the Near West Side. For the most part they did not work or play together. Their meetings foundered on speech-making, circling back to one or another version of "We sure need some good jobs." "Oh yeah." "Jobs, that's it." One grumbled that Negroes had taken their jobs. An old man who never took off his battered fedora, the skin around his mouth puckered like a prune left exposed to the air too long, denounced the Jews.

Matt was stunned. "Is Lyndon Johnson a Jew?"

"Sure he's a Jew!"

Matt couldn't resist: "What about Robert McNamara?"

"Why, he's also a Jew!"

An argument ensued about whether to show this man the door. The wounds of resentment did not align.

The "students," as they were known in the neighborhood, were at a loss. *Even if we found these proverbial leaders,* Matt thought but didn't say, *we wouldn't know how to train them. We don't know how to train ourselves.* Terry was unflagging. He spent days reading pamphlets written by Alinsky organizers and visiting union contacts in that hope that they could introduce them to groups of the unemployed. Those groups did not materialize. If you were willing to work day labor, there was work to be had in the neighborhood.

Winter crept closer, announcing itself in winds that whipped down the streets, shredding away body heat, but Matt, no stranger to winds off the Great Lakes, prided himself on standing fast against them. The wind was not the problem. The problem was lack of focus. The problem was the prevailing attitude: every man for himself.

Matt admired Terry, who always seemed to have something to say to prospective recruits. This was not Matt's strength. He needed a firmer foundation. He needed to think. He told Terry he would take charge of mimeographing but needed time off from knocking on doors. Terry nodded, looking dubious. Secretly relieved to escape the duty of trying to start conversations with strangers, Matt started spending long hours alone in his room. Mornings, Valerie made the bed and headed off with Charlotte's web, and Matt spent the day reading. He read about the rural populists of the last century, trying to extract from their history the promise that Terry had extracted. He read memoirs of union organizers from the Thirties. He'd always wondered about a book by Herbert Marcuse called *Eros and Civilization,* and now he devoured it, making elaborate notes on the utopian potential fairly bursting to explode forth from the human libido into an all-around erotic way of life, and on the difference between repression, which was biological, as Freud said, and surplus repression, which could be overcome by socialism properly organized. The problem was, how to move from a few folks grumbling about the city's lousy garbage collection to a movement of labor against capital that has a shot at making life more generous and cooperative? The problem seemed insoluble. It seemed, in fact, laughable. Too many links were missing. Not wanting to demoralize anyone, he didn't dare say so out loud. He spent time fidgeting with his glasses. His grins were fewer and farther between. Two short vertical frown lines appeared on his forehead, slashing downward.

"Who said this was going to be easy?" Valerie said to him, unhelpfully. "You need to cheer up."

"I do, don't I."

She placed her fingertips on the ends of his mouth and played at bending it into the simulation of a smile.

"Come on," she said. "I knew you could do it."

"Can I siphon off some of your good cheer?" he asked her, attempting a half-smile but abandoning it partway.

"Please do," she said and tapped him on the nose, and pecked him on the lips, before heading off to pass out leaflets.

He felt a bit better for a couple of days and wondered if he'd rather be in graduate school after all. She noticed how awkward he was, which did not always charm her. She felt like addressing him as "Your Grace," but that would have been mean, and she didn't want to be mean, she just wanted him to thrive. Damn it. He wasn't eating well. He took to scooping peanut butter straight out of the jar. One day, walking downstairs, he sprained his ankle. She thought he was losing weight. She was beginning to see, in him, signs of her older sister's dreadful withdrawal, her parched frailty, her refusal of life. Was Valerie possessed of a rescuer complex? To cheer herself up, she turned to reading Colette, more diverting than Doris Lessing. Men need not be tormentors. Perhaps, if organizing didn't work out, she'd move to Paris. Colette was a favorite of her departed Kathryn. Colette did not save Kathryn, of course, but Kathryn had been beyond saving. Valerie had tried. She *did* try.

Terry spent most of his time with the SDS group, trying to stoke up a rent strike in a big brick building ("1-1/2 room apartments" was the advertised specialty) where the boiler had completely broken down in subzero temperatures. Sure enough, Terry located a tenant who was willing to protest directly—"Hell, I got nothing better to do," said Ava, a plump woman in her forties from Arkansas, who left two of her children in the care of her ten-year-old and cradled a two-year-old boy at meetings—but the landlord was on vacation and management was in the hands of Charlotte's Carlos, whose furtive eyes dashed back and forth like a manual typewriter whose carriage was being thrown. He was sorry, but he could not authorize major repairs until the landlord returned.

"Ava here has something to tell you, then," Terry said, and Ava, her toddler asleep in her lap, took the cue. She told Carlos that the tenants were going to withhold the next month's rent, deposit it into an escrow account to be released only when the boiler was repaired and the other violations remedied. Carlos shrugged: "It's a free country, but you're nuts. And with respect, I must tell you something. I come from Havana. To me, private property is *sacred*."

The tenants wanted the landlord to sign a contract. Carlos laughed. This was Cleveland, not Cuba. Terry lined up a lawyer named Applebaum, an old Communist, who (pro bono) would help them draw up the document. Quite a victory it would be to sign the first tenant-landlord agreement in the history of Cleveland! Terry's eyes sparkled.

To keep the tenants free of pneumonia while sacredness won proper protection, the organizers collected used blankets from a local church, distributed them, and convened a meeting. With Valerie's connivance, Marcia got Matt out of his room, took him to the deeds office downtown, and showed him how to look up property records. Perhaps research would be his salvation. They located lots of decrepit buildings, totaling, in one case, two hundred fifty-six recorded violations on the part of a single landlord. A few days later, Carlos came by, poked ineffectually at the dysfunctional boiler, and a few days after that he dispatched a non-union repairman for an equally fruitless visit. Marcia, unfazed, located the landlord's home address, in a western suburb, and they organized a small but dogged picket line in front of his house, chanting "Slumlord!" They drew frightened looks through the curtained windows of neighbors. The local cops showed up, two of whom sat watchfully on their front fenders, heavy flashlights clanking from their thick belts, exchanging smirks with Terry.

For Matt, this activity was not as exalting as Marcuse's *Eros and Civilization,* let alone as invigorating as Alinsky, but two days into the picket line at the landlord's house he perked up at the astonishing sight of a cheerful Ronnie Silverberg—wearing a denim jacket, jeans, and a navy blue watch cap—operating a squarish black pistol-grip movie camera mounted on top of a tripod. He was interviewing Ava about conditions in her apartment, nodding gravely at her tales of woe, laughing along with her. He had trimmed his bushy eyebrows and acquired a crisp on-camera manner.

"I thought you were going to law school, become the next Clarence Darrow," Matt said once Ronnie was done with Ava.

"Didn't work out. *The* law, as they call it, bored my brains out. Death by statute. Case by case." Ronnie shuddered, then added: "A friend of my old man came to the rescue, hired me to travel around and shoot film, whatever looks interesting, for a documentary about the movement. Guy owns a factory now, runs an educational film business on the side. We'll see." He patted Matt on the shoulder. Matt needed all the morale boosts he could get, even when they were wrapped in condescension. Ronnie moved in, sharing Terry's space. "I'm beginning to see what you're doing here," he told Matt one day. "It's far out."

The landlord, a small man named Goldstein, with baggy eyes and the look of a man who has absorbed his punches, returned from vacation with a Florida tan and to everyone's amazement said he was willing to sign a contract in which he guaranteed specified repairs in exchange for the tenants' association guaranteeing the rent. Ava signed for the tenants. When he rolled up his sleeve— was it deliberate?—Matt could see the six-digit number tattooed in slightly fuzzed blue ink on his left forearm. The last two digits were "06." Ava asked Matt later what that meant. He told her this was something the Nazis did. She had never heard of such things. She wondered how a man who had suffered so much could treat his tenants so badly.

After the contract was signed, six more weeks passed without heat. Ava found an apartment in a nearby building, a smaller place but decently heated, and moved. The temperature ticked up a few degrees. Another resident of Goldstein's building, Ava's cousin, also moved out. Applebaum, the tenants' lawyer, charged breach of contract and got a court date.

Valerie, blooming, kept Matt apprised of the doings of Charlotte's web. They had an appointment with the county welfare commissioner. They made contact with a Negro group on the east side of town and met together to draw up common demands. Matt tried to rejoice for Valerie's sake. About the rent strike, he did his best to put on an enthusiastic show, but he had to ask

how many rent strikes, how many picket lines, how much research it was going to take to bind together the tenants of a single
rent-striking building and keep them from drifting away? They
had kids to take care of. They needed heat, not a contract—which
Ronnie, on the basis of a few weeks in a contracts class, doubted
would be enforceable anyway. Inside, Matt felt like a slow-motion cave-in. Valerie had no answers. Where, if anywhere, was this
going?

Terry McKay lumbered through the neighborhood, shoulders
hunched, eyes hungry, in search of young guys who showed signs,
any signs, of perking up with class anger. It was obvious that the
welfare mothers struck up a natural solidarity but the young guys
didn't. He started hanging out at a bar called True Country, where
he tried to turn the conversation to unemployment, only to discover
that the guys who clustered there, drank beer, shot pool, and played
the jukebox, seemed to be enmeshed in a competition over who
could appear most at ease wasting time. Whatever energy they displayed was fitful and dispersed; as a group, they were sarcastic when
they were not listless. They couldn't care less about the American
economy and the future of automation. They'd "done time" in coal
mines, steel mills, warehouses, and a nearby TV assembly plant.
They'd done day labor. Somehow, even between jobs, they could
peel off twenty dollar bills from rolls stuffed into their hip pockets.
Terry had no idea how they managed this, but they did. Even if
they were doomed to the unhappy fates celebrated in country-western songs, they felt lucky.

They recited sayings like, "That's the way it goes—first your
money, then your clothes" and "You can't win, and you better not
lose," and laughed. They bought rounds. They joshed about the in-
creasing brownness of the Cleveland Browns. They got Terry to
join their running argument over which centerfolds in *Playboy* and
Penthouse would best be fucked dog-style. Preening and putdowns
were their style. Sometimes the monotony was broken by strangers,

like the time when somebody shoved somebody off a barstool, resulting in an advisory to hang out someplace else, and a cut lip, and a growl, "Asshole," and more beer, more jukebox action, more stoic looks, more moodiness.

Patrol cars with red plastic domes, like fake crowns, cruised around the corner or stood outside double-parked. The young men glared, clucked, mouthed the word "cocksuckers," and complained about the cop sons-of-bitches who couldn't think of anything better to do than chase them off street corners. One lean, hawk-nosed fellow wearing a wool-lined denim vest—cowlick over his left eye, right arm in a cast hanging from a sling—had been pistol-whipped by a cop not long ago. His right cheekbone was puffed up.

"What for?" Terry asked.

"Mindin' my own business," the man said. His name was Billy Joe Webb.

"Oh yeah?" said Terry, trying to make it sound casual.

"Damn straight, mindin' my own business, workin' TV repair, when a cop come into the shop and asked for his monthly 'installment'—that's what he called it—and I knew this son of a bitch, knew he was no *damn* good, and I said to the boss, 'What's this guy talkin' about?' and the cop said to him, 'Your new guy's wet behind the ears, he don't know the rules,' and boss said, 'Give it to him,' and I said, 'I don't know there's a rule says you get a cash reward for hasslin' people who're just mindin' their business,' and next thing I knew he knocked me upside my head, broke my damn arm, and I was out on my ear 'cause the boss said I wasn't worth anything anymore with only my left hand."

"Maybe we should be gettin' together and put a stop to this bullshit, Billy Joe," Terry said earnestly.

Billy Joe gave him a no-shit stare, like, *There's a great idea, why didn't I think of that?* Terry chose to overlook the sarcasm. Billy Joe went on: "Sure thing, let's go on TV, tell 'em the cops are cocksuckers." The topic of conversation passed over to the Cleveland Indians and the question of whether their infield or their outfield was full of more holes.

Another fellow strolled in, helped himself to a wooden chair he pulled out from under the table and sat down facing backwards. "College," Billy Joe called him, a tall, wiry fellow, cocky, with milky blue eyes and sandy hair slicked back, whose actual name was Wyatt Burns. It turned out that Wyatt had grown up in the neighborhood, showed some smarts, and won a scholarship to Swarthmore. Why he had landed back in his old neighborhood wasn't clear. Did he flunk out? Get caught in the girls' dorm? He drummed his fingers on the back of the chair. He had a muscular torso, contained inside a plaid green sport jacket too small for him. Rumor had it that his father was a hit man for the mob.

Out of the blue, Wyatt snarled about "that fuckin' war," where, he said, his older brother served on an aircraft carrier off the Vietnam coast and wrote him that there was something fishy about that naval confrontation in the Gulf of Tonkin.

"Fishy is right," Terry contributed quietly.

Billy Joe addressed Wyatt. "College, you sayin' you're a pussy?"

"Rich man's war and the workin' man fights it," Wyatt grinned.

"Well, that's for sure."

Over the following days, conversation circled back to the subject of the police. The grousing ebbed and flowed. It was almost symphonic. Terry listened, bought rounds, didn't say much, paid close attention. A moment came. It was like the take-off moment when a date gets serious or an inadvertent bump turns into a fight. They should, Terry said, organize a patrol, follow police cars around the neighborhood, see what they're up to, put them on notice that a guy has the right to stand on a street corner. "They want to watch us? We can watch them."

Terry knew when he was commanding attention. This was one of those times. He spoke in full sentences separated by little coughs.

Billy Joe looked interested.

Wyatt slapped the table. "In. The. End"—for emphasis—"the cops respect one thing—firepower. That's it."

"You're nuts, man," Billy Joe scoffed. "That what they teach you in college?"

Terry invited them over to the staff house the next night to talk about what might be done.

Later, Terry briefed Matt, who was impressed, not for the first time, at the way Terry opened up contact. "You may think Billy Joe's a little crude. He *is* crude. He's a racist, in other words. But he's not stupid. And he's got energy. There's gotta be a way to get this guy together with the Negroes, right?" He pounded his fist in a let's-get-it-on way.

"I guess," Matt said. "Same enemies." He had no idea.

"Also," Terry added, "watch out for this guy they call 'College.' Talks a big game. Might be a gun nut. See what you think."

"So why are we inviting him over?"

"The other guys respect him."

Matt looked quizzical, but he knew there was a lot he didn't understand.

"Like Alinsky says," Terry added, "you take leaders where you find them." And an afterthought: "Interesting that he doesn't smoke." It occurred to Matt that Terry didn't smoke either. Not smoking was rare. Maybe it went with leadership, discipline.

Billy Joe brought along a friend called James. Matt noted that Billy Joe walked coiled, on the balls of his feet, like a leader. "College" he found too eager to impress. They exchanged nods, Billy Joe lifting his right-arm cast as a greeting.

Two of the SDS organizers arrived with Ronnie Silverberg. Steve Coleman was a short, well-built fellow with an impressively black pompadour and a heavy motorcycle jacket; Ben was spindly, blinking a lot behind rimless glasses; Ronnie was in jeans and a denim jacket. When Valerie passed through the living room on her way to the kitchen, she was inspected with admiration.

The guys talked over each other, but Terry was cheered. This might be the affinity moment, some kind of rhythm at work among the guys, so that "the students" would no longer feel like outsiders parachuting into the neighborhood, issuing stilted manifestos, striving to drop final "g's." Wyatt, who drove a big Ford Galaxie, a bright blue boat of a car, volunteered to drive them around on patrol Saturday nights. Billy Joe suggested they keep records of police brutality. Everyone liked these ideas. James made notes for a complaint form, which Wyatt typed out on a stencil. They mimeographed a hundred copies, divided them up, and over the next days started collecting complaints—some crisp, some vague, a few that went on for pages. Matt volunteered to collect them. For the first time in Cleveland, he felt something rolling.

He could envision a march of insurgent street toughs to the police station. The thought grew on him that they might be, in their own way, another band of apostles. His life in bed perked up. He told Valerie that he could feel the guys' moodiness ignite, turn to energy. She felt relieved that he'd dug his way out of his darkness, though she feared he might be getting ahead of himself. Anyway, they were making love again.

Turned out that Billy Joe liked to write songs, and now that he was freed of his cast and his sling, he played the guitar. One evening he trotted out a song about a girlfriend who done him wrong:

> *You said you'd always stand by me*
> *My amazing Grace—*
> *Now look who's there behind you*
> *With his arm around your waist—*

Everyone whooped. They'd all been there.

March crashed in with subzero nights, the wind off Lake Erie slicing straight to the bone, the unmelting snowdrifts turning tarblack, trapping parked cars, their engines wheezing pathetically as neighbors uncoiled jumper cables and sprayed sweet-smelling chemicals on dysfunctional batteries. Life was an assault. Just to ease a car away from the curb and over black ice to get to a meeting or a movie, or out of the neighborhood anywhere, was a major achievement. They postponed the patrols.

Eventually the day came. Big fuzzy dice swung from Wyatt's rear-view mirror as he tapped at the steering wheel while Billy Joe flicked drum brushes with his good hand on the dashboard. Terry and Matt shared the backseat, holding clipboards. They kept a block's distance behind a patrol car until a siren whined. Wyatt winced at the flashing blue and red lights in the rear-view mirror, and pulled to the curb.

"Didn't take long," Billy Joe drawled.

Matt pulled from his pocket a tiny silver-steel Minolta camera that he had bought from a mail-order catalogue for forty bucks, a crappy looking little thing the size of a big cigarette lighter, made of two halves that you pressed together to take a picture. He had had the foresight to load it with film.

Two cops took their time lumbering to the front of the Galaxie while the patrol car up ahead made a U-turn, came back around with its blue and red lights putting on a show, and double-parked on the other side of the street.

The cop on Wyatt's side of the Galaxie, a hefty gentleman, said, "Driver's-license-and-registration," as if that was a single word.

"What's the trouble, officer?" said Wyatt.

"Out of the car."

"Excuse me?"

"You deaf or something? Out of the car!"

Avoiding a direct look, Wyatt complied. He pulled his license and registration out of his wallet. Hefty produced a small flashlight. There was no street lamp nearby. "There a problem, officer?"

Shining his flashlight straight into Wyatt's eyes, Hefty said gruffly, "You know you got a broken tail light." It was more statement than question.

"That so?" Wyatt turned toward the rear. "Funny. Was good this afternoon. Let me look."

"Turn around," Hefty commanded, elbowing him in the right kidney. Wyatt fell forward against the car door, biting his lip to cut off a moan.

"You stay right there," Hefty said. "No steps. None."

"You others, get out of the car," said the other cop, whose hawk face was heavily furrowed, whether by nature or injury was not clear. "Now. Leave the doors open."

Matt scrambled out onto the sidewalk, stepped back a few paces, backed away from the Galaxie, and waited. Terry, on the street side, turned toward the trunk. Billy Joe waited idly. Hawk-Face poked around the rear seat, reached under the driver's seat, found Billy Joe's drum brushes, plucked them out and brandished them as if they were concealed weapons. Matt pulled his camera out of his pocket, pointed it toward Hawk-Face, and squeezed the halves together. *Click.*

Hefty heard. He charged and snatched the camera out of Matt's hands. He was surprisingly fast on his feet.

Matt said stupidly, "Hey!" Whatever fear he had felt, he no longer felt, but rather a bizarre kind of elevation.

Terry, behind the Galaxie, called out: "The tail light is fine."

Hefty strode to the rear, shoved Terry out of the way, and smashed the left tail light with his nightstick. "You need glasses, son. You got a driver's license?"

From across the street, two more cops approached, holsters and handcuffs jingling against thick waists. One held a clipboard.

"What about you other guys?" said Hefty. "You got ID?"

"Don't need no license to ride in a car," said Billy Joe.

"That so? Open your trunk."

It occurred to Terry to demand that the cops show them a search warrant, but instantly he erased that fugitive thought.

Wincing, Wyatt jerked open the trunk with his left hand. Hawk-Face ambled over, felt around in the tire well, picked up the jack, tossed the drum brushes onto the floor of the trunk and, with the jack, smashed them. It was impressive, in a way, how casually he performed his routine. He capped his performance by tossing the jack onto the ruined brushes.

No one said a word.

"Wait there," Hefty told Wyatt, then turned to Terry and said, "Lemme see your operator's." Terry, his face rigid, handed over his license.

"Says here you require corrective lenses."

"I do when I'm driving."

"Well, you never know. You may have to drive if your friend here—" pointing to Wyatt "—turns out unable." He repeated the ritual with Billy Joe and Matt.

If Terry was frightened, he didn't show it. Matt felt fear chewing into his bones. "You don't need a license to take a picture either."

"You're in Cleveland, Ohio, now, Matthew Stackhouse, Jr. We issue the licenses."

Hefty and Hawk-Faced sauntered back to their car and filled out forms. Wyatt pressed the back of his right hand against his lower back and straightened up gingerly.

Two women of indeterminate age were standing on the sidewalk, it wasn't clear for how long. One had tight dark curls under a bright kerchief, the other was tall, broad-shouldered, heavyset.

Wyatt breathed heavily. "You see what happened here? Ma'am? You see them stop us for nothing? Hit me for no reason?" The one in the kerchief shook her head. The longer he looked at her, the older she looked.

Matt had the unhappy feeling that she was thinking: "They should have hit you harder."

Hefty ambled back to the car clutching the licenses, registration, and a ticket. "Better repair that light, Mr.—Wyatt Burns. It's very dangerous when you brake and the car behind you gets no warning. People get hurt. We don't want anyone hurt, do we." Wyatt had worked out how hard he could glare at the hefty cop without inciting more trouble. He stopped just short of the limit.

Matt cleared his throat and summoned his peak politeness. "Officer, my camera—"

"Oh, sure. Here you are, Matthew." He passed it over casually.

They got back into the Galaxie and wordlessly pulled away from the curb.

Terry let out a long breath and asked Wyatt if he was OK.

"Could be worse," said Wyatt. "The first time it happened to me, I peed blood."

Matt slid his finger slowly along the edges of the camera—once, twice—said, "Shit," and clicked on the inside roof light. The long side of the Minolta was visibly and significantly dented. He tried squeezing the two halves together. They were immovable. He shook the thing. Nothing happened. "Idiots couldn't figure out how to get the film out," he said, "so they fucking wrecked the camera."

Wyatt turned around and glowered at Matt. "I saw how you got a picture of them whacking me. I knew I could count on you."

"Hey, there was no light." Matt was taken aback. "Thing doesn't have a flash."

"Didn't stop you from trying to get a picture of them searching the car."

Matt didn't know what to say.

Terry whispered to Matt: "Easy."

"I guess you didn't exactly see what was happening, right?" Wyatt sneered. "Could be he was making nice. Or goosing me."

"Must hurt," Billy Joe said to Wyatt.

"This patrol thing is fucked up," said Billy Joe after Wyatt dropped Terry and Matt at the staff house.

Terry considered. "The camera was a good idea, it got them to back off. Maybe we bring Ronnie along next time, shoot film, tell them to smile, they're going to be in a movie." He paused. "Of course the problem is our guys are not a well-oiled machine."

Matt's heart was clogging his throat, but he saw no sign that Terry felt any fear whatsoever.

Upstairs, Valerie slept, the ashtray at her side holding a single crushed butt, half-smoked. Matt, disquieted, crawled into bed next to her, watched her chest rise and fall, fingered his broken camera like a sprained knuckle, stared at the ceiling, played back the night's events. Some bunch of apostles! Some IMP! It came to him that the cheering insurgents that Terry carried around in his imagination didn't wear polo shirts and leather jackets, or drive Galaxies; they brandished swords and muskets, and waved little

French revolutionary caps at the ends of their bayonets. The movie Terry was watching in his mind's eye was set on the narrow cobblestone streets of eighteenth-century Paris, horses clopping through the darkness, puffs of gun smoke curling up against the walls of the Bastille, which the insurgents, their minds filled with incendiary pamphlets about the state of nature and the iniquity of the king, were about to tear down, one brick at a time, in a century long dead.

To be honest, Matt knew he had been watching the same movie.

He went down to the kitchen and started writing a sardonic letter to Kurt Barsky, telling him what he was missing in Cleveland and culminating in a riff on Terry's relentlessness. "I admire him. I resent him. The more I see of him, the less I understand him. I can't figure out how this guy slides through life so smoothly. When we spend time together, why do I come away feeling pathetic? Did he make you feel that way? Or is it just me? If he's my leader, do I have to like him? You lived with the guy. I thought you'd have some insight."

He tore up the letter, threw the pieces away, and went upstairs to bed.

A couple of days later, Wyatt looked surprisingly calm, sitting feet up on the couch in the staff house leafing through the reports on police misconduct that James had been collecting. Terry walked in lugging two six-packs of Schmidt's Beer and said: "Wyatt, good that you're doing this."

Wyatt peered at him. "Yeah. Got to be some way we can use this stuff."

Terry considered. "One thing is, say whatever you want, the cops are worried about us now. I think we should keep going with the patrols. Next time bring Ronnie along, shoot film."

"I've been thinking," Wyatt said, "we need to get together with the coloreds. They don't scare easy."

"You know any of those guys?" Terry asked. He liked the fact that Wyatt was thinking strategically. Crossing the race line was, after all, the original idea of the interracial movement of the poor. But timing was everything. Terry's intuition told him the time hadn't arrived.

"I don't, not really. I do run into some of their—merchants, though." Wyatt pulled a small, bright metal pistol from his inside jacket pocket. "You like me to get you one?"

Terry begged off. *Not a well-oiled machine,* he thought.

Valerie and Marcia passed by on their way into the kitchen, humming. Terry wondered how Valerie was getting along with Matt. *He must not be easy.* Wyatt watched Marcia go and declared: "Wouldn't kick her out of bed." Nodding at Valerie, he added: "Her neither."

Sometimes the True Country boys dropped in to get a look at the TV news. One summer evening, Matt and Marcia sat on the scarred couch, beers in hand, watching a Marine in South Vietnam torch a thatched roof with his lighter while a second Marine, in a flak jacket, opened up with a flame thrower. Billy Joe sat in a battered armchair and glared.

The reporter, Morley Safer, said: "This is what the war in Vietnam is all about." Vietnamese women, holding babies, staggered out of the basement shelters where they'd taken refuge, weeping and running. Safer asked a Marine if he was "getting fire" from a house that he had set aflame. "Somewhat," the Marine said, "not too much, they were sacrificed." Safer said: "Today's operation burned down a hundred and fifty houses, wounded three women, killed one baby, wounded one Marine, and netted these prisoners—" shown blindfolded as they were led away by Marines "—four old men who could not answer questions put to them in English." Safer addressed the camera: "There's little doubt that military firepower can win a victory here. But to a Vietnamese peasant whose home means a lifetime of backbreaking labor, it will take more

than presidential promises to convince him that we are on his side."
There was a sound of wailing.

Cringing, Marcia stared at the screen. Matt opened a second
bottle of Schmidt's and drained it. Millions of Americans watched
this without revolting. The country was diseased. Matt tasted disgust, something rancid, way back in his throat.

"When did we turn into Nazis?" Marcia howled as she leaped
up and ran out of the room, slamming the door behind her.

Billy Joe swiveled toward Matt and barked out: "Come on!
Fuckin' Commonists."

"What do you mean?"

Billy Joe, flames shooting out of his eyes, said: "Come on! You
can *tell* this ain't the whole story. They don't show what happened
before. They're Commonists there. We're defending ourselves."

Matt anticipated a whole blasted landscape of argument
stretching out before them and decided not to bother. He went into
the kitchen. Marcia looked ghastly. She was boiling a pot of water.
Matt wanted to say something soothing, not that he blamed her for
her reaction. "What you said before—"

She interrupted him: "You have to understand something,
Matt. My parents met in Auschwitz."

"My God" was all he could manage to say.

"It's hard," Marcia said, "it is so fucking hard, you have no idea."

Matt read about a woman in Detroit named Alice Herz, a Jewish
pacifist who fled Germany in 1933, and now, in 1965, in the United
States of America, stood on a busy street corner, doused herself
with cleaning fluid, and set herself on fire. A passing motorist who
stopped to help stamp out the flames said that she looked "like a
flaming torch." In her purse was a letter saying that she wanted "to
call attention to the problems of South Viet Nam" by dying "the
illuminating death of a Buddhist." She had stuffed her mouth with
cotton. She died of her burns nine days later.

"There'll be more," Terry said grimly.

Matt didn't bring up Alice Herz in front of Billy Joe. He didn't want to hear what he'd say.

At True Country one night, Wyatt went on about "the fuckin' war," and Billy Joe said actually he was thinking of signing up because if he wasn't fit for anything else he could at least go and kill himself a Commonist. "Patriot is as patriot does," he said, and Wyatt allowed as how that sounded mighty brave of him, and Billy Joe said, "Yeah? What's keepin' *you* out?" and Wyatt said, "You calling me a faggot or what?" and the next thing he knew he was holding his bleeding nose as Billy Joe walked away.

Having dropped out of school, Matt was notified that his student draft deferment had expired. The subject of the draft dropped into many conversations. Newspapers mentioned alternatives and ruses. There was such a thing as a conscientious objector. If you appeared before your draft board and told them that you believed in a Supreme Being who commanded you not to take up arms, they had to consider your case. If the words "I believe in a Supreme Being" stuck in your throat, you could try saying something else, or you could sing them Buffy Sainte-Marie's great song, "Universal Soldier," best known in the pop version by Donovan but far more grave and angry in her own Indian voice. If the members of the draft board asked if you would have fought Hitler, you could say that so far as you knew, Hitler was dead and we were not going to war with him again. The local board, made up of veterans and small businessmen, would turn you down. You would appeal to the state board. The FBI would investigate. They could interview anybody they liked to determine your character and the sincerity of your beliefs about war. They would write up their interviews and the state board would make a decision. This all would take months, maybe years. Odds were they would decide you were not a conscientious objector, but while they were deciding, they couldn't draft you. If and when they turned you down, you'd have lost nothing. In the meantime, you'd stalled them off and they might forget about you, or the war might end.

Though the war would not end.

Matt had been hearing about how to prepare for the physical. You visit a shrink. You starve yourself or stay awake several days running. You stand in ice water long enough to come down with a cold. You get very, very stoned. You say you're in love with your former gym teacher. You bring proof that you've fathered children or applied to go to divinity school. You show up filthy, muttering to yourself. You feel an irrepressible urge to attack authority figures.

Such tactics were evasions. Matt did not want to evade. He wanted to resist. Some of his peers were starting to burn their draft cards. They did it in public. They put their bodies on the line. Congress passed a law decreeing a penalty of up to five years in jail and a $10,000 fine for "knowingly destroying" or "knowingly mutilating" your draft card. But going to jail would take you out of action. It would look like a confession of guilt. It would confirm the authority of the authorities.

His mind was a broken record of indecision.

Terry, for his part, started seeing a shrink, and recommended him to Matt, who thought this was almost funny, since Terry was about the most stable person he knew. The system would be crazy to draft Terry McKay. Why would they want him running around their army making trouble? Matt didn't want to play evasion games. He wrote to his draft board declaring that he was a conscientious objector to war. He told them he was trying to show young men in Cleveland how to seek their own conscientious objector status. A month later, he was summoned to an appointment before his board. Terry went with him. They sang antiwar songs all the way to Chicago.

On the northwest side of Chicago, wizened old men asked Matt the predictable questions, as well as one that Matt was not expecting:

"Your father is a minister. We understand he was in the service. We understand that he has a Purple Heart. Does he agree with what you're doing here?"

"You'd have to ask him," Matt said quietly.

Terry was made to wait in an adjacent room, where he read a history of the Vietnam war. A cadaverous draft board member wearing an obvious toupee smirked as Matt read aloud the lyrics to "Universal Soldier."

On the drive back to Cleveland, Matt didn't feel much like singing. He doubted he had convinced anyone of his sincerity. Absurdly, his mind drifted back to the Apostles. If they were alive, they would spend their days crammed into caravans, swapping stories, breaking bread, pleading their case, discussing the resurrection of Jesus, figuring out whom to recruit and how to approach the Gentiles—heartened in behalf of humanity.

Matt let Terry in on his interest in the Apostles.

"I know your dad is a minister," Terry said. "Must be strange, you hanging out with all these atheists."

"I fell off the wagon a long time ago. But the story of the Apostles keeps coming back to me."

"Your archetype," Terry chuckled. "I have to say, the whole Christian thing makes no sense to me." He paused. "But I know it helps people deal with their suffering." He was as solemn as a mountain.

The case of the landlord-tenant contract came to trial. Goldstein's lawyer moved for dismissal on the ground that the contract was null and void. It turned out that, by mistake, the expiration date written into the contract was the same as the date it went into effect. No one had noticed. The judge ruled that the contract was, in fact, null and void, and the case was dismissed.

Matt took to burrowing back under the covers as soon as he awoke. By the time he opened his eyes again, nothing would have changed. If there was any doubt before, there was none now: He had no feel for this community, so how could he organize there? He was an alien dropped into the Near West Side of an alien city, and the theories of what was supposed to happen there were, simply put, otherworldly. Those Negro kids in Birmingham weren't isolated when they went up against the police dogs. They were the champions—the apostles—of their community. But Matt had never seen any sign that the elders of the Near West Side regarded the volatile young guys as champions. "Punks" was more like it. They did not elicit especially warm feelings in Matt. As for the young guys, they never mentioned their families. An occasional harsh remark about landlords was all they had to say about the community. They wanted to fight the cops, period. The elders wanted the cops to protect them—from the young guys, among others.

There had to be something else to do—for him, Matt Stackhouse, not Terry McKay, not Valerie Parr, not Marcia Stein or Caroline Caldwell or the SDS guys. Somehow, they kept their batteries charged. But he thought they, too, were organizing with mirrors.

He wrote desolation poetry—Eliotic melancholy punctuated by Ginsbergian howls. The results were not pretty. He was marooned. Valerie was no longer asking him what he was doing with his days—or at least that was his impression.

Where would he be without Valerie? Where is he *with* her?

The pillow that her long hair spilled onto was *his* pillow. But he wasn't enjoying his luck—no energy and only the most fleeting animal delights. By the time he dragged himself out of bed in the morning, she was usually in the bathroom, or downstairs with toast, eggs, coffee, and a cigarette, or off writing leaflets, consulting with allies, talking tactics. They exchanged perfunctory comments about Vietnam, but otherwise she was fixated on the doings of Charlotte's web, about which, in truth, he was sick and tired of hearing.

A few weeks after the abortive patrol, he hauled himself out of bed and heard, through the bathroom door, which Valerie had left cracked open, the squeak of the faucet as she turned off the shower. She was, of all things, whistling. The glow of her green ring caught the morning light on the bed stand. His own grayness was all the more blatant.

"*You're* in a good mood," he called out, which was also a way of saying who wasn't.

"What?"

"Nothing." She no longer sympathized with his aggressive self-pity but didn't want to pretend things were also going badly for her.

Charlotte's web was recruiting and going citywide, she burbled. She only worried whether they were moving too fast, setting up expectations they couldn't meet.

"Lucky you, to have that kind of problem." This was not the first time he envied her Charlotte's web. "Women play well with others, don't they? You get the organizers, and we get the muscle guys in the muscle cars. They also have muscles in their heads."

"It's true," she said, wanting to back away from an out-and-out quarrel, "our ladies are pretty good at cooperation." She didn't need to state the obvious, namely, that women in general were more patient and resilient than men, and better listeners. "But don't get the idea that it's one big picnic for us either."

He headed into the bathroom, which did not accommodate two. She squeezed out sideways past him, face to the wall, wrapped in her towel.

With his fingers, he wiped off a space in the steamed-up mirror. His monkish look had grown more extreme. His cheekbones were more savage. His face looked damaged by gravity.

Having put on a simple flowered dress, Valerie was back at the doorjamb studying him in the mirror. "You know, Matt, *please* take this in a friendly way, but really, the fact that the lady novices are doing pretty well doesn't take anything away from you." She knew—but didn't want to say out loud—that this was not a guy problem, it was a Matt problem. He was the one who was hiding under his covers. She tried to cushion his feelings. Which he appreciated, sort of, though the fact that she saw him at such low ebb made him feel more exposed, more pathetic.

"Come on, Matt, for the hundredth time, cheer up! Get yourself going!" As these words flew out of her mouth, she dimly recollected speaking the identical words to her big sister Kathryn. To Kathryn, too, they must have sounded like rank ultimatum talk—uncomprehending and futile.

The hundredth time. It wasn't her fault that it was so hard for Matt to get out of bed in the morning.

"I know this is hard for you," he said quietly, but with an edge. He really didn't want to drag her into his hole, did he? Or did he? But neither of them could deny that she was thriving while he was diminishing.

He kicked the door shut behind him—or not quite shut. It slammed on her hand. She screamed.

She shoved him away as she dashed to the sink and plunged her left hand under the cold-water faucet. Her forefinger was gashed and swollen, the skin on her middle finger cracked. Her blood, ferocious and cruel, spilled onto the porcelain. Her face in the mirror was distended with pain, rage, astonishment.

Now they both knew what he had inside him: volcanic fury. He got sulfurous whiffs of it from time to time. But he didn't mean to hurt her. Obviously. She lifted her wounded finger and blew on it.

"Don't blow on it," he said stupidly. "Just wash it out. You'll be OK."

"Thanks for the great advice, Matt." She washed the cut. He grabbed a bar of soap only to feel it slip out of his hand. He watched her blood come as if in a movie. He was the monster. She breathed hard. Fair enough: She was entitled to play this for the full melodrama. Matt scrambled for the soap.

"Soap too! I never would have thought of that!" She scrubbed the cut, bit her lower lip, pressed the palm of her good hand against the mirror for no apparent reason.

"Val. Oh Jesus. I didn't mean—"

She said nothing.

"I'm sorry, I'm sorry, I'm sorry. I'm stupid, I'm clumsy. Jesus Christ." She was unimpressed. He might as well not have been there. He punched the wall with his right fist. Plaster flaked off. Pain shot down his arm.

He shook his right hand, reached into the medicine chest, plucked out boxes of gauze and bandages, dropped them onto the side of the sink. He found the mercurochrome, unscrewed the top, held up the glass applicator. She took it from him and applied it to her wound, leaving a screaming orange stain on her skin.

He kneeled on the cold bathroom tile. All he could offer was bad theater. The audience was cold.

"I didn't know your hand was there. You know I didn't, Val. Really."

"You didn't know," she repeated, watching her hand bleed. "I know you didn't know. You barely notice me. You're too busy feeling sorry for yourself."

"I don't know what's wrong with me. I can't tell you how sorry I am. I swear, Val. I'm better than this. We're better than this. I feel so bad."

"Sometimes I think feeling bad is your all-purpose solution," she said.

When they went down to breakfast, her left forefinger and middle finger were snugly bandaged together, her hair combed, her face arranged in a passable blankness. "What happened?" Marcia asked.

"Stupid accident," Valerie said, arms akimbo. "It's nothing." After scarfing down scrambled eggs and coffee, she swept out of the house, head high, to meet Charlotte.

The day was cold, bright, and windless, the winter biting so hard it left bruises. But he could not blame the winter for his foul state of mind. He had degenerated into a dangerous boor. He thought of going to see Terry's shrink.

He trudged down the block in the glaring light, gazing blankly into the middle distance. The worn houses, wooden and sad, stared back, acknowledging that they had nothing else to show but peeling paint, all the sadder for the light's surprising strength. Bleakness was all. As if regressing to childhood, Matt stepped gingerly over the cracks that divided sidewalk sections. Avoiding cracks would be his achievement for the day.

He turned the corner, turned a second corner into the alley behind the staff house. He was a year and three months into this so-called organizing with nothing to show for it.

A car rumbled. A late-model tan Plymouth inched along behind him, keeping a distance. He spun around. The glare off the windshield obscured the driver's face. The car pulled alongside. A bulging headlight beam, unlit, was mounted next to the driver's side. The broad-shouldered, middle-aged driver wore a mud-colored fedora tilted back on his head at an angle that a mystery writer would call jaunty.

"Mr. Stackhouse," the man said, enjoying himself. His smile was thin. So was his mustache, and his green tie. The total effect was villainous.

Matt was startled. "How do you know my name?"

"How're your folks doing in Chicago? Nice town, Chicago."

"Who are you?"

"Your folks know what you're doing here?"

"Why are my parents any of your business?"

"You're an impatient fellow," the man said, sticking out his hand. "John Hlavaty. Sgt. Hlavaty."

The man called Hlavaty waited. Matt said nothing.

"Well, see you next time, Mr. Stackhouse." The Plymouth crept on down the alley.

Back at the staff house, at dinner, Matt told the story. "Congratulations," Terry said, making a sour-lemon face. "You've made the acquaintance of Sgt. John Hlavaty, chief of the Cleveland Red Squad. He wants us to know he's paying attention."

"We should be honored," said Marcia. "We'll be up on the walls of the post office soon."

Matt did not agree. It was not a sign of honor, it was a sign of Hlavaty's cluelessness, and the scarcity of actual Reds in Cleveland, that he should think their lame little project deserved scrutiny.

Some weeks passed. Matt's mother forwarded a form letter from his draft board. The board had turned down his application for conscientious objector status. Under "Explanation" was written the word "Ineligible." Matt filled out an appeal form and mailed it to an address in Springfield, Illinois. Neither Terry nor Valerie thought it was a coincidence that Hlavaty had showed up not long after Matt registered his conscientious objection to military service.

Bless Valerie for her resilience. If Matt was a bottom-feeder, she was a high-flier. She glided through the world with aplomb. No sad-sack boyfriend was going to drag her down.

Charlotte's web hummed throughout the winter and into the spring. She was cheery again—until the day she wasn't.

April delivered sudden spikes of warmth, trees budding overnight, and pollen declaring war on Matt's sinuses. Then came wilder spikes and sudden troughs, humidity bloating up off Lake Erie like the atmosphere of a less habitable planet. Matt refused to be conquered by allergies or all-around malaise. He started his days by doing ten pushups as soon as he got out of bed, then graduated to twenty, then thirty. He tiptoed around Valerie. Now that she was no longer flaring at him, she seemed bored. He saw her point. He bored himself.

Household life settled. The staff house had a new cooking rotation. Valerie and Marcia alternated spaghetti with prime steaks that they slipped into the extra-large purses they found suitable for shopping at the chain supermarket. Terry improvised tacos with refried beans, which could be stored in a huge pot, kept in the fridge, and ladled out, each evening, after refrying in fresh lard for crispness. Matt did his best with hot dogs and beans.

Valerie brought news about Charlotte's web, who now met regularly with the east side Negro women to put together a city-wide demonstration. That cheer circulated for a couple of weeks until the spring turned gelid.

"If we're not moving forward," Marcia said doubtfully, "we're moving backwards. Maybe we should be thinking bigger. A statewide demonstration, or even national. Force Johnson to choose between the Great Society and the Great War." Marcia thought ahead. Her childhood had trained her for that.

One day Charlotte's biweekly check was cut by twenty percent. "They" might be retaliating because she was making a pest of herself at headquarters. "They" might suspect that her boyfriend Carlos was sleeping over and supplying the household with provisions—strict violations of the rules. Charlotte spoke to her caseworker, who told her to speak to her supervisor. This required a trip downtown, where the supervisor told her that it was "against policy" to show her the rule on the basis of which she was being punished. When Charlotte reported on this development—"Can you believe this stuff?!"—Valerie was mind-boggled to see life-experience aping literature, for she had read Kafka's *The Trial*, in which Joseph K. was informed that it was against the law to show him the text of the law that required his punishment.

Charlotte's web resolved to sit-in at the welfare office downtown.

Which brought them to the day when Valerie came back to the staff house late and in tears.

"I'm OK," she told Marcia. "It's just that everything else is a disaster."

Charlotte had come home from the welfare office early and found Carlos in bed with her daughter Darlene. She was hysterical. She was quitting the group. She cracked Carlos in the skull with a chopping board before she went after him with a knife and sent him packing. Charlotte blamed herself for this disaster. If she had paid more attention to her own household, this wouldn't have happened.

Charlotte's life was ruined and so was the web.

Or was it? Early the next morning, Valerie seized the phone. No sooner had she hung up than it rang again. The group scheduled a meeting. She stayed on the phone for hours. Between calls, she smoked frantically. The question was not whether the Campaign for Welfare Rights could go on, but how?

Matt was awed at the sight of Valerie sailing out of the house with her shoulders thrown back and her arms swinging. The woman had the knack. She and Marcia were in tune, like a girl group.

The True Country guys also came back to life. Billy Joe stopped picking fights over Vietnam. A sign-up list for police patrols circulated. The sky was a blazing blue. Unstoppable spring was in the air. Matt's nostrils filled with fragrances. Valerie's fingers were scarless and smooth. She no longer glared at him. He was making it up to her.

It was May Day, the day of spring, revolution, and distress.

Later that day, time would stop.

Waking up in the days and weeks to come—if he slept at all—he would feel, at first, nothing, and then his humiliation would flood back in, and he would be awash, thrashing around in the sewage-filled whirlpool of the world.

There would be times when he would flex his memory, as if supposing he could recreate the precise sequence of events, trace how A led to B, which led to C, he could rewrite the story, pinpoint the crossroads and turning points and points of no return, and thus figure out what exactly he might have done to avert disaster.

Perhaps, if he could see his disgrace as the consequence of his acts, not divine punishment or an unearned curse upon his existence, he would feel better.

Unlikely.

Why did they move to Cleveland in the first place? Actually, by replaying and re-replaying the sequence, Matt was gouging his wound deeper.

But it was beyond absurd to nickel-and-dime your own life. You would never catch Pascal doing that, or Nietzsche.

In the late afternoon of the day when Valerie glided out of the staff house to help resuscitate the Campaign for Welfare Rights, Matt accompanied Terry to True Country, there to meet Steve and Ben from SDS, hang out, plan more patrols, see if anyone had a bright idea how to stop the cops from running them off the corners, which they were now doing regularly. A guy had a God-given right to stand around and watch the world go by. This was America!

Wyatt wasn't around, but Steve and Ben were at a corner table with Billy Joe, his taciturn friend James, and Ronnie Silverberg. Billy Joe was drinking rum and Coke in a tall glass. Terry sensed apathy around the table.

Billy Joe finally told Ronnie, "Next patrol, bring your movie camera along."

"You gonna make me a movie star?" Billy Joe's sarcasm was lost on no one.

They ordered more rounds. They disputed the reasons why the Cleveland Indians were such losers. They laughed at Elvis Presley for recording "Crying in the Chapel." They approached moments of focus, then lost them.

Ronnie was in an ill humor. He felt unemployed. Neighborhood girls posed for him, and sleeping around was interesting until it wasn't. Caroline was too quiet and too bony. Ronnie shot footage of welfare picket lines—not very cinematic.

Matt finally scraped back his chair, said he was heading home. Billy Joe suggested they get some pizza, head over to his place, and play nickel-dime poker.

Sunlight filled the street with a sense of vague expectation. Matt breathed it in. There was promise in the air. Then he heard a sudden screech of brakes. At the far end of the block, a big two-toned car, red on black, had plowed into a pick-up truck. Black smoke steamed from the crumpled hood. Matt quickened his pace. By the time he reached the collision, a couple of passersby were opening up the doors and helping the drivers out. The pickup had West Virginia plates. Matt saw no reason to stick around. Might as well head back to the staff house by an unaccustomed route. Shadows were sharpening, the light was tarnished gold.

He dawdled down a couple of blocks, turned, and found himself in a grand arcade of elms. Life was passable. Cleveland was a place like any other place—what you made of it. Halfway down the next block, he was struck by the sight of a strikingly blue two-tone Galaxie parked under one of the sheltering elms. This piqued his interest. The Galaxie, what a thing of beauty, plush, wide, and long, surely a sign of the time—a rolling icon of affluence and power, exactly the sort of radiant acquisition that young men rush out to buy on time. Who needed a socialist revolution if you could cruise along power-steering your Galaxie with two fingers? Not for the first time he thought that Herbert Marcuse was probably right that a society that "delivers the goods" cushions the chains of servitude and locks the workers into a soft prison, blinded to the fact that the gates are, in fact, unlocked. Who needs a new stage of civilization to have fun?

Matt saw that this particular Galaxie boasted two intact tail-lights. He smiled and kept walking. A shaft of light shot into the car. He saw fuzzy dice hanging from the rear-view mirror.

So many coincidences in the world! This one was not, on reflection, altogether surprising. The kind of young man who loved horsepower, chrome strips and the wide prairie expanse of the Galaxie would be partial to fuzzy dice.

As he pulled even with the front seat, Matt saw, inside, a slightly bent pants leg stretched out beneath the steering wheel, and, toward the passenger side, the unmistakable green jacket and the reddish hair on the back of the head that pressed downward onto another face, and he did not have to look twice to recognize the glowing skein of golden hair that spilled onto the seat as Wyatt's face pressed down on Valerie's.

Valerie and Sally were corresponding regularly. Valerie's letters chronicled the ups and downs of Charlotte's web, complained about Matt, and confessed helplessness in the face of the carnage in Vietnam. About unsatisfactory boys she had much to say. She marveled at their gratitude, satisfied as they were by transient sex moments. The other character in their letters was always Vietnam.

The last word was always torment. Now that Sally's time in ed school was closing out, she'd be moving on to a teaching job in the fall, in Chicago. Valerie invited her to visit.

On the Near West Side, the first thing that registered with Sally was how happy the children looked—riding bicycles, slurping on ice cream cones, scampering around in front yards. The second thing that registered was how worn and aged the parents of those children looked. The third was that Valerie looked triumphant, smiled too much, and was smoking, nervously, like a teenager. The fourth was the ravaged look on Matt's face. The fifth was how quickly he cleared the table after dinner and hustled away upstairs. Valerie took Sally aside and told her story. She had been stuck in a trap with Matt. She had to leap. She was entitled to romance.

Matt had not been given to prayer for many years but he prayed that Sally could talk some sense into her. A ridiculous hope.

Sally slept in the living room downstairs. Valerie moved in with Wyatt, leaving the little cactuses with Matt—a good-will gesture. He neglected them. They died. He told her to take her goddamn cactuses with her.

He spent hours adrift on the expanse of his unmade, unshared bed. Watching him mope around the staff house was not good for Valerie's morale. He wasn't facing reality. He stopped eating. His Lincolnesque creases deepened into crevasses. Sally ached for him. Valerie was an air spirit and Matt was earth, a captive of gravity. They were mismatched. Valerie had done them both a favor, ending it now. Wyatt was what she needed now—pure impulse. Matt was cooked—overcooked—and Wyatt was raw. And then there were Wyatt's melting eyes.

Sally was more than slightly horrified at the spectacle of Valerie flaunting her conquest. She gravitated toward the devastated Matt. She caught herself wondering whether her sympathy could actually turn into something more than sympathy. She canceled such thoughts.

Matt, talk to me, Sally said. Matt did not want to admit that he didn't know which was worse—losing Valerie or exposing his humiliation for everybody to gawk at. Matt was never a fast talker but now he was so slowed down, it was as if he was picking his way up a rock face, painstakingly searching out footholds.

Terry came up to him one day, massaged his shoulder, and said: "She's not worth it." *What the hell did he mean by that?* All women were replaceable? Was this solidarity or pity?

As for Wyatt, Valerie soon realized that what she felt for him was not all-around love, though he was certainly fun—melting eyes, boyish cowlick, rumbling voice, experienced fingers—until he wasn't. She liked his curiosity, not just about her but about Matt, Terry, Ronnie, and Marcia, their backgrounds, how they all met. He regaled her with stories about growing up on the Near West Side. She'd never actually met anybody who'd been a paperboy with his own route. He talked about the art of steering his bike with one hand while wrapped in a baggy plastic poncho when it rained or snowed or, worst of all, sleeted. He made the bike routine sound like a cover of the *Saturday Evening Post*. He talked about accompanying his old man as he went from bar to bar collecting the proceeds from juke boxes, delivering sacks of change to somebody who delivered them to somebody else. He remembered begging his old man to post him as a lookout during high-stakes poker nights.

Valerie lapped up his tales, but there were too many of them and they came too fast and he had the habit of barging into her sentences.

She upped her cigarette quota. Wyatt seemed not to notice. Sally did notice: "I can't help noticing that you're not only smoking a lot but you're trembling. It's like you're a high-school kid learning to inhale." Valerie denied it but it was true.

It came to her that Wyatt was her exit ramp out of Cleveland. Even in overripe summer light there wasn't enough color at the edge of Lake Erie. Mexico's muralists seized her mind. She longed for burnt sienna, burnt umber, blazing yellow, electric blue, ochre. She bought colored pencils and tried to reproduce Diego Rivera's diagonals. She remembered Halloweens when she defied her parents and with Mexican high-school friends took the bus to East

L.A. to celebrate *El Día de Muertos,* painting their faces like skulls, leaving offerings on gravestones, visiting homes where little shrines displayed photos, tequila bottles, beer cans, flowers, unpeeled fruit, all the accoutrements of welcome for the revived dead. A world her parents tried to keep at bay with their lawn and pool and sprawling Spanish-style house.

Eventually, it would become clear to Matt, too, that Valerie had done them both a favor.

But not yet.

Her period was late.

She told Sally. Valerie didn't know whose it was. She did know that it was hers.

She dreamed she was chasing a baby in a red snow-suit rolling downhill. She tripped on her full-length fur coat and fell hard. The baby rolled into an abyss.

In the middle of the night, with a cut-off half-cry, she shuddered awake and felt her cheek for a wound. But the wound was not to her face.

A garbage truck churned down the street. She walked to the window and watched huge, gross raindrops pattering, staccato, on fallen leaves. She was afraid to sleep. She was afraid not to sleep. When she went to sleep, she prayed not to repeat the dream of the glacier, the baby, and the abyss.

Planned Parenthood occupied a gray clapboard house whose three long wooden steps, painted a pallid blue, creaked. Under an eave, two rocking chairs were set at a slight angle to one another. The screen door slammed harshly. Three girls were already waiting in red vinyl chairs. One—slender, pimpled, leafing through an issue of *Reader's Digest*—couldn't have been older than eighteen. The others were in their late twenties or thirties, one with a beehive hairdo, the other a dark bob, and from their easy manner with one another

Sally could tell they were here together, though not which of them might be pregnant. Valerie filled out a form.

A red-haired nurse wearing cat-eye glasses ushered her into a small office with a print of a flower basket on the wall, took her form, smiled briskly and said, "Well, let's see what we have." She took a paper cup from an inverted stack on a shelf, wrote VALERIE PARR on it, held it out like a trophy, and pointed toward the ladies' room.

Valerie left her cup of urine on a shelf and went back to the waiting room, where Sally took her hand.

The nurse ushered them back into the small office.

The word was *Positive.*

"Oh, it's so fast," Valerie said.

A dam burst in her. The nurse handed her a tissue. Would she prefer to talk about alternatives the next day?

"Tomorrow, yes," she said.

"It's going to be all right," the nurse said in a pleasant voice that seemed rehearsed but not inauthentic. "Whatever you decide."

Whatever I decide.

It's nobody else's. It's mine.

"I don't want Wyatt to know."

"Of course not. But what about Matt?"

"I'll think about it."

Carterville, Pennsylvania, 1965

A CLASSMATE OF SALLY'S IN ed school had found herself "in trouble" and found an organized, safe, and affordable way to get out of trouble. The doctor operated a clinic on Main Street in a mountain town east of Pittsburgh called Carterville. The doctor was named Barton. He was no back-alley hack. It was said that his daughter had died from a botched abortion. It was said that he paid off the police. In any case, women—thousands of them, over the years—arrived on Main Street in Carterville from all over the country. You drove there after lunch, got there for dinner, stayed over one night, got it done.

Sally wrote to Dr. Barton. A half-sheet of paper folded in thirds came back by return mail, addressed in block letters, in a small envelope with a preprinted stamp, bearing no return address:

8 PM WED SEPT 1 114 MAIN ST CARTERVILLE
PA CHECK IN FIRST COLLINS MOTEL BRING
$50 CASH

It was like a ransom note in a movie.

After Valerie stopped weeping she was able to swallow a chicken salad sandwich and keep it down. She slept dreamlessly.

She had a plan: a name, an address, an appointment. Doctor Barton: he sounded friendly. Like Clara of the Red Cross, on a mission of mercy.

First there was an emergency. Now there was only a problem. Problems could be solved.

Problem One: get to Carterville. Sally had a car.

Problem Two: get fifty dollars. And whatever one night in a motel costs.

Problem Three: Matt. But Matt could solve Problem Two.

Should she tell him? Of course. It would be only right. Matt would be a gentleman—chastened, accepting. He meant no harm. He loved her in his fashion. But Valerie was one of Doris Lessing's free women. She owed him no explanation. She didn't need Matt's money. Only one uterus was involved.

It rained all night, drops drumming on rooftops and cars and large maple leaves that had come down prematurely, in free fall. The rain thrummed on heaps of leaves in the gutter, making a soggy mass out of what started out a crisp and brilliant red. By the morning the paddling sound dwindled, then stopped. The sky looked like an erased blackboard.

The air in the car was congested with silence for more than an hour as Sally drove east on the Ohio Turnpike, where dips substituted for valleys and overpasses doubled as hills to keep the flat land from pounding you into absolute tedium. Valerie thought about all the surveying and bulldozing and paving that had erased every remnant of history along the route, so that today's Americans could swoop comfortably across the state without being reminded that turkeys and deer lived in the forests and Indians trapped and hunted there before they were driven out and the land commandeered.

Soon a mass of cells would be scraped out of her uterus, where they didn't belong. What she would undergo was a cleansing.

Her mother had once offered to teach her to knit, but Valerie preferred to apply her fingers to the violin. At times like this she wished she had a routine to keep her hands busy. She imagined cuddling a baby; squeals; crawls; first steps; lullabies; joy. She jammed on the mind-brakes. *You've got a life to live. Next time you'll be more careful.*

Sally clicked on the radio. Dusty Springfield with her girl-group backup sang, "I only want to be with you" and "You would cry too if it happened to you." Valerie closed her eyes, bobbed her head. She wanted to clear out the buzz, all the what-ifs and if-onlys, the regrets and anticipations, the trickles of doubt and calculation. She was not afraid. Of course she was afraid. She slipped into the violin surge, the chorus of yearning. Leslie Gore came on. It was still her party and she'd cry if she wanted to. Valerie didn't want to. She thought about Mexico, about floundering Matt, about where she should go to do antiwar work.

The radio ate up the miles. They crossed the state line into Pennsylvania, where the trees were more irregular, and the road narrowed, the center strip shrank, potholes appeared, the curves were curvier, the rises and dips more pronounced. Traffic thinned. It bunched up near Pittsburgh, then thinned out again.

They stopped at a truck stop. Valerie felt a bit queasy. Best to go into this with an empty stomach. Sally stepped outside, diminished by a herd of trucks filling the parking lot. She'd grab a bite and not subject Valerie to the food smells. The cafeteria was a huge shed with a flat roof. The air was thick with the aromas of frying things. On the knotty pine walls, fish and antlers were mounted, and funny signs. A stick figure stepped onto cracking ice: "THIN ICE." Then in smaller type: "GO AHEAD! ... TRY IT ANYWAY ... YOU DON'T WEIGH THAT MUCH." A woman with a Doris Day smile: "PEOPLE SAY I HAVE A BAD ATTITUDE. I SAY SCREW 'EM!" A man with an Archie comics pompadour holding a beer mug: "BEER. HELPING UGLY PEOPLE HAVE SEX SINCE 1862!" "BEWARE OF THE DOG. THE CAT IS NOT TRUSTWORTHY EITHER." "CAUTION." The silhouette of a child running. "STUPID KIDS CROSSING."

Random aggression. Not the focused, murderous aggression of the Mississippi Delta, but diffuse working class nastiness, to which Sally had not been exposed.

It's peculiar, she thought, that stupid people were the butts of most of the gags, like everyone knew someone stupider than they were, which was reassuring if you were afraid *you* were the one who was stupid. She thought about the American mind: the fear that somebody was always looking down on you; the belief that some people deserved to be looked down on; the fear that you might look stupid in somebody's eyes; the need to get one-up on somebody else; but also, the passion for commerce, the movement of things and people, the ever-renewed wish that around the next bend—because you were not stupid—was a place worth getting to, which you wouldn't want to leave.

Valerie had closed her eyes by the time Sally got back to the car. Sally touched her knee.

"Don't worry, girl," Valerie said, "I'm not scared." The truth was: now she wasn't. Her mind emptied. She fell asleep.

About forty miles east of Pittsburgh, the light wore out behind them. Small farms dotted the countryside. Barns neared collapse, bounded by segments of stone walls and wooden fences in various states of disrepair. On both sides of the road, shapes loomed. The road got bumpier. Valerie woke up to see the moon emerge from a cloud long enough to reveal a slope on the right gouged out of a mountain, with a stream on the left. They crossed over a short iron bridge. The tires whirred. They passed a graveyard and flashing lights mounted on sawhorses. The Lions Club welcomed them to Carterville.

Carterville was there to be useful, not scenic. The headlights revealed a bump of a mountain off to the side, and a roadside thick with buildings: a diner with metal siding and a red neon sign, old houses with porches held up by decaying columns, modest churches, stores for hardware, toys, and furniture. There were no streetlights, but it was not hard to find Main Street—they were already on it. They passed numbers 118 and 116, but they didn't see 114 or, for that matter, 112. Number 110 was a clothing store.

Dr. Barton did not put up much of a front. On the other side of the street was a drive-in diner; a few doors down, a movie theater, the Palace; next to the Palace, an antiques shop. Parking was on the street. No meters and few passersby. The street seemed to shiver. Sally navigated through an intersection where a traffic light hung from a wire over the road. Seeing no motel, she pulled into the drive-in lot, went inside, asked the cashier where she could find the Collins Motel. "Next right and up the road a piece," said the cashier, perky.

In front of the Collins Motel, diminutive potted pines stood, forlorn and ragged, on either side of the screen door. Sally noted license plates: Pennsylvania, of course, but also New York, Ohio, Iowa, Kansas. The clerk, a girl with a beehive hairdo slightly askew to the left, and a face full of heartbreaking psoriasis, barely looked at them. Sally stepped up: "We'd like a room." The clerk took out the register. "You'll be staying with us one night, is that right?"

The sidewalk was uneven. Parked cars came from Virginia, Massachusetts, New Jersey, Iowa. It was as if the town were hosting a national car rally. A police car was parked down the block. Surely Dr. Barton paid off the cops. Possibly he was Carterville's chief economic support.

From the interiors of the houses that fronted Main Street, the eerie blue glow of television sets was the only visible light. You could never tell which real-life soap operas were taking place in the houses where people lived.

Right up in front of 114, perpendicular to the street, they could barely make out the sign:

HARRY BARTON, M.D.
BARTON CLINIC
GENERAL MEDICINE

It was a nondescript three-story stone building, mainly dark gray, mottled, randomly dotted by pale gray and white stones. The door featured three tiny rectangular glass windows arranged stepwise. A welcome mat was uncommunicative. The door was unlocked. Two coffee tables held dim antique lamps and copies of *Life, Look,* the *Saturday Evening Post,* and *Collier's.*

Eight women sat in the waiting room on thinly cushioned wooden chairs and two worn sofas. Two were teenagers, one with massively tangled black hair, the other dirty blonde, bony and buck-toothed. Judging from the discreet conversation taking place between pairs of women, some were there strictly for companionship. There were plaques from the American Legion and the Kiwanis Club; a photograph of a dark-haired young man with a high forehead climbing to widow's peaks, the ends of his mouth slightly upturned into a slight smile, wearing an army uniform with brass buttons and a stiff collar. In one print, a doctor in a dark suit with an I'm-humoring-you look held his stethoscope to the chest of a doll held up to him by a little girl in a red beret. The photos included a man with his cheeks puffed up, blowing a glass bowl; a full red moon hanging over the horizon; a palm tree; Niagara Falls. Everything was jammed together as in an antiques shop. The effect was the same: disorderly to the point of chaotic, busy but warm. Framed photos and prints covered all four walls. A quote from Thomas Paine: "The world is my country and to do good my religion."

A door opened and a stocky woman with a long, straight nose, wearing a white nurse's uniform—her hair up in a net—came out and asked for Mrs. Cooper. Mrs. Cooper—pale, mid-twenties, with umber hair and a black headband—stood up and the nurse escorted her inside.

Not many minutes passed before a thin, pale woman, her limp dark hair untidily pigtailed like an afterthought, was slowly half-carried through the interior door into the waiting room by the nurse on one side and, on the other, a short, white-haired man who somewhat resembled Norman Rockwell's doll doctor, but leaner and older—he appeared to be in his seventies. "I'll see you in the morning," he said quietly in a kind baritone voice.

The pale, pigtailed woman shook his hand and thanked him weakly. Propped upright by an older woman in a long sweater-dress, she departed.

The doctor had mild gray eyes, and combed his scarce white hairs back over the top of his head. He wore a white medical coat, and his sleeves were rolled up to his elbows. His glasses were metal-rimmed, and he wore a bow tie as if born to it. He had the elongated mouth of the young uniformed man in the photo, and a milder version of the same smile, unforced and gracious. He brought to mind the words *reliable, respectable, benign.* He would not stand out in a crowd. His shoes had crepe soles, and his gait was deliberate.

Sally read *Collier's* and wondered how, if at all, growing up in Carterville, Pennsylvania, would have been different from growing up in Mt. Harmony, Michigan. "This will be over soon, and you'll go back to your life," Sally said quietly.

Valerie thought: *I should be feeling terrible but I don't. What's wrong with me?* She thought about Diego Rivera's force-fields pivoting on diagonal lines.

Eventually the nurse asked which one was Valerie.

"I'm Valerie, but may my sister come with me?"

"Sher," said the nurse, in an accent Valerie took to be local. "Sher thing."

She ushered them into a corridor smelling faintly of disinfectant, opened a door on the left, which led into a reassuringly professional-looking examination room, where she spread fresh paper the length of the gynecological table. She escorted Valerie behind a screen and asked her to put on a thin cloth gown. The stirrups were, as always, ridiculous—silly though necessary; part of the strange inconvenience of being female.

After a quick rap on the door, the doctor entered and shook Valerie's hand. He inquired into her general health. He took her medical history. He was shorter than the nurse by several inches. His fingers were remarkably small. He asked about her menstrual cycle and last intercourse. He touched the back of her hand and asked her to place her feet in the stirrups. With warm instruments he poked around inside her.

"Good," he said. "Very good."

The moment when metal instruments exited her vagina was always a fine moment. "What's going to happen now?"

"I'll apply a solution of soft soap, mostly, to dilate your cervix. It shouldn't hurt."

Eyes closed, she felt his delicate fingers. There was a sort of paste on them that he smeared around.

"Do you have any questions, Valerie?"

"Actually, I don't."

"Then I'll see you back here at six in the morning. For the curettage."

It sounded so elegant, *curettage,* like "cure," not scraping.

If anyone should ever ask, he said, she should say that he treated her for a vaginal discharge. "Of course, it's very unlikely that anyone will ever ask."

He must have smelled her breath, because he added, at the last minute: "By the way, it would be best if you'd stop smoking."

She nodded blankly.

Afterward, walking down Main Street, Sally took her by the hand and said, "He has a kind face. In the morning it'll all be—"

"I'll never have to go through this again."

"You're in good hands." She knew it.

They went right to their twin beds. It was 9:30. Sally set her folding alarm clock for 5:30.

The morning, blessedly, was a blur.

It was dark—coal dark—when they left the motel, dark as they retraced their steps to the clinic. On the dot of six, the nurse entered, her uniform crisper and whiter than the night before. Valerie told Sally not to worry, and the two women hugged.

The nurse steered Valerie into an operating room—table with stirrups, sink, tables with instruments. The linoleum tiles on the floor were black and white squares set diagonally. The effect was of symmetry but at the same time, flow. On the back wall, tilted at slightly different angles, hung two diplomas, one from Pennsylvania State

College, the other an M.D. from the University of Pennsylvania, along with certificates of awards, paintings of deer, bunny-rabbits, and leaping salmon, and two framed mottos. One was attributed to Benjamin Franklin: "Where there is marriage without love there will be love without marriage." The other read: "The most important thing in the universe is energy." The whole room said: *Energy needs professional help.*

A male assistant with a sandy crew cut and a broad face walked in, greeted Valerie, handed her a light gray gown, pointed her toward a small auxiliary room behind a green curtain. The gown went down to her waist. When she tossed back the curtain and reentered the operating room, the doctor was examining his instruments. The nurse returned. The doctor said, "Just try to relax," as the nurse rolled rubber gloves onto his hands. "This won't take long. You won't feel any pain."

She believed him. She walked decisively to the operating table, lay on her back and fit her feet into the stirrups. Slowly but firmly he inserted a long rubber tube into her urethra and said this was the time to empty her bladder. Her bladder performed. As the liquid rushed audibly down the tube, she felt pleased not to feel embarrassed, and remained pleased as the doctor washed down her whole vaginal region, inside and out, meticulously, using gauze pads soaked in something that gave off an unidentifiable aroma.

He came around the table holding a syringe. She didn't need to be told to close her eyes, or not to be afraid.

"You can relax," he said.

She did. All thought expired.

She came to on a plain hospital bed in a different room, head on a pillow, facing a window covered with beige blinds, and in front of it, the kindly face of Dr. Barton. She had never felt so glad to see a face. "What time?"

After a glance at his watch, he said, "Six thirty-five. How do you feel?"

"Kind of dull."

He held up another syringe. "Penicillin," he said, as if offering her a lollypop. She nodded weakly. He swabbed the inside of her right elbow with alcohol and injected the gift.

"Relieved."

"Good. Just lie here for a while. Take your time. Whenever you're ready, you can get dressed." Her clothes were neatly folded on a nearby chair.

He'd said this a thousand times, but he meant it.

Time passed.

It had not exactly been an ordeal. A loss; a passage; a "termination," they called it; a solution … "Relief" would do. She had no regrets.

She dressed. The doctor came back with a Kotex—"in case there's any bleeding"—and left again. Through the window fluttered the murmurs of townspeople passing by, living their lives. She could be anywhere. She lay down again in the enveloping, restorative fog. The absence of pain was part of what she felt, but only part. Her relief bordered on happiness. Everyone should feel such relief.

She closed her eyes.

Eventually she heard the hush of crepe soles. The doctor said she should rest for a couple of days. He handed her a prescription for birth control pills made out in the same neat hand that inscribed the framed sayings on the wall. She told him that her regular physician recommended against the Pill.

"Well, as you know, there are other ways."

"I do." She paused. "Is it safe for me to drive home to Cleveland?"

"As long as you don't take the wheel. Lie down in the backseat, sher, and relax."

She picked up her purse. "Oh, and how much do I owe you?"

"Fifty dollars." She took out two twenties and a ten, pressed them into his small hand.

"Doctor—I just want to—"

"You'll be fine."

"—thank you."

"You're so impressive," Sally said as they walked down the sidewalk, arm in arm, in Carterville, Pennsylvania.

"You're a wonderful friend. We're both lucky."

"Think of the women who don't find Dr. Barton."

With Sally at the wheel, Valerie wedged herself against the door, her eyes open just long enough to observe the slag heaps bulging up on the outskirts of town, more conspicuous than the evening before, humps of mineral remains lying heavy on the land, hulks of refuse gouged out from excavations long completed and abandoned, left as monuments to a defeated earth and a harsh way of life. In such a place, Dr. Harry Barton practiced.

By the time Valerie woke up, they were well into Ohio. Briefly, at last, she wept—for which she felt relief. The sun cast crisp shadows. The light was undefeated.

Neither of them felt like eating anything but Raisinets and Good & Plenty.

Cleveland, Chicago, and
San Miguel de Allende, 1966-67

O NE MORE MORNING LIKE the one before and the one that would no doubt follow, Matt Stackhouse awoke alone in an unmade bed, sweating, morose, anxious, his mind torqued. All morning he lay there, a slab of self-loathing, arm shielding his head, underarm rancid, thinking about this woman he had loved and whom, it turned out, he didn't know at all. She could have told him straight-out that she was sorry she had hurt him. As if that would matter. But it *would* matter. He touched his forehead with the back of his hand but felt no sign of a fever.

Valerie, having returned to Cleveland, packed up and left again. For good. Without leaving Matt a note. Without telling anyone where she and Sally had gone. Sally, however, left Matt a note with her phone number and address. She would drive Valerie as far as Chicago.

The overactive radiator clanked away next to the wall. Matt got up and turned down the heat. Another winter was near, unbidden. The clanking ceased. A jet of cold air knifed through a crack in the window where the pane had come free of the sash. He went downstairs to the kitchen, brought back a paper towel, folded it in half, then in half again, tore up the quarters, stuffed them into the crack. Paint was peeling on both sides of the pane. He wondered who had lived here before—how they felt there, whether they raised children, whether anyone smashed someone else's thumb while slamming a door, whether anyone died, whether life went better or worse for them after they left, or stayed the same.

A house was a stopping-off point, nothing more.

Outside, a bird, a freakish holdover or an early return, was scooting up the bare trunk of a tree—the bark peeling, like the windowsill—and stood, poised, perched on a branch, jerking its head to the left and peering back at him, equally surprised. What was either of them doing in Cleveland?

The bird was a small, chunky thing, brightly cinnamon-colored on top, orange below, nervous—a big head, not much neck, a white throat and a long white stripe over his eye. Its bill described a narrow downward-curving arc; its tail was cocked upwards, suggesting alertness. It produced a big piercing trill. It hopped, turned around, and stopped still, feet clutching the same spot on the branch where it had started.

The bird got somewhere by hopping. It changed its angle of vision. It flew off in search of more world.

Every incident came wrapped in a moral. *Change your angle of vision, man.*

He stumbled downstairs to the pantry, treated himself to a lunchtime can of Dinty Moore stew—meat and potatoes that tasted like two slightly different flavors of cardboard—and conducted inventory. It was not by chance, not whimsically, that he had come to this pass, but as a man of reason. He had started out on the premise that there had to be radical change in America. Second premise: A radical thrust in America required organizing of an interracial movement of the poor. Conclusion: He should help bring that movement about. But it was always absurd to think that moody, preachy, pedantic Matt Stackhouse had it in him to organize young toughs. What did he know about these footloose guys? What did he know about the Near West Side of Cleveland? What did he know about cops?

He stared into the mirror, picked up his razor. Perspective starts with the face. The guy in the mirror was callow, unformed. He needed a moustache. Thick in the center, tapering gracefully out toward the upturned corners. Eventually he might arrive at Zapata.

Zapata. Mexico. Valerie.

Valerie told Marcia she was leaving for Mexico. She said she needed to get back on her path. "To study art" was the reason she gave. She did not try defending her decision to someone so dedicated to organizing the poor, let alone a woman whose parents had met at Auschwitz. The world was immense and dug-in, Valerie thought. They were few, they were children. Marcia shrugged gamely, wished her the best, and embraced her.

Matt wrote to Sally, trying to sound convalescent.

Sally wrote back that he needed to take care of himself. She wrote that, for fun, she was translating poetry from the French, including Rimbaud, who made her think of Matt: "The march, the burden, the desert, the boredom, the anger."

He wrote back thanking her, saying that he was sorry that he had been so deeply lost inside himself when she was in Cleveland, but he appreciated her kindness even if he hadn't quite shown it. He knew she would understand what he was going through. He wondered how she would feel about a visit from him. He needed a pilgrimage.

She smelled his desperation and wrote back: "Matt, truly I wish I were in love with you. Teaching is hard. I've put my heart in a deep freeze. But here's a word of advice: I'm not sure Valerie is finished with you. If you want to write her, here's her address."

Months passed. Matt astonished himself by rereading the Gospels, not because he believed but because he wanted to see what it might feel like to have faith. He went through the motions of working for an antiwar congressional candidate who was running in the Democratic primary, a professor at Case Western Reserve University, a Quaker with a mild voice and scholarly demeanor. The work of writing up file cards on potential antiwar voters was tedious, but Matt persisted. The Quaker professor ended up with twenty-one percent of the vote against the incumbent, who was loyal to Lyndon Johnson.

A letter arrived from the Illinois state draft appeals board sustaining the local board's decision that he did not qualify as a conscientious objector. They enclosed a copy of the FBI's findings from their interviews, including his onetime Ann Arbor landlord's account of his poor housekeeping habits and the transcript of an FBI interview with Professor Franz Hartmann:

Matthew Stackhouse studied with me, a year-long course in political theory. He was a thoughtful student with a good deal of talent, though an unformed talent. I was disappointed when he decided to drop out of school. Matthew has a good deal of concern about the direction of modern society, and his opposition to war is, without doubt, sincere. He is vague and romantic. I was something like him when I was his age.

When he puts his mind to it, Matthew thinks clearly, but he doesn't always put his mind to it, and I think this is not because he lacks the ability but because he interferes with his mind—he rebels against it. I think this is because he has been seized by an impractical passion to make the world over. At times he understands how poisonous it can be for passion to swamp reason. It is curious and tragic how an intelligent young man will put his skepticism into cold storage, so to say, because it would interfere with his zealotry. As strange as this might sound, he feels embarrassed by the quality of his mind.

No, I have never heard young Mr. Stackhouse speak a disloyal word. He is not a Communist. He is not subversive. He comes from a good family. Whether they encouraged this current path in his life, I rather doubt. I understand that his father is a minister but I have not known the son to be religious, at least in any conventional sense. If I may say so, Matthew strikes me as one of these young religious people whose tragedy is that he lacks a religion.

I have known such troubled young men. Some of them, when exposed to extreme ideologies, get carried along on the currents of the moment and become—I must use the word—fanatics—or even monsters. This can happen. I am not saying that I have observed in Matthew any sign of extreme ideologies. But of this intense passion I am, I must tell you, suspicious. I have seen enough of passionate cruelty and stupidity to last me many lifetimes.

I never saw any sign that he was attracted to men.

He is a fine young man, honest and patriotic—at least I have no reason to believe that he is anything but patriotic. But patriotism is not an opinion one wears and discards as one pleases, like an overcoat. A young man should serve his country.

Valerie had Mexico. Matt needed his own country.

Terry, for his part, lusted for antiwar work. His contacts offered up pet projects and rumors, but no solid idea emerged. A lot of the antiwar action was on campuses. Having left school what seemed like decades ago, he had outgrown students. When all was said and done, they were as provincial as they were energetic. A draft-resistance project for working-class white guys was starting up in Boston, which was interesting, in theory, but for one thing, it was at an early stage, and for another, the thought of counseling would-be conscientious objectors did not excite him.

He and Matt thought of themselves as pilgrims without a portfolio. They drank to that.

Steve Coleman from SDS mentioned one day that the national organization was trying to push its chapters to set its sights on campus war research. The point was to expose "complicity," to shatter false innocence and galvanize action directly against the war machine. Matt started to work with the SDS chapter at Case Western Reserve. It was pleasant enough to spend time in the library reference room. There were a handful of *aha!* moments. Terry showed no interest. To him, "complicity" was abstract, sandbox stuff. The point of antiwar action was to rouse mass action, not to invoke guilt. Matt felt judged.

He preferred hanging out with Steve, whose thoughts were more practical, less grand. One day Steve reached into his wallet and pulled out an American Airlines youth fare card. "Take this." It listed his date of birth as October 21, 1945.

"Don't you need it?"

"Believe me, I have others. Benefits of a baby face: nobody ever looks at me twice. Just practice my signature and memorize your new birth date. Sometimes they ask."

One evening, his mother called.

"Matthew."

"Mom, you sound worried."

"I miss you, Matthew. That's my job. I'm your *mother*. Are you all right?"

"I'm fine, mom," he lied. "What's wrong?"

"I just wanted to say hello." She was as lousy a liar as he was. "And by the way, a letter arrived for you."

"You say that as though it came in a black envelope inscribed with a skull and crossbones."

"Don't joke, Matthew. It's from the Selective Service System."

His heart actually skipped a beat. This was too much of a coincidence. "Oh? Did you open it?"

"Matthew! I don't open your mail. There's another one here for you, too. From Mexico. You're popular. I wouldn't open that one either."

"Please open the one from Selective Service, mom."

She did and rapidly said: "I knew it." Something was caught in her throat.

"What did you know?"

"It says that since you're no longer a registered student, you have been reclassified 1-A and you must report for a physical examination."

"When?"

"September 15."

"Mom, don't worry, it's routine. I'll come home."

"Matthew—" She was sobbing.

"There's a whole long procedure before they—before the Army can touch you. I'll come home."

On the road, in the primitive comfort of his VW bug, Matt's mind churned. He needed to stare at hard facts. He was no longer a student. The state appeals board agreed with the local board that he had no grounds for objection. Professor Hartmann turned on him. The hard facts stared back at him. Now what?

Meanwhile, there was another fact: Valerie had written.

When he had driven most of the way across bleak Indiana, the rain gave up, and for a moment, as night closed in, weak sunlight slanted through slats in the shapeless clouds.

He parked in his parents' driveway and pulled his duffel bag out of the trunk. At the doorway he stood shivering before lifting the knocker, tapping it, tapping it again. He heard his father limp up to the door and turn the latch.

"Come in, son," said Matthew Stackhouse, Sr., soberly. They inspected each other like strangers. His father extended a hand.

That old feeling rammed into his gut—*I have done something wrong.* They shook hands in the cold.

So muscular, his father's shoulders. His left leg was like a stick. But the man lifted weights every day in his garage.

Oven smells, heavy meat, the tang of grease wafted out of the kitchen. What was that line of Robert Frost's about home being the place where, when you had to go there, they had to take you in? Nothing had changed—pale blue sofas, straight-up armchairs, area rugs, some in needlepoint, piano with yellowing keys, framed photos: Matt Stackhouse, Sr., in his army uniform, Matt Stackhouse, Jr., looking as though he'd been tortured into a stiff smile. His mother ran up.

"Oh, Matt. Matt, Matt. It's so good you're here. Dinner's almost ready."

"Smells good."

"And here." She waved an onion-skin envelope, postmarked in Spanish. "Why don't you take this to your room? And freshen up."

In the rear of the house, in his childhood bedroom, carefully propped against the desk lamp, awaited the other envelope, the one with the return address "Selective Service System," perfectly slit open with a sharp letter opener. He left it there. He lay down on his perfectly made bed and read Valerie's gossipy letter—twice—looking for code. A single line grabbed his attention: "It wasn't the right time for us." Meaning there might be a right time. Or not.

Before leaving Cleveland, Valerie had cashed her three most recent trust fund checks—$150 apiece—which she'd kept in her drawer because she had discovered she could live on less. She had started collecting these monthly checks when she hit eighteen—by virtue of having the right parents. With this unearned stipend she would not live a luxurious life, but she had no desire to live a luxurious life.

It was no disgrace to be lucky. Her mother, Roz née Rosalinde, often said that her daughter had "chosen the right forebears," meaning her runaway father, who was a Brewster and a McMartin, just the right pedigree for the State Department. "If I've done nothing else for you," she had told Valerie once, "I arranged for you to acquire some valuable genes." Any child born to Rosalinde Parr and Brewster McMartin would have enjoyed the ballet lessons and the semi-grand European tour and the trust fund—they were the luck of the same draw. Not that the same benefits had cushioned unhappy Kathryn—which was nobody's fault. Nobody earned either bad luck or good any more than Kathryn was responsible for her beauty or talent or the darkness that gathered around her like a velvet cloak.

Kathryn's last gift: the jade ring with the zigzag platinum pattern—for a mountain ridge slashing the whole way around, for the jagged life. "Which is the only life," as Kathryn said on presenting her with the ring on her eighteenth birthday.

After struggling for years with Kathryn's suicide, and concluding in the end that Rosalinde's grief on top of his own was too heavy a burden to bear, Brewster McMartin had declared his family defunct and gone off to launch a different one. For Valerie this was something of a release. Her father had been distant but still somehow lorded it over the household. Now she was free to make up her life as she went along. Women were taught to think of themselves as creators of life, vessels of creation—but to create her own life, that was the thing. And Kathryn, Kathryn had been free to choose her death, which came with the package. It lifted Valerie, somehow—a bit—to think so.

There was no way to know whether Kathryn would have had a better shot at her freedom if she'd lived long enough to read *The Golden Notebook*.

One thing Valerie had learned from her father was that men get a jump on women because they're willing to pull up stakes first. When she broke up with Matt, she notched another marker on her freedom trail. Freedom was, in the end, the freedom to leave.

She thought about these things on the bus from Chicago to Laredo and the train south through the Sierra Maestra and eventually, after a long taxi ride, to San Miguel de Allende, where she rented a small yellow stucco house for forty dollars a month.

She signed up for an introductory Spanish class that met every morning in a school on the top floor of a peach-colored stucco villa high up on a hill. Whenever she gazed out the window, which was frequently, the purple bougainvillea on rose-colored walls screamed. The school was run by a thin-faced, unsmiling American with the improbably old-fashioned name of Horace Malone, a man of few words in English or Spanish, who sported a debonair black mustache like David Niven's but wispier, almost as if scratched onto his face in India ink. When she started developing blisters from hiking uphill, she bought a Vespa with a couple of minor dents in the front fender, for the equivalent of three dollars, and named it Green Goddess.

After school, and on weekends, she rode around the outskirts of town, stopping wherever the place and the light combined to make an impression. Playgrounds of gods and heroes set among battlefields and graves. When she tired of random searches she explored the remains of a pyramid complex, with high walls, which included a cylindrical structure, possibly astronomical. She found a ghost town pocked with the remains of gold and silver mines, reminding her of the coal mine refugees she met in Cleveland. In the high desert, the wind howled through the ruins. She tried sketching Day-of-the-Dead skeletons but gave up; she couldn't get the proportions right.

She enrolled in a course about the frescos inspired by the Mexican Revolution. They were like starbursts from another universe. The instructor, Sr. Vazquez, had served Diego Rivera as an apprentice, assisting him with his famous, or rather, notorious fresco in New York City, the one that, as could easily be seen, pitted capitalism against socialism, where a Russian May Day rally featured a replica of Lenin who looked slightly Mexican—so Sr. Vazquez said slyly.

Sr. Vazquez took his students on pilgrimages to Mexico City to ogle the work of Rivera, Orozco, and Siqueiros, *los tres grandes.* Their diagonals slashed across the walls just as in the picture-books. Sr. Vazquez said that diagonals foretold the future, which did not lie with mechanically repressive verticals or trivial horizontals, but with the unpredictable energies of acute and obtuse angles—the immense, explosive human adventure. He preached that the future of art lay in the insurrectionary Third World, not in the United States, where the collective imagination was shredded by bourgeois individualism and choked by the taste of big capitalists. He told them how Picasso shocked the bourgeoisie when he imported African styles into Europe, only to find his work lionized by the bourgeoisie. He told them that the wretched peasantry of the tremendous Third World, the *tercer mundo,* was rising up, an armada of phoenixes, to liberate the benighted, the wretched, *les misérables,* to triumph—with a panoply of slashing oblique angles—over the decadent West. And so on into references to "forces" and "classes" and "struggles."

Of her visit to the vicinity of the wide open space of the Zócalo, that enormous expanse in the heart of Mexico City, Valerie's most vivid memory would be of a young man with a withered leg, wearing a torn T-shirt and jeans, who, without looking up, painstakingly wheeled a hand truck across the street toward a fruit stand and stepped in front of a bus, while the driver yanked up the hand brake and waited, drumming his fingers on the steering wheel as the crippled man plodded in front of the car, each step an achievement, and Valerie wondered what kind of life this man looked forward to, what Emiliano Zapata or Pancho Villa had accomplished for him, what was his view of Diego Rivera and the successes and failures of the Mexican Revolution, and she noted as the man passed that he wasn't wincing, his face was not twisted in anger, he was not an incarnation of suffering. However much *los tres grandes* had wanted to exalt this man, to honor and elevate him, to cast him as a symbol of suffering and glory, he was who he was, living his damaged life, which was his one and only life, and for all she knew he was not miserable but happy to be alive. Silently she wished him good luck. Many times, she would try to draw this man, but could never get him right.

In the museums Valerie wanted to ask ordinary Mexicans how they felt about these murals, which were supposed to fortify them. She sadly noted how few Mexican Indians she saw there. She tried to imagine what it would be like to discover that you belong, blood-deep, bone-deep, to a conquered nation. Would you celebrate your survival? Would the ancestors crowd around your altar on *El Día de Muertos*?

Thinking of the Day of the Dead led her to think about Matt and his hurt look. He would disapprove of her lounging around even if he didn't glare as Terry would. She wrote to Matt about her life, in care of his parents in Chicago. Occasionally she picked up a copy of *Time* magazine and wondered what Matt was doing. She liked not being needed. She owed the world no more—if also no less—than anyone else. *Terry was right. I'm frivolous.*

Each day was a gift that she did not have to earn. She did not tire of the aroma of orange and wood smoke, or the sight of hummingbirds in the patio beating against gravity, hanging astonishingly in the air, wings invisible, colors resplendent—as if each tree, bush, leaf, bird carried within it a light source of its own, as if every surface was burnished. She sipped coffee with chocolate mixed in and arranged her body to absorb maximum sunlight.

She reckoned correctly that she was employable as a nude model. At five foot eleven, with her freckles and the singular little bump on her nose, she was unusual and not off-puttingly pretty. Her face did not look much lived in, unlined except for (if she looked closely) a fine mesh fanning out from the corners of her eyes. Confusion seemed to slide off her. She could keep her mouth closed without appearing to pout, and hold awkward poses without looking rigid—her whole life, in fact, was a flight from rigidity. She thanked her sister for the ring she wore, her tribute to jaggedness.

As time passed, she was called upon to prime canvases and mix paint, even to fill in shapes in a fresco. Having broken the state hundred-meter track record for women during her junior year in high school, she was still wiry and looked as though she could take care of herself. She could keep the hands of medium-famous muralists off her when she chose to.

Sr. Vazquez approved of her work but told her after three shots of tequila one evening that it was a pity she did not have the "equipment" for a career of her own. "You will never get a wall of your own to work on," was the way he put it. The lush life of *los grandes* was reserved for men. Somehow it hadn't previously occurred to her how much of the world belonged to men.

Whenever she was of a mind for passing stimulation, hot-blooded boys came around to clutch and be clutched by her, though she discovered they were disposed toward mauling episodes followed by ram-jam lightning strikes on her vagina, which were not all that un-pleasant, actually, but nothing she couldn't live without. Whenever it became too disconcerting to wake up staring at a ceiling she did not recognize, or the underwear she had hung, neatly folded, on the back of an unfamiliar chair, she moved on.

One evening, after mixing paints, she went into a bar that featured actual swinging doors. She had passed it frequently and had been told to avoid such picturesque places, but tonight she felt bold. She was on her third *refresco* when a lean American came in and plunked himself down a couple of stools away. She had seen the guy around. He turned and sat straddling his seat. He sported a sleek pompadour, dark shaggy eyebrows and high—possibly Indian—cheekbones. His lined, leathery face had seen better days and his piercing turquoise eyes were bloodshot. He might have been any-where between thirty-five and fifty. The pompadour was his most attractive feature, though his nose, which had been broken—you could see the bump from the side—had healed in a way that made her think of Steve McQueen.

He wore a T-shirt frayed at the top beneath a short-sleeved polyester Hawaiian-type shirt, which seemed like a strange out-fit on a hot day—not scorchingly, grease-on-the-griddle-hot, but placid, starched, blue-sky San Miguel hot. There was a softness around his lower lip which set her at her ease. He lowered his chin like a boxer going in for the assault and talked into the mirror be-hind the bar, as if resuming a soliloquy, in a high, husky voice: "…it's a disaster, colossal, it's like from pillar to post, from post to pillar, but where's the pillar and where's the post? I'm asking you, what are they holding up? Stick up your hands, it's a hold-up!" He pointed his index finger at the mirror, guffawed, turned toward Valerie to see if she also found this hilarious. She did not. He leaned toward her and said, "You look thoughtful."

She swept her hair back and said, "Thank you. I try to be."

"You mind if I move over one stool?"

She liked him. "Come on over."

He did.

His eyes didn't exactly focus. "You mind if I ask you a question?"

"Sure. Go ahead, ask me a question."

"You're supposed to say, *You already did.*" Where had she heard this before?

"What?"

"You're supposed to say, *You already did.* Ask me a question."

"Excuse me?"

"I asked you a question. My question was, *You mind if I ask you a question?*"

"Ha-ha." Terry, she thought. Was there a central depot somewhere where guys passed around dumb jokes?

"You're a fun-loving young lady, I see."

She withheld any expression.

He cocked his head and said, "You're a cheeky one. Cheek to cheek, I guess."

"Check," she said, getting into the rhythm. "What are you doing in Mexico?"

He shrugged. "Now that is one hell of a good question to which I don't know the answer. What does anyone do? Nothing ever happens in Mexico anymore. Really. Ask any Mexican." His eyebrows shot up and he said, "You like a drink," as if it were a statement and not a question.

"No thanks, I'm good, but you go ahead," she said, thinking that this guy was crazy but also original and unthreatening.

He ordered a shot of the best reposado in the house—*ree-posado,* he called it. "So, how you like San Miguel?"

"I like it fine. And you?"

"It's groovy, but you know—" he lowered his voice "—since the States is *all fucked up,* almost, this place is always busy, I'm busy, too, like a bee, bees get a lot done when they get off their asses, but there's a problem for them, you know, because *bees don't have asses,* though that's all right, what I care about is the honey." He held up his shot glass, said "Salud!" and downed the drink. "I don't know what they're doing to the tequila. Mexico lost its soul when they killed the priests. Some kind of revolution *that* was, killing the priests. Now that the priests are dead, who's gonna pray for you? Who's gonna get to the moon? Who's watching the plants grow? You know what I mean. So tell me, are you happy?"

He turned toward her and smiled, or tried to smile. He had trouble pulling his upper lip over his big teeth.

"Kind of," she said, not sure how to play this. "Are you?"

"Happy is as happy does. In an apocalypse, you never know. You *never* know. You got a smoke?"

She felt around in her purse, pulled out a pack of Parliaments, and he took one, looked at it quizzically, as if he had never seen one before, sniffed it along its length, said, "Interesting, int-er-est-ing," ripped the filter off and turned it upright on the bar so that it stood like a fireplug. "Hope you don't mind." He had a long jaw, and when you looked at him directly the jaw seemed to widen and his neck thickened, so that he looked kind of obtuse—or only sad.

"Why should I mind?" She reached back into her purse, took out a lighter, spun the wheel, held the flame toward him. He took her hand, adjusted it upward. His hand was huge.

"Nice ring," he said. "Mountains."

"Thanks."

"You never know, do you? Mexico is where God went to die. That's what they say—" He nodded at no one in particular. "The priests are creeping back, speaking Irish." He squinted around as if he was following a bug as it skittered across the mirror.

Somebody at the far end of the bar said something barely audible about "el gringo."

"Do I bug you?" the man with the pompadour said to her. "You look—" he studied her face "—offended. Or disappointed." He waved his cigarette around, the ash fell onto the bar, he swept it toward him, and she watched it drift toward the floor.

She knew he wasn't dangerous. "It takes a lot to disappoint me," she said. "Let's cut out."

By the time they reached her house, he was waving his hands frenetically and his voice, although quieter, was more frantic. He was now borderline incomprehensible about Lincoln, ghosts, priests, spies. He plucked at his shirt and blinked violently. He jammed his right hand into his pocket, scrunched it around as if feeling for change, or possibly his prick. He was all cranked up, and she was borderline excited as she unlocked the door.

His chest was completely hairless. As she unbuttoned her blouse he plucked at her skirt and kicked away his pants. He was erect. She smoothed out her skirt and shook his prick as if they were shaking hands, then let go, told him to wait a minute, she'd be right back, and he raked his big hand through her hair and said, "I can't wait, but I'll wait." In the bathroom, she inserted her diaphragm. *Sometimes you just need to get fucked.* She returned to find him fondling his prick. She told him he was an eager boy.

He pressed her against the wall, planted his flag in her, shuddered his way to a quick conclusion. He made a small, sharp noise, like a puppy.

He asked for another cigarette, and her name. Again he ripped off the filter. He looked around for a wastebasket. She cupped her hand; he gave her the filter. He used to know a Valerie: a Polack, actually; a dance instructor, short, narrow hips; he was crazy about her. He would have married her if he wasn't already married. "You ever been married?" he asked.

"Not that I recall."

"I've been married. Hell, I *am* married." He broke up, and she laughed with him, or at him, she wasn't sure which. "You ever ask yourself what's a family for?"

After briefly considering that it might be fun to see him again, she made a point of not asking his name. Their eyes didn't meet. He left politely. She had no regrets.

She studied herself in the mirror. She was twenty-five years old; no beauty, but bold; freckled in a way she no longer regretted; spirited; adventurous; long-limbed, big-boned, gawky; that interesting nose; that strong chin; charming; something in the giraffe family, or possibly gazelle. She could take care of herself. She was hungry, though not for a lover who loved his madness more than anyone or anything else.

She thought: *I am a conqueror.*

She thought: *This is my education.*

She knew she would leave San Miguel soon, and the thought was a breeze through her mind.

Whenever she thought that she no longer missed Matt, she found herself missing him. Stutter-step Matt; sad, stuck, compelling Matt; self-cancelling Matt; Matt the ponderous thinker-through; portentous Matt of the deep-set eyes; Matt with his monk face; blinking Matt on his Mount, picking up the thread of a conversation soaked in wine dregs abandoned at the bottom of a plastic cup on a one-in-the-morning kitchen table; Matt gazing through his kaleidoscope darkly; butterfly Matt flitting from one subject or attitude to another, as if, in his mind, there was no change of subject or attitude at all, as if jaggedness was an illusion, as if the world was, if you looked at it the right way, a continuous skein, a Möbius strip of consciousness—and just as surely there reared up, in her mind, the image of Matt of the sudden, delighted high-pitched laugh, Matt who'd just made an *aha!* discovery; the lucky accident of Matt as he sometimes used to be: the moments when he looked his most earnest and burst out in giggles; the fun of never knowing what would come out of his mouth next; his honest awkwardness in bed.

Suppose they hadn't moved to Cleveland. What would have happened? The whole expedition had been crazy, a long shot. Neither of them had belonged there. The world turned, spun them loose. Did she miss him now, or did she miss the lucky accident of love?

He would never forgive her. He didn't even know about the abortion, but he knew what humiliation felt like, and that was enough reason not to forgive her. She would never have wanted his child. But what did she want? *The hardest mind to read*, she told herself, *is your own*.

She bought a fountain pen from a Mexican woman sitting on the steps of the Cathedral, and wrote Matt a friendly, gossipy, travelogue of a letter. She told him that the uneventful pleasantness of San Miguel was starting to pall.

"It wasn't the right time for us." The words replayed in Matt's mind in Chicago.

Chicago and Points West, 1966-67

IS FATHER, WITH A hitch in his step, led him to the dinner table. During the war, Matt Stackhouse, Sr., had taken a considerable number of machine-gun rounds, shattering—beyond repair—his left leg beneath his knee. When he got out of the VA hospital, he had a pronounced limp and a friendly Midwestern nurse for a wife. Her name was Evelyn. He called her Evie, which rhymed, he sometimes said, with heavy, though heavy she was not.

The table was set, like his mother's face. Embroidered white tablecloth, setting off ornate silver candlesticks—a wedding present and their most precious luxury—and the good china.

His mother came from the kitchen bearing a cut-glass serving tray heaped with pot roast. She walked around the table, serving the men, and brought out a second tray, roasted potatoes and carrots, along with a gravy boat.

His parents sat at opposite ends of the table. "Good trip?" said his father, his eyes unsmiling.

Later, after what he would come to think of as The Last Supper, Matt would remember the evening in snatches, as if it had been edited into a trailer for his life—the all-around awkwardness; his father's stony look, as if his head had been carved into Mount Rushmore; his stalling gestures and ensuing abruptness; Matt's struggle to tamp down his own spikes of fury; his mother's labors to placate simultaneously the two men in her life—then the screen going blank, as if the film had slipped the sprockets and flamed out, all the images ashen.

Matt, Jr., peeled child-sized strips of meat off his pot roast. His father examined his water glass, adjusted his knife, his fork, and his spoon, by fractions of an inch, on both sides of his plate, to ensure that they were exactly parallel, and fastened upon his son. Court was in session. "Your mother tells me you received an important letter." He had not yet taken a bite.

It was overwhelmingly quiet, as if a storm had passed, but in fact it was only arriving. Matt shot his mother what she would call "a look."

"Matt, your country is like your father," she said primly, clearing her throat. How long did it take her to come up with that line? "You may not approve of everything he does, but he's your father."

Delicately, Matt laid his fork and knife across his plate.

"You know your father wants what's best." She sounded as though she were handling her words with tongs.

"Uh-huh." He stared at the lump of pot roast—a cheap cut, full of gristle; a remnant; a dead thing. But this was not what had him stopped. Dread had him stopped.

"You know, it pains me to see you hurting this way," she said. Matt knew that she meant it, but the words sounded rehearsed. "Why don't you take the world off your shoulders?"

"You know, mom," he said with as little sarcasm as possible, "you could always help me carry the load."

"Son," said his father, who was not subtle. "We know you don't like this war. We don't blame you. It's a hard thing to understand. But there are things we do not know about the threat."

"Do we have to have this discussion right now?"

"Matt, don't," said his mother, lips pinched as thin as paper plates.

Matt imagined he heard an echo from a memory cavern, an echo that emerged from a portal long overgrown by underbrush, a moment that followed some unremembered defiance of his—the sound of his father standing over him, slipping his belt out of the loops, doubling it, gripping the buckle in his hand, Abraham over Isaac ... *So help me!*

"Matthew, you're going to do—you're going to do—what is required," his father said, at the family dinner table in the middle of an unbearable, unconscionable war.

His father's face was twisted into a rictus. Spite boiled up from deep in his eyes. His jaw muscles rippled on either side of his mouth. He was *ugly*.

"War is hell," his father said in a tone he might have used for "pass the potatoes."

"Nobody knows that better than your father," said his mother mechanically. "But you know, what's best for your country is what's best for you. God knows we don't want you to go over there—"

"You will do the right thing, son. I know you will." Matt, Sr., sliced off a chunk of pot roast and wolfed it down.

Matt did not remember his father's eyes this blue. Ice blue. It hit Matt that his father was a man of the nineteenth century. Life was character. Character was duty. You were called and you went. When Matthew Stackhouse, Sr., was called, he went. He was called to the service as later he would be called to the ministry. There was no war without casualties, and there was no victory, no freedom, no life without war. A man answered the call. If you failed to answer, you were an insult to righteousness. You were nothing.

The words that formed in Matt, Jr.'s mind were, *I will try to do the right thing,* but even before he spoke them, they sounded like a guilty plea or an appeal for mercy; so he said nothing.

His father's voice ratcheted up to command volume. He spat words like nails. He was winding up to pronounce sentence. "Do you know what happens when everyone takes it upon *himself* to decide for *himself* when he's going to listen to his father and when he's going to turn his head and go on about his own business because he thinks he *knows* better? You have small children walking onto the train tracks just because they get the idea into their head. They see a butterfly or something. It's pretty. The next thing they know—" he put up the palm of his hand, like a stop sign, "—they're *gone*. Boom. You have *misrule*. You have *chaos*."

This scene was not chaotic. Order had come over it.

"*Chaos!* It is in chaos that Jesus is crucified. Betrayal and chaos. That's what happens when the country no longer commands the loyalty of its citizens." Imperious, muted, his father's voice swept away the silence. "Do you hear me, son?"

Matt's face hardened. "Dad, are you ready to step down from the pulpit? Do you know what you sound like?"

The rictus was back. "So help me God, I sound like *your father*, who served his country so that you could have a good and a free life as an American!"

A pall hung, a family shroud, over the table. Seconds passed, or minutes.

Young Matt squeezed out his words: "It is not a good life when *the United States of America* sets fire to peasants—*sets them on fire*—whole villages—because—"

"All war is terrible," his father said as if reciting the alphabet. "Our own war against Hitler was terrible. The Communists leave us no choice."

"There's no such thing as 'the Communists,' Dad. They're almost at war with each other. The Russians hate the Chinese. The Vietnamese have been fighting off the Chinese for a thousand years."

"Don't give me this left-wing crap."

This was not an argument about Communists, it was an argument about Matt and his way of life. "Marching off with the good Germans is not the life I want to live."

His mother, distraught, lunged out of her great pained silence. "Matt, do you think I could watch you go with an easy heart? To give what your father gave?" She would not be able to lock down her tears much longer. "Or worse, God forbid?"

"Mom—"

"Listen, Matt. *Please* listen."

"You don't have to say it, mom I *am* grateful. I thank the Lord for both of you and I'm grateful to the entire United States of America—"

"Don't raise your voice to your father!" His mother's voice was a formerly dull blade freshly sharpened.

"Listen! Please! For once!"

His parents subsided. His father's eyes were scorching.

"This is a free country," Matt said, "which means that I grew up to think for myself and to act on what I believe. You gave me that. You both did. You told me it was terrible to lie and just as bad to be a hypocrite. Which means that when my country goes horribly—" he smacked the table with the flat of his hand "—desperately *wrong*, and we *set babies on fire*—"

"And you know what?" said his father. "We did that in Japan! We did it in Germany! We burned down whole cities! Awful, terrible things! And they had to be done!"

"There are things we have to live with," his mother said.

Contempt rose in Matt's heart. He did not approve of it, but there it was.

His father stood and amped up his voice. "I did what I had to do! Does that make me—make me—some kind of *louse*?" For Matt Stackhouse, Sr., this was the strongest possible language.

"I have to live with myself," Matt barked out. In a single motion, he stormed out of his chair, tramped awkwardly into the hallway like a wounded angel, grabbed his duffel bag, and stomped back to the bedroom where he had lived—sometimes in fear, sometimes in comfort—as a child. The slight indentation of his body was visible on the covers. The bed was prepared for his collapse.

He lay in darkness replaying fragments of the dining-room scene, trying out lines he had missed, words with which he might have shielded himself or even claimed victory. But he had said what he needed to say. He was furious but whole. Proud, in fact.

He turned on the lamp to its lowest setting and made animal-head shadows on the wall—a rabbit, a chipmunk, an owl.

He switched off the lamp and watched the kaleidoscope of his mind arrive at the surprising feeling that he had passed through the Valley of the Shadow of Death.

If his father or his mother came to his door he didn't know what he would say.

They did not come. They left him alone in the darkness.

He churned. He could not imagine how to turn these people around, his embittered father and his complicit mother. Even less did he know what to do about millions like them. What did it take to arouse a whole people and get them to cry *Stop!* to the sin and crime of their own government, the frenzy of violence that this monstrosity of a nation inflicted—*we* inflicted—with impunity, every day and night, on the body and soul of a country that most of our good citizens couldn't be troubled to locate on a map? He knew this speech all too well.

Speeches availed nothing. His earnest little soliloquy was nothing but noise.

When he next opened his eyes, it was four-fifteen in the morning, and he knew what to do.

He opened a desk drawer, took out a diminutive pair of scissors with dull blades, the one he had used as a child to cut out pictures of animal heads when he built dioramas inspired by display cases in the Museum of Science and Industry. Musk ox, elephant, elephant seal, polar bear, Eskimos. He took out a bottle of glue—"mucilage," they called it—whose dried crust had hardened. He flexed the rubber nipple so that the slit opened. He was in luck: there were sheets of blank paper and a little packet of first-class stamps in the drawer.

From his wallet he pulled out his draft card—name, number, his classification (2S, for student deferment, now brutally expired), the signature of the local draft board clerk (Harriet Ballard, neatly cursive), his own hasty signature—and carefully snipped it into irregular halves, which, in turn, he halved into irregular halves. He halved the four quarters into irregular eighths. He opened up the letter from the Selective Service System. It was exactly as his mother had said. He arranged the eighths along the page until he had found a satisfying arrangement.

He glued them to the page.

At the top he wrote carefully, in capital letters:

TO WHOM IT MAY CONCERN:
I HAVE KNOWINGLY DESTROYED AND
MUTILATED THE ENCLOSED OBJECT.
THE PERSON TO WHOM YOU SENT THIS
NOTICE IS BEYOND YOUR COMMAND.
LOVE AND KISSES,
MATTHEW W. STACKHOUSE, JR.

He folded the letter back into thirds, tucked it into the envelope, circled the return address, wrote neatly alongside it, RETURN TO SENDER, and Scotch-taped the envelope closed.

His mother deserved to know something. He wrote a note: *Mom, it'll be OK. I need to go. I need to clear my head. Don't worry. I won't do anything foolish. I'll call.*

I love you, your son, Matt

He folded it, wrote *Mom* on the outside, and left it on the desk. He took up another sheet of paper and wrote:

Dearest Val,

I was very happy to get your letter. For a while I thought you were gone from me forever.

We got stupid, didn't we? I don't blame you, I don't blame myself. I hope you're not bitter. I'm not. I was but I'm not anymore. Time stretches us, doesn't it? Bitterness is a sewer. When I ask myself who I want to talk to about what's going on with me, it's you.

But first, about America, because I can't tell where America stops and I start. For all our fancy talk, the problem is simple. It's a shortage of soul. Every day is another gash in a wound that never stops bleeding. America bleeds from the holes in its soul. LBJ says we're not going to "tuck tail and run." Like we're living in a Bugs Bunny cartoon.

I can't turn away from the scene of the wreck. I need to deal with the war head-on. I've left Cleveland for parts unknown. Probably I'll do draft work. A few kids are burning their draft cards. I don't have the guts but I can help. There are sit-ins at draft boards. We're in the streets at the drop of a hat. We've got priests, ministers, rabbis. By the way, my draft board decided that I was ripe to kill Commies because I wasn't conscientious enough to be an objector. I filed an appeal. Appeal rejected. So I didn't burn my card but I just sliced it up and today I'm mailing it back to my draft board.

Mass mutiny is coming. We organize righteous jamborees. We're part dirge and part revelry. You know me—I'm more on the dirge side. I'll find something useful to do. When I have a return address, I'll write again.

I love you,
Matt

In his stocking feet, he picked up his duffel bag and stepped out of the house. He stopped on the doormat to pull on his boots, made a quick stop at the corner mailbox, deposited the Selective Service letter, paused, kissed the envelope addressed to Valerie, dropped it in, and headed west.

Matt had never set foot on the other side of the Mississippi River, which turned out to be sluggish and brown, not majestic. Near Davenport, Iowa, he stopped for gas amid strip malls under construction, gigantic parking lots, 5 & 10 shops, used car lots announcing ROCK BOTTOM SALES, junk yards piled high with rust, McDonald's arches (1 BILLION SOLD), signs of assurance that Jesus Saves. Hot rods, Cadillacs with their spiky fins. Death culture. Flatland, as Ronnie Silverberg used to call it.

Flatland was the name of a book that had caught Ronnie's fancy in high school, written by a mathematician named Edwin Abbott. The world was populated by geometric figures who lived on a plane. Men were polygons, women were lines. Occasionally, circles appeared, swelling up from the size of a dot, then shrinking until they vanished. The circles were the traces of spheres passing through the plane. Only the rulers of Flatland knew that there was such a thing as a sphere. It was forbidden to say there was a third dimension. Anyone who claimed to have seen a sphere, or any other three-dimensional object, was thrown into prison or murdered.

Matt badly wanted to experience another dimension, but couldn't picture it. An apostle trapped in Flatland. What a joke.

The crisp, sunny morning was cold enough to overwhelm the VW's feeble heater. Needing a heavier sweater, Matt stopped, unlatched the hood, pulled out his duffel bag, opened it, and found, on top of his clothes, a small unsealed envelope, containing five crisp twenty-dollar bills and a note: *Matt, This will help tide you over. Love from your mom.* She supported her son the only way she knew how—the way of not making a fuss.

Somewhere in Iowa he spotted a car pulled over on the side of the road, hood up. A clean-shaven, middle-aged white man wearing a dark suit was peering into the engine compartment of his Buick. Matt, in a beneficent mood, stopped. The radiator had sprung a leak. Could Matt drop him at the next garage? Sure, hop in. The man opened his trunk, took out a fat sample case, black, probably vinyl, and laid it down gently on Matt's backseat.

"Was my unlucky day until you stopped," the man said after sizing him up. "You're a Christian."

"I have been," Matt said.

A few miles later, the man spoke again: "You're probably wondering what I have in the case."

"As a matter of fact—"

"You look like an honest man so I'm gonna tell you. Uppers. I'm in the pharmaceutical business. I manage sales. Worked my way up from production. Company makes a fortune. Employees don't and managers don't either. So, smartest idea I ever had, I started going in at nights, running the machines, turning out a little extra supply. That's what I got in there. I sell wholesale. Why should some old buzzard who inherited the business and doesn't know beans about it keep all the profits?"

Matt was silent. This was his country.

"Don't worry about me. They don't keep good records. I should know, I was the one who was supposed to keep 'em. They'll never miss 'em. So."

"Uh-huh,"

"So I believe in free enterprise, see. With what I make from that one case, I'll buy myself my retirement cabin in the mountains."

"I'm curious," said Matt, poker-faced. "Why are you telling me this?"

"Like I said, you have an honest face. Can I offer you—?"

"Thanks, but—"

"You don't need to explain."

He dropped the man at a garage next to a gas station.

"You're a gentleman," the man said. "Thank you." Taking his sample case with him, he snapped a little salute and wished Matt good luck.

Matt's tires were nicely inflated, his oil was holding up. He bought a map, laid it flat on the counter, traced the thickened line of Interstate 80 westward. Nebraska … Wyoming … Utah … Nevada … California. The proprietor glared at him—his stubble, his flannel shirt—knowingly. Matt *felt* suspect.

Always the quandary: How can the few of us move the many of them? Archimedes said: "Give me a place to stand and with a lever I will move the whole world." Where's my place to stand?

He knew that where he was going he would find more pharmaceutical entrepreneurs, more death culture, more Flatland, but Interstate 80, if he kept to it, would take him to Berkeley, California, which, by reputation, might be his kind of scene. They were marching to block the tracks there, trying to stop the troop trains.

Then, Matt thought, at the edge of the Pacific, with Asia in flames on the other side, the United States of America would come to an end.

The skies were overcast, dull aluminum with the look of having been scraped by steel cleats. Underneath, the landscape was a blur. What caught his eye were the uniform bright green road signs with identical white lettering, colors and fonts designed to be read at a distance. The lab that designed them might be the same lab that quality-controlled the munitions destined for Vietnam. To Matt they suggested a country hammered into submission.

He felt surprisingly loose. No one awaited him. *This land was made for you and me.*

Somewhere on the prairie of central Nebraska, in the fading light, he pulled off the road. The darkness was smeared with streaks of a blacker darkness. Americans lived here. He knew nothing of them, though he was curious. They knew nothing of him, though he doubted they were curious. He locked the doors, closed his eyes, dreamed that a group of ragged children carrying cudgels were smashing one piñata after another, all hanging in a row, and he wanted to join them but decided it was incumbent upon him to stand clear.

Further west, in the parking lot of a roadside inn where he stopped for a tasteless breakfast the next morning, he picked up a hitchhiker, a young man wearing a belted green raincoat and sturdy boots—slender, blond, flat-topped—who looked like a farm boy and called him "Sir" until Matt told him to call him Matt.

His name was Gerald. He had a sweet voice. Sure enough, he was a farm boy, he loved horses, he was on his way to bid farewell to his sweetheart in Cheyenne, the next day, before shipping out for Vietnam, where a cavalry division awaited him. He toted his own duffel bag, which he slipped behind the front seat.

Matt had heard the terms "Air Cavalry," and "Air Cav," on the radio, but didn't know if they referred to an actual or a metaphorical cavalry.

The kid had acne spots all over his left cheek and his neck. "You're in luck," Matt said. "I can take you to Cheyenne."

"That's real good. Thank you."

Gerald seemed the taciturn sort, and Matt was relieved that they would not have to talk about the war. They were content to listen to top-forty rock, switching from one station to another during long commercial breaks. "California Dreamin'" came on, full of longing and harmony, irresistible, and Matt sang along, "On such a winter's day / Stopped into a church / I passed along the way / Well, I got down on my knees / And I began to pray—"

Gerald interrupted him. "Matt, you know, it's not 'began to pray.'"

"It isn't?"

"No, it's 'I *pretend* to pray.'"

"Damn!" Matt said, "I never noticed." He was not in a mood to reflect on why this might be. "Do you pray, Gerald?"

"I sure do. Every morning and night." He grinned. "So far, so good. And you?"

"My daddy's a minister, but I'm kinda out of practice now."

"Uh-huh."

"We're everywhere," Matt said, "the former Baptists."

Gerald didn't seem to find this amusing, so Matt went on: "And you?"

"Assemblies of God." Gerald seemed to think that every Christian knew who the Assemblies of God were.

"OK."

"Reach Out, I'll Be There" came along as if on cue. Urgent gospel, good news coming, with a sloppy drum track—

"Kinda *sounds* like the cavalry, you know? Hoof beats?" Matt said.

"One a them boys," Gerald said, "colored boys, I heard he's in Nam now."

"Oh yeah?"

"Makes me think of my girl."

"What's her name?"

"Pat. Sometimes I tease her, call her Patty, but she prefers Pat."

The DJ said something about the special taste of Dr. Pepper and then drew out his syllables to say, "And here ... it ... is" and the next sounds were the pounding treble chords of an organ, honky-tonk style, this could only be "96 Tears," by Question Mark and the Mysterians. He and Gerald sang along for a while but couldn't remember any lyrics beyond "too many teardrops" and "96 Tears." Listening more closely than usual, Matt understood for the first time how vindictive they were. This was a revenge song. Funny he never thought of that before. Valerie came to mind. Her lean frame, her green eyes, her freckles, the little bump on her nose.

He had her address. Draft resistors were always heading to Canada, but he could try Mexico, which would have better weather and probably easier access. He could drive south from Cheyenne, just show up in San Miguel.

"I wonder why it's *ninety-six* tears," Matt said.

"Guess it's the way it comes out, the rhythm, you know."

"Yeah, but why couldn't it be forty-four tears, or sixty-five?"

"That's a good question."

"It's nice that you have a girlfriend," Matt said. "What's she like?"

"Oh, lord, she's so pretty you could cry just to look at her. Looks kinda like that one in the Mamas and the Papas, you know, the blonde one with long hair?"

Then the guitar started slipping the scale downward, *doom-doom-doom-doom—doom-doom-doom-doom*, here came "These Boots Are Made for Walkin'," *yes*, Nancy Sinatra, with her little yips and hollers, her borderline nasty "You keep playin' where you shouldn't be playin'"—and what was *his* side of the story? Matt wondered—"and you keep thinkin' that you'll never get burnt"—did everybody play the great game of what-can-I-get-away-with?—and then "I just found me a brand new box of matches—" Sound-track of our lives.

"Are you ready, boots?" Matt said. "Start walking!"

"Kinda steppin' all over ya." Gerald chuckled.

But there was no time for reflection on the ways of women before the next number began, down from number one but still going strong, "the brave song by the man wounded in battle," the

DJ rattled the name off triumphantly "Staff ... Sergeant ... Barry ... Sadler!":

> *Fighting soldiers from the sky*
> *Fearless men who fight and die ...*

They hummed along.

"I sure like that Green Beret song," Gerald said.

Matt waited it out before he said, "Mmm, let's take a break," and clicked off the radio.

They passed a fenced-off ranch, horses grazing, and further off, a herd of larger, thicker creatures bearing antlers. The horizon opened up, the sky was big and off-blue, and a few patches of snow not yet swallowed up by the prairie. For a while the steady plinking of the motor and the swish of the tires were the only sounds.

Gerald reached into an inside pocket and extracted a perfectly rolled, tightly packed joint. They lit it up and passed it back and forth. Pungent fumes, pepperish but sweet, filled the car. The stuff went to work quickly. Gerald asked if Matt minded turning the radio back on. "Not at all," said Matt. "Long as it's mellow."

"California Dreamin'" came back, and again Matt sang along. "Very nice," he said.

"So, you headin' for California?"

"Could be. I haven't exactly made up my mind. See where the road takes me."

Gerald was maybe twenty or twenty-one, and Matt wondered whether he was drafted or enlisted, but it didn't matter that much. He probably didn't know Ho Chi Minh from Sitting Bull, didn't know who we were fighting or why, and believed—in the words of "The Ballad of the Green Berets"—that the fallen hero had died "for those oppressed," but he was still—or soon would be—an accomplice to an evil war. Matt knew this was the wrong way to think. But he also knew that because people like Matt refused to go, people like Gerald went.

Some apostle Matt was.

"I think it's a gonna take a turn for the better, now," Gerald said, sucking in the grass, holding it in his lungs.

"What's that?"

"Vietnam. We been havin' some trouble getting started, the Communists caught us with our pants down, so to speak, but I think we're gettin' up to speed now."

Matt could see a repeat coming, an upchuck of his dinner table confrontation; he could write the whole script in advance; he could switch parts and play his father for the hell of it ... But he would try a different gambit. "I was just thinking about that line, 'fighting for those oppressed,' how we have oppressed people here in our own country, you know, who need fighting for."

"Oh yeah. That's for sure."

"I've known some awful poor people," Matt stumbled on. "Like where I've been living, in Cleveland. No jobs. Nasty cops. Rats, roaches in the apartments."

"That right? Terrible how people let themselves go, throw garbage out in the street, that kinda thing. Seen it myself."

Matt didn't have the heart to push the argument further. The benign dope and the words to "California Dreamin'" were all he wanted in his head.

"I'm about ready for some shut-eye," Matt said. "How about you?"

"If it's all the same to you," Gerald said, taking the joint back, thrusting the nub of it back in his throat, swallowing the roach, "I'd just as soon keep going, you know?"

"You must be real eager to see your Pat."

"Oh yeah, *real* eager."

Matt pulled off the road, cut the engine, and they stepped outside. Gerald ran up and down in place for a while, shouting "Quick step!" Water vapor, condensed, curled from their mouths. After a couple of minutes, Matt was ready to lie down on the backseat. "Sure you're OK to drive?" he asked.

"Oh, sure. Not exactly a lot of traffic out here."

"Have a blast," Matt said, thinking about the beautiful blonde in the Mamas and the Papas, wondering if Pat was a California girl, thinking that Valerie might be the only California girl he'd ever known, thinking how little she resembled the ones in the beach blanket movies—much smarter, taller, more complicated.

Matt leaned back, said "See ya," and the next thing he knew, he was awake, still pleasantly buzzed, and Gerald had stopped at a red light, tossing back over his shoulder, "Welcome to Cheyenne," then adding, "Hate to tell you, Matt, but you may have a problem."

"What's that?"

As the light turned green, Gerald put in the clutch, shifted into first, and revved up the car, which made, on top of its usual whine, more of a rumble.

"You feel that?"

"You mean the shake."

"Yeah."

"Uh-oh."

"Don't think it's that serious," Gerald said. "Sounds to me like the disk of your clutch is slipping." Gerald was in his element. Matt was embarrassed to know so little about his own car.

"Uh-huh."

"These bugs are built like Tinker Toys. Clutch is a real simple thing to replace. But you're headin' into the mountains, your clutch is gonna get a workout, so I'd get it checked. You don't want to find yourself frozen so you can't shift gears. Worst comes to worst, you won't be able to shift into gear at all."

A flash flood of dread poured into Matt. "Jesus," he said.

"You're probably OK for now, it's not terrible yet. But I'll tell you, you're one lucky guy you're getting this information before you hit the Rockies, which is, you know, downshift heaven."

"Man, you are knowledgeable."

"I've fixed a car or two in my time. That was my job, mechanic, before I enlisted. These little Volkswagens are bad for business, they last forever."

They reached downtown Cheyenne, which looked like a movie set—three-story brick buildings, a couple of bison flags flying, cars parked diagonally. Gerald pulled in across the street from the bus station, in front of a bar whose neon sign read "High Plains." A smaller sign read "Mon Nites R Ladies Nites."

"High Plains. My kinda place. This is where I get off." Gerald got out, yanking up his duffel bag. "Where you gonna head now, Matt?"

Matt thought, *I'm going to miss this guy.* "California Dreamin'," he said with a smile. "Good luck to both of us." Gerald fired off a two-finger salute.

While Matt was dozing, the grayness had broken down and the sky blued up and started to go purple, the sun being well past its zenith. Flat-bottomed cumulus clouds, piled high, floated in from the west. Matt's mind was in a state of high buzz, but his stomach was growling and he needed a decent night's sleep. He'd push on to the next town tonight, find a mechanic, get an early start into the mountains early tomorrow.

What he needed to see him safely to port was a high dose of caffeine and a slice of all-American pie in downtown Cheyenne, Wyoming. He didn't want to intrude on Gerald in High Plains, so he picked up his map and walked into another café, called Good and Hot, sat down at the counter, and (thinking that despite the name of the café the shock of cold liquid would do him the most good) ordered a large glass of iced coffee, black, then inspected the top shelf of the round plastic case and pointed to a wedge of gummy-looking blueberry pie to go with it, and looked up to see the perky, chubby young waitress, holding a stubby pencil to her pad, staring at him.

"Huh?" she said.

Matt knit his brow. "The pie and a big glass of iced coffee?"

The waitress wanted to be polite, but she was struggling. "Uh, sorry, we don't have that."

Matt tilted his head querulously, and his expression shifted to how-stupid-are-you? "You don't have that."

"No sir."

"Coffee with ice in it."

She was fresh-faced, wanted to be conscientious, looked forward to greater things in life, but she was blank. This challenge she had not anticipated.

"Tell you what. Could you bring me a big glass full of ice and also a cup of hot coffee? Black."

She kept her game face on. "Sure thing." She wielded the spatula on a wedge of pie, placed it in front of him, said, "Here you are!" and turned toward the ice compartment.

Matt reflected on the strangeness of a country that claimed the two of them equally and probably drove them to equal distraction.

She brought a large Coke glass of ice, then the steaming coffee. He inserted a knife blade-down into the glass, to avoid shattering it as he poured the coffee. It tasted like leather but he felt the caffeine go to work. He smiled at the waitress and she smiled back. He unfolded the map on the counter.

If he drove west, the next medium-size town was Laramie, which looked to be about an hour away, and was (the map said) a university town, so it would be likely to feature a decent (or at least not too terrible) place to crash. From the look of the twisting roads, little mountain symbols and summit altitudes, Wyoming got more scenic from there on, which was good, but on the other hand he'd be heading further north, which meant colder, and farther from the San Francisco Bay Area, which by default felt like his destination—and for that matter from Mexico, in case dropping in on Valerie came to feel like something other than a lamebrain idea. Moreover, when he came down out of the mountains, he'd find himself in Salt Lake City, to which his only association was the Mormon Tabernacle, starred on the map as a "Special Interest," which he expected would turn out tacky and saccharine. He'd heard about the Latter Day Saints' sacred writings in ancient Egyptian on gold plates, unearthed by Joseph Smith in upstate New York. America was *weird*. On the third hand, if he headed south, he was less than hour from Fort Collins, home of Colorado State University, where he might find a hostel or a kindred spirit. He would meander westward, the Interstate being under construction, but he'd be able to wiggle across the Rockies and pass through a town called Rifle, which seemed worth a look just for the hell of it, before passing into what the map designated as the canyon region of Utah. Canyons made him think of the Lone Ranger, a stalwart of his American childhood.

The coffee sent him to the bathroom, where after a long, satisfying urination, he got a look at himself. His hair was twisted up behind his ears like Satanic horns, his face carried an undergrowth of dark stubble, there was a stain on his shirt above his bellybutton. He washed his face, which helped somewhat. But he could see more clearly why the waitress might have regarded him as an oddball.

Fort Collins, Rifle, canyons of Utah, here we come.

Accelerating from a stop sign, merging onto the highway, the car shuddered worse than before, and when Matt fed the engine more gas, not much happened. Still on the mellow side of stoned, he fought to stay lighthearted. He twirled the AM dial, picked up country music. Every protagonist in the songs had been left, everyone was peeved about it, or in mourning, or resolute.

An uneventful hour later, with a sense of great relief—a run of good luck for a change—he pulled into Fort Collins, where great shafts of brightness were knifing through the clouds as the sun sank. Red and orange leaves carpeted the streets. Skeletal silver tree trunks were on display.

He followed a sign to College Avenue, which sounded promising, and saw advertisements for auto repairs. There were hotels and a bar called "The Real McCoy," with a sculpture made of antlers twisted together above the door. The window featured a neon recommendation for Coors Beer, "Brewed with Pure Rocky Mountain Spring Water." He parked diagonally on College Avenue, thanking the automotive gods for bringing him this far.

The country-western sound pouring out of The Real McCoy made it plain that he was about to enter an alternative universe. The juke box was playing "Your Cheatin' Heart" at high volume through a crowded room thick with cigarette smoke and a low roar of jumbled talk. Knotty pine paneling festooned with mounted elk heads, complete with massive antlers. Buffaloes and a black bear. Posters of John Wayne and Marilyn Monroe, and one of World War II vintage with Uncle Sam posed against a billowing flag urging BUY WAR BONDS. Two pretty girls in angora sweaters, one pink, one white. This place was not his kind of collegiate, not one of those hangouts the likes of which you saw in Ann Arbor, New Haven, or Madison, where the posters featured James Dean, Humphrey Bogart, and the sleek Art Deco French locomotive ("EXACTITUDE") and ocean liner ("NORMANDIE") speeding head-on, almost lethally precise. Between the posters, small metallic signs include "Down with literasy tests" and "Everybody believes in something. I believe I will have another beer." Behind the bar: "Tequila! Helping Women Lower Their Standards For Years." Matt remembered having heard that Colorado's state universities were tops in the nation for partying. Not for antiwar sentiment, most likely.

He felt worn out, scraped; he had a car to worry about; he was in no mood to look for a more congenial hangout. Gerald had been sufficient company for a while; he could live without any more congeniality today. There were affordable looking hotels on the block, and he also liked the look of the full-lipped, wavy-haired (blonde with a reddish tinge), forty-something bartender, who wore a pine-green blouse gathered at the scoop neck, showing a touch of cleavage. Round face, straight nose, large mouth, a touch of plummy lipstick. Perhaps she was looking for a date. Twenty years ago, she would have been a knockout. She'd been around the block but had come back for a second try. Her badge read GRETCHEN.

He sat down on a barstool, ordered a burger and a draft beer, and mused about whether he had missed an opportunity with Gerald. Should he have taken a different tack—made the generals' arguments against getting involved in another land war in

Asia? Talked about the Sino-Soviet split? He needed to tune up for arguments to come. And if the movement was going to grow, it needed to grow in places like Fort Collins. He could see if SDS or some other group needed somebody to organize draft resistance in the mountain states. Berkeley didn't need him; it must be jam-packed with his sort of people; he'd be a fifth or a fifty-first wheel there. Then again, Fort Collins would be another Cleveland, fish-out-of-water experience. He'd be asking for trouble. Suppose a cop asked for his draft card. But was it automatically a bad idea to ask for trouble?

The hamburger agreed with his dope-enhanced taste buds, so Matt ordered another, was on his second mug of crisp-chilled beer, felt encouraged to make a two-fingered beckoning motion to Gretchen.

"Say, Gretchen," he said quietly, "I see your name's Gretchen—"

"Hi there," she said cheerily.

"Hi. I'm Matt."

"What can I do for you, Matt?"

"Well, I have what might seem like a funny question. Do you know anybody around here who's not so crazy about the Vietnam war?"

"Hmm." Her brow wrinkled querulously, then charmingly. "Why do you ask?"

Matt improvised. "Well, tell you the truth, I just got my induction notice and, I don't know, I'm just curious."

She lifted her eyebrows, cast her eyes around the bar room, turned back to him and lowered her own voice. "Well, me, actually, I'm not crazy about it."

Down at the other end of the bar, a young man with close-cropped sandy hair, wearing a crisply ironed western shirt—red, with snaps—was loudly talking about football, as if trying to compete with the country music, to a couple of buddies wearing cowboy hats.

"But I don't talk about it much," Gretchen said.

"Oh?"

"I got a boy over there."

Jesus. She probably wouldn't want to be asked what her boy thinks about the war.

"Hey, Gretchen," the guy in the red shirt shouted, "bring us another pitcher, OK?"

Gretchen said, "Excuse me" to Matt, drew a pitcher of Coors draft and headed down the bar with it. On her return she was not smiling, seemed pulled tight, like an overwound watch.

"Hard day?"

"As a matter of fact," she said, with an accent hard to trace, maybe a touch of the upper South, "you see that sign?" She pointed toward *"MOTHER TOLD ME THERE'D BE DAYS LIKE THIS But She Didn't Say How Many."*

"I know what you mean."

"Oh man," she said, "you don't want to know about trouble." Now that he studied her face more closely, he saw how heavily she was made up, especially around her right cheekbone. Her perkiness had worn off. Her voice was heavier than her look.

Matt hunched forward, elbows on the bar. "Sorry for asking," he said.

"No, it's fine. I don't mind talking."

"Can I buy you a beer?"

She glanced down the bar. "Maybe after work—"

The fellow in the red shirt sauntered over, loomed over Matt, jacked up the sound of his voice, and said—a statement, not a question—"Hey Gretch, this guy giving you any trouble."

"No, he sure isn't, Charlie."

"You sure?" Charlie's defense-of-womanhood voice was right at the edge of belligerent. He stuck out his chest and swaggered while standing still.

"Ye-es, I'm sure."

"'Cause he kinda looks like a hippie to me." He examined Matt up and down as if summoning his inner bad guy. "What's your name, hippie?"

Matt counted off a silent 1-2-3. "It's Matt, and I'm not a hippie."

"Oh yeah? Funny, you sure look like a hippie to me."

Out of the corner of his eye Matt observed one of Charlie's cowboy-hat buddies sliding down the bar toward him.

Stay matter-of-fact, Matt. Neither surly nor deferential. "No, you must be mixing me up with somebody else."

"A faggot, you mean? Gretch, doesn't this guy look to you like a faggot?"

"Cut it out, Charlie." Gretchen narrowed her eyes and glared at prickly-haired Charlie, who ignored her, or was encouraged by her disapproval, it was hard to tell. He narrowed his eyes. "Faggot is as faggot does, but you know, personally, I'd rather be a cocksucker than a Commie."

"Stop it right now," Gretchen said, giving Charlie a dirtier look, but he was undeterred. Chin out, he turned his icepick eyes on Matt:

"Why you want to hang around with a faggot?"

"Charlie! I'm warning you!"

Charlie turned his swagger up another notch. He wanted it known that he was a winner. Matt hoisted himself up from his stool and stepped back, but he was wobbling. Charlie was quicker and weirdly, with the heel of his left palm, smacked him first in his right eye and then in the chin. The sweet taste of his own blood came as a surprise and Matt lurched backward, knocking over his stool, swaying, but steadied himself by grabbing the one next to his, and—too late—stuck out his left forearm to parry the next blow. A moment later, coming up from behind Matt, one of the cowboy hats slugged him in the mouth and knocked him to the floor, where he banged his skull against the leg of a nearby chair. People scattered. Matt's head rang. Conversation stopped although the country-western songs did not.

Gretchen scrambled into a back office and returned in the company of a short man, fiftyish, with shaggy sideburns, sporting a thin scar on his right cheek, wearing a tag that said: MANAGER, AL, WHAT CAN I DO FOR YOU?

"What's going on here?" Al was commanding but unruffled. He'd seen all kinds.

"Al, since when you stop supporting your country?" Charlie was slurring his words. "Why you let queers in?"

"Out," said Al authoritatively, nodding toward the exit. He could deal with assholes like this in his sleep. "Out."

Charlie stood pat.

"You deaf, Charlie? You guys get the fuck out of my place." Al kept his voice level.

Charlie glared at prostrate Matt and said, a little sing-songy, "I don't know, Al. Not good for business. Don't want to get a reputation—"

"Shut up. You and your buddies—" indicating the cowboy hats "—you get right out of here or I call the cops. *Now*."

Charlie snorted triumphantly and with his two buddies, their sneers aligned, headed for the exit. Around the bar room, customers craned for views and asked each other what had happened.

Pain washed around Matt's head—from his right cheekbone, smack against the rough wood floor; from his right jaw; from the back of his skull; and from somewhere in the damaged interior of his mouth. He felt around his top right teeth with his tongue, felt a hole, opened his eyes, blinked hard, blinked again, jerked his head around birdlike, and determined that no new danger had arisen. Gasps and mutters buzzed around the room and nearby customers looked on: "Are you all right?" Matt sucked his lip.

"Oh yeah, I'm fine." Matt made an effort to sit up but didn't really mean it and gave up.

"Don't move yet." Gretchen touched his wrist, possibly checking his pulse.

"I'm OK. Really. Somebody pass me some—?"

Al was holding a wad of napkins grabbed from a metal holder on a nearby table.

"Thank you. Very much." Matt patted down his torn lip, tore off a chunk of napkin and stuck it into the space between his upper lip and the bloody hole where his molar used to be, and held the rest of the wad against the cut on his forehead, from which a narrow stream of blood trickled down his forehead.

Al said, "Let me call you an ambulance."

"No, please don't bother. It's not necessary. Really. Just a couple of cuts and a tooth. But it's kind of you."

"Whatever you say. We've got a room upstairs where you can rest." He exchanged with Gretchen a look that was hard to interpret. "You mind telling me what this was about in the first place?"

"Beats me. I haven't a clue. You'll have to ask the other guys. They had trouble minding their own business."

"I'm sorry this happened, mister."

"It's not your fault."

"Why don't you take him upstairs," Al said to Gretchen. "Let him clean up. I'll take over the bar for a while."

"Thanks, Al," she said.

The bar room quieted down, like a lake where a huge boulder had landed a while ago but the waves were now subsiding.

"Somebody give me a hand?" Gretchen said to the customers in general. One, a stocky man wearing a flannel shirt and cowboy boots carved with a rodeo scene, bent to help Matt up.

Matt lifted his head and said, "Thanks, that's very kind of you."

"Don't mention it, mister. Take it easy, now."

The man's sincerity was soothing. Curious bystanders pulled back and cleared a space. The man cradled Matt's head on his shoulder, and the room reeled. Matt lay back down, closed his eyes to steady the room, stopped time, opened his eyes some seconds later and said, "I'm OK." There was a commotion in his head. The man and Gretchen lifted him by his elbows. For a moment, he felt stable, and said, "I can stand up now." He tried, and went weak in the knees. The stocky man grabbed him by one elbow and Gretchen by the other.

"Easy," the man repeated.

"Whoa, let's slow it down," Gretchen said. "Do you think you can walk?"

Matt patted his lip again and rasped, "Let's find out."

Gretchen took him by one arm, the stocky man by the other, and together, painstakingly, they elevated him and edged him toward the exit and out onto the sidewalk. Charlie and his pals were nowhere to be seen.

The stocky man headed back inside as Gretchen towed Matt along, saying, "We've got our own special recovery room."

Matt sent his tongue to explore his mouth, where the space formerly occupied by his molar felt cavernous.

The street was dark now, though oddly familiar to him, as if he had passed through there in another life. Gretchen clasped his elbow as he got out his key and opened the VW hood. She picked up his duffel bag. He followed her around the side of the building to a padlocked, unmarked wooden door, which she unlocked. Once they were inside, she threw a deadbolt behind her and reclaimed his elbow.

"You sure you're OK?"

"Oh yeah. Fine and dandy."

"You're not dizzy?"

"Not exactly dizzy, no."

At the top of a narrow flight of rickety wooden stairs they faced a door painted bright blue. She unlocked it and, still gripping his elbow, said, "Go 'head in."

Matt stepped into a large room with a bare wood floor, two windows with dark green curtains, a couple of travel posters—one of the Grand Canyon, one of some rocky expanse in multiple colors—and an armchair with pebbly blue upholstery, a matching sofa, equally uncomfortable-looking, and another door, behind which stood a small sink. Gretchen opened a cabinet, took out fresh towels and a washcloth, and left them for him on the sink while she rummaged through a medicine chest and pulled out a bottle of mercurochrome and some Band-Aids. Mercurochrome was becoming the story of Matt's life.

His head rang dully. The jukebox thumping downstairs did not help.

She dampened the washcloth in cold water and held it gently against the bruise that was already making his right eye look as though it had taken artillery fire. The mirror, having lost some of its silver backing, looked like a war zone itself.

"Thanks."

"You should lie down." She led him to the blue sofa, set out a throw pillow there, and gestured that he should rest his head. "How do you feel?"

"Lousy. And better."

"Good. I mean the 'better' part."

He stretched out lengthwise and closed his eyes. The jukebox didn't let up. Neither did the wooziness in his head.

She brought a large Coke glass full of cloudy water and some ice cubes wrapped into a knotted napkin. "Hold this to your eye."

He did. He couldn't stop thinking this was his lucky day except that he had to get unlucky first.

On closer inspection her hair was teased into the sort of controlled swirl he associated with Doris Day. "Do you understand what *that* was about?"

"You know, I really don't. Not exactly. Most of us aren't jerks. Most of the time."

"My moustache set off a hippie vibe?"

"Could be. Charlie's kind of wired, can't hold his liquor. Even when he isn't wired, he's the jealous type, like he's been deputized by my old man to stand guard over me. Or something. Honestly, beats me. By the way, don't take this personal, but you could use a shower."

"Sorry. I've been on the road a long time. Long time, long story. I need to fix my car." Now he felt mildly fortified. "Truth is, everything in my life needs repair."

She didn't bite. "What's wrong with it? The car, I mean."

"Clutch."

"Frank down the street is good. He opens at seven, I think. AM. Or maybe six. Where you headed?"

"You know, that might seem to you like a simple question, but it's got me stumped."

"Uh-huh. Well, shoot, it don't matter. You let me know if there's any way I can help."

He could think of more than one thing but opted for biting his lip, damaged as it was. The day was either real or slipping into surreal country, or he couldn't tell the difference. If he couldn't tell the difference, was that good or bad?

He dug fresh clothes out of his duffel bag and headed for the shower. The jet of hot water scorched his injuries, made them scream. Soap made them scream louder. He patted his face dry, toweled off, put on fresh clothes, and eyed himself in the mirror. Considering the fight, he could have looked worse. His lip was puffing up, a bruise darkening on his forehead, and the area beneath his right eye was going purple, but the noise in his head was more or less subsiding, and although the sting from his wounds was severe, it was specific, which was comforting. He was not so badly damaged. He looked rumpled, which made him laugh.

"What's so funny?" she asked.

"It *is* funny, isn't it?"

"If you say so!" She returned his laugh with her own.

"I'm Matt, by the way. I figured out that you're Gretchen."

"Well, you're no dummy!"

He took the mercurochrome and Band-Aids off the sink and said, "If you'll do the honors," and sat down on the sofa at a neutral distance. The country-western music thumped. He couldn't make out any lyrics. "You know, I kinda feel like one of those country songs," he said.

"I can imagine." She leaned over, examined his face from a nurse's distance, unscrewed the mercurochrome cap, extracted the glass applicator. "It's gonna sting like crazy." Close up, he saw a tiny scar just above, and into, her upper lip. He winced as the mercurochrome went to work.

"And take three of these aspirins," she ordered.

"Thank you. You're expert."

"Well, I've done a lot of this sort of thing."

"Oh, right, you mentioned your son."

"Sons, actually. I got three."

"Really!"

"Really. And you?"

"Me? Oh no. No, no, no."

"Well, *that's* very definite. Never say never. They're the greatest gifts. They're a handful, they're angels, they're devils, boys especially, they make your life a lot more wonderful and a lot scarier, and all kinds of other good things."

She capped the mercurochrome, walked it back to the bathroom, stood at the doorway, arms folded, watching him in a friendly but not much more than friendly way. Her belly was slightly, pleasingly outcurved. "You know, that thing's a convertible," she said of the sofa. "I've been spending time here myself. It's not the most comfortable thing in the world but the rent is dirt cheap. Free, in fact."

"Oh?"

This was not only getting more interesting but—up to a point—distracting him nicely from the condition of his head. He was not sure what he wanted, or what she wanted.

"I've got a long story, too," she finally said. "To start at the end, in case you were wondering, I'm on a little vacation from my old man," was the way she started, and the rest gushed into a cascade of information punctuated by shrugs, grimaces, embarrassed smiles, expressions of self-reproach, and, at the end, a few tears: married at eighteen, high school sweethearts, first baby after a year—he was the one over in 'Nam—her younger boys now in high school and her old man drank and spent a lot of time on his bike, motorcycle, worked on bikes at a garage outside town, and did she mention that he drank too much, and, by the way, he'd taken swings at her (that too-heavily made-up area around her cheekbone), and she was fed up, so she took the two younger kids to stay with her mother nearby, and her old man probably went off with his 'cycle buddies' but she wasn't sure, and now she didn't know what to do. Then her face crumpled and she wept, which broke into Matt's sense of unreality.

"Damn it, I can't do this," she said, mopping her face with a tissue. "I'm gonna have to fix myself up so's I can go back to work."

For what it was worth, she was not wearing a wedding ring.

His aches interfered with the preliminaries of lust. Or was that only an excuse for his indecision?

A coughing fit came over him, buying him time. "Al's gonna wonder what became of you," he said finally. "I wouldn't want you to get in trouble."

"I know. Stand up, OK?"

He did, she waved him to one side, took a sofa seat cushion in both hands, leaned it against the wall, and she was on her way to take up the other one but he stopped her, picked it up himself, carried it over; she pulled the mechanical handle to open up the bed, where the mattress was already made up with sheets and a single pillow. She lay the two seat cushions end to end on the floor, went to the closet, pulled out a couple of sheets and a pillow case, lay the sheets over the cushions, stuffed a sofa pillow into the pillowcase and placed it neatly.

He waited. Her ripeness awaited him. His breathing tightened. She might just be old enough to be his mother. Fine. Her skin was smooth and her cheeks round and her cleavage welcoming. But she had a lot to lose if Al got the idea that she was overstaying her break time.

There was also the biker husband to think about, roaming around somewhere. There were Charlie and Charlie's friends.

Given the complications of her life, a roll in the hay with him was probably not what Gretchen, this decent, generous, and surely attractive woman, needed most.

Hold on, who was he anyway—her shrink, her best girlfriend, her guidance counselor, her psychic? Who appointed him to think for her?

Moment of truth, Matt. You lit out for the territory. Are you a go-for-broke kind of guy? If you don't know where you're going, how can you be lost?

Fucking a multitude of women had never been his particular thing.

Separately they made up their minds to proceed with caution, though this was not easily explained.

"I'd better get on back downstairs," she said faintly. "We close at two, and then I got to help clean up."

"Sure. I'll take the cushions."

"I'll come back when I get off." And she was gone.

He regretted his way to sleep.

He slept dreamlessly until in the small, dark, silent hours he was startled half-awake as a key turned in the door and Gretchen quietly set down her shoes and padded across the room. He opened his good eye. She entered his field of vision. His head ached and the cuts in his face stung.

She lay down, her back against his front, pushing against him. They were separated by a sheet.

His thought was vivid even if banal: *It's good to be alive.* Banality was nothing to be ashamed of.

"Just hold me," she whispered.

He laid his hand on her hip.

A few minutes later, she whispered again, "I wish—"

He whispered back: "You wish what?"

"—wish I could get to know you."

"Yes."

"Some other time."

He knew she was talking straight. Their shadows, in another life, were already making love.

She turned so that she was sitting but his hand was still on her hip. "I've been thinking. You know—Matt—I'm thinking I should be the one who takes your car into Frank's shop. Him and me, we're on good terms, and I got to get up early anyway, go see my boys, so tell me where to find your key, I'll take your car and find out when Frank can get the work done, and come back and let you know."

"Sounds good to me. God bless you."

"Ain't nothin'." She got up. "'Night."

The next thing he knew, morning light was leaking into the room and she was leaning over him, saying, "Frank's gettin' right on it." She sat down beside him. "I got to go see my kids now. Be back when the car's ready." She kissed his cheek and went.

He was awake and clean, with one and a half functional eyes, moderately clear-headed, with two more aspirin at work in him, gazing at her poster of the canyon which was not the Grand Canyon, a canyon filled with spiky red, orange, and pink open-air stalagmites in many shades, a festival of stone, thinking that this looked like a place to see—he still lacked a stopping-off point on his way west—and also contemplating the prospect of breakfast, or lunch, when she returned in the early afternoon, dangling his key on her finger, and said:

"You're in luck. It isn't serious." She was holding an invoice, which she read from: "Had to replace the clutch cable, and something called a pedal hook."

"What do I owe him? Or you?"

"You don't owe either of us a thing. We're pals." She placed the key in his palm.

"You sure?"

"I'm sure."

"I *am* in luck."

"That's Bryce," she said, nodding at the poster. "Bryce Canyon."

"Where's that?"

"Utah."

"Lord. That really exists?"

"Oh yeah. Looks just like that."

"Looks like a forest of popsicle sticks. Maybe you just answered my question of where I was headed."

"Pardon my nosiness, but don't you have to go to work sometimes?"

"I'm not working," he said. "Not for wages, anyway. I'm working against the war."

"You don't mean those demonstrations? Oh, God, Matt, that doesn't do any good."

He had the feeling that what she meant was that her son didn't approve of them.

"Your son. Does he mention the demonstrations?"

"John—John's his name—tell you the truth, they make him angry, he thinks they're worse than a waste of time, and you boys are unpatriotic. I'm not sayin' I agree. I just think politics is screwed up."

"Well—"

"Let's do me a favor and not talk about politics, OK?"

"OK," he said after hesitating a moment. "Let's talk about beautiful things. How long does it take to drive to Bryce Canyon?"

"Mm, I don't know, maybe half a day if you don't stop too long."

The thought of driving half a day in his bug, even with a functioning clutch, improving vision and decreasing pain, did not attract him. He checked his watch. Twelve thirty-five.

"Hold on," she said. "I got a better idea for you. There's another place right over the Utah border. Not only closer but, now that I think of it, a lot less crowded than Bryce. Arches."

"Does it have those popsicle sticks?"

"Different kinds of rocks, and a lot of them are arches, truly." She stretched her arms into a downward-facing semicircle. "*Huge* arches. Really, you've never seen anythin' like to it. Arches National Monument."

"How far is it from here?"

"Oh, maybe four hundred miles, six hours and change—if your bug isn't slowed down too much gettin' over the mountains and you don't get in any more trouble." She winked. "You could get there by nightfall. 'Course, I don't know what the motel situation is. It's a pretty small town, around Arches."

"I've got a sleeping bag."

"Well, great. Then you can go on to Bryce afterwards."

They faced one another. His longing had just about broken up on a reef of regret and gratitude. They kissed moderately and pulled back.

"You *are* sweet," she said. "Just one thing. I want you to make me a promise."

"What's that?"

"Wait right there and hold out your hand."

When she came back from the bathroom she deposited a small, pink flat-sided pill in his palm.

"Uh-oh. But I already stole some more of your aspirin."

She closed his hand onto the pill. "Get loaded on this when you get to the arches."

He knew her too well now to ask if she was serious. "What is it?"

She said something that sounded like "guy." A local variation of "golly"? But asking what she meant would have been rude.

"It's *acid*, Matt," she went on, as if explaining to a child. "Very good, very pure. You take it when the sun is setting over the arches—"

"I've never taken acid."

"Well, it's about time you started." She ignited the room with a smile. "I guarantee you, you'll have a night to remember me by. You promise?"

"I promise." He plunged the pill deep into his pocket.

"And another thing. You have to promise to send me a postcard."

"I might just *bring* you a postcard."

"Mm, that would be lovely ... but I don't think I would recommend it, not now, and no more visits to the Real McCoy till the smoke clears." She tapped him on the nose and laughed. "But when you have an address, you send it, you hear?"

He promised.

"I parked your car a block down, to the right. Don't hang around. Just get in and go. Please. It's a great day for me that you stopped here. I think it was fate. Now go."

They embraced and separated.

Accidents are thresholds.

He lumbered downstairs, steady enough on his feet, mostly unharmed. His cut lip smarted and he kept tonguing the cavern between his teeth, but his skull bore only a sort of echo of an ache.

Down on the street, the sunlight was friendly. He tossed a look over his shoulder. No one was paying him any attention. He was unhappy to be leaving but he had to leave. By the time he got to his car, stashed his duffel bag, turned the key, put in the clutch, and felt the seamless shift of the gears, he felt more joyful than rueful. He had a new friend in Fort Collins, Colorado. He had, in the short term, a destination. America, with some exceptions, might be his country after all. *Good to be alive.*

He located a country-western station on the dial, turned up the volume, and hummed along. The heartbreak songs didn't distinguish between women. All women betrayed you, all women were better than you deserve, everyone sounded plaintive. What a raw country. *Shut up, Matt. You can't live your life by the radio dial.* He stopped at a red light behind a pick-up truck that sported an AMERICA—LOVE IT OR LEAVE IT bumper sticker. A couple of blocks down he saw a rusted-out Chevy bearing the same message. He thought of Valerie. She might have had the right idea about leaving. Why did he need a country to love?

Without question he did love America, ruptured as it was. Gretchen's America was not Charlie's America.

Further down College Avenue, a stooped old man with a weathered face that vaguely resembled Bryce Canyon, wearing a heavy leather vest and a nicely pressed work shirt, crossed the street in front of him, taking all the time in the world. Peering down into the VW he shouted, "Filthy hippie!" Did him proud.

Just outside town, Matt stopped at a hamburger joint, bought a boxful, topped with ketchup and a scatter of diced-up onions, and a bag of moderately greasy fries, a giant-size Coke (with ice) and a large cup of coffee (without), a couple of packs of beef jerky and three Hershey bars with almonds.

The German engine did its work smoothly, and he headed south toward Denver, where he would bend westward to skirt the metropolis. The limitless sky beckoned him, tested him, comforted him—immense, seductive, relentless—a billboard for God's first and faultless country (excluding some of its inhabitants), unbound and unbounded, calling out: *Keep going, though you'll never arrive, and you're not safe yet.*

In the wind, the bare aspen gleamed in the open sunlight, and shuddered.

He ticked off the weirdly precise summit signs along the highway—8219 feet, 8712 feet, 9058 feet—keeping both hands on the steering wheel. At the sight of a sign reading, "Truckers, you are not down yet," he clutched the wheel tighter. As the road twisted, hair-pinned, swerved, the gears engaged flawlessly, and impatient as he was to make Arches by nightfall, he was not sorry to get stuck behind trucks for long stretches, because their great bulk sheltered him from gusts of mountain wind, because the mountains offered up snowcaps to his thirsty eyes as he filled his stomach, avoiding the cut on his lip, chewing slowly for the sake of his jaw, drinking Coke and coffee alternately. He wondered why country-western songs were so obsessed with broken hearts at the expense of everything lasting around them—sky, mountains, valleys, snow, waterfalls, wildlife. We listen for the companionship of the unlucky, he thought, for the fires of revenge and the cool water of absolution. The music tells an inescapable truth: It doesn't matter how big your national sky is, even a patriot's heart will be broken.

He felt light-headed. He could live without guarantees. Not everyone could. For now, he loved the feeling. But Gretchen's heart was not safe in Fort Collins, Colorado, and might never be so. As for Valerie, the émigré, the exile, the voyeur, whatever, he did not know. Did she preserve her American heart in Mexico, or cancel it? *Valerie, Valerie—will we ever break through?*

A sign announced Rocky Mountain National Park and the highway became Trail Ridge Road, which was the right name, for it twisted wildly, and he needed to shift a lot more—up and down, back and forth between third gear and second, in love with his new clutch—and the view from the mountain ridge over the precipice dropped off to his left and sometimes to his right. He thought switchbacks were a fine metaphor for life because as you proceeded, the view changed in one way but stayed the same in another. Some other time he'd come back and go camping, possibly with Gretchen.

Probably not in the town of Rifle, though, which offered its share of wide-open spaces, barbed-wire fences, and grazing cattle, but otherwise nothing to speak of besides a gun store called AMMU NATION with weathered wood siding and a sign saying, "We Have What You Need."

On the other side of Rifle, he stopped at an overlook to pee against a mostly denuded aspen, its residual leaves flapping in the wind like a crowd waving farewell. He was breathing a little hard. He sat on a fallen tree-trunk and took in gallons of cool, thin air. A mountain pass off to the east glared so brightly he had to squint. As the wind picked up, a faintly vanilla aroma reached his nostrils from an evergreen vastness, and he was caught up by a distant roar. He stood, felt steady, took a few steps downhill, rounded a bend, and the roar intensified, he found himself staring at a whitewater river, charging down the mountain, around a scatter of boulders and over them. The river always resumed on the other side of the rock, he thought. The rock was damp but intact. He tenderly contemplated his jagged life and thought that, as life swept over him, he too was dampened but intact.

He passed into a time tunnel, his thoughts fugitive and forgettable, as if the wind were not only rousing his skin but cleansing him, sweeping dust out of his head, rearranging his mental furniture. He wolfed down three burgers, fries, and a candy bar, and soon he was closing in on the Utah state line and seeing signs for Arches National Monument, and the next thing he knew, with two hamburgers and a dozen fries left on the front seat, he was pulling into an unpaved parking area. A sign warned that the area was closed from sunset to sunrise, but he had not come all this way to care. There was no sign of a ranger. Two battered Chevvies and a pickup truck were parked there.

The moon was up, swollen. Looming above the parking lot were the huge stones that Gretchen had promised, pillars of stone, walls of stone, some rounded, some flattened—fingers, towers, upright bludgeons. There was one—no, two—visible arches. The stones went on and on, up the hillside, as far as he could see. The deepening red was a color he had never before seen.

He tried to formulate words for this extraterrestrial color but gave up. The close-to-full moon staggered him. His head was no longer thundering, his wounds were no longer of interest. Reality began, or resumed, here. It made his skin tingle and filled his nostrils with promise.

From his glove compartment, he pulled out a small black notebook, clipped a retractable ballpoint pen onto the cover, stuck it into his back pocket, lifted his bagged-up sleeping bag out of the trunk, jammed the remaining beef jerky and candy inside, along with a sweater, plugged a half-full Coke bottle with a stopper he fashioned out of a bunch of rolled-up leaves, dug into his pocket to make sure of Gretchen's pill—it was there—checked that the car was locked, and gazed at a bulbous, more or less vertical rock that shared a base with a grander rock which, as he watched, came to resemble an elephant. A shadow deepened down the crevice that ran between the two rocks.

On second thought, the Coke bottle didn't belong in this landscape. He was making a getaway from Coca-Cola country. So he took the pink pill into his mouth, swallowed some Coke, washed down the pill with the rest of the bottle, went back to the car, unlocked it, tossed the bottle onto the floor, and locked the door again. If he had been better prepared, he would have brought a canteen. But if he had been better prepared, he might not have gotten here after all.

The wind was gusting and red-orange light was soaking deep into the stone and putting out radiant heat. The trail to the arch area was obvious. He checked the time, 7:48, unbuckled his watch, jammed it deep into his pocket.

The sunlight dwindled and the moon bulged like an ornament of slightly tarnished silver. He made his way up switchbacks, over a dry stream-bed, past bunches of tall grass, scrubby low bushes and spiky plants that it would be wise not to brush up against. He took his time. The exertion of his climb, and the residual heat of the day's sun coming off the rocks, kept the chill at bay. Every direction offered a different shade of sundown. He smelled a slight, indefinable sweetness, probably herbal. Shadows darkened fitfully. Like the second hand of a cheap clock, they stood still for extended moments, then suddenly lengthened. He gazed at one particular hump of rock, where a long slash of horizontal shadow resembled the mouth of a cave. He had lost track of time.

His skin tingled and he felt a tautness around his head, not exactly unpleasant, a kind of alertness, a tang, along with a flicker of fear, and with the opening of his senses knew that the acid was working and that the boundary between himself and the world was softening. This was the real McCoy. Time deepened. The world quivered. Every lengthening shadow suggested an animal—a lizard, a rabbit, a squirrel. Should he expect rattlesnakes? Did they sleep at night? In Westerns they dozed in the sun. Did that mean that at night they crawled around? He would tread carefully. He stared at the cave-like shadow. He concentrated, but heard only the sound of the wind rustling the spiky plants.

The earth made contact. When the wind died down, he heard the earth. It was not making any sound in particular but he heard it. When it slept, it breathed, like him. It blew minds. It *was* a mind. It weathered the fearful and strange. As Gretchen did. The stillness was uncanny. And natural. Absolute stillness emanated from this place and time as assuredly as the barroom noise of the Real McCoy in Fort Collins emanated from its own place and time. The universe was folded and the folds made contact—

Was this what awe meant, knowing along the whole range of your being that the earth was alive in the way that you are alive but endlessly so and far grander? Baptists did not believe in a living earth, so far as he knew, but there was a lot the Baptists didn't know. The earth was alive, he was alive, he was alone.

He was not alone. He was coated in solitude, and the solitude had a memory. The native people lived here. The white men drove them away, force-marched them into submission, but something of them remained. This place was *crowded*. Not with ghosts but—something.

In the silver moonlight, a stump curled backwards, like a huge and twisted armadillo. Around it arose spiky plants, blades of the obscure. He could not have imagined such a living thing.

Behind the stump, a monumental stone reared up against the sky, its edges silvered, a huge balancing rock, taller than wide, like a granite mushroom, dark gray going red, a boulder balancing on top of a band of white, chalky stone, which in turn rested on a wider, thicker stretch of gray stone. Head on neck on torso. The torso was a sort of sprawling pedestal. There were no other human beings in sight.

He walked around the stone, taking his time. From one angle, it was a Norse God holding a tremendous hammer; from another, an impassive head, an Easter Island prototype (he'd seen pictures), but with a flatter nose, worn down, craning forward for a better look at the mountains. Or a tomahawk?

Erosion produced these shapes and their dignity. The implausibly balanced rock was America.

There was nothing to fear. He had enough courage. The gods may not have lived here but the people who believed in the gods did.

The tingle working its way around his skull was insistent, and not unpleasant. He was all nerve endings.

Before the sun was completely gone, he scouted around. The arches were all around—long, short, higher, lower, thinner, thicker. They soaked up the dwindling light. Arches from here to somewhere, ground to ground. He stared. He saw bloodstains, and bloody faces. Blank, bloody faces. Wide foreheads, broken noses. Fossils from ancient battles. These were not the faces of angels.

No, these were the children of erosion. The irreversible evolution of things, water devouring rock.

His stomach growled. He had brought nothing to eat besides beef jerky and a candy bar. But the thought of food made him retch. The best idea was to sleep. He circled the balanced rock until he found a shallow indentation about his size. Looking one way, he faced the rock; looking the other way, a long arch. He rolled out his sleeping bag on some soft scrub, bulked up his sweater for a pillow, tucked his notebook beneath it, crawled in, looked up at a billion stars, and slept the sleep of a stoned-out lower-case god.

He dreams of Indians with bandages gagging their mouths.

When he awakens, a tire is inflating inside his head, pressing on his skull. Inner volcanoes rumble.

A breeze is up, carrying an aroma—something like cinnamon—into his nostrils. The balancing rock casts a moon shadow. He squints to narrow his focus and watches the great head nod ever so slightly. It is for this moment that he has come here. The draft notice … the broken clutch … Gretchen … Charlie … all culminating here. He lifts his head, transfixed.

His mouth is dry. How stupid of him not to have brought water.

It occurs to him that he might have suffered a concussion at the Real McCoy. He does not know what the symptoms are. He touches the tender places, but they are not the sources of the tightness and tingles running around his skull.

His stomach is hollow. The beef jerky tempts him, but he does not succumb. He's groggy. He must have slept a long time. He pulls out his watch, holds it up to the moon. Nine forty-two.

The unseen do not speak.

The moon is, actually, precisely, full.

The arch is the Ark. The Ark whose exact specifications were prescribed by the God of Genesis.

He is always suspicious of straight lines. Nature abhors them.

The rock is perfectly balanced. Preserved. Asymmetry is not chaos. Equipoise is what he lacks, what he needs. Or the opposite—the breakout, the breakthrough. To what?

Order is what remains from a previous rupture.

The rock is humanity. As he stares, it teeters.

Is this the moment when he breaks through to—what?—the gods in whom he does not believe? Or perseverance? You don't break through to perseverance. You persevere. You gave chaos time to break down. Down to earth. The Second Law of Thermodynamics. Stone endures. Until, at an infinitesimal pace, it dissolves. Human beings do not endure. Even wars do not endure.

The war is the crucifixion. Jesus of Hanoi.

This is crazy. Crazy is what he hungers for—the courage for the right kind of crazy. He might just dissolve the membrane that seals him off from the world.

The rock no longer teeters. Its moon shadow is long and slender; fuzzy at the edges. Let happen whatever happens.

But the skin around his skull grows more taut. He is holding on to something that will not let go of him.

The air has grown chilly, but the wind has died down. The mountains ripple, coated by blackness.

The mountains have been eaten away. Matt Stackhouse, Jr., is alone with the balanced rock.

There is only the rock.

Nothing surprises him. Except for the tenderness of his dissolution.

There is nothing to fear. Let go.

Nothing to fear.

He is freaked out of his mind.

He can do this.

With supreme concentration, he enters the rock—he *is* the rock, which has no core, no shape, which is a chaos of consciousness inside an unconscious thing. None of this makes sense. He closes his eyes.

The story of his life: always the urge forward, upward, off the scale; always the fervor; always the call to liftoff; always the fugitive energies, the flickers of incandescence, the sparklers that emit shimmering particles of light until the light is extinguished.

Always the fear that at the last moment, the moment of truth, he will pull back.

When he next opens his eyes and digs into his pocket for his watch, it's a few minutes after four in the morning, the morning light pallid, the aroma of cinnamon strong. He is wrung out, something sounds wrong. A small high-squeaking tone goes off. Something pings at the top of his skull. It was as if he has stepped into an express elevator on its way up. Doors closing. Takeoff. Ascent. Pure velocity.

I'm on the threshold. I'm taking leave.

The balancing rock is stable, but the long arch resembles the gaping mouth of a ravenous, toothless beast. Further away stand huge rippling shapes impenetrable to the light: the jagged mountains.

His body is a cauldron. His heart thunders.

He stares as, in the distance, the whole mountain range slides sideways, left, right, left, a breach opens up, water pours through, the waterfall fans out, a mile wide, two miles, immeasurable miles, and the water sparkles, phosphorescent, an aroma of chocolate wafts through the high desert air, and Gretchen appears, dressed in a bright red top now, and says softly: "Wait for me."

The phosphorescence vanishes. She's gone. His stomach rumbles. The sensation around his scalp tightens—a vise that will not let go.

I can hold on. But—but nothing. This is the butt time. But time. Everything is despite. The spite. History, mystery, all in a row. Pressure is no pleasure. If losing is winning, where's the beginning? My mouth is my valve.

Why am I doing this to myself?

In time all things are possible, except what is out of time.

Suddenly the waterfall shuts down and the mountains stop swaying and the distant spikes sharpen into stalagmite teeth while, from the heavens, stalactite teeth plunge downward, he is no longer Noah, he is Jonah, sealed inside, the saw-toothed mountains will shred him. He hasn't dissolved. He could *be* dissolved.

Ain't it just like the night, t'play tricks when you're trying t'bih so quiet.

Defy it.

I do not want to be chewed to pulp.

The thought makes him gag.

Whatever the altitude, the air is brisk, oxygen swirls.

I can't be sealed up. I won't be sealed up.

Nothing to fear. The sky is obscenely blue, the rocks brightening to the color of pale rust.

I must have come west to die. I'm going to get what I wanted: the final liquefaction.

The roof of his head rips away. His mind is about to blast out of his body.

There it goes, up and away, shedding his remains—like a snakeskin—leaving the earth behind—losing himself—his mind—

He needs to reel it in. But that is impossible.

How much courage does he need to face the impossible?

He shudders, a personal earthquake. He sits bolt upright, cries for help, swallows hard, again, again, wretched, at wit's end, straining, swallowing, *haul, haul again,* haul it back—

If I pull hard enough, I can reclaim my mind—

He shakes, retches, protests—until, somehow, he succeeds in yanking his mind back into his body.

He leans against a rock. The rock makes an impression on his back, the backs of his thighs, calves, heels.

Give it time. Time is on my side. Yes it is.

A chill. Outside his skin, inside his skin. He trembles. He waits. A time will come when he should move. Not yet. Then the time comes. He takes a step, his legs go rubbery, he falls back. Waits. Waits longer. Breathes. Stops. Firm enough. He is still trembling, but less so.

Take your time.

Step.

The world is not the world he used to know. But it is close.

He stumbles around until he finds the trail down to the parking lot. He climbed this way as the sunlight expired, a very long time ago.

Down at the road, only one other car, a rusty pale-yellow Pontiac, is parked near his own. He pulls out his notebook, stashes the rest of his stuff, leans against the hood and writes down everything he can remember.

He hears an engine. Approaching is a blue Chevy Impala with a license plate that says DEATH.

The Impala slows down as it nears him and he sees that the license plate is actually DE 478. The driver waves.

It hits Matt that what he was holding onto at the balancing rock was fear. Fear is the cap pulled tight over his skull. The fear of dissolution he knows intimately. But perhaps it is not fear at all. Perhaps it is a *longing* to dissolve. Perhaps this longing is not dangerous. Perhaps it is his instrument. Great chords of fear, thunderous vibrations. *Let go.*

It comes to him that he needs the membrane that protects him from the world. His head is ruled by a dynamo of pure, essential, rock-bottom fear. If he lets the membrane dissolve, there will no longer be anyone left to be frightened.

Matt Stackhouse, Jr., exalted and unnerved, no longer trembling, wondered if he would ever again see and feel what he saw and felt at the balancing rock. Was it possible to bring the rocks and the arches into his life? And if the answer to both questions was no, were they any the less real?

There was a sense in which even to ask such questions was an imposture, a gimmick. Asking was the closest he could get to an answer.

He drove on for hours. At Bryce Canyon, he stopped at the park headquarters, gulped two large glasses of ice water, devoured a plate of scrambled eggs and toast, discovered to his relief that he could keep food down, and chose tea over coffee. The air was compassionate. He drove into the tourist loop, shifting between second and third gear, peering into the canyon at every turn for as many seconds as he could spare from the road. He parked at overlooks and let the canyon come to him. The divine-demonic chemical was still in his system, and last night's explosion of color sense was still detonating in slow motion. The sky was ultimate blue, the stone pillars tangerine, the spikes of stone flame-orange.

However glorious, Bryce after Arches was anticlimactic.

He hiked around the canyon's edge, stared at the pillars and spikes, grabbed a fistful of memory out of the night before—it was already fading—and on his way back to the car groped for words, a formula he could communicate, a statement, a proposition.

On his way out of the tourist loop, he stopped to buy a picture postcard of the canyon at twilight, the vista saturated with blazing reds and oranges, colors raised to a higher power, and wrote out a message:

> *Dear Gretchen,*
>
> *Arches was all that you promised and more. I owe to you a memorable thrilling night and I am forever grateful. It was wonderful to meet you. Thank you again for taking care of me in all the ways you did. I hope our paths cross again.*
>
> *Love,*
> *Matt Stackhouse*
> *P.S. I hope everything goes well with your John.*

This felt lame, but he couldn't think of anything better. Gretchen would know what he meant. On second thought, he bought an envelope, stamped it, enclosed the postcard, and mailed it to her c/o the Real McCoy.

The mountains had given him what they had to give. Love flooded his heart. He could wander here for days—weeks, months—but more would not have been better.

Greenwood, Mississippi, 1966

MELISSA HOWARD, DEPLETED, CLUTCHING a folding carpenter's rule in one hand and a bottle of warm Coke in the other, was taking a break from her task, which was to measure the radius from the central tent pole to the spots in the ground where the stakes would be pounded in. It was a torrid June 16. She was sopping wet from humidity and had already changed clothes earlier in the afternoon. She asked herself why, after two years of organizing, she remained in the Delta, stuffing cotton into the bleeding heart of Mississippi. She gave herself the standard answers—encouraging local people to stand up, registering voters, feeling her membership in a community, which was more family to her now than her own in Detroit—but today there was an additional element: the March Against Fear was on its way into town, because Greenwood, gateway to the Delta, was still a movement epicenter and an unavoidable stop.

For the Greenwood SNCC staff, the work of welcoming the March was a huge hassle. It disrupted their plans though arguably it was still worthwhile, since it had already inspired hundreds of new voters to register, and Melissa knew that God laughed while men made plans, and so for more than a week she gave the March everything she had.

The March had started out ten days earlier as the brainchild of James Meredith, the Air Force veteran who had integrated the University of Mississippi in 1962 and was now, four years later, a law student at Columbia University. Meredith was the opposite of an organization man, in fact the word around SNCC and other civil rights groups was that he was gutsy but more than a little bit Lone Ranger, or a loose cannon, or maybe a bit, you know, erratic, for when he had filed suit to be admitted into Ole Miss, it was him by his lonesome, not a member of any group, and he remained on his own when Federal courts ruled in favor of his right to attend, and still again when the Justice Department sent five hundred U.S. marshals to accompany him onto the Ole Miss campus, and he was still no organization man when, four years later, he set out, solo, on a two hundred twenty mile walk from Memphis to Jackson. None of the civil rights groups cared a whit.

On his second day out of Memphis, Meredith was gunned down. While he was recovering at a nearby hospital, SNCC, CORE, and the SCLC decided they were obliged to continue his march, in the spirit of refusing to be shotgunned into lassitude or even the appearance of it, which is how the press would play a failure to march on to Jackson. Unlike Meredith, the organized marchers would be accompanied by armed security guards, the Deacons for Defense, whose men would be packing firearms though you'd have to look closely to see them. The police, figuring that Mississippi had reaped enough bad publicity for a while, decided to leave them alone. Dr. King was not happy about the Deacons but he had worked out a deal with SNCC: they agreed to let white people march in exchange for his willingness to tolerate the Deacons.

He disagreed with SNCC's recent decision to exclude white folks from the movement on the grounds that they dominated and intimidated black folks whether or not they intended to. But in truth, Dr. King was fond of SNCC's recently elected new chairman, Stokely Carmichael, thought of him as a rambunctious kid brother. Stokely had a fierce side, Dr. King knew, which had surely spurred the movement during these terrible and wonderful last years, but a deal was a deal. Stokely could be trusted to keep his agreement. Dr. King had been around long enough to know that in a messy world even the world's best known apostle of nonviolence has to make deals.

Speaking of deals, when a few hundred marchers strode and limped and drove into Greenwood, Stokely told the police that the march's advance party had a right to set up their tent at the Stone Street Negro Elementary School, whereupon he was arrested. Melissa knew that on the wall of the police station was a plaque honoring Tiger, a German shepherd famous for nipping at civil rights demonstrations in Greenwood. While Stokely was in jail, the SNCC folks decided that the important thing was to make sure that the rally took place, so they started setting up in a park across the street from the remains of the old SNCC office where (as Melissa well knew from James Turnbull) a bunch of buildings had been destroyed by arson in 1963, the same year Tiger became the rednecks' folk hero.

Stokely, with his buoyant Trinidadian accent, his precise elocution, his banter, his bulging, flashing, somehow feral eyes and his whitest of white teeth—Melissa was excited to see him again. A year and a half ago she got involved with him for a few days. That's how she thought of it. Not love but involvement, she was fine with involvement, involvement was a movement thing, a rocking and rolling thing, and it was all she had time for. Stokely trailed a big reputation for coming and going but he was gentle and playful with her, and she knew he had been kidding when he said that "the position of women in SNCC is prone" and so did most of the other women in SNCC even though there was some truth, a lot of truth, in the joke, which became notorious as if Stokely had meant it seriously.

After the Selma-to-Montgomery march last year, which was not SNCC's idea either—SNCC was *way* beyond protest marches—Stokely had moved on to Lowndes County, Alabama, where he had helped form the Lowndes County Freedom Organization, with its little Black Panther symbol that for all its awkwardly drawn leap and protruding claws looked to Melissa like a pussycat. Move on over, the poster said, or we'll move on over you. Stokely put on denim overalls, *overhauls*, with their snaps, but he looked like he was down-dressing from his natural elegance, striding out of the Greenwood jail in his short-sleeved white shirt, although it was rumpled from Mississippi sweat and six hours behind bars. A local lawyer had put up the astonishingly low bail of one hundred dollars, the Greensboro establishment having decided to play it cool for a change.

People were wondering whether the thin-lipped middle-aged white man named Byron De La Beckwith would show up again, having already been spotted lurking around the march. Melissa knew who he was because she had sat in the courtroom during his second trial for the murder of Medgar Evers, when the former governor, Ross Barnett, walked up and shook his hand while Medgar's widow Myrlie was on the witness stand. The murderer had got off not once but twice after all-white juries couldn't agree on a verdict. But somebody must have delivered a message to De La Beckwith because he didn't show up today.

Melissa had no trouble recruiting a bunch of kids who'd been playing baseball in the park to help put up the tent, the kids clamoring to join in, thrilled that the March Against Fear was coming to town, and so much adrenaline flowed that they got the job done in half an hour. By the time Stokely got to the park, the tent was up, along with a speaking platform, and a few hundred folks were there, people still drifting in at the edge of the crowd, and the city, bless its white heart, had left the bright lights on, around the tent, and the whites were on good behavior—and nobody seemed upset that Dr. King wasn't there, he'd gone off to Memphis to appear on some network TV show, no surprise, SNCC had for quite some time been referring to him, behind his back, as "De Lawd," and more recently as "Black Jesus." For Stokely, Dr. King's absence was a big opportunity.

Melissa rushed up to Stokely, who gave her a delicious smile and a "How you doin', girl?" and she had half a mind to see more of him later, but Bobby Hicks was hovering nearby, and she didn't want any part of Hicks, a local hothead with a big round face, though a pleasing smile when he decided to smile, which was not often—Melissa even felt scared of him sometimes, she wasn't sure why, maybe because he wore sunglasses even at night, but in any case she avoided being alone with him and behind his back called him

"Dark Bobby." Here was Bobby Hicks with his big hand around Stokely's shoulders, telling him, "We're going for Black Power. Don't hit too much on Freedom Now, but hit the need for power," and when Stokely got up on the platform, the electric lights around the park glinted off the whites of his eyes, he was in no mood to banter, he went straight-out:

"This is the twenty-seventh time I have been arrested. I ain't going to jail no more. I ain't going to jail no more."

He said:

"They take Black boys to fight in Vietnam. We shouldn't go fight in Vietnam. Our fight is here!"

—and Melissa thought, *Amen*—

and Stokely went on:

"We have begged the president. We've begged the federal government—that's all we've been doing, begging and begging. It's time we stand up and take over—"

and somebody in the crowd yelled, "Tell it, brother!" and Melissa thought, *Oh yeah*, but it was not her place to shout, it was the local folks' park, it was their place, they were going to be here long after she and Stokely had moved on—and then Stokely was shaking his fist:

"Everybody owns our neighborhood except us. We outnumber the whites in this county; we want Black Power. That's what we want—Black Power! From now on, when they ask you what you want, you know what to tell 'em. What we need is Black Power. What do you want?"

and the crowd roared, "Black Power!" and Bobby Hicks jumped up on the platform alongside Stokely and shouted, "What do you want?" and again, louder, "What do you want?" and the response boomed, "Black Power!" "Black Power!" and Stokely went on, sweating profusely: "Ain't nothin' wrong with anything all black, 'cause I'm all black and I'm all good." *Well, he is good*, Melissa thought, *and he certainly is all black*, and something very big and very good, probably very good, was happening here, though it also made her nervous—

"The only way we gonna stop them white men from whuppin' us is to take over. We been saying freedom for six years and we ain't got nothin'. What we got to start saying now is *Black Power!*"

and Bobby Hicks shouted, "Black Power!" again, Stokely shouting along with him, growing hoarse, and the crowd shouted back, and Stokely went on:

"Every courthouse in Mississippi ought to be burned down tomorrow to get rid of the dirt and the mess—"

and Melissa, startled, thought, *Stokely, hold on, oh my goodness, I don't know exactly what kind of Christian I am now, I'm not so much for turning my cheek anymore, but one thing I do know is that burning down a courthouse or even threatening it is not such a great idea, it won't sound so great on the evening news, this is not the beloved community, this is not the overcoming, this is not Ida Mae, it is not Pete Seeger. Stokely, Stokely, where are you going with this?*—and Bobby Hicks shouted again, "Black Power!" and the crowd was right there with him.

Afterwards, Stokely went off with the local leadership, the other march leaders took down the tent, Melissa directed folks to clean up, and she looked up to see Bobby Hicks glowering, near the platform, arguing with a white guy wearing a broad-brimmed hat, his head down and obscured, a guy who looked up momentarily and glanced in her direction, head cocked, and when she got a better look at him, not only did he bear a resemblance to Terry McKay, damn if it *wasn't* Terry McKay. Last she had heard, he was in Cleveland, trying to get somewhere with the interracial movement of the poor, which she always thought was a fine idea (as did Stokely, who probably came up with the idea in the first place), though about its practicality she had her doubts. What was Terry McKay doing here?

Now Terry was pulling a cigarette out of his jeans jacket pocket—she didn't remember him as a smoker—and as Bobby Hicks leaned into him, waving his finger around like a pistol, scowling, eyes concealed by his dark shades, she heard him berate Terry: "Self-determination, that's what it means. Self. Not you, Mister! Us! It's *our* struggle."

Terry stuck the cigarette between his lips and Bobby Hicks reached out his big hand and snatched it.

Terry felt like slugging him but he understood that the last thing anyone needed to see at a Black Power rally was a race brawl. Over Hicks's shoulder he saw Melissa approach and waved to show that he recognized her but shook his head slightly to signal that it would be best if she stayed away from this scene.

Bobby stuck the cigarette in his mouth, unlit.

Terry calmly studied him and let a moment pass before beginning his lecture. "Look, man, *we're* not the problem. The white radicals aren't the problem. We have the same problem with white liberals you have. Liberals sometimes take you to lunch but radicals pay the check."

"You know what I think?"

"What do you think? Tell me."

"I think you're *afraid* to deal with the crackers. You want us to shelter you in the bosom of our loving Jesus." Hicks spit out the words. "You don't know who you'd be without us."

"That's not it"—Terry thinking that he actually was OK with Black Power, thinking that this moment was unavoidable, thinking that what Stokely meant, what he *really* meant, was taking power through elections, not burning down courthouses, though the time would come when some people *would* burn down courthouses, and lots of people would throw kerosene on the flames, which would kick off all kinds of mayhem, and God knows what would happen then, maybe it would be defeat at Armageddon because the Blacks would be way outnumbered and outgunned, but still, Stokely and Bobby Hicks and, let's face it, most of the SNCC staff were right that the moment of Black Power had arrived, and now, even if white people trembled, this is the dynamic of revolutions, they flow on tides of emotion and they go to extremes and they're painful and dangerous and they don't turn back.

"Listen, Mistah White Radical," Bobby Hicks snarled, "you come back and we'll talk oncet you got a whole army of poor white people behind you, you understand? Don't go around preach' your paternalism. We don't need no speech from you about racism. You go tell the people who need to hear it. This ain't your movement no more. You hear me?"

By now Melissa had circled around Terry so that Bobby could see her stalk up, chin set, and bite off her words: "Bobby Hicks, cut it out *right now. Now.* You crazy?" Bobby clenched his jaw and stomped away.

Terry threw his arms around her and thought it would be delightful to spend the night with her but under the circumstances it would not be a good idea, and Melissa was thinking the same thing.

For months Terry had looked for an off-ramp out of Cleveland, an antiwar project that felt right, but couldn't find an obvious exit, there were too many cloverleaves. Uncharacteristically, he was baffled, knocking around, weightless.

Cleveland had run into a wall. The Billy Joe-Wyatt group on the Near West Side had fallen afoul of personal quarrels. Terry couldn't figure out whether the trouble was girls, or power rivalries, or both, but whatever the reasons, the hope of organizing around police brutality was stalled. After their absurd defeat in court on the technicality of a mistake about the contract's expiration date, rent strikes looked impractical. Meanwhile, riots broke out on the East Side, the Negro side—*that* was only a matter of time—and prospects of cross-race coalitions had to be shelved.

It was different for the women. The sustained energy of their work in the neighborhood was a marvel to behold. Marcia Stein, bless her, remained hopeful that welfare organizing might recover from the collapse of Charlotte's web. Terry was still getting it on with her nicely, but as an organizer, he was no help. Some of the SDS people talked about putting together a citywide training school for black and white organizers, show folks how to do power structure research, teach the history of the city, raise money, and so on, but to Terry this sounded like treading water. *If you can, do. If you can't, teach.*

He was floating. So, when James Meredith was gunned down and Terry heard that SNCC, CORE, and SCLC were carrying on with his march, he packed a bag, bought a youth-fare ticket for Atlanta, and from there picked up a ride to Memphis and another one south into Mississippi, to join up.

So here he was, setting foot in murderous Mississippi for the first time. In 1961, when Tom Hayden published his SDS pamphlet, *Revolution in Mississippi*, Terry had gobbled it up, it left a bonfire burning on his mental map. If there was one thing he scorned in movement politics, it was theatrical stunts, especially parachuting into a hot spot just to make an appearance before the cameras. But the actual state of Mississippi, here and now, was the testing ground, Mississippi was where it was at, because SNCC had put out the call, and SNCC was more than his inspiration, it was his lodestar, the incarnation of conscience, the measure of what was called for in their time, and the proof of what you could do—had to do—when you abandoned illusions.

The air was a hot dead weight, fat with moisture, the sidewalks were blazing, he was striding his way into myth—*Terry McKay walks the streets of Greenwood, hot damn!*—and he didn't care if he was self-dramatizing. He was a bit player and his personal marker didn't mean anything to anyone but himself, but still, it was not nothing, and anyway, the march was mythic though the heat was punishing, and Terry was glad that he had brought along an extra pair of sneakers and a supply of Band-Aids. The whites kept off the streets but some peered out from windows and storefronts, sullen, smirking, or unreadable. He drew dirty looks. Downtown, on his way to the rally, he passed a couple of middle-aged white guys sitting on fold-up chairs on the sidewalk accompanied by a police dog in front of a cotton broker's shop. One of them tilted his chair back against the wall and said, "Brutus likes the breast of a chicken but he don't like no black meat." Terry understood that Brutus was the dog. "We got a law on our books that says you can't rape," the guy said. "Every so often they forget it. The only way to stop that is to put a gin wheel around a nigger's neck and let him swim the river with it."

Terry had learned a lot from Jean-Paul Sartre, knew that Sartre had studied in Berlin in 1933 and wondered if this is what it felt like—the visitor's shadowed half-knowledge of the bone-cracking, mind-crushing assaults taking place around the corner; the need not to know; the pretense of normality; the churning fright; the impulse to theorize. Except that in 1933 the worst was yet to come, and in 1966 the worst was probably over.

But not certainly. For this leaflet appeared in Greenwood after the rally:

> *The world first heard the revolutionary cry of BLACK POWER shouted from the mouth of a sunbaked Ubangi named STOKLEY CARMICAL right here in Greenwood during the 'Mississippi March.' If any of you should allow yourselves to become intoxicated with this revolutionary brew, rest assured, you will be promptly sobered up with massive doses of BLACK POWDER, already in the hands of we white, Christian patriots. Do not be fools black men. We will live here with you in the future as we have in the past or we will fertilize the soil of our beloved Southland with your remains. Remember, the choice is yours and ours.*

East Palo Alto and Dallas, 1967-68

THE COUNTRY WAS TILTED, somebody once said. Everything loose rolled west, to San Francisco, Berkeley, L.A.—the end of the line, the edge of the continent, the imperial terminus where America gave out. He might be superfluous, one more freelance apostle roaming around, but surely Cleveland was over for him, and Chicago was out of the question, and he couldn't think of any particular reason to go anywhere else, and he had come too far to stop. He thought he might try his luck in Palo Alto, which might not be so oversettled with radicals as Berkeley. At forks in the road, he headed westerly, through deserts, back into mountains and back down, stopping long enough to nap and grab a bite, for the wonder of his mind-trip at the balancing rock faded and the best mood he could find now was vague excitement that kept receding into dull confusion tinged with dread.

He passed through a town called Gilroy, central California's odd exception to the rule of towns called San This and Santa That, where he smelled something surprising, opened his windows and breathed in, full blast, the warm all-around thick aroma of garlic. He had been ready for orange trees but not garlic.

Traffic began to bunch up as he headed north up Route 101, a full continent away from Route 1 that ran along the Atlantic, so that he had to slow down and sweep glances around the San Francisco peninsula, perked up by glimpses of the Bay to the east and titillated by the spine of hills scraping the sky to the west—if he wasn't mistaken there were actual *estates* lining those hills— and a chain of suburbs taking their names from natural features

("Sunnyvale," "Mountain View," "Los Altos Hills"—but wasn't that redundant, "Heights Hills"?). He parked and walked onto the radiant, Romanesque, unreal Stanford campus, that vast, sumptuous, sun-saturated, sprawling playpen of tawny sandstone and Spanish arches, where big money purchased tennis courts, big skies, and the right to knowledge. He breathed in the pungent eucalyptus aromas and gawked at the first palm trees he had ever seen for real. The light was bright, abundant, somehow deep.

It wasn't long before he spotted a student wearing a button bearing a large Ω, the universally recognized symbol for electrical resistance. It turned out that his name was Mike Starr, he was a senior from Texas, he wore a bushy but trimmed moustache and his dark hair was cut surprisingly short, as if he had only half finished assuming his disguise, and he proudly volunteered that he had burned his draft card and now worked full time with a group that called itself, not surprisingly, The Resistance. They lived collectively on "the wrong side of the freeway," as Mike called it, in rattletrap East Palo Alto. They lived cheap.

A year earlier, Mike had been drawn to Trotsky—until he came to understand that he, Mike, was an absolute pacifist, while Trotsky drew a sharp line between "their morals and ours."

The collective, four or five of them at any given time, occupied a sprawling, minimally furnished house, as if all the furniture they needed was high-powered sunlight. They were intense but somehow careless, not grave. In a conversation that came and went, they argued about what Trotsky had meant by his 1918 slogan, "Neither war nor peace," and whether "permanent revolution" made sense, and if it could be nonviolent. They cheerfully welcomed Matt, who seamlessly folded in, helping plan draft-card burnings and turn-ins, compiling press lists, setting up concerts for their ardent supporter Joan Baez (who soon enough was even more ardently connected, having partnered with the blond, broadly smiling *echt* Californian David Harris, in his granny glasses). They reminisced about civil rights work in Mississippi. Now they helped fix resisters up with fresh starts in Canada, even Sweden. There was talk about raiding a draft board, nonviolently, to destroy files—a notion they put off for the time being. Matt told them what he had done with his draft card. Mike thought that was "far out," but was surprised to learn that Matt hadn't thought out what would happen from then on. Mike had taken a draft counseling course from the Quakers and told him that when Matt's board in Chicago got around to it, they wouldn't beat around the bush, they'd order him to report for induction.

They were underway, like a caravan. New people showed up at meetings. Matt felt more or less at home. There was gravitas, spirit, generosity. Was this a California thing? Matt's mustache grew to Zapata proportions, flowing the full width of his face. There was a flow to conversations, too, which often looped into discussions of the motives for, and limits of, civil disobedience. Should Cuba disarm unilaterally? Should the Jews have sat down on the German railroad tracks? And then what, as the corpses piled up? Voices rose, clashed, fell. They listened to Jefferson Airplane and Janis Joplin. The real-life Joan Baez, ebony hair and shining intensity, came by the house, smiled beneficently upon them and sang "Oh Freedom" and "This Little Light of Mine" but also "Runaway" and "Donna" and "Little Darling," her riffs running up and down the octaves like wild horses at dawn. In the mornings, the same arguments resumed, like rehearsals for a show that was not yet ready to open.

There was momentum. There was strong, smooth grass and jugs of rough Red Mountain. One day little purple pills appeared inside the tea spoons in everyone's place settings. When everyone else swallowed their pills down in wine and spaghetti sauce, Matt demurred. For him, acid was not the stuff of everyday rites; it deserved special occasions. He couldn't help feeling a touch superior as his new friends crawled around the house and onto the lawn muttering "Wow" and staring at ants. He watched them with sympathy and some envy. He could appreciate that inside the brilliant silences that ensued, the Resistance was bonding, and it was not that he didn't want to belong, but that this was not his way. He walked outside, lay down on the grass, and thought about the stone arches of Utah—so much more stirring than the perfect symmetries adorning the Stanford campus.

Days passed. He was ducking the question of what to tell his parents. He called midday Chicago time, when his father would not be home. His mother was worried sick. She couldn't sleep. Was he going to go to jail? Was he keeping healthy? Was he eating well? Yes, he was healthy. Yes, he was eating well.

"What are you doing with your life? How can you treat your parents—?"

"Mom, stop right now, or I'll hang up, I swear I will."

She slipped into tears of abandonment and reproach.

"It's OK, Mom, it's OK."

"It's not OK. It'll never be OK."

"Never is a long time, Mom. It's going to be OK. Listen, I'm fine."

He didn't think she believed him, but she had to pretend. "You sound all right. Thank God."

She told him she was all right, too, though "a bit of a nervous wreck." His father had back problems. Matt told her he had a good (though nondescript) job in California, he liked the people he worked with, and by the way, had any more mail come from Mexico?

None.

"Mom, I really know this is hard for you. I know." The subject needed changing.

"Promise me, Mom, that if I get any more mail, from anywhere, you'll forward it to me." He gave her the East Palo Alto address. She promised.

"Matthew, do you know what you're doing?"

"You know, Mom, I actually do."

"You'd tell me if you were in trouble, wouldn't you?"

"Of course I would."

Three days later, a letter from her arrived. He opened the envelope to find three crisp hundred-dollar bills.

He was not exactly lonely but he was alone, alone and horny, contenting himself with dalliances, making more or less love with girls at equally loose ends; and even, at one point, a mid-afternoon surprise. He didn't always properly understand the signals. Were they really so cheerful, these California girls? When Amy leaned back on her sofa, when Barbara offered him a joint, what did they mean? He wasn't very good at the psychic maneuvers—the "what-do-you-really-think-of-me," the "why-don't-we" and "be-in-the-now"—the gropings, the *do this* and *please* and *no* and *don't let go*. Sometimes he'd just as soon take care of himself by himself. This kind of life could go on forever. So could the war. His life dwindled into a dream that the war and the Resistance were, between them, dreaming together. He missed Valerie.

The thought of her receded. He thought it might be nice to get back in touch with Gretchen. But most likely he wouldn't be doing her any favors.

Militancy was in the air, like an endless chain of midwestern thunderstorms.

Matt helped recruit for The Resistance's draft board sit-ins, though he avoided taking part himself, since getting busted without a draft card would be very bad for him. "Raise the stakes" was the name of the game. One of the Resistance founders, Steve Hamilton, a soft-spoken fellow with a wide downward-curving mustache and soft lips, came by the Resistance house to recruit for a regional action to shut down the downtown Oakland induction center in October—they called it Stop the Draft Week. No pussy-footing around! "Nonviolence is last season's costume," he said. "We're gonna shut the mother down." Mike Starr was astonished. "Last I saw Steve," Mike told Matt, "he was studying Gandhi."

Matt and Mike met with Steve's group in Berkeley, but got nowhere trying to talk them out of the idyll of street-fighting that shaped their imagination. "You fight the pig or the pig eats you," said one of Steve's group, a handsome, wiry fellow called Tom-Tom. The militants had picked up the Black Panther epithet "pig." Everyone was growing bestial. To Matt's eyes, Steve, Tom-Tom, and the rest of them had all the verve and resolve of lemmings. "Let's get it on," Tom-Tom said, pounding his fist into his palm with a smirk. That's probably what the chief lemming would say if he could speak. In truth, Matt recognized in them the élan of apostles. Velocity ruled. In for a dime, in for a dollar.

The Resistance won a concession from the Berkeley group: They were allocated a day of their own, Monday, to sit nonviolently on the sidewalk in front of the Oakland Induction Center. From Tuesday on, for the rest of the week, the scene metamorphosed into taking the streets, blocking traffic, turning over planters, fighting the cops. Chagrined, Matt would have to avoid all these activities. He hated avoidance as much as he hated getting outflanked by militants.

So did they careen into October.

And then it turned out that Mike Starr knew somebody who knew somebody who ran into Valerie Parr at a women's liberation meeting in Dallas—but there must have been some mistake, Matt thought, since Dallas was an unlikely place for *his* Valerie Parr, yet Mike's contact checked and confirmed that this Valerie Parr used to work with a certain Matt Stackhouse in Cleveland, and she sent along a hello, and one thing led to another, and soon the two of them were in phone contact, thanks to that miraculous toy, the whistle that came in Captain Crunch cereal boxes, which when blown into the receiver of a pay phone generated a tone of precisely the right frequency to trick the system into hooking you into a long-distance line at no cost. To add to the serendipity, it turns out that another friend of Mike's, a freak engineer in Palo Alto, was the guy who had discovered the whistle's powers—known, of course, as Captain Crunch.

Explaining the whistle, Mike winked and said out of the side of his mouth, "The future is free," and relayed news about Matt's whereabouts to the person who knew the person who knew Valerie, who located a convenient payphone and passed its number back up the chain to Matt; and so, during the months leading up to the Democratic Convention, Matt and Valerie made payphone-to-payphone calls every few days. Their conversations started out heavy on politics and awkwardness, but soon enough they had slid through the tentative stage and their conversations were running an hour or longer.

Valerie sounded a bit formal at first, her "Hi there" scripted, as though she was straining to freshen up a language that had dried out from disuse. Afraid to say the wrong thing, Matt listened, mostly, to her voice, which was as richly colored as before, or if anything, creamier, and pictured her (as lean as before?), and asked questions. Evidently he passed her test. They laughed. She relaxed. After a stretch of Mexico stories, and a long pause, she said: "Matt?"

"Uh-huh."

"I know you're afraid I'm going to hurt you again."

"Uh-huh." He waited.

She waited.

"I think we can get past it," he said.

"Can we?" Her voice caught—so it seemed to him.

"I hope so. I think so. We'll see."

"I—I really want to."

"Let's see." He thought they could.

She addressed him as if he were a dear old friend, no more but no less, and resumed her report on her sojourn in Mexico and her decision to return to the States, which was where the struggle was—her struggle too, whether she liked it or not, because she had no other country besides heartbreaking America—even though she wasn't sure what to do next except that she hoped to combine her political work and her art.

"But Dallas?" he asked. "Why Dallas? Since when are you the Dallas type?"

"You mean bouffant hair and pearls? No, I haven't changed *that* much."

She explained that one day in a San Miguel bar she had run into an elderly expat who wanted someone to comfort him about his granddaughter, roughly her age, smart as hell, who had, he groused, gone hippie and was wasting her life, working for a silly paper called *Big D*. *Big D!* You'd think they could have come up with a better name! She was a good kid, he said, no Communist. They called it an underground paper like it was illegal. Nonsense. It was just noisy. He told me that if I got to Dallas, I should look her up, said I would like her. He scribbled her name on a napkin— Doris-Ann Dawson—and Valerie stuffed it into her pocket.

Matt listened for the moment when something would change in her voice, send a signal that she was ready to address him as something other than an old friend. It didn't arrive, but he could live with the suspense.

She got into a rhythm when she got to the part about how she had wearied of San Miguel's expat world of purposeless self-satisfaction. She had stored her belongings except for her sketch pads and toured around central Mexico by bus. "Tell me about it," Matt said. She did: bare, parched hills, fields of dried grasses, needle-like palms shooting up randomly, villages spare on the tawny earth, full of squared-off stucco-faced buildings with rebar poking out from their tops, looking as though they were slapped up the day before yesterday and left to be finished tomorrow. She climbed the pyramids at Chichen-Itza, in the Yucatan. It troubled her that the Mayans were such a brutal people. It horrified her that they killed some of their enemies by ripping their hearts out of their living bodies. Maybe it was not altogether bad that they succumbed to the Spanish *conquistadores*. But this was an onlooker's question, not a native's. She would never get used to being an expat. All her days she would speak exile with an accent.

Mexico had finished with Valerie Parr.

One day, an unopened envelope from Matt's draft board, inserted in a larger envelope from his mother, arrived in East Palo Alto. He had been ordered to report for induction, in Chicago, on March 27, 1968. In her note, his mother wrote: "Promise me you'll tell me if this is serious." No way in the world was he going to report for induction on March 27. He stalled.

It was clear to him, as Valerie told her stories, that Mexico would not solve his problems.

Valerie figured that Dallas might give her a new start, so with no particular reason to go anywhere else, she had gone there.

Big D, a tabloid weekly with a four-color psychedelic front page, was published by an oil company heir, a serious pothead, in his garage. Doris-Ann Dawson moved on, and the paper was short-handed. Valerie jumped at the chance of being their first art editor, making pen-and-ink drawings about the horrors of war, rough approximations of William Blake, along with collecting information about upcoming concerts and demonstrations and so on, putting that stuff in order every week. She learned to set type and to lay out the pages to be photographed for the offset print job. She savored the sweet fumes of rubber cement.

On her own time, she took part in antiwar actions. The publisher was stoned into stupefaction, and his sidekick editor was irascible and erratic—and also stoned—but she got along nicely with the women, who were calm and reliable, and did most of the actual work. After a while two of them, Annabelle and Susie—both girlish, quiet, and short-haired—invited her into their women's liberation group, where four or five of them talked about how women always end up doing the shit work. Valerie didn't feel that what she did at the paper was shit work, but she was fascinated—horrified, really—by the stories the women told about their upbringings, all the abuse they suffered, two of them in East Texas, one in Wichita Falls, one in Oklahoma. Valerie felt acutely her own privilege, but there wasn't a damn thing she could do about that except work harder against the war and the whole system.

When Annabelle, after hours, printed up a booklet of her whimsical poems, Valerie was flabbergasted to discover that the two women were lesbian lovers. This was, she thought, odd. Not wrong, just odd, even interesting—a new fact in the world. They traded stories about unsavory men they had known. Eventually, they were weeping as they talked about the adults who had abused them when they were children. But over the weeks—she told Matt—she found herself drifting away from the group not because she had anything against lesbians but because whe wasn't one, and she didn't feel angry at men, not the way they did. The group came to feel ideological, like there was a "correct line" you had to adhere to. Women had never turned her on. She didn't understand the lesbian thing. She wanted intimacy with women but not in bed—she wanted to go hiking with them. Soon the group made her feel more lonely, not less.

There came a point where she felt easy enough on the phone with Matt to confide that she wasn't meeting any men worth more than an occasional fuck-affair, which made Matt gulp. The intimacy of buddies—was that she he wanted? She held back from telling him that she fantasized about joining him in California. But what would she do there? Rushing off to orbit around Matt sounded like a terrible idea. Possibly she could look for another underground paper—but no, she was done with that.

Valerie told him about the morning she had pulled up in front of the *Big D* office and found the garage door splayed with a tight constellation of bullet holes. The cops had interrogated the staff as to their whereabouts the previous night, and wanted to know if any of them owned a shotgun. None did.

"Any enemies?"

"Well, as a matter of fact," said the publisher, "you folks aren't exactly our friends, are you?" That got him busted for disorderly conduct and resisting arrest. No one was charged for shooting up the garage.

But the shotgun attack was not the reason why Valerie came to realize that *Big D* wasn't the right place for her. The firebombing of Annabelle's car soon afterward gave her pause, but even that didn't drive her away. If anything, the fact that they were under fire made her want to stay. But what she wanted to write and make art about was the Vietnam war, while the paper was all over the place—a screwy mish-mash of local reports, atrocity stories from Vietnam, tidbits on the idiocy of straight society, assassination lore, satirical cartoons of varying quality, paranoid bulletins about the FBI and the police, reports on the price of drugs this week, and on bad drugs to look out for, and pictures of Huey Newton and Eldridge Cleaver and fierce-looking Black Panther women with magnificent Afros, all kinds of out-there stuff.

Matt told her that it drove him crazy that Americans only heard about *American* casualties; that nobody seemed to care how much unthinkable pain came to how many Vietnamese when white phosphorus burned through their skin into their bodily organs until the fire exhausted all available oxygen; or when they were burned alive by napalm, which melted through their skin at temperatures that matched the eruptions of volcanoes. He reflected upon the absurdity of thinking that this was happening on "the other side of the world," since the world had no sides. In Washington, educated men spoke to each other crisply and thousands of miles away, villages went up in flames.

He filled her in about his draft situation, and his flight from his family, and about Utah (leaving out Gretchen), and what he felt at the Arches, how on good days he felt like a sort of pantheist. They shared excitements and apprehensions about the Pentagon and Oakland demonstrations. He talked about how the Resistance was growing and predicted that the military was going to have a harder and harder time filling their draft calls, how more and more young men were "following the drinking gourd," heading north for Canada, and how draft counselors were hearing from growing numbers of GIs who wanted to file conscientious objector claims and get the hell out.

After a while they passed with surprising ease around, or through, leftover tensions, into the tender areas. He knew she was right to say that they did not live in a world where relationships endured. That was how things were, another sign of the ruling disorder—or perhaps it was natural. Anyway, she was not "in love" with him, and dismissed what she had come to think of as "pit-ter-pat" feelings. Still, although she was not quite ready to say so, she knew that Matt was her soulmate.

As Matt traveled for the Resistance, he would call her from his stopping-off points at the same payphone near her apartment. It was a sensible arrangement. If, on the other hand, she moved to East Palo Alto, would they really have time together? She did get lonely. He thought about visiting Dallas but didn't want to press. He didn't want to screw anything up.

Valerie wasn't any more Texan than Mexican—aesthetically, even less. If anything, Dallas was more alien than San Miguel—its own kind of ideologically walled enclave. She wanted to talk with someone she trusted, someone besides Matt who had known her for more than five minutes. She asked Matt if he'd been in touch with Sally. He knew that Sally had moved back to Ann Arbor, and thought she was still teaching. Valerie located her.

The two women talked in cascades, gushing with stories as if they had never ceased talking. Sally liked teaching high school English, helping the kids solve problems, even if they were "only aesthetic problems," relishing the tiny nitty-gritty triumphs of the classroom; explaining what Emily Dickinson meant by telling "all the truth" but telling it "slant"; and exploring why Melville might have wanted to slide all over the place stylistically in *Moby Dick*; and reveling in the look on a kid's face when he figured out why Mark Twain warned that "persons attempting to find a moral" in *Huckleberry Finn* "will be banished"—except that when the kids wanted to talk about what was going on in America she was afraid she'd only deepen the despair and rage that had taken up residence in their hearts. She talked about two of her students, good students, best friends, who the day after graduation enlisted in the army rather than wait to be drafted. She talked about how she got trained as a draft counselor and now worked after school for the conscientious objector group. She talked about helping to write a high-school history curriculum about Vietnam. She read poems about the war, found them too bombastic, and tried to write better ones. Valerie told her about her Blake-inspired drawings. Perhaps they could find a way to collaborate.

Sally was pleased—and surprised—that Valerie was back in touch with Matt. She didn't tell Valerie that, after she had left for Mexico, Matt had come on to her—any more than she would ever tell Matt about the abortion. They were held together by their willingness to keep secrets. Of Terry, Ronnie, Kurt, and Marcia, she knew nothing. Sally had talked to Melissa, though, knew she had returned to Greenwood, and not only envied but admired her for knowing just where she needed to be. They did not need to remind each other of the price that Black people paid for such clarity.

Sally had an affair with her vice principal, who was married, and told her that her body reminded him of a Rubens. It ended badly. She didn't exactly understand women's liberation, didn't like the clamor and sloganeering, though she agreed with a lot of the criticisms women were making of men. Her crowd could agree, anyway, that it was fine not to be married.

Sally and Valerie rejoiced in Lyndon Johnson's decision to beg off from another term, though they weren't sure what it meant. Four days later, they were driven to hot fury and holy grief by the murder of Dr. King. They felt whiplashed. They talked about violence as a plague. They stuttered with fury at the meager men, the loners, the lurkers—the Lee Harvey Oswalds and James Earl Rays—who slithered forth out of the dark, indecipherable, guns blazing, extinguishing the light. They did not comprehend how these men succeeded in grabbing hold of history. Maybe there was something to be said for conspiracy theories. (*Big D* ran a regular feature about the logistics of Dealey Plaza and the grassy knoll and Oswald's Mannlicher-Carcano rifle.) They talked about how you couldn't let the monsters trample your hope; how you had to keep going, even when it was all you could do to go through the motions. They staggered through the ruins of their broken hearts, dumb and mute, watching the light fade.

Valerie couldn't imagine anything getting better—*ever*. Sally agreed with her inwardly, but couldn't bring herself to admit it out loud. The country was a dark, curdled, misbegotten monstrosity. They didn't know how to relate to it, they didn't know how to sweep it out of their minds. Someone in Sally's study group was talking about going to Chicago to protest at the Democratic Convention, in August. This sounded to her like walking into an ambush. She was getting too old to put her body on the line. Still, after King's murder, she had to do something besides weep. Despair was a luxury.

Valerie didn't know what to think. But she liked the idea of reconnecting in Chicago. "I could take a crash course in first aid," Sally said lightly.

"You'll be the one who writes the poems we need about the antiwar movement," Valerie told her. "And persistence."

Meanwhile, Matt felt good—better than good—about Valerie: He felt accompanied. He wanted to see her. "I'm up for it," she said.

Neither of them thrilled to the notion of a "Festival of Life" that the Yippies had called for in Chicago during the Convention—*Big D* had overdosed her on the notion that antics changed the world—or the more conventional protest announced by Tom Hayden and other movement types. Matt had heard that Tom was saying that the Democrats had to be resisted "by any means necessary." This struck him as bonkers. Not that the Democrats should be allowed to conduct their convention in a business-as-usual manner. There had to be loud, conspicuous protest. The Democrats were hidebound, blind, gutless, morally bankrupt. But it was stupid to respond by dashing headlong into a trap on Mayor Daley's turf. As for the Black movement, the Panthers were in a combative mood, and God knew they had piles of good reasons to hate the cops, but what did it mean to chant "Off the pig"? Did they think the cops were going to sit around and wait to be ambushed? How could they not notice that they were way outnumbered and way outgunned? Chicago would be a fortress. The movement was ragged and—face it—small.

But there was a force field pulling the movement—a destiny. Energies were converging. Vectors were lining up.

Matt and Valerie did not talk about Cleveland or Wyatt. They talked about antiwar projects that might make sense when the summer was over and it might even be possible to insert the question of war into the presidential campaign. Valerie wanted to find a community coalition, one that encompassed ordinary people, not just radicals and freaks. Dallas didn't offer any such thing. Preaching to choirs didn't turn her on. Matt was committed to the Resistance. Valerie did not want to join a women's auxiliary for a men's movement although she thought the slogan "Girls say yes to boys who say no" was cute.

At least Valerie knew she had done right to come back from Mexico. She needed to be here, in the American cauldron—not just to protest but to live her American life.

Johnson exited, King died, Kennedy died. Rough beasts rampaged over the corpses of best-laid plans. The script of their lives was being written by invisible hands. Later, neither of them could remember who made the first suggestion that they rendezvous during the Convention. The force field did the deciding. On Tuesday, August 27, they would meet in Chicago—for righteousness, for moments of truth, against ugliness and lies, for the chance of love reignited.

Chicago, August 1968

NOT LONG AFTER THE murder of Dr. King, Matt picked up the phone at the Resistance house and to his surprise, heard the assured voice of Terry McKay. That Terry should look him up was a welcome surprise—the master acknowledging the apprentice. A long time since Cleveland, a longer time since Ann Arbor. Well, fine. The world turned.

They met at a raucous bar near the Stanford campus, where they were seated next to a table of fervent students wearing black armbands and buttons for McCarthy and Kennedy, one of them also a "Free Huey!" and another a Ω. Somebody said something inaudible about Chicago. They ordered beers from a tiny blonde wearing a McCarthy button on the belt of her miniskirt.

"The students look twelve years old, they make me feel ancient," Matt said.

"I just turned a hundred," Terry shrugged.

Terry looked a bit haggard, his hair was thinning, and the thought crossed Matt's mind: *We were supposed to be young, but this thing is aging us.*

No time was wasted in chit-chat. Like generals, they reviewed the state of the war. They hoped that the Tet Offensive marked the beginning of the end. They noted with satisfaction that Johnson was refusing to give his generals all the fresh troops they wanted. They reviewed the state of the movement. Neither expected much good to come out of the Democratic Convention, which would be locked up for Humphrey. They both expected street-fighting in Chicago, which would excite some people and horrify others, so what was the point? Terry brought up the Black Panthers, who were all the rage on the campuses now. You had to hand it to them—they were organized like an army. What was the *strategy*? They thought they were the Apostles, Matt said, though neither Huey Newton with his bookish rhetoric nor Eldridge Cleaver with his trail of rapes qualified as Jesus Christ. Matt thought the Panthers were basically a media stunt, with their guns and their sleek leather coats and their big talk. The Yippies were another kind of media stunt, though they were more fun. As for SDS, it no longer spoke American; it spoke in Marxist-Leninist tongues.

Matt raved about The Resistance, which was spreading in Portland, Seattle, L.A. Terry wasn't terribly interested. Surprisingly, he agreed with Matt about the Black Panthers. He thought they were living inside a cartoon. "I feel like I'm coming out of a trance." His head quivered.

"I could think of a better trance," Matt said, and waited for Terry to ask him to elaborate, but Terry didn't. He had gone through his own changes on strategy. It came to him that the movement was heading over a cliff. He wondered whether the FBI or the CIA or some other government agency was pulling the strings. Matt thought that if Terry was thinking this way, the danger must be serious. What to do about it was another question. Terry, like Valerie, wanted to build local federations—clergy, unions, liberals—to widen the movement's political base. That might insulate them from provocateurs—help insulate them, at any rate. *Not more militant, more convincing*—that was his slogan.

Terry rolled on, as lucid as ever, making so much sense you wondered how anyone but a dolt could disagree. King's Poor People's Campaign was a good idea but it was only symbolic; it lacked pizzazz; hell, it lacked poor people. The King people were planning to send a mule train to Chicago, show that the protest wasn't just for white folks, which was symbolic too, but fine, let Chicago be a carnival of symbols. Melissa Howard had brought folks from Mississippi to the tent city in Washington, D.C.—"Resurrection City," they called it—and was working on the mule train. Terry doubted the mule train would lead anywhere. Matt thought trying something was better than trying nothing, though he severely doubted that Congress was in any mood to deliver anything to the poor.

And if this wasn't bad enough, they agreed, the crazies would have the run of the streets in Chicago, and who could control them? The right wing was coming off its leash—look at George Wallace piling up support in the North. In head-on confrontations, no matter who struck the first blow, the cops would win the "hearts and minds" of the public, as Lyndon Johnson would say. The papers and TV would collude with the government goons. The cops would emerge as the golden boys, guardians of peace-loving America, while the movement would look like a ragtag army of reckless brats, assuming that the war was basically righteous even though there were regrettable excesses. Crazy stuff flying everywhere, a whole universe going haywire.

To Matt, the interesting thing about Terry was not that he changed his mind—a lot of movement people were going through changes—but that as he changed his mind he never gave an impression of having thought differently before. He always had six strong reasons for thinking whatever he thought.

Matt feared a massacre.

Sunday morning, August 25, dawned benignly in East Palo Alto. The world felt mild. Matt was well aware this was an illusion. He had been reading obsessively about Chicago—the demonstrators' siege talk, Mayor Daley's siege plans, bravado everywhere. The National Guard was running exercises to practice defense against "hippie attacks." The Yippies, more Marx Brothers than Karl Marx, announced a plan to release greased pigs, dose the delegates' drinks with LSD, and seduce the delegates' wives. Their women would pose as prostitutes, and kidnap the delegates in fake taxis. The *Chicago Tribune* and Mayor Daley believed them. The Army readied to send units from Fort Hood in Texas. (Matt wondered what Gretchen and her son John would think.) Matt lived by twinges, careening from anxiety to excitement to dread. Surely some apocalypse was at hand. Chicago wouldn't be boring. How could he stay away?

Mike Starr dropped him off at San Francisco Airport. Matt carried a single carry-on bag and a light suede jacket. His jaw felt tight-wired, and he had not slept well. His hair was trimmed to military length. His mustache was obliterated. He did not want to call attention to himself.

As he got out of the car it occurred to Matt that a warrant might be out for him in Chicago, since he was almost five months late for his draft call. Should he worry?

"I doubt it," said Mike, the draft counseling expert. "They probably have their hands full. Or—" Mike winked "—you're not important enough to rate an all-points bulletin. Sorry, man. But you might want to avoid getting busted anyway."

"Why didn't I think of that?"

"And by the way, don't do anything crazy."

"Good idea."

Mike clasped him on the shoulder, then reached into the backseat, said, "By the way—" and handing Matt the latest English-language edition of *Granma*, the Cuban paper, added grimly: "Read this and weep." Matt stuffed the paper into his carry-on bag. Since Cleveland, he had been carrying Steve Coleman's youth fare fifty-percent discount card in his wallet. He set it down on the ticket counter, dashed off a reasonable approximation to Steve's signature, and paid cash for a standby ticket.

"Gate 26, Mr. Coleman," said the expressionless clerk, who— Matt worried—might have hesitated an instant before passing him his ticket. *Might have.*

Airports once excited Matt, promising to lift him out of the mundane, out of the world. Now they scared him.

"Have a pleasant flight."

Having fastened his seat belt, Matt started reading. The jet engines roared, gravity loosened its grip, it was too late to turn back.

The whole of *Granma* was a transcript of Fidel Castro's speech defending the Soviet invasion of Czechoslovakia. By the time San

Francisco Bay had slid away like a dissolving dream beneath the wings, he'd read enough.

Fidel, cunning behind his bohemian beard, had seen fit to deliver thousands of words to justify the invasion. It was not Fidel's view that the tanks had rolled into Prague to wipe out workers' control and free speech and to crush the efflorescence of "socialism with a human face." No, said Fidel, they had rolled in to thwart a NATO plot. This was Fidel, the rebel supreme, whom the gangster-faced Russians had been treating like an annoying little brother. How could he believe this crap? Or was he now a run-of-the-mill cynic, dishing out bullshit propaganda to get back into the Russians' good graces, so he could buy their cheap oil and sell them millions of tons of sugar? So the vanguard was now the rear guard. Unbelievable.

Matt's mind churned. When he returned to consciousness, he put Czechoslovakia aside and watched as the Rockies yielded to great green squares of pastureland. He wondered how Gretchen was doing. He thought about how much more complicated his life would have become if she'd accompanied him to Utah. He avoided chatting with the guy sitting next to him, a freckled, redheaded fellow with long sideburns. But the redhead would not take hints. He was on his way to a convention of actuaries.

"Oh yeah?" Matt said. "I'm also going to a convention."

"Which one is that?"

"The Democrats."

"Oh."

"Don't get me wrong, I'm against them."

"That's OK then," the redhead said noncommittally, and went on to muse that there was always money to be made out of trouble. For example, you could insure against it, or you could be like his granddad, who ran guns in the 1890s, in South Dakota. "He was for the Indians, man! Sold the crappy guns to the whites and the good ones to the Sioux. Can you dig it?" He reminded Matt of the drug company thief who had hitched a ride with him in Iowa.

The TWA jet circled over O'Hare. The Chicago area looked like a broken necklace dropped on the floor, its baubles scattered. In the terminal, soldiers walked by like wind-up toys. One of them carried a copy of *Stranger in a Strange Land*. Matt noted it in his mental file of auspicious signs.

He hadn't lined up a place to stay but the underground papers said that a registry was being kept at a "movement center"—a Methodist church near Lincoln Park—where affinity groups and loose individuals could rendezvous, coordinate, find out where to crash.

It was a surprisingly mild and not overbearingly humid afternoon outside the squat brick church, across the street from a Polish sausage stand. In front, a rail-thin Black man in a three-piece black suit, with a long, scraggly white beard tucked into his vest, was passing out pamphlets made of mimeographed sheets unevenly stapled and folded down the middle. Matt took one. On the cover was a crude drawing of Tyrannosaurus Rex bearing an obscure symbol on its snout. Matt thanked him, folded his copy without inspecting it and stuffed it into his back pocket.

At the church door, a skinny kid on a high stool, wearing a white armband torn from a sheet, looked Matt up and down, then nodded, "Welcome, brother," and directed him to the basement, where a cavernous, whitewashed space was thick with the pungent odor of spray paint, Magic Markers, and sweat. Women were making signs: "Welcome to Czechago" was a favorite; also "Dump the Hump" and "Stop the Racist War." On the wall, a silk-screen poster featured a porcine Mayor Daley looming above a file of soldiers holding fixed bayonets: "Chicago, Aug. '68. A Closed Convention in a Closed City. S.D.S." Another depicted a chubby man in a black leather jacket and white helmet, wearing shades: "HOT TOWN / PIGS IN THE STREETS ... BUT THE STREETS BELONG TO THE PEOPLE!" and below the photo, beneath a cartoon fist, the words "DIG IT?" Anxiety hummed, people clustered, talking earnestly, low-key, about logistics and meeting places, about bail bonds, about the question of whether Vaseline was good to smear on your face before you got hit with tear gas or whether that was the worst possible thing to do. A guy with a dagger-shaped beard and an eye-patch sported a mock Humphrey button, showing three H's interlocked into barbed wire.

A hastily drawn poster declared that a seventeen-year-old Indian named Dean Johnson, just off the bus from South Dakota for the demonstrations, had been shot dead by a cop who had (he said) caught him violating curfew. The kid had pulled a gun first (the cop said). It figured, Matt thought. He'd seen the movie. The Indian kid was always outgunned. He thought of the redhead's grandfather from South Dakota.

A lot of people looked vaguely familiar, though in a generic way. The stage was being set, the props put in place, the orchestra tuning up; the waiting. The curtain would soon rise. They themselves were the performance. Fragments of rumor floated around the room: "National Guard's coming in tonight. Heard it on WCFL." "It's bluff." "You wish." "I'll tell you what's not bluff. The cops have dogs. Daley's called out the dogs. They'll have a dog in every patrol car." "Well, you know what we have to do?" "What?" "Carry portable hydrants." "Stay away from the Mobe office. Fuckin' cowboys just blew in here acting like generals. Watch. When the dust has cleared, they'll zip out of town just like they zipped in, and we gotta live with the heat." "You hear Johnson's gonna come in at the last minute, dump the Hump for us?" "Meet on Michigan Avenue catty-corner from the Hilton at six. If nobody's there, the drug store on Wabash, six-thirty, or any half-hour after that." Furies would be loosed.

On a huge bulletin board were tacked dozens of note cards, offering spare beds, recruiting monitors, recruiting medics, recruiting legal observers, announcing meetings. You had to search painstakingly, since the newer index cards obscured older ones. If you succeeded in arranging for a spare bed, you were supposed to remove the index card. Matt was working his way through the spare bed section when, from behind, he was wrapped in a bear hug. He spun around half-fearfully.

199

Terry McKay was grinning at him. Matt felt a rush of unbridled joy. He expected Chicago to be full of wonders, but even after their friendly encounter in Palo Alto, an extravagant greeting from Terry McKay was still a surprise and a pleasure. Plainly their relationship was in an advanced state of metamorphosis. Having agreed that Chicago was a trap the movement had set for itself, they embraced like brothers who agreed that the family rendezvous would be difficult but wouldn't miss it for the world.

Terry was red-eyed with too little sleep. "Hey, man! Couldn't stay away!"

"Pigs in shit. Lucky us. Party time."

After using the church phone to reserve a bed on the Near North Side, and leaving a note for Valerie with the address and phone number, Matt found Terry in conversation with a tall, lean fellow in a green T-shirt smeared with black paint, his olive skin deepened in the fluorescent light, a cigarette in his hand, his back turned to Matt. Ronnie Silverberg was giving a rundown of the day's events, saying evenly, "Nuts," as if that were a plain description. And then: "Oh you better believe I'm ready." Ronnie tipped his ashes into the cellophane wrapper.

Matt, Terry, Ronnie, with Valerie on her way—it was a Cleveland reunion.

Ronnie flashed Terry his quicksilver smile. "I heard Dick Gregory speak last night. Supercharged. I went up to him afterwards and told him he sounded like a Panther. You know what he said? 'Whatever it takes, man.' Dick Gregory, Mr. Nonviolence! Whatever it takes. Far out."

Ronnie was on his way to the Hilton, to check out the delegates and scout locations. Ronnie's camera served as a sort of passport into and out of tight spots. Matt envied him that.

"You're going to the Hilton dressed like—?" He pointed at Ronnie's outfit spotted with ashes and squiggles of black paint.

"Don't worry, man, I have a change of clothes. And hey, I've got a sound man with me, we're going to shoot around the city tomorrow. I'm looking for wheels to drive us around. Anyone interested?"

Terry volunteered: "Sure, I'll be your chauffeur." This did not require extensive thought. "It's overdue. We never did get around to cruising around Cleveland together."

"Yeah, too bad."

Terry couldn't remember why they hadn't gotten around to it. Things came up.

They would meet in the early afternoon the next day.

As Ronnie dashed off, a big blond fellow strode up.

"Hey, Carl," Terry said without great enthusiasm. "What's the plan?"

Carl had an impressive mustache, the full Zapata, and boots, wore a big shit-eating grin, stood with his hands on his hips and his pelvis stuck out, and said with a hillbilly twang: "Plans aren't shit." His lips curled. "Hey, Terry, I dig you. I want you to meet my cadres. I recruited them. Greasers. They're far out. Seeds. Spread the seeds."

"Heard the area around the Hilton is an armed camp," Matt said. "Be careful."

Terry said, "See you."

"Be gentle but tough," Carl said. "Remember: seeds."

Ronnie returned, wearing a white suit, a white tie, and seriously polished patent leather shoes. He exuded readiness. The suit set off his skin gorgeously. He was holding the green clothes crudely wrapped in butcher paper.

"Don't worry, man. Dressed like this, I look like an Italian movie star." Which, Matt reflected, was true—like Mastroianni slumming his way through the ruins—but no, that was a half-truth, and unfair. Ronnie did not impersonate anyone but himself. He casually commanded the space he filled, making himself up as he went along. He flourished in transformation and danger. Which was why all the people crowding this basement were here—which was, in truth, why he was here. He had traveled a long way to arrive at this clarifying moment. He was not playing a role; he was at last living his life.

Matt thought: *We've all been heading this way, toward this vortex in Chicago, for a long time. We're not overgrown kids anymore.*

We're the marauders. We're the barbarians at the gates—inside the gates. We're the action.

Matt headed for Lincoln Park, where several hundred people had gathered for a concert—a lovely afternoon for a concert, he thought, as if the world weren't going to hell—and breezes stirred off the lake, as if leaks had sprung in the iron dome of the bright day, but in a flash the quiet waiting exploded into noise—the popping of vicious farts from three-wheeled motorcycles: The cops were feeling festive in their own way, reveling in their belligerence, squads on a rampage, scowling, looking daggers, exulting in the panic they caused. This was *their* moment. Matt watched, aghast, as a young mother pushing a stroller slipped to the side like a ballerina as a cop came within inches. The cop was wearing neither a badge nor a nametag, and a kid standing nearby, long brown hair tucked under a headband, yelled, "Motherfucking fascist pig!" and the cop swiped at the kid with his nightstick, smacked him on the shoulder, and when a photographer with a press pass hanging from his neck lifted his camera and started clicking, the cop jumped off his cycle, clubbed down the camera, and smashed the photographer on the skull, blood trickling down his forehead, while the kid shouted, "Far out, far out," to no one in particular, and then "You see that?" and then "You believe this? Wait till your kid finds out what you do for a living!" and blurted out to Matt that the cops had been letting people stay in the park until the 11 PM curfew, but today was different, something real heavy was about to come down. "See you at 11 tonight," said the cop who had jumped off his three-wheeler, flashing a "V" sign, then folding his index finger down, leaving his middle finger raised. Wearing glasses beneath his helmet, he looked like a conquering extraterrestrial. His voice was a dagger of ice.

Matt's rage spiked. This was beyond his control. But he knew there was nothing useful about such rage. All he could do was flee with some dignity. Twilight arrived, strangely luminous. He picked up his pace and headed westward out of the park into Old Town, reminded of the times when he used to take refuge there from his parents and from school, taking particular note of the club where he had celebrated his reaching the drinking age. He had gone there to hear a bluesman named Terry Callier, whose whispery baritone laid out a mist of lamentation, voice as soft as a chamois cloth, and who, unable to get customers to shut up, had closed his eyes, *closed his eyes,* and gone on playing, plaintive, climbing a mountain of inward silence with his acoustic guitar, a conscientious objector consecrated to the blues.

In a mood of reprieve, with shreds of a Callier riff working its way through his memory, Matt made his way to his destination, a fourth floor walk-up apartment. Two handsome young McCarthy supporters greeted him cheerily: "Good timing!" They were just leaving, wearing white armbands with Red Crosses, medical students heading for their rounds as medics. A woman, in pigtails and a busy look, pointed out the serviceable wide-enough futon on the floor, showed him the towels, and urged him to make use of the electric coffee pot and the refrigerator which, on inspection, contained ice cream, strawberry jam, a bag of bagels and bunches of carrots. "Stay the whole week if you like," she said, placing a key in his hand. "We have a lot to do."

Having nibbled at carrots, bagels and jam, Matt plucked from his back pocket the pamphlet he had stuck there at the movement center. It was the Book of Revelation, with Tyrannosaurus Rex on the cover cast as the Beast of 666, which put him in mind of his father, who was surely on Mayor Daley's side. Matt leafed through, in amazement that John of Patmos, or anyone, had ever been so whacked out as to write such a gush of monstrous tales, and wondered if his father really believed all this stuff about the throne of God, the great thunders, the earthquake, the angels bearing sickles and the angels bearing plagues, the trumpets heralding the end of time, the sea of glass and the sea of fire, the whore of Babylon rewarding accomplices with the blood of saints and prophets, and all the nations that drank of "the wine of the wrath of her fornication," and finally, deliverance, the Word of God, the King of Kings, Lord of Lords, astride a white horse, bringing a new heaven and a new earth, and the end of all night—

Did Matthew Stackhouse, Sr., really believe that a giant whore, a throne of God, and battalions of angels one day would make themselves at home on earth? The wrath that burned in his father, was that his way of longing for history to come to a screeching halt?

A new heaven and a new earth—what was wrong with the old heaven anyway?

Matt closed his eyes and cast his mind back to the balancing rock in Utah, thought that the rock bathed in red-gold light was more astonishing than the throne of God; thought that even rumors of the old heaven and truths of the old earth were wonders enough for him; thought about the magnificence of the glowing array of the stone arches that were, in their origin, unplanned by any intelligence; thought about the tranquility that would outlast any afterlife; thought how much more wonder and equilibrium were to be found in the actual world than in the Four Horsemen of the Apocalypse or the frenzy of abandoned St. John of Patmos, banished by the Romans—his father had once said—to a rocky island in the Aegean, a stranded nutcase languishing with no company but his own fevers.

Flares streaked through the pressure-cooker night as Chicago's festival of misrule and chaos churned through the park and spilled into the streets. Matt felt oddly meditative. Was it like this before a battle, your mind emptied of everything but your duty and your orders? Had his father felt this way the last time he had his own two legs to stand on? In the dark, every deployment was a crescendo, every crescendo was a collision, every collision entailed a moral emergency, every emergency shattered nerves. Wreckage was preordained. Tracks had been laid, engines tuned up. Now came the uproar, the unpostponable long-overdue boil-over into torrents of rage and fright, sardonic glee, conversion, revelation, epiphany, and purification, as the shock troops of order slammed down their terminal judgments, crowds erupted, long-lost friends and lovers found and lost each other again, barricades arose in the streets, the streets were theirs.

Adrenaline roared. Frenzied joy filled the night. Complexities were stripped bare. What emerged was elegant simplification, as if leaden clouds had cleared and a spotlight shone through mists of dry ice. From one side, the lovers of love swept onstage, in the name of peace. On the other side, the legions of control swooned with their own comradely loyalty, locking, loading, aiming. To Matt Stackhouse, Sr., there was no such thing as frenzied joy. To him, and President Lyndon B. Johnson, and Mayor Richard J. Daley, this week was nothing but tribulation and Armageddon, with Gog and Magog gathered by Satan for the final of all final battles, with the seething and writhing of the seven-headed snakes gathered at the feet of the Son of Man, from the pit of hell, at the loosening of the seven seals, and the quaking of the earth that would usher in the redemption, salvation by cleansing fire.

This festival was not a frolicsome carnival where the last became first and the first, last, and joy erupted from the knowledge that when the day was over the world would have settled into a new order. The big tent had collapsed. The spotlights cast long shadows through clouds of tear gas. The police tapped their nightsticks against their palms, straining to come off the leash, to give the barbarians a taste of barbarism themselves, in the name of everything they held dear—their fathers, their flag, their commanders, their city, their courage under nonexistent fire which, while it didn't exist, was none the less real to them, a mash-up of desire, war movies, and their own fury. For them the brute question was whether they would be permitted to break loose and trample their enemies once and for all—the Commie kids and hippie freaks flashing their ridiculous "V" signs for the cameras, the glaring lights where only darkness had been permitted to gather, the reporters stabbing with their pens and pencils for words that might be commensurate with what they saw but couldn't quite believe.

On the far side of the police lines, facing the legions in their robin's-egg-blue helmets and sweated-up short-sleeved shirts, there assembled a few thousand stubborn, audacious kids, blazing with righteous desperation. There was myopia, there was terror, there was yearning for victory, or finality; there was freedom, truth, wildness, fuck-it-all giddiness. From all the mad spirits loosed in America, from all the dinner-table showdowns and this-far-and-no-further battle cries, Chicago was the long hungered for showdown. The bleeding incarnation.

In the benign early afternoon of Wednesday, under a too-placid sky, Terry McKay picked up Ronnie Silverberg and his sound man, Barry Moses, in front of the Hyde Park apartment which Ronnie had borrowed from his cousin Evan, a graduate student at the University of Chicago. In June, Evan had bolted to Israel to fight in the Six-Day War and stayed on in the Holy Land to celebrate victory. These days, many radicals cheered for Yasir Arafat's guerrillas, but Evan saw things differently, saw Israel as a diminutive, beleaguered country with a people's army, like Cuba and North Vietnam, so that, even though allied with the U.S., it was on the side of the angels against Goliath. Ronnie did not know what to make of this argument but did not feel the need to engage it—in fact, he saw every reason to duck it—so that when Evan wrote him and laid out his theory of worthy underdog countries, Ronnie replied politely and changed the subject to Vietnam, where, he said, even as America continued the slaughter, the remarkable and crucial thing was that the Viet Cong and North Vietnam were winning, just as Israel was smashing its way to a resounding victory in the Six-Day War.

The war was glued to Ronnie Silverberg's mind; it *was* his mind; it filled his void; it *was* his void; his war against the war was his mission. There were days when he caught himself conversing about revolution when he had to admit that he didn't know what he was talking about, and said to himself, *Listen to what's coming out of my mouth!* And he responded, *Go with it. This is your one and only jump-cut life.*

Ronnie could master the whipsaw. He spent June and July burrowed into the family cabin on a slope in southeast Vermont, near the New Hampshire border, surrounded by fir trees where, in his childhood, his parents spent stretches of time avoiding each other while Ronnie complained about boredom. Now that his father was gone and his mother's legs were crippled, she had no use for the solitude of the back woods, so he could retreat there, well supplied with firewood and dope, to study up on Vietnam and the other Third World revolutions with the same disciplined fervor he once brought to articles in *Popular Mechanics* on how to build portable radios. He had unearthed a scholarly book called *Viet Cong* written by an American government expert who, though no fan of the Communists, respected their warrior spirit and explained, in detail, how they structured their organization, ran liberated areas, fought a people's war. Ronnie also read Carlos Castaneda's *The Teachings of Don Juan*, which celebrated the shaman's kind of warrior spirit. In Ronnie's eyes, *Viet Cong* and *Don Juan* rhymed. He read each of them straight through and then reread them in alternate chapters. With mescaline procured from a dealer at a nearby farm, he got in touch with his warrior nature.

At the current rate, the war was going to go on for the rest of his life. What was that somebody from SDS had said, how many years ago? "We have to stop the seventh war from now." Fair enough. Look at Ho Chi Minh: He was unfazed by the prospect of war until victory, no matter how long it took. Plastic America couldn't dig a depth so deep. Americans hated revolutions, Ronnie came to think, because in truth, whether they knew it or not, they were trapped in Flatland and unwilling to face their own misery of spirit. They thought they were already free. They dared not rise up against their own overlords. So they projected onto Vietnam—and Cuba—their own disowned rebelliousness, which they had to crush. Something like that. His Park Avenue shrink, Alan Bernstein, had taught him to think in these Freudian loops, and while Bernstein didn't have any insight into why an intelligent young man might be legitimately disgusted by the thought of a life in Flatland, Ronnie had to admit that he had learned a thing or two during his three, four, five, whatever-it-was years of psychoanalysis.

Ronnie's correspondence with Evan had warmed to the point at which Ronnie felt relaxed enough to ask what plans Evan had for his Hyde Park apartment during convention week. Evan replied that he had sublet his apartment through the end of July but had no objection to installing Ronnie—and, if he liked, a few of his friends, why not—for the last week of August. Ronnie, pleased, called around. Convergence!

Effervescent, ready-to-go, what's-our-next-project Marcia Stein was hot for Chicago. She'd heard that Terry would be there, too, she couldn't possibly stay away, this was the *climax*, what a gas it would be to live through it together. Marcia called Sally Barnes, who had moved back to Ann Arbor. When Sally expressed her distaste for getting smacked in the head by a nightstick, Marcia assured her that Chicago would be a twenty-ring circus, everybody could do their own thing, anything to fight napalm and fascism, doubts were cool but the question was always what you were doing while you were doubting, and anyway, their old friend Ronnie had the use of a whole big apartment in Hyde Park, and Sally was welcome to stay there, too.

Sally always struck Ronnie as the sedate type, cut out to be a librarian or a high-school teacher. Indeed, she *was* a high-school teacher, which was work that somebody decent had to do. Marcia had, if anything, become spicier since Cleveland. So it was that, in one of the several bedrooms of Evan's sprawling apartment, Tuesday night, she and Ronnie consummated their long-dangling flirtation, leaving Ronnie with an impressive scratch down his left shoulder blade. This might or might not go beyond a one-night stand. He didn't know where she stood with Terry McKay.

Now, Wednesday, August 28, a mild and breezy day, Sally was dressed in a gray mid-calf skirt, a soft-collared white blouse, and flats—if there was a catalogue for teacher's outfits, she had ordered from it, Ronnie thought—while Marcia, planning to flirt with the National Guard, was wearing an off-the-shoulder silky white top, a white headband, a miniskirt, and kitten heels. Sally was apprehensive, at first, but Marcia assured her that, at the last moment, the previous day, the city had granted a permit for a rally at the Grant Park band-shell. The two women took the Illinois Central train to Grant Park, across Michigan Avenue from the Hilton. Later that afternoon they would march to the Amphitheater on the South Side, where the Convention was taking place, the same place where, in 1957 (or so Marcia said), Elvis Presley had performed in his gold lamé suit for the first time. This news brought a giggle from Sally, because she realized that she and Marcia might have been in Elvis's audience then, if they'd been old enough, and the guys gazing down on them from the cheaper seats might have grown up to become the cops who would be glaring at them today.

Marcia knew things like that about Elvis, and enjoyed bestowing her knowledge on friends. She also took pleasure in secrets. She refrained from telling Sally that permission to march to the Amphitheater had been denied by a Federal judge, who was named Lynch, of course, and if that wasn't enough, he used to be Mayor Daley's law partner. Marcia couldn't care a hoot whether there was one permit, two permits, or none.

The temperature was moderate but nothing else was. The air seemed to sweat.

Dangling around Ronnie's neck on a lanyard was a plasticized press pass that read CLEVELAND DAILY NEWS. He jammed a Gauloise into his mouth, took a matchbook out of his shirt pocket, bent a match in half with his thumb, scraping the head against the striking surface, and lit up one-handed. In a khaki shirt and slacks, he sat on a step in front of Evan's building.

"Only time I've ever seen anybody do that, it was a truck driver I hitched a ride with," said Barry Moses, walking up. "I never got the hang of it myself."

"You have to learn from somebody who understands that getting it right is a matter of life and death," Ronnie said, self-approving and self-deprecating at once. "I learned from a GI at Fort Hood."

"Well," Barry drawled, "they say the army's a good place to learn skills." Barry, taller than Ronnie, gangling and with slightly pocked skin—wearing a work shirt and a sailor cap, a Nagra tape recorder in a leather case slung over his right shoulder—was moonlighting from his day job as a network sound man.

"Like killing gooks," Barry said, with a tiny curl of his lip.

They were talking about film stock, shutter speeds, and the sensitivity of the mic when Terry drove up. Sweat dripped down his forehead. His armpits already stank. Ronnie and Barry climbed into the back seat. Terry asked himself why he had volunteered for this fool's errand. The song running through his head was from *High Noon:* "Do not forsake me, oh my darling..."

"I don't remember any Daily News in Cleveland," he said.

"Sounds more kosher than Independent Film-Maker Documenting the Movement, don't you think?" said Ronnie, poised.

There was, around Ronnie, an aura of magic. He knew how to make things happen. The camera extended the aura. Ronnie inserted a camera between himself and the world, Terry reflected, and the world became more manageable. For his own part, Terry had never been able to view the world through a viewfinder. This was both his strength and his weakness.

Driving north, Ronnie talked about sequences he'd been shooting: a draft resistance project in a working-class section of Boston; a community group trying to find its footing in the Newark ghetto after the 1967 riot; most recently, the coffeehouse at Fort Hood, Texas, where, over espresso, organizers rapped with disgruntled GIs, helped them distribute antiwar newspapers, and collected 'Nam stories about necklaces made of VC ears, and white racists, and guys who freaked out and started shooting at trees.

"You realize thirty American soldiers and pilots die every day?" Ronnie said earnestly. He almost sounded as if he cared. Terry was impressed; Ronnie had come a long way from cheap good-guys-bad-guys anti-imperialism. In the coffeehouse, Ronnie went on, the Black GIs were the angriest, the friendliest, and the most curious about the antiwar movement. Ronnie even had footage of a hundred soldiers—one hundred!—who, on hearing that they were being sent to Chicago for riot control, got together and pledged not to go. Forty-three of them, all Black, had been busted.

Ronnie's working title for his film was: "Rome Wasn't Destroyed in a Day."

"What's our mission today, chief?" Terry flecked the word "mission" with delicate quotation marks.

"Planning is like trying to see around corners," Ronnie said. "The mission is readiness. Drive around, see what we see, hear what we hear, watch it all go down." He sounded like a docent in a museum. "I had a nice little shoot the other day. Marcia and some of our other friends went to the Federal building in their sundresses, carrying purses big enough to hold spray-paint cans. You want to know where the CIA has its office? Check out the door: 'CIA ASSASSINS.' I went in with the press. Got it in here." He tapped his camera. "I'll be sorry to have to miss the stink bombs—"

"Stink bombs," Terry says, impressed. "I didn't hear that—"

"At the Hilton. Later. It's a week of surprises. Frolic in the airlock to hell."

A police car zoomed up behind them, headlights flashing, red, blue, siren imperious, like an earthbound flying saucer. "Louder than Cleveland," Terry said coolly. "Shit" was Ronnie's reaction, but Terry said "false alarm" as the cops passed uneventfully. Sirens blurred into background noise. Inhale, exhale. Ronnie tossed his cigarette out the window, where it smoldered. Barry rolled down his window and stuck out his microphone. Ronnie crouched forward.

"Let's go around the block again."

"Aye, aye."

In the sunshine, Black people waited for buses; kids scampered and played ball. These kids might well wonder, Terry thought, what shit was going to come down on them because the white kids were having such a swell time.

Traffic thickened as they neared the Loop. They passed a parked red Mustang convertible sporting a McCarthy bumper sticker. A police car had pulled up in front of it, and a cop was kneeling next to its rear right wheel.

"Son of a bitch is slashing the guy's tires." Terry was matter-of-fact.

Ronnie filmed steadily, taking in evidence. "Idiots," Ronnie said, "they haven't the faintest idea that they're playing walk-on parts in the scenario." Ronnie had written plays in college, performed to some local notoriety.

"The scenario," Terry said.

"They stomp around like Cyclops, they panic, they kick ass, they radicalize more kids, and they move the spiral onward. It's the way of the warrior."

Terry looked quizzical.

Ronnie explained that after digesting *The Teachings of Don Juan*, he had started reading Sun Tzu's *Art of War*, which advised turning the weight of the enemy against him.

Terry was silent. If this was war, they would lose. Chicago was teetering on the brink of hysteria. Nothing was scripted. They were all in a fog. Ronnie was running on pure swagger. Terry wiped sweat out of his eyes. "Hold on a minute, Ronnie. I've got questions."

"Good."

"OK, this'll be a picturesque week, granted, it'll make a great movie, we prove the Democrats can only govern at the point of a bayonet. Fine, great, we expose them."

"Exactly. We strip away the façade. The McCarthy kids don't know where they're living or what time it is. Middle-class kids came for the fun, like this is Fort Lauderdale. They'll learn the hard way."

"So we expose the ruling class," Terry said. "We expose them again. They're overexposed. Look, there they go again, misbehaving! But they still run the show. So we stick a burr up their ass and send them storming around like lunatics. For an hour or so. Does that bring us closer to ending the war?"

"Well, you know, as a matter of fact, it does. The Vietnamese love what we're doing. The troops will have to come home to patrol the streets." Ronnie might have been lecturing a child.

Terry glowered into the rear-view mirror. "Ronnie, you ever worry that we're going to elect Nixon?"

"Pardon me?"

"Nixon," Terry repeated. "Richard Nixon. Remember him? You want to talk about scenarios? That's *my* scenario. He wins. We're screwed."

"So? Come on, what the fuck is the difference?"

"He'll bomb the dikes. He'll mine Haiphong. He could go nuclear, for Christ's sake."

"Come on, man. Play it out. Nixon, Humphrey. Humphrey, Nixon. Humphrey Dumpty is Johnson's lapdog. Nixon snarls louder. So what? What's eating you, Terry?"

"Nixon's eating me, Ronnie. And Wallace is waiting in the wings."

"Get over Wallace. We're supposed to shriek—" going falsetto now "—Ooh, George Wallace, how scary!" Ronnie flapped his hands around. "We'd better be nice boys and girls or the bogeyman is gonna get us! That's Humphrey talk. Surrender talk. Look, the Vietnamese lose territory all the time—*until they win*. They take over the countryside at night. That's the plan. They have the long view. They think in centuries. That's why they'll outlast Johnson, Nixon, and the Nixon after him. The weight of the monster brings him down."

"And pulverizes us."

"Well, if that's what it takes, let us be the sacrifice," Ronnie said lightly. "That's in the scenario. Look at Mao. He picked the party up from oblivion after they got slaughtered in the cities, and pulled off the Long March. They hid in caves till the coast was clear."

"That was them. That was there. We have to be where the Americans are. Organize—" His voice trailed off. To his own ears, he sounded like a machine. He didn't like the cards he was holding, though they were the only cards he had.

Ronnie went on: "When the beast thrashes around, America crashes and burns, everything grinds to a halt, we bring the war home, and whoever's running the government has to end the war. *Whoever.*"

Terry thought: *This has poetry and scary logic if you're willing to treat the movement as cannon fodder.*

"You sound real Christian, Ronnie. I thought you were Jewish."

"Funny man," Ronnie said, leaning forward, his chin on the back of the front seat. "Listen, Terry. I was in Cleveland with you guys. I went to your meetings. I hung out with your tough guys. I saw what happened. Nothing happened. The steadier working class is bought off, they're racist, they're cool with the system, and if I remember correctly, we recruited one guy. Wyatt Burns, remember? Wyatt is good. He's here, by the way. I saw him yesterday."

"You mean," Terry said mockingly, "Rome wasn't destroyed in a day."

Marching down the sidewalk up ahead was a straight-look-ing detachment, dressed more like McCarthy kids than Yippies, holding up a banner made out of a torn sheet. Reading the words backwards, Terry made out: COMMITTEE OF RETURNED VOLUNTEERS. They were shouting words he couldn't make out.

"Peace Corps kids," Terry said. "Reinforcements."

"Back home for the revolution," Ronnie said. It was hard to know whether he approved or sneered.

Behind him, Terry heard a zipper pull open. Metal clinked against metal. Traffic was bunched up in front of them. He adjusted the rear-view mirror. Ronnie was looking down into his lap. More clinking.

"Ronnie, what are you doing?"

Ronnie extended his fist out the window and tossed things onto the pavement.

"Ronnie, what the hell?"

"Spike balls." He dangled two little metal spheres with sharp points, resembling the jacks that little girls play with, but larger. They tinkled.

Terry cast his mind back to the time four or five years ago when Ronnie had been a blowhard and a kibitzer. Now he thought he was a guerrilla, armed with jacks.

Ronnie reached for another fistful of spike balls, suspended them outside the window, and tossed them to the side so they landed to the rear of the car. Voice clipped, as if reading aloud from Sun Tzu, Ronnie said: "Traffic's a public nuisance. Rome's eating itself. Attack when auspicious. Like lightning. Move the scenario along." He scattered more spike balls onto the pavement. "Don't worry about your tires, we're clear, safe, beautiful." The moment was beautiful. An art form was happening. Peering out the window, Ronnie felt like a Viet Cong general surveying his battlefield. From somewhere behind them, sirens blasted the air.

They neared a steel bridge over the Chicago River, sunlight glaring from car roofs, everything going metallic, and the chants ahead were discernible: "Dump the Hump!" "The streets belong to the people!" People streamed onto the bridge, some wearing folded bandannas, some rubbing their eyes. Ronnie panned the crowd. V-signs jabbed the air, and fists. A couple of McCarthy buttons appeared, along with a small white one with green lettering that Terry recognized as WHERE IS LEE HARVEY OSWALD NOW THAT WE REALLY NEED HIM? Barry stuck his mic out the window. "Dump the Hump!" caromed through the crowd in a roar of euphoric rage. Two exuberant freaks bore on their shoulders a rapturous moon-faced girl wearing a beret and army fatigues, stoned on glory, waving a Viet Cong flag tied to the end of a stick, yellow star on a half-red, half-blue field. Faces bobbed up around the car like riotous balloons. One young longhair had a white kerchief tied around his head, reading FUCK. Terry understood this was how to keep your picture out of the paper. A brown-skinned kid stepped up with a sign inscribed: "This is the hour of the furnaces, and only light should be seen—José Martí."

"I love that," Ronnie said.

Terry wondered what was burning in those furnaces. Sometimes, in this strategic phase of his life, he surprised himself. And questioned himself. What's eating me?

A staticky transistor radio squawked that the Democrats had voted against the proposed peace plank.

The crowd was in love with itself. Terry could tell from the faces who was terrified and who was thrilled. There was some plane of emotion on which those poles met. The wheels of history rolled. Flatland crumbled. Ronnie got that.

"Fuck the draft!" "Hell no, we won't go!" "The whole world is watching!"

"The Third World is winning!" Ronnie shouted from the back seat.

This was original, Terry thought. Too bad it wouldn't catch on with the crowd.

Traffic cramped to a flat-out halt as the crowd swirled like a white-water river ahead of them and alongside, churning over fallen boulders, rolling into rapids and whirlpools. To the stopped cars the demonstrators turned radiant faces, as if they were on the threshold of victory. The girl with the Viet Cong flag looked orgasmic, turning her face slowly this way and that as if facing the flash bulbs on a fashion runway. She had reached her life summit. The bridge was blocked.

"Streets belong to the people," Ronnie intoned.

In the rear-view mirror Terry saw him half-smile—possibly ironically, possibly not.

"Off the cars!" Ronnie yelped.

A siren blasted close behind them and Terry yelled: "Shit." Then: "Ronnie, get the fuck out—"

Ronnie was already getting to his feet and talking fast: "OK, look, Barry, take the spike balls, leave the Nagra. You go left, I'll go right. Terry, catch you later." In a flash Ronnie was gone, plowing into the crowd in his patent leather shoes; Barry darted the opposite way. A pot-bellied cop stormed up on the driver's side, waving a gun in his left hand and a nightstick in his right, peered inside, noted the empty back seat, did not note the equipment on the floor, burst out, "Cocksuckers," raised his stick and smashed the car door, smashed it again, and chased after Ronnie.

Terry, immobilized, flashed back to the aborted patrol in Cleveland, but this time he was surrounded by demonstrators with electrified-looking crazy-shocked-savage eyes, celebrating themselves, glorying in their moment of truth, while behind him a trail of flattened tires had turned the street into a parking lot. Cars honked, possibly rooting for the crowd, possibly against. It took the cops ten, or twenty, or who knows how many minutes to clear the bridge, clubbing and jabbing. "Fuck you, pigs!" resounded.

Terry felt like running, but for him running was not an option, he was stuck behind the wheel. Whatever was coming was out of his hands. The good or not-so-good citizens of Chicago, whatever they thought about the war, would hate our guts for blocking their streets. They agreed that the streets belonged to the people, but never doubted that the people the streets belonged to were themselves.

The cops were gone now, but the crowd had the car boxed in. Terry flicked on his radio (the crowd easing closer to listen) and heard a frantic announcer recap the afternoon news. He picked up snatches: "disorder" at the band-shell rally ... several thousand ... a "Yippie" lowered the American flag ... police "cleared" (the announcer's word) the area ... tear gas ... bridges from Grant Park over to Michigan Avenue barricaded by National Guardsmen ... sprayed Mace ... 30 caliber machine guns and grenade launchers ... streamed over an unguarded bridge ... converged with a mule train from a Poor People's Campaign ... crowd bunched up outside the Hilton ... somebody chanted "Kill, kill, kill" ... pitched battle ... smashed a glass window ... streamed into the Haymarket Lounge ... barricades ... several arrests ... several injuries ... turned over a paddy wagon ...

In his mind's eye Terry saw clubs hammering skulls. He feared for Ronnie. His back ached.

At that moment, a few blocks away, Melissa Howard was af-
flicted by sharp pains in her lower back from bouncing on the plank
of a mule-drawn cart, clip-clopping down Michigan Avenue and
telling herself, *I'm getting too old for this, I do not want to be here.*
She wore overalls and a ragged straw hat that all afternoon had
failed to keep the sweat out of her eyes, which burned even more
fiercely now from the hellish fumes pouring out of Grant Park, and
she feared that the mules might panic, though she was somewhat
reassured by the coolness of the mule-driver, Avon, who came from
Marks, Mississippi, and had in the course of his life passed through
many valleys of the shadow of death.

The demonstrators, almost all of them white, were panicking
worse than the mules as they streamed out of Grant Park in several
directions at once, each leading from gas to more gas. The simple
answer to what she was doing there was: *Carrying out the last will
of Dr. Martin Luther King, Jr.* Last March, when Dr. King started
putting together the Poor People's Campaign, he had invited her
to accompany him to the Delta town of Marks, and she showed
him around, and there, in the lunchroom of the decrepit school-
house, where she picked up thick, nasty splinters just from resting
her right hand against a wooden column (as if she had petted a por-
cupine), she and Dr. King watched as a teacher fed children a meal
consisting of a slice of apple and crackers. Dr. King wept, and the
janitor, a young man named Avon with a light in his eyes, brought
him a glass of warm water. Dr. King was so, so tired; so tired; worn
down to a ghost of himself, a walking defeat, so that while she was
so proud and joyful to be there with him, while there was nowhere
else on earth she would rather be, she thought he needed to get
away, he couldn't bear the weight he was bearing. That day, Avon,
who knew his way around mules, volunteered to take charge of the
mule train.

When Dr. King was dead and buried, Melissa told herself: *I'd
rather be naïve than cynical. We have to go on, we have to go on, we
have to go on. We have to bring these people to Washington, give them
some comfort, display their courage, show that they can endure one more*

valley, and maybe the press will pay attention, sort of in honor of Dr. King. That will be real 'Black Power,' Bobby Hicks, not a rant or a chain of curses, and not just Black Power but poor people's power; they have to march, have to campaign, have to demand; not strut around toting guns like the Panthers. But in truth, Melissa thought, *none of what we're doing is going to put a decent lunch in these kids' mouths. This is the end of the road. Conscience has bled to death.*

She thought about bright-eyed Stokely Carmichael, the hot-blooded man in a hurry, the clever, quick man who came up with the Black Panther symbol two years earlier—which seemed like a century—that looked kittenish then but didn't look so kittenish anymore, Stokely a TV star now, his picture everywhere, snarling, as if he had transmuted into a panther himself, so much so that he was said to have become the Black Panthers' "Honorary Prime Minister," which to her, whatever exactly it meant, sounded mighty pompous. She doubted that he teased anymore. She didn't think she would enjoy seeing him again, she didn't think she would go to bed with him, no, she definitely would not, he wasn't helping, he was screaming with fury and pain. She understood how people burning with anger decided to stay up all night in front of church with shotguns in their laps, offering their own kind of comfort, but she didn't understand why they had to turn into beasts and carica-tures of themselves.

At the same time she was thinking, *The mule train is a relic. Tent cities and mule trains are not the future of the Black people of America. We're a reenactment for tourists. The movement is receding into the past. It has nothing left to offer.*

But she was damned if she was going to walk away from Dr. King and three consuming years in damp, sweltering Mississippi towns, registering voters and integrating swimming pools and schools and bowling alleys and buses and all the places the law said could no longer be lawfully segregated. People like Avon had not thrown in the towel. For that matter, Bobby Hicks had not thrown in the towel. The bitter-end killers had not thrown in the towel. She would not throw in the towel. So she traveled and sweated with

Avon's mule train all the way from Texas to Washington, and sat alongside him when a thousand cops blasted them with gas to clear them out of Resurrection City—with Bobby Kennedy's body barely cold in his grave—and now she found herself enveloped in tear gas again—because she could not think of anything more to do for, or *with* (*with* would be better) the poor Black people who needed so much more than what the movement had to offer them right now. She knew that white America was sick of the niggers and all their agitation, it wanted them to *go away*.

She was tired of waking up in unfamiliar beds clutching boys who were as burned out as she was—Black boys whom Stokely accused of not being tough enough, white boys who wanted to know what it really felt like to be Black. There had to be something else.

Maybe her mother was right: She should go to law school. Whatever the movement decided to do, it was going to need lawyers.

But America was a madhouse, not a courthouse.

The gas scorched her eyes and razor-bladed her throat, she coughed up a fury, and looked up, and suddenly saw, dashing across Michigan Avenue, in front of the gallant mules, Matt Stackhouse, or the spitting image of him—she hadn't seen him for an age and a half—pressing a handkerchief over his eyes. Over the uproar of the street she shouted, "Matt!" but he didn't see or hear her. She would not have thought she would see Matt in the middle of such a crazy scene. Had the whole world come here to go berserk, or die?

And if Matt was here, was Terry here also? If Matt thought it wasn't crazy to be here, then Terry might not think it was crazy to be here either. Dynamo Terry, unstoppable, who when he looked you straight in the eyes saw all the way down to the bottom of your soul, it had been so fine to see him in Greenwood back when Stokely came through town with the Meredith march and shouted out "Black Power!" which made the press and everybody think the world was coming to an end—and that nasty Bobby Hicks was acting like such a jerk, as if the whole Negro people had appointed

him their avenging angel, to treat Terry McKay as if he was Byron
De La Beckwith or some other ignorant cracker, as if a man was
nothing but a void inside his skin.

Whoever it was, Matt Stackhouse or whoever, darted away and
the mule-train clopped on down Michigan Avenue through clouds
of gas.

Matt Stackhouse, in a white shirt saturated with gas and thick with
sweat, was trapped in the chaotic crowd that scrambled away from
the band-shell after the cops charged—taking pains to bash the
skull of Tom Hayden's most loyal lieutenant Rennie Davis—and
scrambled between rows of National Guardsmen standing fast,
looking authoritative with their bayonets. The crowd spilled into
Michigan Avenue toward the Hilton. Matt's vision was blurred, his
throat raw. He was so right about not wanting to be here, but now
that he was unmistakably here, there was no exit, there was only the
imperative to keep moving.

He passed a water fountain, stopped to wash out his eyes (without rubbing them, a nice trick) and dampen his handkerchief, which
he was rolling up to cover his nostrils when he looked down and
saw Marcia Stein performing the identical ritual, sexy in a headband, showing her sweaty shoulders, and they laughed because they
had to lower their handkerchiefs to speak, and hugged.

"Look who's here!" he exclaimed stupidly.

"Great place for a reunion," she said, cocking her head wryly.
"Hey, I was with Sally Barnes, but we got separated. We're staying
together."

"Far out. Give me your number, OK?"

On a blank check, which was the only piece of paper she could
find in her purse, she wrote out the number of Evan's apartment in
Hyde Park.

He took the paper, quickly let go of her hand because her fingernails were so sharp, and guffawed: "Nice to cross paths with you
in hell."

They lowered their heads and she led him into the clotted street, slipping around the stately, or perhaps only indifferent, mules pulling the rickety wagons driven by overall-wearing black men and women of the Poor People's Campaign—*Wandering through the human wilderness in search of their forty acres*, Matt thought—and he took the lead as they waded deeper into the teeming crowd, toward the Hilton, where the gas remained palpable, though thinning, and the atmosphere was thick with bodies and terror. It was small comfort to realize that everyone was afraid. Try as you might, it was impossible to stand your ground here. You were inside a cage that was closing in, it was "The Pit and the Pendulum," surrounded by hundreds of cops, pressing in, jamming a pitiful, helpless mass of human beings toward the façade of the hotel.

Time slowed. Marcia jerked around frantically, and only now did Matt see that she was wearing a miniskirt, for Christ's sake! Some yards behind her, an attack line of billy clubs flailed toward them. A huge cop with a red face wound up like a pitcher on the mound before smashing a skinny boy just behind her.

Time revved up again. Matt scrambled to keep his footing as the great beast of a crowd stampeded ahead toward the big window of the Haymarket Lounge at the north end of the Hilton. A foot landed on the back of his right shoe—How easily could he be trampled? Where was Marcia?—and as if lightning had struck, he heard the sharp *crack* of glass smashed, and as if in slow motion saw a young man in a cowboy hat kick his bootheels through the shattered window into the lounge, or being shoved, it was hard to tell, and now cops like mad bulls were charging through what remained of the window, so that he and Marcia had no choice but to be shoved inside, too, Marcia stepping lively over shards of glass, Matt ducking to avoid a descending club. Inside, people lay on the floor bleeding from head wounds, whether from broken glass or billy clubs was not clear, and shrieks ricocheted as if they were ripples in one unrelenting scream. He grabbed Marcia by the hand, never mind her fingernails, and they clambered out of the Lounge and through a thinning crowd of demonstrators mixing with delegates and delegates' wives and tourists and God knows who else, into the lobby, where thinning wafts of tear gas were mixing with something more putrid—stink bombs to freak out the delegates, they would later learn. Everyone looked bewildered and panicky, even—or especially—the Democrats who looked dressed for a cocktail party.

They scrambled back out onto Michigan Avenue and fled northward, as did most of the refugees from the Hilton, seeing that most of the cops were heading the other way, southward toward the Amphitheater. Somebody on the other side of the street was screaming, "Fuck! Fuck!" and somebody else, "Fuck the draft!" Despite the gas and the stink bombs, the air was less viscous in the street, more like oxygen, but Matt had to blink a lot, trying to see straight. The window of the Haymarket Lounge was smashed to pieces, people were still writhing and screaming inside.

The two of them lurched onward, running and staggering. The gas was thinning and so was the crowd, until it bunched up again.

Ahead, on the next block, a paddy wagon was surrounded, trapped by five, six, seven young men in jeans who had cleared a space around it and were shoving it left with their shoulders and outstretched hands, rocking the big blue-and-white beast. One of them, a muscular blond guy, shaggy-haired, wearing a short-sleeved blue plaid shirt, a red bandanna over his mouth, was grasping the door handle, as behind him frenzied teenagers darted out of the crowd to help as sandy-haired men in black leather jackets moved in, displaying their overheated faces, and Matt recognized one of them as Carl from the movement center, the big guy who had been rattling on about seeds. Matt could see, in the wagon, two cops, one of them looking frantic. He swiveled around looking for Marcia and heard her scream: "What!"

He thought that was what she was screaming but when she repeated it, he heard the trace of a second syllable. What she was screaming was "Wyatt!"

The man with the red bandanna lurched toward the sound of his name, couldn't see who was calling him, but spotted Matt, who was dumbfounded when he beheld, above the bandanna, the ghastly eyes of Wyatt Burns, who blinked hard, recovered, grinned, and then, startled to be recognized, lost his balance, whereupon a buddy who sported major sideburns grabbed him by the elbow before he could hit the pavement, and caught him, but in the next moment, Wyatt twisted sharply so that something, a flat object, fell out of his shirt pocket and lay on the pavement glinting in the sunlight, as Marcia approached, unseen, from behind Wyatt, who was stabbing around on the pavement trying to get his fingers around the thing, which she could now see was an identification card in a plastic case. She peered over his shoulder before Wyatt picked up the card and jammed it into his right rear pants pocket.

She made a small indecipherable noise. Her headband was gone, her hair was flying witchy-wild, her short, bare legs were churning as she led Matt for some reason back toward the Hilton. Others were running too, in opposite directions, some faster, some slower—greasers, longhairs, people in suits who might have been delegates. Matt strained to keep up, his lungs still hurt. As they passed in front of the stone-lion-patrolled Art Institute, Marcia turned back toward him, eyes like platters, blood-shot, flaring, and said something he couldn't make out.

His eyes burned from sweat and gas. "What?"

Panting, she yanked him up the steps, behind the southernmost lion, haughty on its pedestal, superior to all human commotion. "Matt, I don't fucking believe it. Son of a bitch Wyatt Burns is a cop! ID from the Cleveland Police, Bureau of Special Services."

"Holy shit. That's the Red Squad."

Matt's mind raced. Suddenly everything made sense. *This is real. This happened.*

"Motherfuck! He set us up!" she yelled. A couple of passersby stared at her and she lowered her voice. "Went after Valerie. Knocked you out of commission. Knocked her out of Cleveland. Two birds with one stone. God, were we stupid."

His mind's eye was stuck on a scene of Wyatt Burns' demonic grin and a rocking paddy wagon, and out on the street, a pot-bellied cop flooded with adrenaline, fresh from smashing a Yippie, poking him with the end of his stick, a man who, the next moment, would be counting his overtime pay and thinking about how soon he could get home to fuck his wife.

Later, a mile to the north, Thursday now—midnight having come and gone—a flare, then another, a third and a fourth flare sliced through the blackened sky over Lincoln Park, and a helicopter smacked the air overhead and unspooled filaments of light onto the churning protest as the National Guardsmen charged through the park. The headlights of police cars swooped in and out of view through the bushes. Branches snapped under the wheels. "They're cleaning out the park," somebody yelled. "Go!" "Move!" "Over there!" Rotor thwacks, biker rips, human roars, and indeterminate noises congealed into blocks of frenzy. Spears of light slashed through the darkness. This was a war-of-the-worlds spectacle with gas grenades hurtling, unidentifiable forms and objects reflecting the light-shafts, and the gas haloing strobe-lit figures of coughing, earthbound angels. A tall, gawky longhaired boy collapsed from a nightstick to the head, started crawling, senselessly, and when he saw a camera raised his fingers in a V and, bleeding from the mouth, grinned, whereupon the cop, wearing neither a badge nor a name-plate, lugging an immense paunch in front of him as if honored to bear such a trophy, turned on the cameraman, smacked him, left him thrashing around on the grass, and turning to see who might be watching, caught sight of Matt Stackhouse and barreled toward him, jabbing his nightstick toward his midsection, as Matt pivoted and darted away, wanting to be anywhere but on the wrong side of that nightstick—and there, standing nearby, a swear-to-God angel, was Valerie Parr, freckles and green eyes, aghast and thrilled.

A white-clad medic wearing a Red Cross armband came running, but two cops reared up behind him and smacked him down, and when the medic tried to stand up, one of the cops shoved his knee into the medic's throat, shoved harder, and started clubbing him in the ribs. From the sidewalk at the west edge of the park, a mobile Fire Department spotlight ignited the wounded sky, while ironically urgent chants of "Walk, walk" tried to compete with choruses of "Oink, oink."

The moment permitted only a brief, though serious, kiss.

Matt took Valerie by the hand as tightly as she took him, and they hustled out of the park, chanting "Walk, walk." Looking back, they saw silhouettes, tableaus, against the lit-up gas fumes and couldn't tell whether those were demonstrators or cops.

He stank. His white shirt was starched to his body, parts of it stiffening. Sweat seemed to pour into his skin from the inside.

To no one's surprise, the delegates voted down the peace plank by a vote of sixty percent to forty percent—a Pyrrhic victory unless you considered it miraculous that the dissenters could amass forty percent given the fact that so many of the delegates were hand-picked by party bosses that nobody voted for—but so far as the park people were concerned, the exact degree of the Democrats' ugliness on this particular day didn't matter a damn, they were not paying close attention to the convention maneuvers, all that mattered was that the party was hell-bent for damnation whether the demonstrators got to sleep in the park or fought the cops. It was a matter of dignity to stay in the park, not get shoved out without a fight, but if they were to be shoved, they wanted to make it happen in front of a camera. The police had a different idea of dignity. They were the forces of order, enforcing a legal curfew, repelling barbarians, refusing to let a bunch of spoiled smart-ass kids get away with thinking they were above the law.

Now, some of the barbarians slowed their headlong flight, but most were closer to running than walking, slowing to catch their breath or tie kerchiefs around their noses, looking for running room on the battlefield. Spears of light ignited the McCarthy and Czechago buttons and the disbelieving eyes. As the glint of flashlights passed across dazzled faces, a collective derangement flowed across the park. Matt reached for his handkerchief and, crossing the street, coughing, gagging, passed it to Valerie, who thanked him kindly, she was already fixing her own handkerchief over her nose. Park people, looming up out of the gas, drifted past him like ectoplasmic emanations. What looked and smelled and sounded unreal was real. Periodically Matt called out "Walk!" No one was in a mood to walk. He wasn't either.

Then, from out of a clamor of shouted commands and generalized whoops, he heard his name called, whereupon he wheeled, and for the second time that day had a jarring half-recognition—a guy he knew, or used to know, but his name took a moment to come to mind; this was someone he knew from another context; he was astonished to realize it was Kurt Barsky, face shadowed by stubble, almost a start-up beard, haggard-looking, the tails of his white shirt pulled out of his pants, waving to him from within a cloud of gas. If Matt had made a list of acquaintances he would have least expected to see running around in Lincoln Park, Kurt would have ranked high, what with his intelligent, fixed skepticism, his tentativeness, his suspicion of "the herd" and "the mob."

They clutched each other.

"Holy Jesus!" Kurt said.

"Unholy. Wild. Terry's here, Marcia's here, Sally Barnes is here—staying together, on the South Side, at Ronnie's cousin's place—Ronnie's here, but I wouldn't have thought—"

"My route was circuitous," Kurt said. Kurt looked, if anything, taller than ever, seeming to peer down at Matt from a height, like the Art Institute lions. Trust Kurt to use the word "circuitous" in the thick of a mob scene.

Kurt surveyed clumps of people fleeing the cops, drifting past like human smoke. *Sally was here.* He asked Matt for the phone number at Ronnie's cousin's place. Matt pulled out Marcia's check, where she had written the number, ripped off a blank section, and copied the number for him. Sally Barnes. Unfinished business.

Kurt, Matt, Valerie, larky together, ran westward, hard-charging away from the park, the lake, the cops.

The helicopter flapped overhead again like an angry pterodactyl, and from ahead, on the street, came more sounds of mayhem:

glass shattering, glass crunched under tires, nightsticks against steel, nightsticks against bodies, car horns, distant sirens, sirens close-up, whoops, screams, ululations straight out of *The Battle of Algiers*. Cars of civilians were under assault from cops looking for some human meat to crack down on. A teenager in a headband tripped and fell directly in front of Matt, who stopped and helped him scramble to his feet. "Thank you, man," the kid said, and ran on. On the other side of the street, a bus full of cops, lights extinguished, got its taillight smashed by a well or luckily aimed rock. The bus turned a corner, sped up, stopped short next to a knot of young people chanting, "Pigs eat shit! Pigs eat shit!" and disgorged a dozen or more helmeted officers, who rushed onto the pavement, billy clubs raised like swords, to smack heads and poke their clubs into the guts and groins of anyone fleeing too slowly or screaming too loud. Matt caught the fright in the eyes of a boy fixed in the beam of a police headlight that suddenly flashed, but Matt didn't see what Valerie saw, namely, another cop bearing down on him from behind, and then suddenly blood was streaming down Matt's face from a cut opened up in his scalp, and he thought, *this is too fucking much, like lightning that strikes twice in the same spot.*

He froze in immobilized disbelief and rage until Valerie grabbed his hand and yanked him to the sidewalk. They stumbled in what he thought was the direction of the walk-up apartment. Valerie caught a glimpse of Kurt trying to slip between parked cars onto the sidewalk as a cop moved in and bashed down at him from behind, but he darted at the last moment and the billy club missed his skull. Then he was gone from her sight.

"Hold on," Matt was saying, pulling at her. "I don't feel so good."

"What?"

"Woozy."

"Do you want to sit down?"

He leaned against a wall. "No. Just woozy. Is this what a concussion feels like?"

"I think—I think—you get blurred vision. You lose memory. Headaches." She didn't know why she was saying these things.

She didn't know what she was talking about. "Can you find the apartment?"

"Yeah."

"OK. Slowly."

The wound in his scalp stung, and his feet screamed, but he found the apartment building. On the way upstairs, he squeezed the banister and was drawn to the thought that this was the chaos his father had warned him against; and assured himself that if he had a concussion, he probably wouldn't be able to formulate such a thought.

Inside the apartment, Valerie took a wash cloth, drenched it, soaped it, parted his hair, mopped off rivulets of blood, cleaned off his cut—he was getting used to this, women repairing his damaged face—and said, "What's this?"

"What?"

"There's a scar right next to this wound. You had another en-counter with a nightstick?"

"It's a long story. I'll tell you later."

"Anyway, this one's not so bad. Your hair took most of the blow." She paused and lit up the room with her smile. "Your *beautiful* hair."

He kissed her. "Valerie."

"Back to business. I don't think you need stitches. Stay away from emergency rooms. They'll bust you for assaulting a cop with your head. See how you feel in a while."

"OK." He collapsed onto the futon, and she inserted a pillow under his feet. She rinsed out the washcloth with cold water, held it against his scalp. "Just hold this for a while."

"OK." He was clear-headed enough to take note of her freckles.

"I think I saw this once in a movie," she said. "And now count backwards from 100. By sevens."

"What?"

He got down to sixty-five before she stopped him.

"You're fine. Is there a fan?"

"Over there."

She turned it on. The air felt good to him over the damp washcloth..

He needed to tell her. He was in no mood for an excavation but she needed to know what he now knew. He didn't know if it would be good for her to know—or whether it was good for him to know what he now knew—but she had a right to know.

He told her about Wyatt and his ID card.

"What!"

She stomped to the window as if corroboration or refutation might be found out on the street, then turned back to face him, mouth gaping, eyes wide with disbelief, and stared.

"I mean *what?*" She made an animal growl of the sort he had never before heard from a human being, burst into tears, and ran to him. He reached for her with the hand that was not holding the compress against his head.

She shuddered into his shoulder.

"That's unbelievable."

"And it happened."

"But hold on." She propped herself up on her elbow and flung her hair away from her eyes. She stared down at her hand and clutched her ring, Kathryn's ring, the ring that tethered her to reality. "The cops beat him up."

"Yup—"

"—when you guys were out on patrol."

"Made us all the more inclined to trust him."

"I can't—"

"Think about it," he said quietly. "The gun talk. The supermilitant talk."

"Stop."

"You have to wonder: Did he intend to bust us up in the first place? Or was that an afterthought, a sort of perk?"

"A bonus," she said. He'd never heard her sound bitter before.

More sobs ensued, and solace, and silent interludes, a closing of eyes and a clutching of bodies. After all the groping and explaining, Matt muscled the image of Wyatt out of his head and made love to Valerie on the futon.

They fell asleep weeping at some unknown hour only to be jarred awake by a pounding at the door. The fan clanked, it was dark, and Terry McKay stood there, sweating, panting, biting off chunks of words—

"Ronnie was busted ... Michigan Avenue ..."

Matt poured Terry a glass of water. Terry gulped and gagged, Valerie whacked him on the back, he thanked her. She brought him a paper towel, he mopped off his sweat.

"Where is he?"

"Don't know ... Legal team's on the case ... They've got bail money ..."

"Is he hurt?"

"Don't know," Terry said. "What an unholy mess ... Listen, can I crash with you guys?"

"Of course," Matt said, flashing on Ronnie—how many days ago?—telling him not to worry because he looked like an Italian movie star.

"There's nothing we can do tonight," Terry said. "We have to wait." He took note of the wound slashing down from Matt's scalp past his hair line. "What happened to you, man?"

"Nothing much. I'm fine. You fine, Terry?"

"I'm great."

Valerie ushered Terry into the barely furnished bedroom, brought him another glass of water, closed the door, and wondered what Hieronymus Bosch inferno the medics and lawyers were trapped in on the street, wondering whether the message she was getting was that she should go to medical school or law school.

Later on the futon, with Valerie curled up next to him, her palm against his chest, Matt lay awake, clammy, into the streaky hours of dawn, listening to the drone of the window fan beating the dead air.

"Are you really fine?" she wanted to know.

"In a way." He adopted a casual tone to tell her about his forth-coming date with the U.S. Army.

"Good lord! You're crazy to be here. Aren't you worried there's a warrant out for you?"

Matt repeated what Mike Starr had explained to him: that this was not a big concern, that the word around The Resistance was that the Feds were inundated with draft cases, and the U.S. Attorney in Chicago might not even have gotten around to indicting him, his case not worth the bother, what with their backlog of work. Matt's assurance sounded so tight that even he believed it. "And by the way," he added, "do you have any idea how glad I am to see you?"

But his mind drifted back to Ronnie, wondering whether headstrong Ronnie, action-freak Ronnie, Ronnie the prince of provocation, would stay cool—would *want* to stay cool—would re-frain from smart-talking a couple of dead-on-their-feet cops. He could imagine Ronnie getting blackjacked and smashed up in some holding cell somewhere, because everything was the fucking hip-pies' fault, and the freaks were hurling rocks and bags of shit, that's what kind of animals they were. Honest people had had enough from these so-called peaceniks; they'd think twice before setting their cloven hooves back inside the hard-working city of Chicago, Richard J. Daley, Mayor.

After ducking the billy club aimed at his head, Kurt veered sharply down the sidewalk and melted into a crowd. By the time he stopped to turn around, he had lost sight of Valerie and Matt.

Kurt's route to Lincoln Park was, as he told Matt, circuitous. It was very Kurt to put it that way, and it was accurate.

Kurt had started graduate work in philosophy, but the theory of language failed to thrill him. After one semester, he let his mother prevail on him to come home to New York and consider the family glove business, which she'd taken over after her husband died. "Just keep an open mind," she said. He let her set up a meeting with her husband's (and now her) partner, a fellow named Arthur Lichtman, who had joined the company in 1938: walked in off the street, unemployed, and talked his way into the business, showed he had the knack, rose to become his father's partner. Kurt met Lichtman at the glove factory, which occupied the second floor of a manufacturing building below Houston Street. Lichtman, paunchy and affable, greeted him at the gate of the freight elevator wearing a classy Panama hat, and they strolled westward into Greenwich Village, passing a number of comfortable-looking Italian restaurants featuring black-jacketed waiters using their horizontally extended arms as racks for white towels, but every time Kurt thought they had reached their destination, Lichtman kept walking. This was strange, but Kurt didn't want to be rude, so he didn't object.

Eventually they found themselves down near the Hudson River, Lichtman chatting away about leather imports and how well the company was doing and how many interesting problems came up in business, good for the mind to grapple with, until at last he led Kurt into a huge wood-frame warehouse of a building with high ceilings and sawdust on the floors where rough-looking guys sat at long tables with paper napkins and plates filled with hunks of meat and baked potatoes and canned corn. A roughly lettered sign said "GOOD FOOD." Lichtman promptly answered the question that Kurt was about to ask, explaining that he had discovered the place in the thirties when he was out of work and trying to organize longshoremen, which got him beaten up and fired, whereupon he got a job on the dock and tried organizing again, and got fired again. It was only then that Lichtman decided to try a different route, and made the acquaintance of Kurt's father. He still liked the sawdust feeling and camaraderie of Good Food, it kept him in touch with the people.

Lichtman had no regrets. The glove business was good to him. Kurt felt sad for Lichtman and was unconvinced that gloves were his own destiny. After kicking around for a while, he took up an invitation to write for the *Southern Gazette*, a weekly paper in Alabama, founded by some of his college acquaintances to report on the civil rights movement. After a few months of that, he felt restless, intellectually undernourished. He was visiting his mother in Brooklyn when he met a young woman, a neighbor, fast-talking and *zaftig*, whose mother worked in the office of a liberal Congressman named Joe Zaretsky, an old-time New Dealer and onetime Army sergeant whose twenty years in the House of Representatives had earned him a spot on the Foreign Affairs Committee, which was now looking to hire a staffer who could do research and write position papers on ways and means of digging the U.S. out of the nuclear arms race. Kurt took an immediate liking to the weathered Zaretsky, who dropped more and more of his terminal "r"s ("befaw," "brotha") the more beers they drank; liked his twinkly manner, liked the unapologetic way he was letting himself go bald without any combover, liked his habit of calling Kurt "Professor" and insisting that Kurt call him "Joe," and shared his respect for Senator J. William Fulbright and also for General de Gaulle, who was appalled that the U.S., in Southeast Asia, had decided to relieve the French of the colonial burden they could no longer afford to carry, and followed them into the swamp. Zaretsky worried about where this war in Vietnam was going even though he had taken the path of least resistance after the Tonkin Gulf incident and let himself be talked into voting for Johnson's war authorization. Kurt was flattered that intelligent, earthy, Joe Zaretsky took him into his confidence. It came as a pleasant surprise that a politician could be thoughtful, popular, and a *mensch*.

During his last months in Ann Arbor, Kurt had tired of ideological talk in the manner of Terry McKay and even the more abstracted Matt Stackhouse, who thought with their blood and their longing. Conscience needed brains! Passion needed brakes! Kurt had wearied of grand visions and splendid mirages—not that they had tempted him so much to start with. The question for Kurt was not what was morally desirable but what, in a given political situation, might be feasible. Clean hands were no hands at all. The movement's moralism and confrontational style appealed to him less than putting his brain to work crafting policies that might win political support. He liked the idea of being paid to read books and write analyses, and he was willing to try out Zaretsky's hypothesis that hardly anybody in Washington knew much about anything, so you might as well roll up your sleeves, outthink them and—not least—outwork them. Dirty hands were hands at work.

Zaretsky liked to be kept informed about what his staff and his colleagues were saying behind his back, and introduced Kurt not only to Capitol Hill gossip but decent $2.98 steaks and fine cigars from Castro's Cuba that had slipped through the embargo, and soon Kurt had graduated from beer to pretty—and then very—good brandy, and discovered, among the young ladies of the Hill, a range of body types, accents, and hair styles new to him. Flings failed, or succeeded, it was the same thing. He concluded that Washington was a place for casual dating that got heavier or lighter according to perceptions of X's or Y's upward mobility prospects. He rented a one-bedroom apartment near Capitol Hill, and studied Southern Africa as well as Southeast Asia on the government dime, wrote position papers and took pleasure from seeing them published in the *Congressional Record* under the name of one Congressman or another.

Washington was no place for romantics. Working on policy hardened him—diminished him—because everything had to be done by committee, you had to hold back your most interesting and original thoughts; the question of what was workable kept intruding into the question of what was good, even if workability was his preferred option. He was devoured by complication, and relished it. He got his feet wet slopping through the miasma of Washington, even when he wore practicality like galoshes.

Zaretsky teased him but perhaps he was right—perhaps Kurt was learning to relish complication too much. He endorsed Gene McCarthy early. He was a delegate to the convention. Would Kurt like to come along? Hell, yes. For all his disaffection from the Democrats—hell, his *disgust*—Kurt was excited at the chance to be at the scene of the crime. When the Democrats had last held a convention, in 1964, it was the end of Freedom Summer, which had begun with the murder of the three civil rights workers, and turned into Johnson's coronation and the murder of the dreams of the Mississippi Freedom Democrats, the opposition which Melissa Howard had worked on in Greenwood. Kurt and Terry had watched on TV, disgusted, as the Party honchos patronized the Freedom Democrats. The Democratic Party murdered ideals but outsiders commanded hope, Kurt had thought at the time. Now it was Gene McCarthy's turn to martyr himself. Well, that seemed a worthy project.

Now, three years into the horrors of war, the party was not just a betrayer of ideals but a slaughterhouse, and McCarthy had come straight out and said so while Bobby Kennedy was dithering. That whole hopeful-desperate, manic-depressive spring of 1968, even as haywire history took over, there remained the slenderest chance that Johnson might come to his senses, that McCarthy might administer the antidote. Johnson had not given up on Zaretsky, after all, he briefed the Congressman on his peace talks, futile or phony as they might be. The Congressman thought it was his duty to subject himself to Johnson's sweet talk in the hope that he could get a word or two in edgewise. It was Zaretsky's job to stay alert, hope for the best and plan for the worst.

In fact, even as the movement was arranging to converge in Chicago, so were Joe Zaretsky and his allies in the McCarthy campaign arranging their caucuses and their credential challenges, mobilizing against the Johnson-Humphrey charade, because with Bobby Kennedy dead, the whole fate of this wretched moribund beast of a political party was left in their hands. Joe and his peers, Terry and Matt and Valerie and *their* peers, all swallowed up together.

Kurt had a front-row seat, and a Congressman to write speeches for, and incidentally his own room in the Hilton.

As it turned out, there was next to no use to be made of Kurt at the convention. Zaretsky was so worked up, he decided to compose his own speeches, mapping out points in capital letters on yellow legal-size pages. At one point, Zaretsky summoned Kurt to his room in the Hilton and started reading him a draft, only to take his pages, crumple them, wad them up, and toss the wad at the window, saying: "This is pure bullshit, Kurt, you don't have to say it," but when Kurt asked if the Congressman wanted him to take a shot, Zaretsky scowled, "If I can't speak my own words about what this war's doing to my country, I should resign." When Zaretsky did take the floor, his passion was so fervent, he made clichés sound like epiphanies. He pulled out the stops. In an officer's voice he told the delegates to listen to George McGovern—"Jawj" it came out—who flew bomber missions in World War II. "Don't you dare call Jawj McGovern a nervous Nellie!" And as for himself, don't confuse Joe Zaretsky with somebody who drove a desk! "I drove a tank, and no one is going to sit there and tell me who a patriot is or isn't ... but the Vietnam war is the wrong war in the wrong place at the wrong time, sheer desolation, and it costs America the respect of the world ..." Kurt had no work to do in Chicago but warm up in the bullpen.

Came late Thursday morning, August 29, and Kurt, weirded out by the scene the previous night at Lincoln Park, was unassigned for the evening. He was unharmed except for a bearable twinge in his shoulder, but the appeal of running around in the streets again was minimal. His mind turned back to Sally Barnes.

He would have thought her too levelheaded to be in Chicago this week. A woman full of surprises. Well, everyone went through changes.

He rang the number Marcia had written down for him. The phone was busy. He called back.

She picked up after a single ring.

"Kurt Barsky here, looking for Sally Barnes."

"You found her."

"How great to hear your voice!"

They compared notes about which park was more intense, Grant or Lincoln. They exchanged guided tours of their recent years. He told her he was working for Joe Zaretsky.

"How sensible of you!" she said. "You're useful!"

"I try," he said, feeling foolish. "This is insane, isn't it?" They shared a laugh. "I imagine you're smiling, I think."

"I am." Her voice had, if anything, deepened.

A giddiness rose between them. He told her he was at the Hilton. She said she would just as soon stay away from the Loop, the police, and the National Guard, and anyway, she wasn't dressed yet, she'd slept in after the gas-saturated night, but she would certainly be delighted to see him. Would he be willing to leave the war zone and come down to a quieter part of Chicago?

He would certainly be willing.

He shaved, showered, and flagged down a cab to Hyde Park. The driver was a cheerful round-faced Black man with thick shoulders, wearing a black T-shirt and a beret. Kurt asked him where he had acquired the beret, leading to a conversation about how the French were so much better at wrecking their government than Americans.

"Let's face it, man," the cabbie said, shifting directly from first into third gear. "What's going on here this week is theater. Theater, man."

"Theater."

"Theater's all it is. It's like the Black Panthers. They strut around, it's a freak show, niggers with guns, you hearing me? White man gets all worked up, and the Panthers think they've got a revolution, but it's more like a show, you know what I mean?"

It turned out that driving a cab was his way of making ends meet between acting gigs. "It's an expensive hobby, acting," he said.

Disheveled, bleary-eyed Marcia opened the door of Evan's apartment and was astonished to see Kurt Barsky. Scattered around the bland living room were cardboard containers from Chinese takeout, chopsticks, beer cans, Coke and Dr. Pepper bottles. There was a damp-looking area in the corner of the carpet. *My old crowd,* he thought. *Love 'em, living as though they're still college students.*

"I might have known you'd show up here," Marcia said ambivalently.

"Sally invited me."

Marcia lifted her right eyebrow. "Right. Don't worry, she hasn't fled. She's getting dressed."

Ronnie stepped gingerly into the living room, in socks, no shoes, a bandage snug over much of black-and-blue cheekbone, and wearing a T-shirt through which his tightly bandaged torso was visible. "I heard my name taken in vain," he said with aplomb. "But no hugs. I still have some ribs intact."

Kurt had a speechwriter's professional admiration for phrase-making. Ronnie's savoir faire had improved over the years.

"Are you all right?"

"Terrific," Ronnie replied, deadpan, and narrated his day, skipping the part about the spike balls but including the nightstick in the Loop and his ending up in a holding cell where two cops wearing tight-fitting black gloves—they must have been filled with buckshot—smashed up his cheekbone, played catch with him, tossing him back and forth, finally leaving him alone to bleed all night on the cold concrete floor before they mopped off his face and took him off to get arraigned. A waiting volunteer lawyer bailed him out. Two medics swooped him off to a friendly doctor's office in Hyde Park and got him X-rayed—better than one of the hospitals, where the cops would be watching.

"Ronnie," Kurt said, "somehow I always knew it would come to this."

Ronnie half-smiled. "You mean I needed a publicity shot for my doc? Well, I didn't exactly go looking for broken bones."

Kurt had his doubts.

Ronnie went to a three-quarter smile. "*Welcome to Czechago.* Adds to the all-around crappy look."

"What do you mean, crappy look?"

Ronnie explained that he was shooting on outdated film stock liberated from sources he was not at liberty to specify, so it would have the look of footage from Vietnam that activists had smuggled into the States. "Crappy" looked "authentic," made the audience "question its presuppositions," "interfered with their self-satisfaction."

Kurt doubted that movies actually worked like that but didn't want to argue with a wounded man.

Marcia brought Ronnie a glass of seltzer. "This is all I get?"

"Very funny."

To defuse the situation, Kurt composed half a smile. "Hey, Ronnie, I commiserate, really. But forgive me if I ask you a simple question. Nothing personal."

"I forgive you. Ask."

"OK. What does this accomplish, fighting the cops?" Kurt felt like a prig but didn't care much.

"Well, so that's your question."

"Bear with me for a minute. I'm thinking about millions of Americans who watch these confrontations on color TV and decide that they're on the cops' side against the scruffy Commie riff-raff who throw rocks at them."

Ronnie winced. "Well, well." There was a glint in his eye. "Poor cops, they never heard anybody say 'cocksucker.'"

"I didn't mean—"

"Kurt, listen, I'm not into short-term results. Truly I'm not. The tactics aren't the point. The training is the point. I don't know what *you're* doing, but *we're* going to war. Some will, some won't. That's where it's going."

"Get off it, Ronnie." Kurt realized he was rising to the bait, but what difference did it make? He set his jaw. "You listen, Ronnie. I work for a congressman who's moving heaven and earth to cut off funding for the war. Cut off weapons. The *actual* war. It's people like him and Gene McCarthy and all their law-and-order-loving sub-urbanite supporters who are going to end the fucking war if anyone is. It's something else when you go to war with the cops—"

Ronnie had the confident air of a chess-player thinking one move ahead. "OK, Kurt, think about it a different way. When we go to war with the cops, we strengthen your boss's hand. You should celebrate—"

"When you go to war with the cops, you undermine us. You win a million votes for Nixon. You look like thugs and losers. You look like a suicide squad. Why pick a fight on the enemy's turf? This is no goddamn game."

"Far out," Ronnie said crisply, glancing at Marcia. "Is this how they teach you to talk in Washington?" Ronnie was enjoying himself.

The door opened. Sally walked in, groggy, hair damp, and made straight for Kurt rising from his chair, eyes meeting, lips meeting too briefly—Kurt who had lost a bunch of hair, his widow's peaks soaring, but his old earnestness was in place, and the hint of a twinkle. The wrinkles fanning out from his eyes were downright dignified.

Ronnie had pushed Kurt into a corner, and the fact that he had to contend with Ronnie at all, barging into his reunion with Sally, left him annoyed. "Well, Sally, it's terrific to see you, and let me bring you up to date. Ronnie imagines he's hunkered down in a tunnel outside Saigon with the National Liberation Front, waiting to attack. Whereas I had the impression that we live in America—"

"You know, Kurt, really—" Ronnie jabbed his index finger toward Kurt's chest, wincing from the effort, "—I'd rather be wrong with the NLF than right with Gene McCarthy."

Kurt noted that Ronnie used the official name, NLF, not Saigon's insulting "Viet Cong."

"That's cute, Ronnie, but for Christ's sake, the NLF doesn't want a bloodbath in Chicago. What they want is a Congressional vote and Americans getting the fuck out of their country. They think we should love the American people, not freak them out. You sound like you're on such close terms with the NLF, why don't you ask them?"

Sally watched a blood vessel pulse in Kurt's right temple. She wanted him. It was thrilling to see him charged up, although this was not the rendezvous she'd expected. For all Ronnie's drollery and elegance, he was the voice of macho self-indulgence—a coming-of-age scarification ritual for boys. She asked herself again what in hell she was doing inside this mayhem. There was no way she could write about it. She understood what drove Marcia. Let's face it, Marcia was born into violence, no fault of her own, it was her heritage and it pointed straight to the heart of her commitment. Ronnie was thinking with his trophy scars. But Sally Barnes of Mt. Harmony, Michigan? She believed in kindness and blossoms. She was born to appreciate, not to wage war. She brought peace, not a sword. Did that make her a liberal? She wanted to help kids grow up and teach them how not to get into wars. She didn't want to teach them to fight cops any more than she wanted to send them to prowl through Southeast Asian jungles.

This was like a reunion with long-lost cousins who'd grown into hostile strangers. Kurt's mistake was to think that he could nudge a momentarily errant cousin into seeing the light. But it was not a family quarrel because they were not a family.

It occurred to Sally that this was an argument between a guy who had to work for a living and a guy who probably lived on a trust fund, since nobody else could afford to make documentaries. She wanted to see Kurt, not Ronnie, not even Marcia.

Ronnie dragged himself up and trudged toward the bathroom. Marcia followed discreetly, closing the door behind her. Kurt eased onto the sofa. Sally wanted to get out of here with Kurt. He moved closer and whispered: "What do you say we head up to the Hilton? I have a room."

They were on their way out by the time Ronnie returned, flashing one of his irresistible smiles: "Hey, really, it's terrific to see you guys. Really, let's get together sometime when I have an easier time breathing."

"For sure," Kurt said.

In the back seat of the taxi, Sally and Kurt leaned, shoulder to shoulder, holding hands, and they kissed the kiss they did not get to kiss in Hyde Park.

As they neared the Hilton, prowling down Michigan Avenue toward a phalanx of riot police came a parade of National Guard jeeps bearing barbed wire grids like monstrous cattle-catchers. Guardsmen in riot gear lined up in neat ranks, alert, tense, facing Grant Park, where a desultory rally was in progress. More

Guardsmen lined the sidewalk in front of the hotel, and despite the barbed wire, they looked harmlessly young—*could be McCarthy kids,* Kurt thought. *Maybe some of them are.* One of them was biting his lip. The doors were guarded by cops who defiantly did not resemble McCarthy kids. They looked impatient, ill-humored. Several looked drained. One looked feral. In riot gear—helmets and plastic visors—they looked Martian. Short sleeves made them look even more Martian. Their nightsticks were poised at nearly identical angles.

Kurt approached a Black cop who was shorter than himself, and held out his hotel badge and room key. The cop's face was as revealing as the wall. He examined the badge, turned it over, reexamined it, turned to Sally. "And you, Miss? Do you have business here?" His voice was milder than his glower.

"She's with me," Kurt said blandly. "Officer."

"Miss, you can speak for yourself." He glanced at her ringless left hand.

"Like he said, officer, I'm with him. There's no law against a honeymoon, is there?"

The cop smiled. He got the joke. "No, ma'am, there certainly is not."

Not yet, Kurt couldn't help but think. The cop waved them through the door.

"Not yet," Sally said, sotto voce, once they were in the lobby, which was still laden with the faint puke smell of the previous day's stink bombs, made more palatable, however, though no less bizarre, by an overlay of disinfectant that was about as convincing as lavender sprayed on a decaying corpse. Guests, faces drawn, were checking out. Uniformed personnel were vacuuming corners of the lobby and emptying ash trays. Plainclothes cops sauntered around. Middle-aged men in suits sat in armchairs trying not to look like security guards.

"The whole world is stinking," Sally said in the elevator on the way up to the fifteenth floor.

There, across from the elevators, an earnest young fellow in a short-sleeved white shirt, wearing a McCarthy button and a tie, knot slightly askew, was manning a table. Kurt greeted him by name: Bob. Bob, who didn't look old enough to vote, waved them on.

Down the corridor Kurt led her, and unlocked a door. His suitcase lay open on a low table. Inside, his belongings were jumbled. He closed the suitcase, grinned sheep-faced, and laid his Congressional staff ID on the desk. A book lay on the night table: a worn paperback of Camus' *The Rebel*. Sally was not used to hotel rooms, or enamored of them—and there was also the quiver of a memory of a motel room in Carterville, Pennsylvania, which she tamped down. The bed was enormous, the headboard and frame resembled mahogany, the flowers in the painting above the bed had a funky Woolworth's charm.

She drew back the curtain across the window and gazed out over Grant Park. A few hundred people milled around a speaker who squawked away indecipherably over a feeble public address system. The crowd was ragged at the edges, dwarfed in the wounded expanse of the park. Lake Michigan was preternaturally tranquil. There were muffled chants and placards she couldn't read, but from this height and distance, the scene appeared weirdly composed, like a Brueghel landscape. It was disconcerting to look out over what, just yesterday, was a battlefield. She had never visited a battlefield. Perhaps they always looked peaceful once the corpses were carried away and the grounds gussied up.

Kurt walked up behind her, slipped his arm around her waist, and they watched together, in a state of grace.

"So peaceful," she said. The skin of her arms felt as though a breeze had just blown over her.

"Whitman, remember? The learn'd astronomer. Perfect silence. No stars, but another kind of perfect." If she spoke another word it would only subtract from the moment. She thought: *He's the one I've wanted to be with.*

Sally turned around. "Kurt, one thing. This is just here. Just now." She drew the curtain. He turned the bed covers.

In bed, she said one word: "Slow." Then: "Make it last."

It lasted, skin to skin, delicate, urgent, giggling boy-girl love; nothing fancy. They swallowed their outcries. The poignancy of this moment, the sharp point of the sword.

Terminal love, most likely, Kurt thought afterwards, as they lay on their backs, hand in hand. Would anything that happened this week last?

Sally floated. "Are you real?"

If this was not only hello but farewell, Kurt thought as he drifted away from toxic Chicago, it was perfect. "I'm so happy to be here, for real, with you," were his words to her.

An uproar from the corridor, a storm of indistinct shouts and banging, jolted them awake. Kurt grabbed his watch—5:10 AM. He jumped up, pulled on his pants, picked up the room key from the bed stand, stuck it into his pocket, went to the door, peeked through the eyehole, and saw nothing. The uproar resumed, subsided, resumed. Sally said muzzily, "Kurt?"

"Stay here." He peered through the eyehole again. Nothing. He cracked the door open. Down the corridor, several yards to his right, a young man in white socks and no shoes sat on the carpet against the wall, holding his hands over his forehead, looking stunned. Behind him another young man with a scraggly blond beard holstered a metallic object that Kurt deduced was a can of Mace.

"Holy Jesus." Kurt darted back into his room. "Hey, can you bring me a damp washcloth?" Sally pressed it into his hand. She was wrapped in a bath towel. He turned her around by her elbow and said, "Better stay in here."

She tossed him his shirt—"You might want this"—then snatched up her own clothes.

Shoeless, buttoning his shirt—buttons and buttonholes misaligned, he realized, and didn't care—he stepped out into the corridor, shut the door behind him, dashed to the young man, who was squeezing his eyes shut with an expression strangely compounded of pain and astonishment. Kurt placed the washcloth over his eyes. "Hey, just keep your eyes closed and don't rub them and don't touch them. *Don't rub them.* Just blink a lot. Keep blinking. You'll be all right. Stay here, OK?"

Kurt didn't know what he was talking about, but what he was saying sounded logical. In any event, it would do the kid good to hear some plausible advice.

The kid thanked him and lapsed into a coughing spell.

Boots clomped down the corridor toward them. In a split second Kurt turned, whipped out his key, made for his room, unlocked the door, pushed inside, and fastened the manual lever contraption. Cops stomped up, some uniformed, some not—the one with the Mace among them—pounded on the door. Kurt said nothing but turned and put his finger to his lips. Sally nodded. Another knock, more imperious. The sound of a passkey in the lock. They held their breath.

The door shuddered. More pounding. "Police! Open up!"

Sally stood next to him, speechless. Kurt was real. So were the cops. Seconds passed. They heard footsteps, blessedly stepping away.

Another burst of tumult outside. Kurt, at the eyehole, saw only a blur.

"Look at you," Sally whispered. She pointed to his out-of-alignment shirt buttons. "You're all askew." She eyed him with a look that was hard to interpret, then refastened him.

They heard, in the corridor, other doors flinging open, knobs banging against walls, indistinct grunts, bangs, and moans. Kurt inched the door open. The boy who had been Maced was blinking frantically. On either side of him, doors stood open. Uniformed cops were shoving two boys and a girl toward the elevator, their arms twisted behind them. Kurt thought he recognized them as McCarthy volunteers. One of the boys howled as the cop in charge of him kneed him in the small of the back and yelled "Move!" The boy staggered, writhed, banged into the wall. Two National Guardsmen and three smirking plainclothesmen, one with hair down to his shoulders, formed a gauntlet along the walls.

From a distance came a shriek.

Bob, the McCarthy kid, ran up to the door of Kurt's room, out of breath, with another McCarthy kid tagging along, half of a pair of glasses on his nose and the other half clutched in his hand.

Sally pushed in front of Kurt and addressed the McCarthy kids:

"Our people were sitting around in their room, talking, drinking beer. The cops smashed in, said we were throwing junk out the windows."

"Junk?"

"Who knows, beer cans, maybe an ashtray. Somebody said something about a ball bearing denting the hood of a jeep."

"Somebody said a typewriter," said the second boy.

"Wow," said Kurt, ambiguously.

"I heard that was earlier," Bob said, as if it mattered. "Anyway, they decided this stuff was coming from our room. The cops had passkeys and busted in and woke people up who weren't even *in* our room, cracked heads, completely nuts. It's unbelievable."

Another commotion flared up as more cops stormed down the hall toward the elevators. "Downstairs," a cop the size of a small truck said to no one in particular.

"I'm going to the twenty-third floor," Bob said. "That's where the Senator is staying."

"Excuse me, you hard of hearing or something?" the cop said, coming up to where Kurt and Sally stood with the McCarthy kids in the doorway to their room. "I said *downstairs. Now.*" The McCarthy kids spun around and headed for the elevators. The kid with the broken glasses stage-whispered: "And to think that on the march yesterday I was calling out to these guys, 'Join us!'"

The cop swiveled, but after a split second determined that this was the phase-out part of the exercise and rotated toward Kurt: "You too. And you."

Kurt stared. It didn't seem like a good time to remind the cop that he was a paying guest. This cop was not in a mood to argue. He was not wearing a nametag.

Footsteps clumped closer, behind Kurt, and a voice he recognized said breathlessly: "Hold on, officer. This man works for me."

The cop swung around to confront a man in leather slippers and a seersucker jacket who was a head shorter than he was.

"And you are?"

"Joe Zaretsky. Congressman Joe Zaretsky. I'm a delegate to the Democratic Convention." Zaretsky glared at the uniform where the cop's nametag was supposed to be. Zaretsky had a Purple Heart from his army tour of duty, Kurt knew. "And what didja say your name was?"

Their eyes locked in staredown.

Zaretsky won. "*This* man—" Zaretsky pointed to Kurt "—is my employee, and he's staying in *this* hotel," he added, pointing down toward the carpet. "He belongs here. This woman—" pointing to Sally "—this woman is his guest." "*They* belong here." Zaretsky's eyes were hard. "*You* don't!"

"We been called by the management." The cop dialed his tone down a notch.

"Well, officer, you have a choice. One, you can arrest me and explain to your C.O. why you busted a congressman. Or two, you go on down to the lobby with the rest of your unit and give him the good news that you successfully kept the peace on the fifteenth floor."

After due consideration, the officer wheeled and departed.

A few minutes later, as Kurt and Sally rode down to the lobby, Sally sniffed up some tears and said: "Get me out of here. Please. I need to go back to the world."

New York City, 1968-69

RONNIE SILVERBERG GLIDED ALONG on the wings of his scenario. Turbulence was to be expected. Rome continued to be destroyed. All good. Picturesque. His mission was to collect the elements and quilt them together to reveal the pattern of things—a pattern that was, if you looked at these things in the right way, already underway. His documentary would be a little masterpiece of jagged montage, a sort of off-balance equivalent of his jump-cut life.

Hell of a great year for Ronnie. First, along with Marcia, Terry, and Valerie, he was invited to Hanoi to meet with North Vietnamese and NLF officials. To be invited on one of these trips was a badge of honor. Ronnie, in high school French that improved with use, interviewed Party cadres who had fought against the French and been tortured by them. He shot footage of peasants guiding their water buffaloes out of rice paddies at the sound of an alert and rushing to man anti-aircraft guns against B-52s. He shot workers rebuilding hospitals and bridges. The North Vietnamese supplied him with footage of children reading textbooks in underground bunkers, civilians rescuing American pilots, soldiers lugging equipment down the Ho Chi Minh trail on bicycles. Ronnie almost convinced an NLF delegate to let him tag along on a trek back to Saigon, so he might put together an hour-long doc that would bring an honest-to-God Vietnamese Communist alive for American viewers. In the end, the NLF decided it would be too dangerous, but the fact that they took months to say no Ronnie took as a compliment.

Remember, the Vietnamese kept telling the Americans, *you need to win over the American people. It is your government that is the enemy. You are a good people.*

No one was going to argue with the Vietnamese. Terry did not believe that the Americans were a particularly good people, but it came as a revelation to him that the Vietnamese were going to win—eventually—because they knew how to act as if they were right about the Americans. The four Americans were moved to tears, epiphanies, and fervent rededications. They came back to America wearing aluminum rings made from the carcasses of B-52 bombers shot down over North Vietnam, slipped onto their hands by the surprisingly small, soft fingers of the gaunt but smiling chief of the delegation, Mme. Nguyen Van Chu. Chu smiled beatifically and trumpeted: "We congratulate our American friends for their struggle toward the inevitable victory!" Of her sincerity there could be no doubt. Ronnie thought they had passed over to a part of the world where people believed the words that came out of their mouths.

They returned to an America that knew nothing of such people. The four of them argued among themselves. Marcia and Ronnie said it was time to raise the stakes. Now that Nixon was ensconced in the White House, the country would have to be shaken to its foundations. Valerie sided with Terry. The confrontation strategy was deadended. It was over. Shaking foundations would not end the war; neither would tying up traffic. Congress would. Terry would keep his B-52 ring on a chain around his neck, tucked into his shirt. *You need to win them over.*

Valerie wore hers on her pinky, next to Kathryn's jade-and-platinum gift. She thought about how uneven a movement is, how it goes by fits and starts, how you should never let the mood of the moment overwhelm you. When the Mexican government massacred hundreds of students in October, she thought about how the crazy American she met in San Miguel had assured here: "Nothing ever happens in Mexico." *We used to say the same about America. And look where we are now.*

To edit his documentary, Ronnie borrowed Barry Moses's New York loft, below Houston Street, for the winter and spring. Barry was in South Vietnam recording sound for stories about American GIs preparing to come home because Nixon was said to be "Vietnamizing" the war. Filthy snow was slathered over Manhattan sidewalks, slushing up at the corners, melting into wretched ponds; windows were splotched with soot; bleak water towers lurked over the rooftops like bloated sentries—these sights suited Ronnie Silverberg's February mood. America was finished, though it wouldn't go easily. On the Lower East Side, he passed a snowed-in playground as the kids, just released from school, whooped and joshed around, and he thought of Hanoi kids evacuated to underground schools. His film would pay homage to them, and to the peasants cultivating rice under the B-52s. The way of the warrior was to refuse the death that history sets out for you.

At the Gem Spa on St. Marks Place—now known as St. Marx Place—where underground papers from all over the country were sold, Ronnie picked up an issue of *Fifth Estate*, published in Detroit. The cover showed a skeleton gazing outward from a sun whose rays displayed the words: "A Philosophy of Life and Death: wars, crimes, divorce, prejudice and insanity are mirrored on a river of blood whose trickling is the music of a skulled violinist and it washes into the sea of fear within your own mind." Yeah, that about covered it. Amerika, never-ending source of grotesque material. Ronnie had worked hard to drain the sea of fear that engulfed him in the back room of a police station in Chicago. He shot a slow crawl of the *Fifth Estate* cover. It might work as a voice-over.

"Our ground," he told Marcia one night—post-coitally, stoned, on the floor mattress, which was wedged into a corner against two walls—"is our own fear. That's where we fight. We win when we turn our fear against itself." He looked through a barred window at a street light slashing away at the blackness. "That's what we need to learn from the Vietnamese."

"Righto, boss," Marcia teased. Actually, she agreed with him, though she wasn't sure what he meant.

Ronnie reflected on his good fortune in finding a woman as serious and saucy as he was, and also as financially cushioned, what with a father who owned a blouse factory specializing in fast turn-arounds on late-breaking specials. Ronnie prided himself on the scars she left down his back—proofs of ferocious fucking that inspired him to think about the complex relations of love and pain. The Vietnamese knew a lot about love and pain.

All spring and into the summer, Ronnie sat—caffeinated, focusing the high beam of his intelligence—at a long editing table made of lumber-yard scrap, facing a brick wall, scribbling scripts, cutting his assemblies apart, splicing them, trying this, trying that, inching toward a rough cut. At the end of the table stood a battered Royal portable holding a sheet of mimeograph paper, which fluttered in a breeze that was reliably stoked up by a rusted fan that rested on the floor next to the mattress.

On the far wall, Malcolm X in black and white, on semi-gloss paper, flashed his eyes and pointed his thin, accusing finger at honkie America, while next to him, Che Guevara lit up the room above the stenciled words, "AT THE RISK OF SEEMING RIDICULOUS, LET ME SAY THAT ALL REVOLUTIONARIES ARE GUIDED BY GREAT FEELINGS OF LOVE." Ronnie nodded at the martyrs: *Good morning, comrades.*

Once in a while, Marcia permitted herself to think: *There is every risk of seeming ridiculous. Do not dwell on their deaths, dwell on their lives, breathe in their resurrections. The Vietnamese are not dumped into crematoria. They know they'll win. That knowledge is their armament.*

On one wall, Marcia hung embroidered Japanese motifs: a solid white mountain with blue shadows, and a lake with a turquoise border. She placed them symmetrically, but Ronnie, preferring the absence of symmetry, moved the mountain over. He called her Lady Symmetry. For all that her childhood must have been hellish, she knew how to mellow him out. This she had tried—and failed—to do for her mother and father. She told Ronnie he ground his teeth in his sleep. He was not surprised.

Near the bed, on stubby little legs, stood a match-scarred hatch-cover coffee table, on which lay a folder of Zig-Zag cigarette papers, a large ceramic ashtray holding trails of ash and several roaches, and two paperback books: Régis Debray's *Revolution in the Revolution?* and, in French, *Feuillets d'Hypnos,* by René Char. Against the wall, next to an ancient turntable and upended orange crates serving as record cabinets, were propped three Rolling Stones jacket covers: "Get Off My Cloud," "Aftermath," and "Between the Buttons," along with Ravi Shankar's "Sound of the Sitar" and "West Meets East," a collaboration with Yehudi Menuhin, a nice Jewish boy.

Sometimes Ronnie set up the record player to replay an LP till he couldn't stand the sound of it anymore. The ragas pumped him, calmed him, and anointed him. Jim Morrison's leathery moan alternately scared and stirred him. "End of the line, end of the line." The words reverberated in his mind: midnight, soul, whiskey, want to kill you. Kill the death culture. Dead buffalo on the prairies, dead buffalo in the rice fields. Flatland. He kept a buffalo nickel, a childhood trophy, on the windowsill by the bed.

Marcia was often around, watching him at his editing table, but feeling restless. When he was done working, they smoked dope and watched old movies on television. Sometimes they started in on the dope earlier in the day. When she was on fire, they rapped about people's war. She helped out here and there, but it bothered her when he didn't feel like taking the time to explain things to her. He started to feel responsible for dreaming up tasks she could carry out. He told her she needed projects of her own. She flared up, accused him of patronizing her. "I don't need you to schedule my life. I have my own rhythm."

"OK, OK."

Such moments of turbulence passed. They decided that they were fuck-buddies; *compañeros*; one unit in an army of lovers that could not be defeated.

She read Mao. She read Régis Debray about organizing guerrillas. Her heart swelled. They were going for broke. She dug how

Debray struggled to divest himself of bourgeois assumptions. Ronnie was like that. "I'm giving myself the education they didn't give me in school. But who," she asked, "is this René Char?"

"A French poet who fought in the Resistance. Those are the poems he wrote underground. You know, he wrote an article later saying that everybody in France after the war was going around saying they fought in the Resistance, but that was horseshit. The Resistance was tiny—brave but, you know, minuscule. A speck of dust." He blew on his hand. "Most of the French got along just fine with the Nazis."

She snuggled up against Ronnie and said that talk about urban guerrilla warfare got her wet. Ronnie licked his lips in a half-parody. "I like kinky," he said, and playfully yanked her ponytail on his way to going down on her. He was learning to be more thoughtful in bed. The way of the warrior was thoughtful. Ronnie used to be called a "hot-blooded boy" for his tendency to come wham-bam. The first time he heard that, he took it as a compliment. God, sometimes it amazed him how stupid he could be, and so recently. On the Times Square shuttle late one Saturday night, he was sitting near a bunch of teenaged chicks in tight skirts, suspenders, and halter tops, they'd drunk enough that they didn't realize how loudly they were jesting about some guy they knew as a "cream puff." The culture was turning.

A local dealer named Gary, a friend of his cousin Evan, dropped in one day. Gary had the air of knowing his way around. One thing led to another, and they found themselves talking about premature ejaculation. "Let me do you a favor," Gary said. They went to a drugstore that had a Thermofax machine. From his wallet, Gary pulled a slip of paper containing a list of herbs, in Chinese, and made Ronnie a copy. Ronnie found an herbalist in Chinatown who would fill the "prescription," a mixture of herbs and powders that he ground in a mortar and wrapped in improvised envelopes made of folded paper.

Wonder of wonders, the herbs, which smelled like ginger, formed a paste when moistened, and the paste slowed him down quite beautifully, kept him hard all night, fuck after fuck, cum after cum, fuck in the ass, fuck in the cunt, fuck America.

The time came when Marcia realized there was a limit to the number of hours a day she wanted to sit and watch Ronnie edit, even stoned, though he was sometimes willing to break into his schedule for a fuck on the floor, or a blowjob, at which she was artful.

Once a week Marcia visited her great-aunt Sarah in the Brooklyn Hebrew Home for the Aged, though the elderly little lady, with her flesh hanging off her arms, called Marcia "Linda" and thought she was a *landsman* from the old country who had worked in the sweatshop with her (but by Marcia's reckoning had been dead for twenty years). The place smelled like many layers of old soap. Marcia was kind to Sarah and usually walked out the door sobbing.

The city was noisy with opportunities. Marcia was often bewildered. She got in the habit of checking the weekly listings in the *Village Voice* and *Rat (Subterranean News)*, the New York underground paper started by a bunch of radicals from Austin. Third World coalitions were pushing for ethnic studies programs; defense committees formed for the Panther 21, who were charged with planning to kill cops and blow up buildings. There were women's liberation groups in several varieties; art gallery openings; anarchist and poetry gatherings; Puerto Rican and Chinatown groups; chapters of the National Welfare Rights Organization (which made her wonder whatever happened to Charlotte); campus and high school SDS chapters, and an at-large chapter for people like her who floated. There were meetings to pull together a post-student organization to be called MDS, Movement for a Democratic Society, as well as collectives of medical students, young lawyers, radical architects, city planners, teachers, social workers, journalists. Holy shit! Not to mention the study groups and collectives that produced comix, alternative textbooks on Vietnam and American history, puppet shows, pamphlets about lousy hospitals in the

Bronx, Hudson River pollution, and what to do if you got busted. She darted here, she darted there, hit-or-miss, more miss than hit, and nowhere did she find a place that, for her, felt right. Of her passion, and the intensification of the struggle, she had no doubt, but her own path forward was a blur.

It was only a matter of time before she made the right connection. At a Panther 21 defense meeting in the Village, she reconnected with Caroline Caldwell, the willowy girl from Texas with whom she had worked with Charlotte's web in Cleveland. Vague about what she was doing in New York, Caroline took Marcia to the Empire Diner on Tenth Avenue, a onetime elegant dining car turned greasy spoon whose name tickled them, where they gossiped about the movement, and celebrated how far they had come. Caroline bubbled about a rising faction of SDS called the Revolutionary Youth Movement. She couldn't wait to go to the SDS convention in June, to have it out with the Maoist-Stalinists who were trying to take over the organization. Marcia thought she would rather be tied down on a hill full of red ants than go to an SDS convention with all its organizational bullshit. Caroline was mildly shocked and teased her that she was unserious.

When spring showed up, lush and humid, blossoms arose on the trees, as if the universe were expressing a will to ripen, and Caroline said that this was what she believed about revolution as well, it was a process with a built-in dynamic, and for this reason, martial arts were in the air, and so Caroline invited Marcia to take aikido classes with her. Once a week they went to a dojo on Fourteenth Street, a second-story room decorated with iron flowers and Japanese paintings, accommodating a dozen students, where, on entering, they took off their shoes and put on loose-fitting white robes. Even though the aikido talk felt to her like gobbledygook, Marcia appreciated the need to learn self-defense techniques, and got a kick out of the Japanese lingo, especially because the instructor was a beautiful blue-eyed hunk named Jonathan, who (in an Appalachian accent, weirdly enough) spoke frequently of "son-keh," with an elongated second syllable, which meant respect. He spoke also, in English, of "the joy of movement" and "overcoming the will" and "meeting aggression with compassion," all of which, in Japanese, required many syllables, impossible to remember.

Marcia told Caroline she liked the sound of "the joy of movement" but was not so sure about "meeting aggression with compassion," since for her part she felt a lot of righteous aggression, which translated into "energy for the struggle," which she refused to give up. "Compassion" reminded her of admen gliding fecklessly around the city in mutton-chops and bell-bottoms, coming on to women on the street. Caroline responded that she felt the same way originally but was coming to understand that the way of aikido was to empty out your ego, to strive to do so, anyway, and that compassion for the enemy had nothing to do with surrender, though the Western mind had trouble differentiating the two. Marcia was inspired to write a ditty, which they sang to the tune of "Joe Hill":

> *I dreamed I saw Uncle Ho last night*
> *At a dojo in Soho*
> *He said, "Kick the ass of the ruling class"*
> *And I said, "Right on, let's go!"—*

Whereupon they broke into giggles.

"By the way," Caroline said, "I think Jonathan is paying special attention to the swing of your pony tail when you go through the movements."

Marcia, a mock-ravenous beast, roared.

Caroline welcomed Marcia into a study group which met weekly for pizza and beer in a ratty studio apartment on Sixth Avenue to read about Cuba, China, Algeria, and the decadence of capitalist culture. Twice they went to see *The Battle of Algiers* at an art film theater where, Marcia thought, a lot of the customers looked like they were taking notes for their own study groups—how to organize cells, how to plant bombs. Marcia invited Ronnie along for

The Battle of Algiers, but he'd already seen it twice. Other nights, six or eight of the study group stuck around, got stoned, and played nickel-dime poker. Callie Barnstable, a writer at *Newsweek*, hip and articulate, kept saying that they needed to talk about what kind of change made sense for America, not Algeria. She had been hired to tell *Newsweek*'s readers what "the kids" were thinking, what their music and clothes meant, and what new careers were opening up. At *Newsweek* she was considered a rising star, but she called it News Weak.

Their meetings moved to Callie's roomy West Village apartment. On the living room walls were Klee and de Kooning lithographs, and the SNCC poster that showed a Black man snapping his fingers while the word NOW magically appeared in his grasp. Callie's husband, an executive at a liberal foundation, attended one meeting, said nothing, and didn't return.

A French *gauchiste* with a round face took up Callie's suggestion to change their discussion focus. Oddly named Laurence, she wore granny glasses and had long-straight black hair and a ripe mouth; she favored low-cut white peasant blouses with little embroidered flowers, and pronounced the word *movement* as if it were French, *moov-mawn*. She wanted to talk about *les événements* of 1968, which she believed were more pertinent for America than China or Cuba, and she convinced the group to read a new book by Danny the Red—Daniel Cohn-Bendit—and his brother, called *Obsolete Communism: The Left-Wing Alternative*, though there was some grumbling that this book was, well, anti-Communist, which was a bad thing. The left-wing alternative was anarchism. Laurence was confident that, even after the Communist Party had sold out and Charles De Gaulle got reelected, "the struggle continued" and that "this revolution has showed that stupid Communism is a stinking corpse." The book did not arouse enthusiasm.

Anarchism was not on the group's agenda, though Jerry—a young, balding assistant professor of sociology with a vaguely German accent—maintained that the old industrial working class was dying and that what took place in France, and at Columbia, and the Democratic Convention, and was now spilling out into Italy and Germany, suggested that a new working class was emerging, its potential power resting on knowledge, and it was reaching its greatest crescendo (finger jab) in the Chinese Cultural Revolution, so that the preconditions for what he called "post-scarcity anarchism" now existed *for the first time in history*. If Marcia could follow his argument, what was emerging was a skipping of stages in the liberation of mankind from the twin evils of bureaucracy and labor because the collective intelligence of mankind, harnessed by capitalism, was crystallizing through automation, a development forecast in an unpublished volume by Karl Marx, the *Grundrisse*, only just now translated into English. Jerry proposed that they read excerpts from Marx's *Capital*, the whole three-volume set that could be purchased at Four Continents, the Soviet bookshop down near the Battery, for three dollars. Marx was "economistic," Laurence objected. But no, said Jerry, you had to read the *Economic and Philosophical Manuscripts of 1844* to see how simplistic that charge was. Laurence proposed that they read theorists of the new working class or the new middle class or the educated class, translated from the French. There was an extensive debate about which Marx to read.

Marcia tried to hold the theoretical distinctions in her mind but they flitted away, and she felt stupid. She confessed as much to Ronnie. He had spent a summer at the Sorbonne and occasionally leafed through *New Left Review*. He glanced at a couple of articles and said these guys were playing a theory game. You entered the game by stamping the world with your own terms. Your vocabulary was your calling card. The French were especially good at this. She urged Ronnie, not for the first time, to join the study group and bring it down to earth. He says he was too busy cutting his film, and forgive him, he was not interested in a circle jerk.

"Rome wasn't destroyed in a day," Marcia grinned and clicked her tongue.

On the first night of Passover, a cousin of Marcia's, several times removed, invited her to celebrate the seder with great-aunt Sarah at the Hebrew Home for the Aged, but Marcia couldn't see the point, since Sarah didn't know whether she was living in Brooklyn or trooping through the divided Red Sea or fleeing a Nazi death march in Poland. Anyway, the study group met the same night, and Marcia had her priorities straight.

That night, Caroline swore them to secrecy and distributed a draft of a long manifesto called "You Don't Need a Weatherman to Know Which Way the Wind Blows," written for the SDS convention in June and issued by a group called, no surprise, Weatherman. They passed the mimeographed text around and took turns reading aloud, like portions of the Haggadah, except that they had to share a single copy of the text, which read as if it had been composed by a million monkeys on typewriters.

… the main struggle going on in the world today is between US imperialism and the national liberation struggles against it … The goal is the destruction of US imperialism and the achievement of a classless world: world communism.

Caroline paused a beat. *This is funny. But also serious.* After some responsive giggles, she added: "And it's right on." Which she mostly meant.

Pot-luck dinner included a ceremonial breaking of bread dedicated to the defiance of all organized religion, and the opening of the door to permit Che to enter. Several points were disputed. Callie skimmed the manifesto, thinking: *This is crushingly stupid.* For years the movement had attracted her for its brains, but this thing was a hodgepodge of bristling and empty phrases. The touchstone was the magic word "struggle." The manifesto spoke of "opening up fronts." Though it frequently invoked "the people of the world," it read as though translated from a language that no one in the world had ever spoken. America was "the heartland of a worldwide monster" except for "the Black Proletarian Colony," which "because of their centralness to the system, economically and geo-militarily," could wage "a people's war for survival and national liberation" without any white help, even as fake revolutionaries were being bought off by "anti-internationalist concepts of 'student power' and 'workers control.'"

Callie couldn't take any more. Over a fourth or fifth glass of wine she burst out: "People, we've been reading it the wrong way. It's not a sequence. It's like a Burroughs cut-up, or the *I Ching*. You're supposed to read it at random."

Caroline's jaw dropped.

"Come on. It's fact-free. There are no human beings in it, except for the overstuffed American masses, and the 'pigs,' and 'the blacks,' who are 'anti-pig.' What does it mean to say that there's a 'protracted struggle around self-defense which becomes a material fighting force'? What is this about 'tying citywide motion back to community youth bases' pushing the 'highest level of consciousness' about 'imperialism, the black vanguard, the State and the need for armed struggle' and 'centralized leadership' and 'an integrated relationship with the active mass-based Movement,' and 'a "Marxist-Leninist" party.' I mean—"

"You don't think it has a certain ring?" Caroline chortled. "It's better if you're stoned."

The group ran out of gas. Callie dropped out. Laurence decided the important thing was *praxis*—which Marcia couldn't quite distinguish from *practice*, except that *praxis* sounded grander. So Laurence dropped out too, but for the purpose of starting her own collective, to be called "Art is Life." She had no trouble recruiting help—especially male—to produce a mock comic book whose full-color cover read:

AFTER LATE CAPITALISM!
LATER THAN YOU THINK!
YES, NOT A MINUTE TOO SOON;
COMIX WITH SUBTITLES!

At the bottom right-hand corner a white circle, like a sticker, read:

CAUTION: CONTAINS DANGEROUS
ANARCHO-SYNDICALIST VIEWS!

The inside pages consisted of Xeroxes of comic strips with the original speech balloons whited out and replaced. Bugs Bunny chomped on his carrot and said: "As long as the working class prostrates itself at the feet of the commodified pseudo-happiness industry, it only nibbles at the edges of the big capitalist cheese!" Elmer Fudd chimed in: "The expropriation of human creativity is the linch-pin of the imperial edifice of misplaced longing and bureaucratic cruelty the world over!" Dick Tracy said, "It's not the end of the world!" and Superman replied, "It's the beginning of the world!" Vietnamese peasants in conical hats fired artillery shells from anti-aircraft guns, which burst into balloons that read: "THE DEAD END OF THE BOURGEOIS IDEA OF ETERNITY!" and "THE DISPOSSESSED, FOR THE FIRST TIME IN HISTORY, TAKE POSSESSION OF THEIR LIVES!" and "THE POLITICS OF RUPTURE IS THE POLITICS OF RAPTURE." Each strip ended: "To be continued" or "This is a work in progress." The back cover was also in Day-Glo color and declared:

THE CONSUMER SOCIETY CONSUMES SOCIETY

Toward the end of Passover, FBI Director J. Edgar Hoover testified before the House Subcommittee on Appropriations Regarding Communist, Racial and Extremist Groups. His mouth, slightly crooked, was jammed shut for the cameras, even as muscles twitched around his jaw and his fleshy chin quivered. He clamped his jaw shut between sentences. He was the incarnation of head-quarters, the unconquerable chief of the Bureau that was the great love of his life in a nation that would never submit—a nation that scowled its way to freedom.

One study group member had a journalist friend in Washington who produced a copy of the Director's not-yet-published testimony. Hoover testified:

> *The New Left movement is a new specter haunting the Western World ... The basic objective of both New Left and old-line Communists and their adherents in our society is to completely destroy our form of government ... There can be no doubt that the New Left movement is a threat to established law and order ... Through it a comparative handful of revolutionaries have displayed total disregard for the rights and privileges of the overwhelming major-ity of millions of dedicated and responsible college students. It has impaired the successful and speedy prosecution of the Vietnam war effort; jeopardized the struggle for civil rights and increased animosity between blacks and whites; severely disrupted the normal processes of our academic system; and has served to advance Communist causes both national and international ... Through informants we have been able to penetrate the organizations at high levels, both locally and nationally. The services of these men and women in their informant capacity have also enabled us to continue our deep penetrations in the intelligence operations being con-ducted in this country by representatives of the Communist bloc particularly Russia, Cuba, and Red China.*

Marcia thought that Hoover looked like a monument to himself.

After Chicago, Kurt Barsky permitted himself to feel buoyant for a change. From Washington, he called Sally and asked if she'd like to help with his new project. She was deep into teaching and draft counseling in Ann Arbor, and she wasn't going to quit her job, but told Kurt in no uncertain terms that he should talk to Terry McKay.

Calling Terry was a good idea, so Kurt did that, invited him down to Washington to meet Congressman Zaretsky and talk about how to generate grass-roots pressure on key Congressmen to cut off war spending.

Terry listened. It sounded as though the days when he had found Kurt an unsteady flame were over. Terry dry-cleaned his college blazer and bought a new tie. They met in Zaretsky's office on Capitol Hill. High ceilings, echoes, ponderous statues, dusty dreams. Scenes of the crime. Scenes of what now.

Kurt briefed Terry: "Look, if we had a Congress full of Zaretskys, we wouldn't have gotten trapped in the crazy war in the first place." He briefed Zaretsky on how to appeal to Terry. The two of them had to learn to speak each other's language. This wasn't so hard after all. Zaretsky said to Terry, "Let's go down to the cafeteria and conspire, my friend," treated him to burgers, praised his civil rights and antiwar work, and urged him to lean on a couple of Ohio Congressmen in particular.

They agreed to talk again soon. Meanwhile, somebody came up with the idea of a national strike against the war, which sounded good; the word *strike* sounded like percussion and vigor, resistance crossed with strength, as in *strike three, strike while the iron is hot, strike, strike, strike!* But after trying it out with antiwar folks in Cleveland and Akron, Terry decided it was a bad idea, sounded too screechy-militant, too *thirties.* Then somebody popped up and said, what if we just had a day when people stop doing business as usual, stop it cold, and do *something* against the war—whatever suited them locally, something respectable, depending on where they were at, all on the same day. Do their things. Veterans and clergy in full regalia would lead parades, waving American flags. Organize teach-ins. Write letters to the editor. Meet with editorial boards. Pass out leaflets in the town square, or in front of the post office, or picket the draft board. Whatever worked, as long as it was nonviolent. One day in October, two in November, three in December—as long as it takes.

Moratorium, the finest five-syllable word in the English language. Kurt was enthused. "Great fucking idea. Should have thought of it in the first place."

"If we always thought of the right thing from the get-go,"Terry said, "the universe would explode from sheer joy."

Terry's gone lyrical in his old age, Kurt thought. They talked nuts and bolts—which Congressmen and religious leaders to pursue, even businessmen; which arguments to stress. Downplay atrocities and "the war is an imperialist crime," play up "we can't win" and "it's a failed strategy" and "our boys are dying for nothing."

Could it be, Kurt thought, *that after a lot of detours we're the future again?*

Ferocious rains blasted the soot out of the Manhattan air. Oxygen was reborn. Lungs expanded. Overcoats suitable for Siberia got stuffed into the back corners of closets. Miniskirts reappeared, like crocuses.

One afternoon in May, on Broadway, Marcia Stein, wearing shorts and sandals, ran into Terry McKay, overdressed in a jean jacket, across the street from Columbia University.

"Hey, Terry McKay. What are you doing here?"

There was a lilt in Terry's heart, seeing her. "Organizing the revisionist revolution,"he said. "Long time since Chicago." He wiggled his eyebrows, Groucho Marx style. In front of the huge, dingy, smoky, clamorous West End Bar, they grabbed at each other and headed inside.

"I like the revolution part. You'll have to tell me about the 'revisionist.'"

Terry had been traveling around the Midwest. He and his entourage were drawing good crowds in churches and synagogues, and in ladies' clubs, not just colleges. The newspapers didn't sneer so much anymore. Antiwar flyers showed up on telephone poles in suburban strip-malls, and downtown, and in the ghetto, and in the hospitals, and in buses and subways. Medical students, architects, teachers, historians, psychologists, ministers, rabbis, priests passed antiwar resolutions. Terry had never worked harder or drunk more. He was living the right life—a frenzy, one meeting after another, town after town, Cleveland to Akron, Akron to Youngstown to Pittsburgh, sleeping on couches when he wasn't getting laid. He got loaded. He slept less than ever, which assured him that he was doing something right. So did the scratchy noises on his phone line. He got the highway blues. He was a circuit-riding preacher of the movement, carrying a toothbrush in one pocket and condoms in another. It came to him to try writing song lyrics as he drove: *I'm a circuit-riding dandy,* to the tune of "Yankee Doodle Dandy." He tried rewriting lyrics from The Band:

> *I pulled into Columbus, I was feelin' about half past dead*
> *Just need some crash-pad where I can lay my head ...*
> *Hey, missy, can you tell me where a guy might find a bed?*
> *She just grinned and sucked my cock and "Sure" was all*
> *she said ...*

His blood turned to alcohol and coffee. Other people burned out, but Terry did not though he did smoke too much dope and drink too much Scotch. An elegant bronze water pipe allowed him to infuse the dope with the woody aroma of the whiskey. You could feel the wave.

No surprise, Nixon was unrelenting. So far. The war was not shutting down though Nixon succeeded in pushing it off the TV screens. Fewer corpses, fewer body bags. The air war was invisible—to Americans. The movement screamed the truth, choked on the truth. The truth got chewed apart by the entertainment machine. The truth was dust. But some truth filtered through. Members of Congress, including Republicans, were paying attention now. More patience, Terry, less bitterness. The time would come—might come—when Nixon would grit his teeth and, still lying, budge.

At the West End Bar, the jukebox sent out the delicate, psychedelic, and weirdly stirring tones of "A Whiter Shade of Pale." Terry and Marcia ordered beer and she tried to read his mind. Was he playing it cool? For all she knew, he still resented how she had gone off with Ronnie. He would never admit it. She was not sure whether he was not possessive or didn't care.

"I can't figure out their lyrics," Terry said, "but I love these guys. The universe loves them. They're incomprehensible."

The skin under his eyes was carrying extra weight—*not unattractively*, Marcia thought, *and since when was Terry McKay talking about the universe?*

"If the universe is capable of love," Terry snickered after skipping a beat. He and Marcia had understood each other when they were young in Ann Arbor, and they might still. Or might not.

He declined her offer of a cigarette. She lit up and blew smoke out of the corner of her mouth. "Procol Harum," she said. "What the hell does that mean?"

"We're supposed to know the meaning," Terry said. "And if some people don't, so much the worse for them. Sounds like the Weathermen's 'Fight the people' to me."

She glared at him, not without sympathy. "Terry, why are you playing these self-destructive games?"

"We've already played them. Now we're just naming them," Terry said.

She let it go. She didn't feel like picking a fight. "Terry, I worry about you."

"Meaning what? I'm great."

"Really?"

"Really. Surreally, superreally, really."

"I'll take your word for it."

The jukebox moved on to the sprung, disrupted rhythm of the Beach Boys' "Heroes and Villains," its melancholy downturns trying, and failing, to revive the spirits of the T-birded Beach Boys who'd come a long way from their surfboards. The song said there were heroes and villains but didn't say how to tell one from the other. And what was this "burning on Thursdays," this "working on turnstiles," this "sunny down snuff"? Terry shook his head. "Obscurity is the zeitgeist. The Marxist-Leninists get that."

"Uh-huh. I'll let you get away with that one." After a pause, she went on: "So what's your analysis?"

Terry stabbed the table with his forefinger to drum out each sentence. "Look, Marcia, our people get high taking over buildings. It's a gas. But America doesn't want to take over buildings. America wants to *live* in *nice* buildings. America wants jobs *building* them. America doesn't want to jam up the streets. America wants to drive through the streets. America roots for the cops. America went for Nixon. We have to smarten up. People are turning against the war and we have to—"

"They think that Nixon's *already* on his way out of Vietnam."

"We have to change their minds," he said.

Weak, Terry. You're tired of your own stale lines. "In the end, Terry, when push comes to shove, we have nothing to work with but our defiance." He had grown middle-aged before her eyes. Memories of the old Terry McKay came up—the one who was ready for "Jail, no bail," the one who heralded the interracial movement, the one who could talk the pants off every girl in the group, all that. *What happened to people?*

"The people I work with around the war—you remember Kurt Barsky?—"

She sure did. *Fussy. Intellectual. He always had it in him to become a suit. Terry's becoming a suit.*

Terry went on talking, pedantically. "—Americans don't want a revolution, they want to get out of Vietnam. They're not interested in people's war or armed struggle, or Che, or this crazy Weather thing coming down the pike. That's loony tunes."

She licked her lips and stared. "Terry, you've got the respect-ability blues."

There was wildness in her eyes—the wildness he fondly remembered from some pretty fancy fucking. She remembered when his favorite word was "urgency."

Terry had heard that Marcia was with Ronnie Silverberg. It made sense. *Ronnie's a romantic in love with an image—the revolution. He looks in the mirror and he sees the revolution. He's an actor who believes in his own act. Nice for him, to simplify his mind. Maybe because he's movie-star handsome. But it's one thing to sprinkle spike balls in traffic, it's something else to believe that urban guerrilla war is coming to phony-baloney Howard-Johnson-Brady-Bunch-Bonanza America."*

"I have to tell you, Terry, I think the Weather people are way right. More right than wrong. And they'll get better, give them time, they're learning. Remember the pig with commitment? Terry, I'm really, really sad to see you turn into an anti-Communist."

They'd failed each other's tests. "Come on, Marcia! What's got into you? The only line in their thing that makes sense is the title, which they didn't write. I can't tell you how sorry I am to hear you talk this way."

She licked her lips again. The beer she had drained agreed with her. "Terry, someday you're going to find yourself on the wrong side of the barricades." She found that she liked how much satisfaction it gave her to say that. She added: "It won't be a happy day."

"You want to know what I think? I think their slogan ought to be, *Crazy power to crazy people.*"

"Stop right there." *Terry's become a sour old man. Like his life is over. Like all our lives are over.* "You should drop acid, Terry."

Ronnie thought the Weatherman manifesto, though high-octane, didn't make a whole lot of sense; it must have been written on acid. But he did like the sound of the slogan, "Bring the war home." God, was he tired of street skits and papier-maché puppet shows! And surely it meant something that this Weatherman thing was attracting the foxiest, sexiest women, girls, whatever. Like Marcia, who'd had it up to *here* with namby-pamby liberal shit. She was not interested in cultivating a Ladies Garden Society against Imperialism, or hippies sticking flowers in gun-barrels, or a women's group debating whether Jacqueline Bouvier Kennedy Onassis was an oppressed woman. Enough! Marcia wanted to leap into the raging river and rage with it. Feeling real meant courting death. A death culture couldn't be consciousness-raised away.

Fired-up Caroline was planning to go to the SDS convention in Chicago, and Marcia was tempted. Ronnie thought all organizations were a drag, conventions were a drag—*anyone's* conventions—all procedure, muddle, and pretense. When something real went down on the streets, SDS would be the last to know. Maybe there'd be a revolution. Maybe there wouldn't be. The thing is, you couldn't live your life as if you could read the future. That was historical opportunism. The point was to live a revolutionary life. You had to live as if you were the revolution incarnate. You had to make a move, observe the enemy, and practice aikido moves. *I really love the way his mind goes,* Marcia thought. *So much more alive than Terry in his current incarnation.*

Weekends, they dropped acid. Sometimes she brought Caroline, who sometimes brought along her new boyfriend, from the study group, name of Chuck Tremaine, an acne-scarred bus driver who had put in time in the Air Force at a missile base in eastern Turkey. Chuck hadn't read much, but he was eager to learn. They read aloud from *The Teachings of Don Juan* and the comix coming out of the "Art is Life" collective. Mostly their trips were not "oh wow" sort of things, where you dug the weirdness of the universe, as much as speed-raps erupting into belly-laughs and roll-around sex on the mattress, the old-new in-out screaming fuck, the tongue-cunt, cunt-prick, *here, here,* and *yes.* This was the way to live. *The more I make love, the more I make revolution.* They loved that French slogan of May '68, even if the French kids had gone back to their bourgeois sleep since then. *La lutte continue! The more I make revolution, the more I want to make love.*

You can't kiss away a death culture, Ronnie thought. *Fuck death in the ass. We're going all the way.*

On June 22, the SDS convention in Chicago ended—or rather, two SDS conventions, the Weathermen (Caroline Caldwell with them) having bolted and declared themselves the real SDS.

The next morning, the cover of the *New York Daily News* shrieked, JUDY GARLAND DIES IN LONDON, and Marcia and Ronnie were invited to a wake at the loft of a homosexual poet friend, Eric Grossman, on the Lower East Side. A dozen people lay on their backs on a fraying Persian carpet, smoking strong dope and singing "Over the Rainbow." Eric was there in the ample flesh, sitting on a little round pillow in full lotus position, and intoning in his sepulchral and reverberant baritone, in short phrase-bursts, oddly precise in contrast to the bushiness of his beard: "O blessed queen Judy has left this planet—for a higher sphere—so it is just and proper that we gather in this lower sphere—honor her mightily—may she live forever—in the excellent heartbreak she has given to us—on this blasted earth, which cannot be conquered by Richard Nixon, demonic president of these United States—benighted states—which is burning babies—and the Cuyahoga River is also on fire—humanity is convulsed—so I must take leave of you—as soon as I take a leak—" and explaining nothing more, he abruptly headed to the bathroom and a few minutes later, wandered out of his own loft.

When the Stonewall riots broke out a few days later, Ronnie grabbed his camera and ran over to the West Village, where a wide-eyed Eric Grossman grabbed him by the shoulder and exulted, wide-eyed: "I was mistaken when I said that the spirit of Judy was gone. She's down here with us flaming mortals. Right here, right now."

"This is out of sight," Ronnie said. *Flaming faggots, they call themselves. Far out. Flatland is going up in smoke.* "These are the farthest-out faggots who ever lived," he told Marcia that night. "They're not scared."

"Dare to struggle, dare to win!" Marcia shouted, not ironically.

Is this what a new civilization looks like when it's scrambling out of the womb? Viet Cong, Don Juan, and the flaming faggots? Sounds like a rock band. Procol you! Ronnie sucked on a tightly-packed joint and said, "It's not the revolution of yesteryear, is it? Well, that's cool."

The word was: Start the world all over again! Leave all the corrupt and stupid institutions! Just walk away! Start counter-institutions! There were rural communes, urban communes, midwife collectives, free schools, free universities, open classrooms, free churches, food coops, dope coops, wicked comix, high school SDS chapters, GI newspapers, underground railroads, newly concocted psychedelic drugs, new therapies. There were factions. There were political prisoners. There were overdoses. Women were organizing "consciousness-raising groups." Puerto Ricans called themselves Young Lords. There was an insurgent Chinatown group called Yellow Peril. The world was on fast-forward. Ronnie couldn't figure out how to get everything into his movie.

Their culture was way ahead of politics. They were off to see *2001: A Space Odyssey* for a second or third time, preferably stoned, preferably lying on their backs in front of the seats and staring upward into the huge curved screen. Was it about the end of the decrepit world or the new one striving to be born? They were off to see Sam Peckinpah's movie *The Wild Bunch*. Ronnie looked up from reading a review and said, "It's about the death of the Old West. Just our style. We're about the death of the New West."

Blood spurted on the screen. Children killed scorpions with ants. Afterwards, Caroline said, "Yuck. Everyone's scum. Human life is worthless. I don't see how this is revolutionary."

"It's a Western," Chuck Tremaine said aimlessly.

"No," Ronnie declared, "it's the ultimate anti-Western."

Ronnie collected interviews with Sam Peckinpah and typed excerpts onto index cards, which he Scotch-taped above his editing table:

"I feel a wonderment in the face of violence. I believe that we, human beings, are awed by it. Ravished by it."

"I am neither for nor against violence. I think violence is ugly, but if we don't recognize violence, that we are violent people—we all are, every one of us standing around here—we're dead. We really and truly are."

"I am always criticized for putting violence in my films, but it seems that when I leave it out nobody bothers to see the picture."

Terry had not been paying attention to the Apollo 11 moon mission. He'd been on the road—Cleveland, Columbus, Cincinnati, Louisville, Indianapolis—meeting with local coalitions promoting the Moratorium, keeping up morale, speechmaking about the courage of the Vietnamese and their longtime struggle against invaders, and when necessary, stroking the outsized egos of protest leaders and trying to figure out how to get them to cool out their infighting. Clergymen delivered moral appeals while he stuck to facts. He was methodical. He stripped away White House propaganda lie by lie. Nixon was not phasing out the war when he said the war was being "Vietnamized" and announced the withdrawal of twenty-five thousand troops. The air war was more savage than ever.

He looked out as his audiences—the peasant blouses, the jackets and ties, the Episcopalian collars—and couldn't tell if he was rousing them or numbing them.

This could very well flop was a refrain he struggled to get out of his mind. Sometimes he feared that he was turning a white shade of pale.

Valerie Parr heard about his city-to-city caravan, and signed on. Thinking that her old welfare organizing networks might be reactivated against the war—after all, war spending was draining money away from the poor—she decided to base herself back in Cleveland. But she couldn't locate Charlotte. Nobody on the Near West Side was excited by the fiscal argument. She contented herself with putting together meetings of antiwar dissenters in the unions and churches.

July 20 found Terry in Cleveland, in a bad mood because, on the radio, he kept hearing that fatuous John Lennon-Yoko Ono song, "Give Peace a Chance." Valerie thought it would only help build the Moratorium, and Terry looked at her cockeyed, as though she'd gone mushy. Rather than argue with his mood, she convinced him to accompany her to a spacious bar and watch the moon landing, so they did. The whole place was jammed, buzzing, beery with joy, so they sat at the bar and ordered draft beers and watched Walter Cronkite go gleeful, and the barroom was flooded with whoops: "We did it!" "America!" "Victory!" As the TV panned across the exuberant faces of the short-haired white-shirted men in Houston, one of them wiped away a tear, and Valerie said that she couldn't believe she was saying this, but she was glad the short-haired guys in Houston had something to rejoice about, and she rejoiced too.

"I wonder what all those kids who pooh-poohed this program are saying now," Cronkite said, and Terry leaned over to Valerie and whispered: "Pooh! Pooh!"

She smiled, but as they walked to her apartment, she felt the joy drain away and the alienation and dread settle in. If they weren't careful, the barroom crowd would be throwing rocks at them soon. She remembered Matt's story of the guys who jumped him in Fort Collins. She missed Matt. She wondered how he was managing the U.S. Army. *It's OK to feel lonely,* she thought. *Loneliness I can live with.*

They stopped at a liquor store. Terry bought a small bottle of Rémy Martin. They went to her place. She placed two wineglasses on her desk, reached way back into a file drawer, brought out an envelope full of excellent grass, rolled two joints, and put *Sgt. Pepper* on the record player. They sat on the sofa and theorized about the songs: Was Harry the Horse heroin? Was it Kennedy who blew his mind out in a car? Terry was playful, as in the old days. She'd been too suspicious of him. She liked his chin—did he always have that dimple?—and his cockeyed smile. There were times when he got off the stage and looked right into her. Sometimes he was so damned little-boy vulnerable.

She remembered that once he was very good in bed.

He thought her face no longer agreed so well with her freckles, and she was too thin, but her legs were as long as ever.

His fingers went for her blouse and hers went for his shirt. They groped for places for fingers and hands, and found them.

Matt, forgive me. We didn't make any promises.

Then, cuddling on the couch, she suddenly stopped, thinking, *I don't want this.*

"No," she said. "No," louder.

She doesn't mean no, he thought. It was too late. He was inside her.

He's not as good as he used to be, she thought. He came very quickly. *We're too drunk.*

Maybe she's still with Matt, Terry thought. *Maybe she feels guilty. I don't have time for guilt.*

Afterwards, she said to herself, *I can't believe I put myself in this position. I'm bad.*

She would put this night out of her mind. It was a quickie. It was OK. Later they would not speak of it.

They were too busy with Moratorium organizing to go to Woodstock, though they thought about it for a second.

After running into Terry at the West End Bar, Marcia Stein lost interest in arguing with people who thought they had the luxury of stalling. Her blood was running with revolution. Though she had the good sense to skip the annoying internecine politics of the SDS convention (*Ronnie, you were so right*), Caroline kept her apprised of the Weathermen's doings. Toward the goal of "building a fighting force," they had called for "Four Days of Rage" in Chicago, starting October 8. They had declared that thousands of revolutionary kids would join them. They would "go wild in the streets." They would "do it in the road." They would fuck hard and fight hard. They were invincible. Marcia knew that "fight the people" was a crazy slogan, but there was nothing like the feeling of being "a crazy mother-fucker." She was getting her shit together. Aikido was her antidote to fear. Her parents had been paralyzed by fear, which was why they didn't try to leave Poland until too late. She wasn't afraid of her fear. Fear was her fuel. She wouldn't gripe and whimper about the cops and the ruling class. Vietnamese women—live like them.

So she jumped at the chance to go to Chicago with Caroline for the Days of Rage. By September, Ronnie was nearing a rough cut of his movie. It was so long, he toyed with the idea of bringing it out in two parts: "I. Rome Wasn't Destroyed" and "II. In a Day." He decided to steer clear of Chicago, since there was probably a warrant out for him for skipping out on his charges from 1968. But Marcia would serve nicely as an assistant director. Ronnie had taught her the rudiments of the camera. She could run with the Weathermen, and she could shoot, see what happened, hope that Ronnie would find room for her footage in his rough cut.

In Chicago, she and Caroline crashed near the SDS national office on Skid Row. They wore boots. They were part of a squad of righteous women who blitzed into a high school; barged into a classroom; locked the teachers out, or knocked them around, or both; rapped to the kids about the revolution that was happening all around them, and how the last would be first and the first would be last. They shouted "Jailbreak!" Afterwards, they felt serene. If they weren't already stoned, they got stoned. She taught aikido to an all-woman cell named for Harriet Tubman. She went to the beach, planted a Viet Cong flag in the sand, and dared the local toughs to fight. Revolution was a kick. Dare to struggle, dare to win.

Came October 8, in the evening chill, the wind gusted off Lake Michigan and Marcia was out and about with Ronnie's camera as two or three hundred Weathermen, fresh from a workout in an ai-kido studio, took the police by surprise in Lincoln Park, as if to redo August 1968 but this time the right way, as no-bullshit warriors. This time they chanted "Off the pigs!" like they meant it. They wore helmets, stomping boots, and goggles, they swung lead pipes and chains, they carried crowbars inside their coats. They dismantled park benches, built a bonfire, stormed along the Gold Coast in formation, arms linked, pausing to smash car windows—a Cadillac, a Jaguar, and because they felt like it, a Volkswagen. They were a motherfucking gang-bang of a gut-check.

The storm troops of white working-class youth did not show up, so fuck them for not being ready. *Even if we had a faulty analysis, we're ready. One who's ready is worth a hundred who aren't. Fuck a thousand pigs and a thousand second thoughts.*

The next morning Marcia was back in Lincoln Park with the camera, wearing a motorcycle helmet too small for her that gave her a headache. She was part of a "women's brigade," some seventy "cunt cadres" to use their term they preferred, intending to march on a draft board, but the police had learned a lesson and today outnumbered the crazies ten to one and penned them up. Caroline carried a wooden pole that she grabbed from a coat rack at the nearby church that served as a movement center, but an adroit cop twisted her arm behind her back so hard that she not only dropped the pole but dislocated her shoulder.

Back in New York, Ronnie would tell Marcia that the white working-class toughs strategy was seriously mistaken, but Marcia glowed in the clarity and euphoria. For all the damage the cops had done to them, it could have been much worse. Somewhere from among the multitudes of the aroused—from among all those who had more in them to give—who were willing to live with their fear, stare it down, melt it down, forge it into a weapon—the boldest would step up…not to plead with the good and decent to stop the war, not to whine, not to beg, but to *stop it themselves … ourselves … with our own bodies … by any means necessary.*

Their lovemaking, later, left bite marks. Ronnie Silverberg and Marcia Stein: avenging angels.

In the run-up to the first Moratorium, on October 15, Senate Minority Leader Hugh Scott of Pennsylvania said that "those people who want to demonstrate ought to demonstrate against Hanoi."

Possibly tongue in cheek, Scott and House Minority Leader Gerald Ford called for a sixty-day moratorium on criticism of Nixon's war policies.

The Moratorium was a grand success, revealing the Weatherman Days of Rage to be a marginal freak show. A thousand high schools saw protests. The Moratorium was front page everywhere, a middle-class jamboree of dignified protest. Walter Cronkite called it "historic in its scope." Antiwar sentiment mushroomed in Congress. Plainly the movement had reached takeoff. On November 3, Nixon, plainly worried, gave a speech saying he had "a plan for peace."

Valerie and Matt burbled, payphone to payphone, about press coverage, agendas, endorsements, amusing denunciations, and internal hassles.

"And did you hear?" Valerie said, psyched. "Paul Newman and Joanne Woodward said they're thinking of moving to Britain because America's in the grip of 'a certain kind of insanity'—that was their phrase—don't you just love it?"

"I'm crazy about it—"

"—a certain kind of insanity—"

"—certain, not uncertain—"

"I miss you, Val. Really miss you."

"Miss you too, Matt."

Two pauses overlapped and resulted in a lull. Matt cleared his throat: "But Val, listen, I need to tell you something. I have to go away for a couple or three weeks."

"Oh no!"

"Yeah—I've got to go incommunicado—for a while. Not long. I wish I didn't have to." Matt had edged his way up to a subject that he would rather have avoided, but could not. "Just something I have to do. I'll be back."

She paused. "Something going on in The Resistance, I take it."

"You know I can't talk about that."

"Or is this your shy way of telling me you have a new girlfriend?"

"Don't be ridiculous."

"Well, Mr. Stackhouse, I don't know what to say. This isn't like you."

"There's more. I have a proposition."

"This is getting weirder. But I have to say that I like it when you proposition me."

"That makes two of us. But here's the deal."

"What's the deal, Matt Stackhouse?"

"I want to talk about us. Beyond tomorrow and the day after tomorrow. You know."

She felt suddenly flushed and swallowed hard. "Oh that."

"Yeah, that." *But then why so somber, Mr. Stackhouse?*

"We haven't ever had that talk, I don't think."

"I thought we've been sort of having it without having it. Between the lines."

"Sort of," Matt said. "I guess. But here's the thing. We need to be in the same room to have that talk. I want it as much as you do. I have a time and a place in mind."

"A summit meeting." She couldn't shake her teasing tone. She didn't know why. "Shall we meet in a Paris café next door to the peace talks?"

"Vermont in mid-December."

"Did I hear you say Vermont?"

"I'm thinking of Ronnie Silverberg's place."

She was already thinking, *That works. I can go to my mother's in California for Thanksgiving first. Where, not for the first time, I will plunge into the absence of my beloved sister. How she would have loved the lives we're living.* She stared at her jade-and-platinum ring, and her aluminum one.

In the New York loft, Ronnie Silverberg was inspecting, arranging, rearranging, and re-inspecting scene outlines and shot sequences described in short phrases on thin stacks of index cards that he had tacked up onto his oversized bulletin board and Scotch-taped to the wall, for the excess had long since spilled over. Once in a while he took Polaroid shots of the wall, so he could reconstruct it, if necessary, after the next rearrangement. He clothes-pinned strips of developed film along a plastic-coated cord that ran the length of the loft. Rome had not yet been destroyed, but a finished product was heaving into sight. He was inches away from a complete rough cut—four hours long, but it was called a rough cut for a reason. The script needed to be revised for the n+1st time—the final time. He looked gaunt, feverish. He needed to get away.

As Marcia's commitment had snowballed, her life had been stripped to essentials. She ate, drank, smoked, and increasingly slept with Weather, or the Weathers, as she called them alternately, including Caroline. Weather and Ronnie, this was her life—over time, more Weather, less Ronnie. Her sister Rose, an architecture student, reserved a seat for her to get to the November 15 march, but at dinner their conversation about the war quickly flamed into a confrontation between "What the hell is wrong with you, you're so fucking bloodthirsty" (Rose) and "You are so bourgeois and fucked up" (Marcia). Rose and, for that matter, most of the people she had known over the last few years, were branches that needed pruning.

It was more or less cool with Ronnie that Marcia was immersing herself in the Weather maelstrom. If anything, his feeling for her was engorged. Perhaps because his parents' marriage had been so volatile and ugly, he was OK with smashing monogamy. Twinges of jealousy he could convert into work-energy. Marcia turned him on as much as ever. What was happening between them was folded into the mysterious pre-apocalypse that was happening all over. For the two of them, less frequent sex was fiercer sex. The way of the warrior was to dive way down to the deep current. To court astonishment. To work yourself into a white heat. To rise above yourself. To destroy the bourgeois ego. So he understood why, after the Days of Rage, Marcia needed to go off in her own direction. They were, and would remain, comrades. She moved to Detroit with a Weather collective.

Ronnie lived on Chinese takeout, multiple daily cups of espresso, peanut-raisin gorp, high-quality dope, and Gauloises, which he bought by the carton from a tobacco shop in the West Village. For recreation, he got stoned and watched bad movies, studying their pacing, how they linked scenes and dealt with marginal characters. Everywhere there was a lesson. In Marcia's absence, he was not in the mood to prowl around in search of substitute fuck-buddies. If they showed up, nice, but he strived for detachment. Time was limited.

He hired a half-time editor. A couple of friendly film pros visited, one of them a Frenchman known for his use of bleached-down color stock. The phone rarely rang; friends knew better than to intrude. Sometimes he answered every other call. Sometimes he didn't answer at all.

One afternoon it was Chuck Tremaine calling, the ex-Air Force guy Caroline had been hanging around with. Chuck wanted to know if Ronnie could put him in touch with her, or at least with Marcia, who would probably know where Caroline was. But Ronnie thought that if Caroline didn't want Chuck to know where she was, he was not going to help.

That evening, Matt Stackhouse called. It had been a long time—since last summer. He liked Matt.

Matt needed a favor.

"Shoot."

"Mmm, Ronnie, about your place in New England."

"Vermont, yeah."

"Vermont. Good. Ronnie, how would it be if I meet up there with Valerie for a couple of days in early December?" Matt forced himself to sound blasé, as if alert to a wiretap.

Well, fine. Matt was one of the best kind of movement people, the ones who take the initiative. He reminded Ronnie of himself a couple of steps behind. Ronnie didn't need to ask questions. "Sure." It occurred to him later that he was also expecting a visit from Marcia in early December, but that was cool: the cabin had two bedrooms; Marcia and Valerie were pals.

Matt's voice for a moment threw Ronnie back to Cleveland, when Valerie had walked out on Matt and Matt had crumpled. From then to now, warp speed, the calendar drunk on velocity.

Mansbridge, Vermont, December 1969

THE WIND DUMPED GREAT flurries of snow onto the firing range, which Ronnie had set up in an abandoned gravel pit a few minutes' walk downhill from the family cabin. He was pleased enough with his accuracy, all the more so because he had been firing into an erratic wind. Now he was bored from setting up bull's-eyes, and his right shoulder ached from his M14's recoil despite the padding he had stuffed under his army jacket. The snow was starting to stick, and his big toe had worn through his left sock. He'd call it a day.

His boots crunched into the icy skin that had formed over the snow, a satisfying sound punctuating the silence, as he trudged uphill, clutching used targets in his left hand, thinking about his movie and his distribution problems. His mind drifted over to some GIs he had met at Fort Hood, poor bastards, not old enough to vote, eyes glazed, some of them, who underwent basic training with M14s like his own (purchased from Army surplus) and watched propaganda films depicting a glutinous red tide sweeping across the globe. America offered up a never-ending supply of such young men, the eager, the walled-in, the credulous, the lost, the dutiful, and the ones who wanted to blow up the world. They heard horrendous stories about what happened over there, and the rage and trembling that came over the mildest of soldiers, and they understood they'd been swindled. They read the GI underground papers. They fought like imperial legions, but more and more of them, were realizing that there was more to life than a suburban house and a big-screen color TV to watch ball games. *This film will light fires.*

Nearing the cabin, Ronnie caught his breath, absorbed the silence, considered the evergreens that were the winter's saving grace, and gazed up at the great oak, which was starting to collect snow on its grand bare limbs, and he contemplated the ruins overhead of the ladder and the tree house—built for him by a local carpenter at the expense of an indulgent father who long ago wanted Ronnie to have a place of his own when he was away on business trips, which was frequently. From his platform on the oak Ronnie would look up from his sci-fi books, watch the chipmunks and squirrels scampering after acorns and the deer at twilight working their way through unprotected flower beds. Once, memorably, he was transfixed by the sight of a huge flat-faced barn owl standing motionless and soundless in a clearing in the moonlight. He watched, and in his mind's eye watched himself watching, and felt thankful that he was an only child who shared the world with all creatures and not just the one or two humans who happened to be at hand.

The tree house was now a dilapidated husk, a termite-infested shell of battered boards, sagging, fifteen feet off the ground, at the top of a ladder whose rungs had seen better days. Ronnie tripped out on the subject of decay. *Decay is the law of life. Rome burned out, America is burning out, and eventually, the sun will burn out. A lot of people are afraid of nature, the great maker of ruins. If you thought about it the wrong way, you could feel besieged out here. The Americans have dwindled into a plastic-wrapped people freaked out by mystery and wildness, by thunder and silence, the whole unboundedness that dwarfs you, reminds you that, whoever you are, or think you are, you're alone and redundant. This must be the origin of property. You look out at the universe, you feel tiny and temporary, so you take possession of things rather than wait for them to take possession of you. The next thing you know you're holding a deed and putting up NO TRESPASSING signs.*

Fight to carve out a living space in time, or start dying.

The first signs that he had company were the footprints—women's boots by the look of them—leading to the front door.

Through stick-like, sick-looking leafless trees, dangling his M14, muzzle down, Ronnie peered and saw a parked, blue Ford Falcon with Ohio plates. He poked the cabin door open.

Marcia, on a kitchen stool, her hair cut short in a shag and dyed reddish brown, turned toward him, holding *LIFE* magazine in her lap. Ronnie's copies of *The Teachings of Don Juan* and the *I Ching* were on the counter in front of her, along with a cup of coffee. She was patting her cheeks with a tissue.

"Hey, kiddo!"

"I decided to make myself at home," she said dully. A small green suitcase stood on the floor nearby.

"Very good," he said lightly, standing his rifle next to the door, muzzle down. Unable to read her expression, he approached, cupped her shoulder, said lightly, "Hi." She was pale and did not look happy to see him. There were tear lines down her cheeks.

"What's wrong?"

"You hear the news?"

He didn't like the sound of that.

"You mean the massacre, what's it called, My Lai? Here." He riffled through the magazine, found the photos of the bodies—in vivid color, heaped in a trench—and dropped the magazine back into her lap. "Check out the pull quotes."

She read aloud in a monotone: "The order was to destroy My Lai and everything in it," and turning the page: "You don't call them civilians—to us they were VC." "The orders were to shoot anything that moved." Ronnie had enclosed those words in a black felt-tip box.

"Sounds like *The Wild Bunch*, doesn't it?" he said.

She grabbed the magazine and hurled it against the wall. "Motherfuckers!" Then she looked at him crookedly. "Fred Hampton," she said.

"What about him?"

"They killed him last night. In his bed."

"What?!"

She was ashen. "The pigs stormed the Panther apartment, in Chicago, in the middle of the night. Fifteen pigs. I heard it on the radio. Dozens of bullet holes. A hundred, who the fuck knows. And another Panther named Mark Clark. Head of the Peoria branch."

"Christ! How old is Fred—*was* Fred?"

"Twenty-one."

"Fucking shit." He exhaled; inhaled; exhaled; arranged his face in a simulation of calm.

"Another dead Black kid," she said.

"The younger they are," he said, "the more extra credit the cops get when they off 'em." *We expected this. We expect worse.*

"Oh Ronnie." He embraced her, and she exploded into tears.

Could it be that this was the first time he'd ever seen her weep? She had raved about eloquent, vivid, brilliant, street-wise Fred, next-generation Fred whom the Panthers, under siege, were grooming for national leadership. No blind follower of Huey Newton or Eldridge Cleaver, he was a work in progress, went from supporting the Weathermen at the SDS convention in June to denouncing them in October, said the "Days of Rage" were "Custeristic"—a terrific term, Ronnie thought. *Follow us, people, as we lead you straight into an ambush*—and also "adventuristic," which sounded right. Adventure was the way of the warrior, but it had to be the right adventure at the right time, and if you were just in it for the rush, you were worthless. The Vietnamese weren't in it for the rush.

Weariness seized him, and his shoulder ached. Fortunately, he had laid a fire before going out to shoot. He lit a kitchen match against the stove and ignited a blaze, watched with satisfaction as the bunched-up newsprint caught and the twigs popped.

Later, staring into a fat green candle he had placed next to the bed, they were silent under the covers.

"He was so right on," she said grimly, "the Days of Rage *was* Custeristic. Marched right into a trap. Fucking idiots we were."

"Light me a cigarette, would you? My shoulder's fucked up."

She did, and put it to his lips.

"Thanks. Did you know him? Fred?"

"Yeah. He understood things we didn't. We're new to armed struggle. We were right about needing to toughen up but we went about it the wrong way." She was trying to sound resolute and almost, but not quite, succeeding. "He had beautiful long fingers."

With his left hand he stroked her hair but it felt odd, mutilated. They were now, themselves, almost strangers. The fire snapped and flourished. From the other side of the room they stared into the flames.

"Hey," he said, after a silence, "do me a favor and massage my chest near my armpit? Sore as hell." Wincing, he extended his left hand to the floor and picked up a green bottle. The label said "Omega Oil." She poured a dollop of the green glop onto the damage. He recoiled from the cold of it.

She worked the oil into his muscles with the power of her grief. "I can tell you've been getting in lots of practice."

"We're under siege," he said vaguely. Then: "We can shoot tomorrow. I have a private firing range."

Her jaw was set. "I don't need any more practice, Ronnie. I'm here only two nights. Caroline's meeting me here Saturday."

"What day is today?"

"Thursday. Oh Ronnie, this is hard and it's going to get harder."

"Mao was right. A revolution's not a tea party." His smile was no more than a flicker on his lips.

What really went on in Ronnie's head? At least with the Weathermen, everyone was naked, everyone faced the gut checks and the acid tests, all the shit came to the surface, every infant squall and night terror, every jagged sliver of the bourgeois self, no one held back. You were wide open.

The next morning, under three itchy blankets and an opened-out sleeping bag, they slept in until an engine sputtered outside. Snow crunched on the driveway. Marcia snapped upright. "It's a VW. Putrid green." She was wearing a granny-style flannel nightgown.

"Matt," Ronnie said. Pallid color patches had formed on the opposite wall where sunlight had climbed into the cabin through the burned-out, thinned-out hulks of candles on the window-sill.

Marcia shivered. She saw cobwebs in the corners of the ceiling. "Matt Stackhouse? No shit."

"No shit. He's meeting Valerie here. I thought that'd be all right with you."

"Sure," she said, slightly disconcerted. She didn't like surprises anymore. "We'll have us another regular little Cleveland reunion. What time is it?"

He glanced at his watch. "Quarter to eight."

"Too early."

In her nightgown, she padded into the bathroom as a knock came at the door and Ronnie, pulling on long johns, called, "Come ahead."

Matt, red-eyed, heavy-booted, stubbled, shorn of his mustache, looked haggard. He wore a puffy, faded blue jacket and jeans, and there was a toothpick stuck into the corner of his mouth, which he tucked into his pocket as Ronnie grabbed his own jeans and jacket where he had dumped them.

Ronnie got up, wrapped him in an embrace, and kissed him on the cheek. "It's really good to see you, man."

Matt's eyes were spectral and globular.

"Coffee?"

"Damn straight."

Ronnie prepared the drip, put water on to boil, and said: "So."

"So."

"So I have to say you look a little ragged,"

"I drove here straight from Montreal."

"No shit."

"No shit."

"Help me with the logs here, would you? We need to wake up the fire."

By the time Marcia appeared, the room was almost lukewarm and the coffee was hot. *Christ,* Marcia thought, *he's so gaunt now, he looks like Preacher Casey in* The Grapes of Wrath, *as depicted by El Greco.*

"So you don't know if there's a warrant out for you," Ronnie was saying.

Matt had lost none of his intensity. "I don't. A lawyer in Chicago told me he could get in touch with the U.S. Attorney, say he represents me, flatly ask them if there was an outstanding warrant, and they'd give him a straight answer. Said they have to tell you if there's a warrant."

"And?"

"I decided I'd rather not remind them that I exist. At all. So I don't know. Maybe I'm the eleventh most wanted."

"What was your big crime?" Marcia interpolated.

Matt turned his big sad eyes on her and coaxed a little smile to the surface.

"Sliced up my draft card, sent it back to them."

"Nice one," she said.

He appreciated the sentiment but was not sure whether she was condescending or not. "Right on." He said, "What about you, Ronnie?"

"What *about* me?"

"Your draft status."

"Funny thing. I'm 1-Y."

"What's that?"

"Temporary 4-F. Means my student deferment wore out but they never got around to upgrading me to 1-A. Somewhere they got the idea I wouldn't be much of a soldier, but they reserve the right to change their minds. Whenever they feel like it. But why Montreal? Can I guess?"

"It's a pretty good scene. A lot of resisters. You just drive in, easy in, easy out. Customs isn't paying attention. You tell them you're a tourist. They like that."

Ronnie got up to poke the fire and remembered that he had forgotten to clean his rifle the previous night, what with Marcia arriving and all the drama. "Excuse me," he called back over his shoulder, "I'm listening, just keep talking." He crossed the room, picked up a sheet of Masonite leaning against the wall, laid it down on the table, then picked up a metal box—like a fishing tackle box, but longer—from which he extricated a can of lubricant, a can of solvent, cleaning rods in various shapes and lengths, brushes, long Q-tips, and a bottle of cleaning alcohol. He laid everything out on the Masonite, confirmed that the chamber was empty, fit the cleaning rod into the barrel. "Go 'head, Matt," he said without looking up. "So tell us about our neighbor to the north."

"Sure." Was it Marcia's imagination or did Matt look squeamish?

"So there are a lot of Americans up there, it's not hard to make connections. Canadians help, they're pretty organized, they find you places to crash, temp work, stuff that pays cash, odd jobs, so forth, because you can't legally work until you get Canadian papers. Which is not supposed to be so hard. Even if there's a warrant out for you in the States, the Canadians don't care, they like being independent."

"Well, God bless 'em," Ronnie said dryly, "even if they did start out as Tories."

"Once you get papers—they call it landed immigrant status—you're good to work. You're a permanent resident."

"Far out," Ronnie said.

"I like that," Marcia said. "Landed immigrant. They give you forty acres and a mule?"

Matt smiled for the first time since he'd arrived. "Actually, doesn't mean homesteading, it just means you've already landed. One of those quaint Canadian customs."

Ronnie looked up from his rifle. "And what—?" He interrupted himself. "Ssh!" The churn of an engine was heard from the driveway.

Before the knock came, Matt was on his feet swinging the door open, enveloping Valerie.

"Looks like a house party," she said. "Mind if I join?"

"You look beyond great," Matt whispered. His arms were around her waist. His hands nestled in the small of her back. He had the strange sensation that she had grown taller. She filled the hole in his heart. His hands slid down.

"Oh, Matt, Jesus, I'm so glad." She thought: *He looks so terribly worn. Not defeated, but worn. He's not eating enough. He's not cut out for the life he's living.*

In the kitchen, a general hug-fest ensued, and then, as if at a signal, everyone migrated around the table and the atmosphere shifted. They were no longer a gathering of friends and lovers but a meeting. Ronnie waved toward a rickety-looking chair standing against the wall, and Valerie pulled it up to the table. "So—"

"I was just telling everyone about my visit to Montreal," Matt said.

Of course, Valerie thought. *It couldn't be more obvious that he wants me to go with him. That's what I'm doing here. It should have been obvious all along.* "It's so terrific to see all of you," she said, with a small brave smile.

Murmurs of agreement rolled around the table.

"Powerful," Marcia said, and waited. *Valerie, girl, take this where you want to take it.*

"So what's it like, Montreal?"

"Beautiful. Old. Here's what it's like. So one day, a couple of weeks ago, middle of the day, a clear day, I'm walking across the street and I look over to the other side and there's a big Mountie standing there at the end of a parking lot—Royal Canadian Mounted Police, right—broad-brim hat and all, and he's staring straight at me. He's singled me out. There's nobody else around. So I say to myself, Hold on, how did he spot me? You know, is there an American flag painted on my chest? Is it the way I walk? Should I run? That would be stupid. The guy is trim and he's all muscle. So I think, well, I've got a Canadian driver's license that the Montreal folks arranged for me. I'm not *really* worried about it, I'm Mr. Cool, what-me-worry, I'm just going on about my business—"

"Jesus Christ," Marcia burst out. "Were you freaked?"

"Freaked? At the thought that I was on my way into the arms of the FBI?" Matt guffawed.

Marcia was, for a moment, relieved that he still had a sense of humor.

"Actually, I wasn't as freaked as I expected to be. He didn't look aggressive. Noncommittal, like, 'I'm just here to enforce rules.' Not playing 'Come on, fuck with me,' like a Chicago cop. Or Cleveland. He's just standing there, all business. So I keep walking, like I'm just ambling along across this parking lot."

"But—"

"Matt, stop!" Valerie said.

"So I keep walking until I'm maybe ten, fifteen feet away, and he says very politely, 'Pardon me, sir.'"

"Sir," Ronnie said.

"Sir, yes. 'Pardon me, sir,' those are his exact words."

"Christ, what did you do?"

"I did the obvious. I got ready, 'Yes, officer?' In my head I went over my false ID—name, date, place of birth, mother's maiden name, all that. And I told myself to stay calm. At a moment like this, the interesting thing is that you can be calm."

Ronnie nodded. "So what did he say?"

"He looks at me, completely bland, and he says, 'You were jaywalking.'"

The whole table cackled.

"Holy Jesus."

"So he writes me out a warning and goes on his way."

When the cackling subsided, Matt thought: *Let's turn this whole thing into a comedy episode, even though what I'm talking about is ripping up my life. Well, why not? I'm going to be a refugee, God knows for how long. I'm drawing a razor-sharp line through my life. I'm already marooned in my own skin. I'm no longer here with these people though I love Valerie beyond reason. Everyone sympathizes. I'll miss Ronnie, I'll miss Marcia. But I'm far-gone already, this is no longer my scene, I have to cut myself off. Hello, America, and farewell, I came back to pass through. I'm a ghost in the shape of my body, going through the motions.*

He was on the brink of tears which a deep breath stifled.

Later, in the guest room, Matt's head lay in Valerie's lap as she stroked his hair, as if something might break, each of them thinking the other was the more nervous, though it was a close call. The thought of Matt in Canada made her think of herself in Mexico, except that her exile was voluntary and she had ended it when she felt like ending it. "It's a strange thing to live out of your car," Matt said "People are kind. I don't know. It's like here, but it's not. No direction known. But I can do this."

"Of course you can."

He perked up. "I like hearing people speak French, even though I barely know what anyone's saying. I like puzzling out the signs. I've always wanted to learn French."

"What else?"

His eyes lost focus. "OK, here's what it isn't like. I'm not a hero. There's nothing glamorous about it. Nobody showers me with petals or confetti. I'm a refugee, that's all. There are lots of us. Life goes on. Most people are polite. Some are just people. It's all right."

Their silences were wrapped around each other.

"Matt, am I here so you can say goodbye to all your nearest and dearest?"

"Val, am I too subtle? You know perfectly well what I want. I want you to come with me."

Well, of course, Valerie Parr. What did you think he wanted? "You want me to come with you."

"Of course I do."

His eyes softened. He reminded her of a deer startled to a standstill, head up. Make a sound and he'll bound away. She searched his eyes for clarification, but if ever clarification was to be found in the eyes of a loved one, depth to depth, there was none to be found in his. It occurred to her that a foraging deer is a hungry one. *Matt is ravenous. For her, for comfort, for solace. For comradeship in exile.* "You want me to answer right now."

"No. No. You need to think about it."

Lovers striding forward into the sunset ... Well, Canada had sunsets too. Why *not* Canada? Why *not* make a new start? Think about what Mexico did for her. She declared independence there, for real. In Mexico, she was free, not reactive. She dealt with things as they came up. She made her mistakes and she moved along. Which brought her, eventually, to this moment. "The work I'm doing is good work, Matt. We're getting somewhere in Washington. We're picking up decent Republicans who know Nixon is lying. We talk to Rotary Clubs, 4-H, you name it. We're reaching new people. It's a real movement."

"I know, I know." He spoke slowly. "It's wonderful work. It's exactly right."

"So—"

He wished he felt more confident about what he was going to say. "Val, the movement is big and it's global. It's got to be global. God, if there's one thing we've learned from these years of organizing, it's that there's no magic key to ending the war."

"But Matt, think about it. What would I do there?"

"So many useful things to do. Montreal, Toronto, Vancouver—final stations on the underground railroad. We've got a lot of friends up there, moving deserters around, and draft resisters, getting them papers. Some go to Europe. They all need support. You could find work that suits you—you, not the all-around, abstract, generic antiwar organizer, but you, Valerie Parr."

He's thought it through. He's resolved. But have I come all this way to join the women's auxiliary?

The two women walked, bundled up, hoods in place, aroused by the sting of the near-freezing air and the pine scents. The padding and crunching of their boots on the packed snow reassured them that the ways of the world went on, though the ways of their particular world were about to change radically. Valerie asked Marcia what she thought.

"Do you really love him?"

"Yes, I really love him."

"But what does that mean?"

"Well, I know what it doesn't mean." Valerie was no more enthusiastic about "pitter-pat" than before. "I don't want to be the tail that pins itself on the donkey."

They took their time strolling along the road, gazing at the hills as they went. But for the tracks of something that might have been a dog, or a coyote or a wolf, the snow, a couple of inches worth, was pristine. The wind had died down. The shadows were lengthening early. Mysteriously, a single bird, some kind of wren, appeared on the bare limb of a sugar maple and brought forth a half-hearted squeak.

"What's *he* doing here?" Marcia said. "Doesn't he know about winter migration?"

"Today's theme. Migration." Valerie's eyes were not laughing.

"You know, girl, I'm so impressed by how you take to adventure. I know it's crazy, but I used to try to dream up scenarios in which my parents left Poland in time ..." *But of course in that case, I, Marcia Stein as I am, as I turned out to be, would not have existed.*

Valerie cast her mind back to Kathryn, who used to talk this way about the Jews who failed to get it together to escape Europe. When she descended into her obsessive-depressive spiral she would talk about the million slaughtered children as if they had been *her* children. Or herself.

Valerie was silent. She thought about Fred Hampton, who never had the option of fleeing.

Marcia thought: *In novels and movies about the Jews of Europe, it's as if a gong sounds the definitive warnings and the smart or lucky or unimpeded ones sell their jewels or abandon everything, and line up their exit papers, or bribe somebody in the Gestapo, and clear out, while the unlucky ones, the gullible ones, the sick ones and crippled ones, and the optimists—another kind of cripple—don't hear the gong, and die the worst of deaths along with everyone they love. But there was no gong, no announcement: "Achtung! Tomorrow, precisely, is the day when it will be too late." Some people simply saw an inch further than others. That's all.* This might be the hundredth time, or the thousandth, that Marcia had rehearsed these scenarios in her mind.

"Do you remember telling me, before I left for Mexico, to expect the unexpected? And I did, and here I am again."

"So what do *you* think?"

Valerie stopped.

They looked at each other, perplexed.

"That is the question, isn't it? What *do* I think?" *We're strung together,* Valerie thought. *She's my sister, but it's my life we're talking about."*

They walked on in the overwhelming silence until Marcia came out with: "Ronnie's got a copy of the *I Ching.* You could always— you know—throw it." She burst out laughing, and Valerie laughed along, and here they were, on a road in Vermont, absurd sisters.

"Great. It'll say something like, 'Opportunity begins on the far side of an obstacle.'"

"So, would you like me to read your palm?" They came to a halt. Marcia took one of Valerie's mittened hands and turned the palm upward. "I have magic powers, you know. I can trace your lines with your mitten on."

"No thanks. I tried the palm thing in Mexico. A wrinkled old lady told me I was going to have eight children but I shouldn't worry, I was going to prosper."

An engine, or a tractor or snowplow, belched in the distance. "Let's keep walking," Valerie said, "I'm getting cold."

They walked on, and after another pause, Marcia said quietly: "I'm going away, too."

"Oh?" Eyes reconnected as they went on walking. "Why? You seem so—I don't know—at home in your life. Integrated."

"Really?" Marcia badly wanted to believe that she had it together, but needed Valerie to confirm it.

"You know," Valerie said, her voice dropping into an intimate register, "sometimes I used to think there was some obscure pain inside you, like a little animal in a cage, and once in a while it would, I don't know, squeak. You'd be rattled for no obvious reason. You'd told me about your family, so I thought I knew the reasons. I thought you were entitled. But you don't seem that way now."

"Well, thank you, that makes me feel good."

"You seem—I don't know, sure of yourself."

"It's true. I'm resolved."

"So why go away? Where?"

Marcia took Valerie by the hand and wheeled her around. "Everything I'm going to say now is between us, OK? *Strictly* between us."

"Sure."

"I don't know where. In a couple of weeks, Weather is going to hold its last public event. We call it a Wargasm. Then we're gone. Under. Away."

"Under."

"Don't ask me where. If I knew, I wouldn't tell you. Might be behind that tree. Or on a bus. Really."

"Christ. Is this really happening?"

"This is really happening. There's no other way."

"Deep breath." Valerie took one. "You know I'm the soul of discretion."

"And don't ask me what we'll be doing, because if I knew, I couldn't tell you that either."

Each of the two women was a surprise to the other. They clutched each other.

Is she flirting with me? Valerie wondered. Just as suddenly, Marcia let go, they separated and walked on, but when Valerie looked at Marcia, Marcia was already watching her.

"You know, Val, we're very different, but I trust you," Marcia said after a while. "There's stuff you could do with us."

"You're kidding, right?"

"Do I sound like I'm kidding?"

"No, but I'm not big on armed struggle, Marcia. You know that."

"I know. But there's other ways you could help. Liaison. Fundraising. Communications."

Valerie's eyes widened. "Are you telling me you want me to pass out communiqués for the revolution? 'Attention, world! The central committee has an announcement to make! The masses gather force for a general strike! That rattling sound you hear is the sound of the ruling class shaking in its boots. Stand by for further instructions.' That kind of thing?"

Marcia could have taken this as an insult but laughed anyway. She was not looking for gratuitous fights. "Not exactly, but—"

"Forget it, dear. It's not my bag."

"You know, as I don't have to tell you, there are going to be lots of ways to—contribute—"

"Thank you, but no."

They passed, on a hillside, a scatter of fallen logs, and as if at an unheard signal started to climb, heels in, toes out.

"You know, Val, so many things are coming unstuck—evolving—or revolving—It's breathtaking—I don't know—But—"

"Aren't you scared?"

"Am I scared? I'm *dizzy* scared."

"But you also sound—I don't know—excited."

"I'm *thrilled!*" Marcia paused. "So let me ask you a question. Have you ever been with a woman?"

She is flirting with me! "So, you're telling me you're going through some other changes?"

"Damn right I am. Opening up. This is my one and only life!"

"You mean, you're riffling through life like it's an encyclopedia, something new on every page?"

Valerie was always sort of bookish. "I don't think of it that way. I think of it like coming alive, landing on earth for the first time, like it's an unknown planet. But did you ever want to?"

"What?"

"Don't you want to see what it's like with another woman? It's so different—"

"Actually not. Marcia, *are* you coming on to me? You're so insistent—"

"No, not really. Just wondering." Marcia cast her eyes at the bare trees along the road. "It's more like, I'm coming to understand all the ways in which I was brought up—we were all brought up—I don't know, deformed. Under surveillance. It's not just brainwashing, it's worse. It's *crippling*. Parts of us were *amputated*. We were punished for coming alive, we were refused permission to be ourselves, it's like we were forced to grow up inside a box. Twisted, like bonsai trees. The lid came down. 'Welcome to life, we've prearranged it. Smile, date, fuck, give birth, cook, clean, smile more.'"

"You're reminding me what I fled. What we all fled."

"Then we felt guilty because we weren't doing it right. That's their game, to keep us delicate. Him Tarzan, you Jane. 'No, little Janey, that's not for you.' Well, that's over. Weather's only the beginning. We're the vanguard—"

"The vanguard of self-destruction."

"The vanguard of reconstruction. The question is not whether we're damaged. The question is what we're going to do about it." She paused. Valerie had the eerie feeling that Marcia was trying to recollect a catechism.

"We change the world, we change ourselves. We become new women. We love ourselves."

"So—what's it like?"

"Women with women? It's different. More tender. I don't know, sweeter. Men want to ram you, show you they've got the stuff. Women don't have to dominate."

"I get that. I do. But you tell me you don't want to be rammed? At least sometimes?"

Marcia grinned broadly. "Sure. But it's different in other ways. Hard to say—"

Eyes bored into eyes, grazed around, asked questions, searched inconclusively. "But you're not coming on to me."

"Not really."

"Let's leave it at that, then."

The snowfall was picking up, the chill scraped at their faces. They halted.

Marcia stared at Valerie head-on.

"What?"

"You know, Val, there's one thing I've been meaning to ask you for a long time. You're going to laugh. How come *you're* the one with a Jewish nose? Sort of."

"My mother, actually. But you know, we're all sisters under the skin."

They agreed that they were getting hungry.

Ronnie—crouching, poker in hand, stabbing at the fire, rearranging logs—was earnestly posing a question to Matt ("Where would we be without guilt?") just as Marcia pushed open the door.

"Huh?" Marcia stomped snow loose from her boots. Valerie followed behind her, thinking that Ronnie sometimes sounded like a Samuel Beckett monologue.

Matt sounded peevish. "I'm saying that your 'armed struggle' heightens panic and ratchets up guilt." He thought, *I sound as though I know what I'm talking about. Ronnie demands that kind of certitude. But I'm in over my head.*

"So? If you're privileged, you *ought* to feel guilty. The question is what you do with it. If I didn't feel guilty, I could spend the winter sailing around the Caribbean, or head back to law school, like a good Jewish boy. Let somebody else finish up the doc and let Rome destroy itself on its own merry way." It took Matt a moment to see that Ronnie was being sardonic.

"Ronnie, you're scaring me!" Marcia said. "I thought revolutionaries were guided by great feelings of love."

"You can't fit everything onto a single poster. At the risk of seeming ridiculous."

The abstractions irritated Valerie. Here she was facing a huge life-decision, which was also a love-decision in her one and only life, and the boys were swapping preachments and gags. *It's not a question of who's right or wrong, but why is this conversation worth having?* "I have a radical question, people. Can we resolve this over dinner? Or am I the only hungry one here?"

"You are not," said Ronnie, poking the logs apart, crushing the fire. "Further discussion awaits large pizzas. And—" He dug into his breast pocket, extricated a perfectly rolled joint, and waved it around. "Here's my contribution."

Valerie stayed Ronnie's hand as he reached for his matchbook. "If you'll permit me, comrades, I'd like to raise a toast, if you can do that with dope—"

She's avoiding me, Matt thought. *I'm going to lose her again.*

"To Chairman Fred," Marcia said gravely.

The room went silent. It was all too much. *Loss is our destiny. In Mexico, a year ago, they massacred hundreds of students. I don't believe in destiny.*

Ronnie lit the joint one-handed. When it rotated around to her, Valerie cleared her throat: "We'll miss the brother. Oh, we will." She sniffled. Her eyes filled. Wherever we end up, wherever we go—" a long look into Matt's dogged and hopeful eyes "—we're in this together, may we stay that way."

"*Wherever we go …*" *She's not coming to Canada. I'm on my own.*

One after the other, they inhaled, captured the smoke in their lungs, reluctantly let it go, tried to think of something to say.

Matt's gloom hung over them. Outside, in the chill, sleet poured down, and darkness began erasing the evergreens. They exhaled vapor trails into the overripe glow of the declining day on the way into Ronnie's VW bus, Ronnie at the wheel, Matt next to him— "It's like the old days," Ronnie said, "boys up front," but Matt was in no mood for banter—and Ronnie switched on the windshield wipers, craned over his shoulder, rested his right arm on the seat top, and backed carefully down the driveway, crunching on thin ice and for a split second sliding a few inches sideways until, after a scary moment, the brakes held. They came to a full stop at the bottom of the driveway. Onto the bare tree-trunks poured more of the dusky glow, the last reward of the day, as the sun flashed a brief reminder of its existence before the earth rolled away from the light. The defroster took its time. Ronnie grabbed a bandanna out of his back pocket, wiped off his side of the windshield, shifted into first and eased down the road. The engine rattled healthily. The snow tires hummed. As the glow dwindled, darkness became the world.

This group needs a pick-me-up, Marcia thought, and started to sing: "We all live in a yellow submarine—"

"A red VW bus—" Valerie interposed.

"... a red VW bus ..."

Matt did not feel like singing. *It was a long shot. We spent so much time apart, more apart than together, she got used to separation, and so did I. But hold on. This reluctance of hers, I might be overinterpreting it. I just sprang Canada on her. Give her some time. Don't rush her. It's a huge decision. Although she might have already guessed that this is why I wanted her to meet me here. Maybe started thinking about it before she got here. It doesn't matter. Look how long it took me to get the thought of Canada through my own head. Well, who was it who said that love is what abides when all the obvious reasons slide away? We weathered Cleveland and Wyatt, we weathered Mexico. Whatever this thing is between us, this charge, this reliable, electric quintessence of love, persists. Separation is nothing. We're knitted together.* He knew what wishfulness sounded like.

Valerie's hand was tender on the back of his neck. He touched, she touched. Touching, they waited.

The song faded. The engine rattled. Kuh-*slick*, kuh-*slick*, went the wipers. The wipers, the wetness, the engine, the snow tires. The passengers went silent.

The balancing rock of Utah. There is an equipoise that lasts, even as nothing lasts—which brought Gretchen back to mind. *You never can tell where you're going to run into a fine woman.*

Down the road Ronnie steered carefully, stoned-slow, through the sleet, from second to third gear and back, clicking the high beams on, passing a sign—curves ahead, with a little picture that showed a truck skidding. He slowed down, passed a concealed driveway, mindful of the 25 MPH speed limit, soon raised to 35, then down to 30, 25. *Come to think of it, every place has its proper speed, the world takes its time.*

They came to an intersection, Ronnie stopped, turned right, accelerated again. Off to the right side lay a long slab of a rock, striped with more or less parallel fissures tilted at fifteen or twenty degrees, running the whole length of the slab. Valerie traced the jagged platinum band in her jade ring. Ronnie thought: *Look at these stripes where the strata separate … The world and its discontinuities … Is this what the Marxists mean by the dialectic? The way continuities break apart? Quantity becomes quality? That's the natural world, like society, time goes in lurches, it doesn't inch along, it doesn't erode gracefully … Ruptures throw new species at you … That's how the world gets remade: in violence … Violence in the wild, and dynamite, the human contribution. Dynamite exposed these stripes to the open air. Violence makes beauty …*

Around a curve, the rock and the stripes ended, they'd come to the bottom of a hill, a smaller road interrupted, headlight beams crossed theirs—

Behind them, a swirling red light exploded in the rear-view mirror. Ronnie's reverie was mocked. High beams pulled up behind him. A jeer of bright light. Wide car. What looked like a shotgun mounted next to the driver. One cop, alone. Ahead, nothing visible but a sharp curve.

Ease onto the gravel shoulder, slow, *calm, calm,* stop. *Just a guy taking his friends out for pizza.* Gravel crunched. Wordlessly, Ronnie killed the engine. And remembered: "Holy shit, I left my wallet back at the cabin with my license." Turning to Matt: "Gimme yours, quick."

"Forget it. You can't pass for me."

The cop was walking toward them beaming his flashlight. "Too late to switch seats," Matt said. "Just play dumb."

"Fuck!"

Ronnie rolled down his window, felt the sting of the sleet against his cheek, left a few inches' gap, summoned his Flatland voice. "Problem, officer?"

"Evening. License and registration, please." Young, clean-shaven, steel-eyed, he scoured the front seat and the back.

"Sure." *Put on a show, feel around in your pockets, come up empty.* "Was I going too fast?"

"Your brake lights are out." Expressionless. A statement of summary fact.

"Really? Are you sure? That's strange."

"Oh yes, they're out."

"I guess it's not my day," Ronnie said, after rehearsing the line. "Can't seem to find my license. Must have left it back at my place."

"You live around here?"

"Sure do. In Mansbridge." He reached in front of Matt, opened the glove compartment, pulled out the registration, passed it through the slit in the window. The cop studied it as if he'd never seen one before. He looked at Ronnie, looked down at the registration as the sleet beaded up on the windshield, looked back at Ronnie, tucked the card into his glove, peered back into the car, said: "You'd better get out of the car."

"All of us?"

"All of you."

The cop stepped back. Ronnie and Matt opened their doors. Valerie slid the rear door open. Marcia got out. Valerie got out. Headlight beams came up behind them, another car, slowing— they were a roadside curiosity—then passed. The cop walked back to his car, where he picked up the radio transmitter. Everything happened slow-motion.

"Hang loose," Ronnie said. "This is bullshit."

"Fuck, it's cold," Marcia said.

"You all know me from Columbia," Matt said. "I'm a student, OK? The Canadians are very good at making ID."

Marcia said, "They don't have shit on us. It'll just be a stupid ticket."

"Brake lights, for Christ's sake," Valerie said.

Expect the unexpected.

"I feel like an idiot," Ronnie said.

"Forget it," Matt said.

The cop came back. "Let me see your draft cards, boys." Holding the registration, the cop turned to Ronnie. "This you? Silverberg?"

"That's me. My draft card's back with my license in Mansbridge. You're welcome to follow me back there. Stupid to leave my wallet and all my stuff. But it's not far."

"I know where Mansbridge is."

"My parents' place," Ronnie said in answer to a question no one had asked. "I spent a lot of time here when I was a kid."

"Uh-huh. And now, how do you make your living?"

"I make documentary films. Not much of a living, tell you the truth."

The cop, unamused, turned to Matt, who was already pulling his wallet out of his back pocket and extricating one card, then another, passing them to the cop, who inspected them with his flashlight. Ronnie tried but failed to see what name Matt was using.

"Henry Kennedy?" the cop wanted to know.

"That's right." Mildly.

"You're not related to—"

"Afraid not." Smiling.

"What's your address, Henry?"

"556 W. 112th St. New York. Manhattan."

The cop made a show of studying Matt's license, then turned to the second card. "Tell me, Henry, what do *you* do for a living?"

"I'm a student." Casual. *Don't sound arrogant. He's studying me like I'm an eye chart.*

"Oh? Where is it you go to school?"

"Columbia University."

"Oh, right, this says you're 2-S."

"Yeah, student deferment."

"Uh-huh." Then, after a pause: "So just out of curiosity, Henry, what do you think of those radical groups down there? Off the record."

Matt affected nonchalance. "Don't pay much attention, to tell you the truth. I'm too busy taking my classes." The cop considered this.

"What is it you study?"

"American literature."

"Uh-huh." The cop looked up at Valerie. "And you, ma'am?" She passed him her license. "Valerie Parr. What brings you here, Valerie."

"I'm a writer. Freelance. I've worked for *Newsweek* and the *L.A. Times*. I'm here to research an article about city people moving to Vermont."

"Oh yeah? I've been noticing that," the cop said, with interest and a hint of scorn.

"Sign of the times sort of thing," she says.

"Right," the cop says. "Some of these young men are said to be on their way to Canada."

"Yes, I keep hearing that, too," Valerie said.

"And you, ma'am?" He turned to Marcia. She passed him her license.

"Marcia Stein. You live on West 106th St., I see."

"103rd."

"Oh yeah, 103rd."

The cop gazed at them, one at a time, as if he'd surrounded them. "Empty your pockets, please. Open the sliding door, and put your things on the running board. You first," he said, gesturing toward Ronnie.

A bandanna, a rabbit's foot, a half-emptied box of roll-your-own smoking tobacco, cigarette papers, change, keys. The cop sorted through these objects as if he was panning for gold. He sniffed the tobacco and seemed satisfied. "You can have them back," the cop told Ronnie. "Now you. Henry."

Matt deposited a handkerchief, his wallet, and an unlabeled vial of pills.

"And these are yours?"

"They sure are. I have a pre-ulcerous condition."

"Uh-huh. You got a prescription for these?"

Matt smiled crookedly. "Tell you the truth, officer, I got them from a doctor who lives in my building—"

"The name of this doctor?"

"Eli Jacobs."

"Are you aware that the law frowns on carrying drugs without a prescription? How do I know this isn't LSD?"

"I think you can tell just by looking—These pills are stamped Pfizer. It's a big, legitimate company. They don't make LSD."

The cop stared at Matt without blinking, and said: "Oh, you know what LSD looks like."

"As you do, officer."

The cop nodded and said, "You wait right here." Holding the pills and Henry Kennedy's license and draft card, he walked back to his squad car.

"Goddamn fucking pills," Matt whispered.

"It's cool," Ronnie said.

"You know, they are what I said they are."

"Don't worry, man."

Valerie, more ruffled than Matt, squeezed his hand.

They waited. The interior light of the police car was on. Neither the cop's face nor his hands were visible. The police radio squawked indecipherably.

"Why is he taking so goddamn long?" Matt said.

"I think it's a good sign," Valerie said. "He's just writing a ticket."

Matt peered ahead, down the road, as the revolving red light ignited the tree trunks several yards into the woods. but beyond lay great swathes of darkness—no features, no distinct anything. The unknown. *Easy, baby. The Pfizer thing did the trick. He's fishing. He has nothing. He'll move on. He gets points for broken brake lights, he gets nothing for a phony drug bust. Calm. Think of the balancing rock.* The night wind of Vermont raged and stung. *I don't belong here. Stillness is stagnation, is surrender. Get going.*

Now, the four of them were transfixed by bright headlights that swept and swung wildly in their direction, around the curve, on the other side of the road, and brakes screeched, an engine roared toward them, and Matt thought, *He's distracted, I can dash across the road, plunge into the woods, free and clear, in a flash I'm invisible, and this cop won't follow me, he's not going to leave the others standing here, this is my chance,* so, sucking the frigid air into his lungs, Matt stole a look at Valerie, squeezed her hand, caught the reflected light of the oncoming car in her eyes, and nodded, *there's time, I can do this,* and sprinted onto the pavement, the woods were *right over there,* but the oncoming car, a big car, a full lane wide, was skidding out of control, one of its front wheels sliding off the slickened road, its rear end swinging around, *coming at me, he doesn't see me, or can't stop, it doesn't—*

His last thoughts were—*Free. Finally. No.*

Afterwards

THE NEXT DAY ARRIVED dry, subzero-crisp, emptied of everything but grief. Brutal sunlight glared off the crust of hardened snow. The survivors staggered around, stunned, striving to comfort each other—for a long time wordlessly.

Valerie located a phone number for Matt's parents, wrote it down for the police, and retreated into the cabin's back bedroom, unable to speak.

When Caroline Caldwell and Chuck Tremaine pulled up in an old blue Volvo, Ronnie had gone out walking, so they were greeted by Marcia, her face puffy with grief. Caroline cried out, "What a waste!"

It was her suggestion that they light all the candles, the thick ones and the thin, fix them on small plates, and set them up all over the wood stove and the floor. Deposits of wax in a hodge-podge of colors muted the incoming sprays of light. Eventually they told stories about Matt, spoke of his "innocence" and "intelligence" and "shyness" and "resilience," and his love of the land, and his fascination with the Apostles, which none of them but Valerie had known about, though they disagreed about how seriously to take it, or even about how seriously *he* took it. Only Valerie knew that Matt Sr. was a Baptist minister and a one-legged veteran. Marcia spoke about Matt's guffaws of delight, the sheer mention of which elicited sobs. Ronnie came back from his walk and said morosely, "I never thought of Matt as having parents." Wrapped in an army blanket, Valerie said on the floor, cross-legged, trembling. The stories petered out.

The next morning, Caroline and Chuck drove off to buy dynamite, fuses, blasting caps, and roofing nails at a nearby construction supply store, and, without telling Ronnie, buried it on his property, in a waterproof wooden cabinet sealed inside an abandoned refrigerator. The stuff was still there, in a corner of the gravel pit, when, after a townhouse on W. 11th St. in New York blew up from a poorly constructed dynamite bomb on March 6, 1970, Chuck led an FBI search party to the premises. Ronnie claimed to know nothing about any dynamite, and no evidence could be found to connect him to it. No charges were filed against him.

On leaving Mansbridge, Marcia intended to join the W. 11th Street townhouse collective. As previously arranged, she arrived there on the evening of March 5. When she found out, early the next morning, that the plan was to assemble dynamite bombs studded with nails to plant at a noncommissioned officers' dance at Fort Dix, New Jersey, to inflict maximum possible damage on dancing human beings, she was incredulous, and shouted, "This is nuts, you motherfuckers! These officers have dates!" She swore to keep the secret and stormed out. No one in the townhouse could figure out what to do with her besides let her go. She hitched to the West Coast, changed her name, joined a commune in northern Oregon, made a living growing marijuana and running a nonhierarchical school, became a Buddhist, and raised three children. One of her grandchildren became a stalwart in Occupy Wall Street.

What was not known in 1970 was that on March 6, the day the townhouse went up in smoke, a Weather Underground collective in Detroit had planted two time bombs of their own. One, consisting of nine sticks of dynamite, was placed in an alley between the headquarters of the Detroit Police Officers' Association and a popular restaurant, where it was uncovered in the nick of time by the Detroit Police and the FBI. The second bomb, consisting of thirty-five sticks of dynamite, was discovered midmorning at the 13th Precinct, just about the time that the townhouse exploded in Greenwich Village.

Had the townhouse bomb and the two Detroit bombs gone off as planned, hundreds of people would likely have died.

The FBI's Assistant Director for Domestic Intelligence, William Sullivan, wrote to Director Hoover in March that the Weather Underground was "a menace of national proportions." This was the same Sullivan who in 1963, two days after Martin Luther King Jr. delivered his "I have a dream" speech in front of the Lincoln Memorial, called King "the most dangerous Negro of the future in this Nation from the standpoint of Communism, the Negro, and national security," and soon thereafter, as King was about to receive the Nobel Peace Prize, sent a package of telephone wiretaps to King's house, purporting to contain evidence of his "sexual orgies," calling King "a colossal fraud ... a dissolute, abnormal moral imbecile ... an evil, abnormal beast," and suggesting that the only way to prevent this information from being "bared to the nation" would be to kill himself.

Had the Weather Underground's three bombs gone off as planned on March 6, 1970, President Nixon would surely have declared a national emergency. The FBI was dragging its feet, since many of its agents were loath to abandon ordinary crimefighting in favor of a political crackdown. Still, later that year, high FBI officials proposed to Director Hoover that preparations be made to place some eleven thousand radicals in internment camps. There was, the memo said, "a state of national emergency." Hoover agreed, saying: "I cannot overemphasize the importance of these cases," and ordered the reopening of the concentration camps—in Arizona, Arkansas, California, Colorado, Idaho, Utah, and Wyoming—that had between 1942 and 1946 held almost 120,000 Japanese-American citizens. The emergency was grave enough, Hoover said, that it was necessary to suspend habeas corpus and intern eleven thousand radicals who had been under scrutiny for years, a list known to the FBI as "the Security Index."

Terry McKay, Kurt Barsky, Marcia Stein, Valerie Parr, Caroline Caldwell, Melissa Howard, and Ronnie Silverberg were among those listed in the Security Index.

The Vietnam war withered away. In 1975, after eastern Cambodia had been ravaged by an American bombing campaign directed by Richard Nixon and Henry Kissinger, the Khmer Rouge took over the country. Obsessed by a purist dream of creating a brand new society on the fresh bones of the old, they put to death some 1.7 million Cambodians, stopping only when, in 1979, the Vietnamese army invaded and drove them out of power.

Valerie Parr learned Khmer and helped start a school for orphans outside Phnom Penh, which later expanded to take in children whose parents were still alive. The children believed in ghosts but taught her to remain calm when ghosts invaded her house. She had the support of her stepfather, who resigned from the State Department in protest over the U.S. policy of supporting the Khmer Rouge's claim to be the legitimate government of Cambodia. In 1980, she moved back to California, had two children of her own, became a lesbian, and worked for human rights organizations, mostly in reconstruction projects in Guatemala and Nicaragua. Over the years she tried to write a memoir but, unable to get very far, abandoned it in favor of a museum installation composed of sketches, photos, watercolors, and lithographs, dedicated to the memory of her late sister Kathryn and to Matt Stackhouse, Jr.

Melissa Howard settled in Seattle, became a community organizer, had a child, married a former Black Panther leader who, having been acquitted of felony charges in the murder of a police officer, began to empty whole bottles of Wild Turkey daily, and beat her. After divorcing him, she won election in 1983 to the first of twelve successive terms on the City Council, where she became a leading proponent of affordable housing. "There's more to America than Ronald Reagan," she liked to say, "and there's more to Seattle than rain." She joined the Baha'i Faith, whose premise was the unity of mankind. When asked why she had made this decision, she liked to say: "I got my Christian, I got my Jewish, my Muslim, all together under one roof. One-stop shopping!"

She supported school busing for racial integration, and more funds for special education, having been spurred by the system's failure to do right by her dyslexic son. Later, she won some conservative support by backing green building codes, tax incentives for crowd-sourced development projects, and alternatives to incarceration.

When the war was over, Terry McKay remained in Washington, D.C., working with a religious coalition to establish normal diplomatic relations with Vietnam and deliver reconstruction aid. He stopped drinking and ran marathons. In 1981, he started teaching political science part-time, in Colorado. He joined a local campaign to create a municipal market where local farmers could sell food directly to customers. As a result, he was accused of Hanoi-style socialism. He made an unsuccessful run for the city council and another for Congress. He worked in national campaigns against American intervention. His speaking tours were not very well attended.

When he lectured in Seattle, Melissa Howard showed up. She was struck by his composure on the platform. It was hard to say which of them was happier to see the other. Talking afterward, over hot chocolate, she thought of their last meeting, in Greenwood, when their fondness for each other had been evident but Bobby Hicks had gotten in their way.

She asked him, "What do you see when you see me?"

"I see the beautiful woman who saved my ass from Bobby Hicks."

"Not the beautiful *Black* woman?"

"I see the smarty-pants who gets a kick out of messing with my mind."

They married, and adopted a Vietnamese orphan.

Ronnie Silverberg's "Rome Wasn't Destroyed in a Day" was a success on the international film festival circuit. He went on to make films about the successful revolution in Angola and the unsuccessful revolution in Portugal. Years and many films later, he told an interviewer: "Everything I do is a sequel to 'Rome.'" He moved to Paris, where retrospectives of his films frequently played at art houses.

After serving a year in prison, Carolyn Caldwell was released on parole, taught women's studies courses, and struggled with the question of what feminists should do for women who live in Muslim countries.

After a series of failed business ventures, Chuck Tremaine became a regular on the right-wing speaking circuit, warning first against the McGovern forces who had taken over the Democratic Party and later against left-wing professors who had taken over the campuses. In the early nineties he ran across Wyatt Burns, who had become a private investigator, was well on his way to becoming a full-blown alcoholic, and would die of cirrhosis of the liver.

After 1969, Malcolm X came down off walls, as did Che Guevara, and Huey Newton on his wicker throne, and Eldridge Cleaver wearing shades. A wide photo of a little girl on the beach went up, gazing out at the waves; the words saying: "This is the first day of the rest of your life."

The time came when children asked: *Who was Malcolm the Tenth? Who was "Chee"? Is it true Paul McCartney was in a band before Wings?*

As for Kurt Barsky, having served his multiyear sentence in the Nation's Capital—first as a speechwriter for the good and the great, next as a legislative assistant and "policy analyst," and finally as a lobbyist for nongovernmental angels, or NGA's as he liked to call them—he passed through the age of self-satisfaction through the age of regret to the age of rumination. The country was mired in Ronald Reagan's dream world. Joe Zaretsky had a serious heart attack and retired. Kurt's labors in behalf of increasingly irrelevant members of Congress felt stale. His causes were gasping for breath. Stopping the worst outcomes so that the next-to-worst outcomes might hang on by their fingernails was meritorious but held dwindling charms.

He started scribbling on evenings and weekends, and before long, realized that the lore he had picked up around town made for a genre—government noir. It was fun to satirize the obnoxious, the climbers, the naïve, the bullies and bullshit artists. Washington offered plenty of material.

His first endeavor, published under a pseudonym, concerned a closeted neo-conservative who cultivated the fine art of backstabbing until outed by a vengeful ex-CIA agent who had an affair with him in Saigon while also sleeping with a Viet Cong infiltrator. Commercially, the book was a flop, but it was recognized here and there as having a certain "flair," despite—or because of—its ridiculous premise. It brought him a contract for number two, which concerned a onetime pacifist turned Pentagon hotshot who apparently committed suicide after leaking classified documents. To his astonishment, this one, whose plot seemed clunky as hell, sold rather well, and the third—involving a bisexual Chinese double agent seeking asylum in Washington—did even better. He had the pleasure of seeing his paperbacks show up on the Metro and in Capitol Hill lunchrooms.

But as his proficiency grew, his formulas wore thin, like coins gripped too tightly and too long. A couple of reviewers called him on it. He had edged past sixty-five, an age which, while no longer an automatic sign of impending mortality, put him in mind that he might have reached the point where he should find new material and stop repeating himself. Casually he made notes and discarded them.

He married, produced progeny, divorced. He read Kierkegaard and Kant for pleasure. His older son was a hedge-fund tycoon, his younger a conceptual artist. They could take care of themselves. He had no pension but with the help of his son he had invested well. He was cushioned with a rent-stabilized apartment near his father's old glove factory in Tribeca, a neighborhood that did not exist when he was growing up. Medicare was satisfactory. He was in reasonably good health and found that the costs of waking up to an otherwise empty bed were outweighed by the benefits. He could afford to coast. He could take his time—take the bus, for example, instead of the subway.

Eventually it dawned on him that his material was hiding in plain sight. He detested the word "legacy," which made him think of overpriced antiques. But OK, a legacy. The longer he waited, the more difficult it would be to get a handle on Terry, Matt, Valerie, Ronnie, Melissa, Sally, and the rest. There was more past to contend with all the time. Trying to reconstruct the world of the sixties was not like sorting old photos into an album. It was more like excavating and shoring up a Roman ruin. Excavation changed the site. Archaeologists debated the meaning of this unavoidable truth. His mind kept drifting back to what he and the others did and didn't do.

He kept up with the obits and started a new section of his notebook called *Who were we? And what the hell was that?* He made notes:

Who were we? What did we amount to? We? They? A passion play, a conceit, a reality show, a shared hallucination, a festival of performance art where the audience, wearing masks, weaves through the rooms of an old hotel watching obscure events take place amid nostalgia-inducing props? An evanescent fringe? Lives and connections were fitful, ridiculous, obscure, unsteady; the rhythms uncanny, ethereal—electronic blurs, like "Sgt. Pepper," ephemeral, incomprehensible, and right.

You come to measure time in births, marriages, divorces, miscarriages, graduate degrees, comings out, conversions, elections, marathons, half-marathons, bicycle trips, elliptical machines, breakups, breakdowns, grandchildren, hip replacements, heart attacks, cancers, nursing homes, and funerals.

We were center stage. It wasn't pure bravado to think so. The bravado came in thinking that we were *the* hinge of history, the pivot point. How grandiose to think that there's such a thing as *the* hinge, *the* pivot! History is full of pivots and hinges, and if there is anything to learn from even a cursory glance at the past, it is that more pivots and hinges are on their way.

Our lives were entwined. It was as if a consciousness emerged from us and hovered, a sort of collective emanation, a spirit floating around our bodies and more than the sum of them. We embraced it, we were embraced by it, we carved out roles in it, we rebelled against those roles. We were a family; we weren't a family; we were a false family; we aren't a family anymore. We had wild ideas about making the world more decent, and crazy ideas that blew up in our faces. They, we, succeeded; they, we, failed. Who keeps the books? We were decent, we tried. Organisms wear out; so do civilizations; so do movements. Later, no surprise, when the stampede was over, and the pressure was off, we diverged.

And now look what's happened. Everything remains to be done.

One day a woman of a certain age—Kurt's age—*zaftig*, with rounded features, loose white hair spilling out from under a bright red tam o'shanter, walked carefully onto the bus. She glanced down the aisle, sat down across from him, smiled the smile of a friendly stranger, looked away, swiveled, stared, and said: "Kurt?"

She had seen his photo on book jackets. He was no longer completely astonished to be recognized in public, and he couldn't deny that the experience was mildly pleasurable. But this was different. In her face, as if within dotted lines, he saw the outline of her younger face.

They were wide-eyed.

This *was* Sally Barnes, whom he loved when they were young together, and who might have loved him.

On her ring finger, she wore a turquoise stone with rounded corners, set in a gaudy silver enclosure. It didn't look like a wedding ring. They kissed cheeks discreetly.

They went out for coffee.

It occurred to him that more years had passed since he and Sally first met than had passed between the Civil War and World War I.

"Are you still teaching?"

"I left the public system, too grueling. I tried a private school. That was too much for me. So I moved to L.A. and retired."

He remembered that she became a teacher because she wanted to—with air-quotes—"make a difference," teaching useful skills to actual kids. But the system had burned her out. Married twice, gave birth twice, divorced twice, raised two daughters, both also divorced, both in California, one in Silicon Valley, the other designing fashions in L.A.

They played the game of Whatever-Happened-To. "Have you heard that Terry McKay passed?" she said. "Had a massive heart attack."

He had not heard. *Terry McKay, silver-tongued devil; captivating; audacious; convinced—often for good reason—that he was indispensable, that minute to minute he knew what needed doing and, if that failed, knew with equal assurance what needed doing next. Terry whose approval you craved even when he didn't seem to care much about yours. All the good he did.*

Kurt thought about how many people he didn't particularly feel like seeing at a memorial service—the dull, thickened, unrecognizable ones, the walking wounded, the ones he had slept with, the ones he had wanted to sleep with, the ones he couldn't remember whether he had slept with or not. He did not want to listen to pompous speeches striving for eloquence, or self-congratulations disguised as tributes. He had never signed up for Veterans of Domestic Wars. "So what brings you to New York?" he asked Sally.

"Well. You won't be surprised to learn that it's Emily Dickinson and Whitman. There's a joint exhibition on at the Morgan Library, lots of originals, also variations. They set them up A-B-A-B, so they can be 'in conversation with each other.' I'm making my second visit. Would you like to come along?"

At the Morgan Library, she pointed and whispered:

"After great pain, a formal feeling comes—
The Nerves sit ceremonious, like Tombs—'"

"Then some of her lines I don't begin to understand," Sally said, "so I'll skip to this:

"A Quartz contentment, like a Stone—
This is the hour of Lead.'"

"Jesus," said Kurt.

"She wrote it," Sally said, "in the middle of the Civil War." And get this at the end: '... then the letting go.'"

"Are we letting go?"

"We're not letting go."

One thing led to another. For some months after the bus en-counter—"meeting cute," they would call it at first, and later, their "summit meeting"—they talked about the book Kurt wanted to write, was trying and failing to write. They remembered people and encounters long forgotten. They talked about how the novelists, the pundits, the movie directors and textbook writers—not to mention their own offspring—got so much wrong about the sixties. They talked about all the texture that was missing from all the attempts—the wild, half-believable ideas, the family fights, the little and big betrayals, the freedoms, the back rooms where the scenarios were scripted, the intermissions when the actors threw away the scripts. They talked about their illusions that the world was new, and their late realizations they had only been new in the world. They talked about how chance had brought them together, and illusion, and possibly something more than chance or illusion. They marveled at the onetime luminosity of the skein they had composed. They talked about the weirdness of it, and how they recovered, and about the history they would never recover from.

One morning Kurt woke up early and found on his desk a few sheets of legal-size yellow paper headed: "Kurt: A few thoughts." He sipped coffee and read:

The past is vapor—No sooner have you caught sight of it than it blurs—You're not sure you saw what you saw—But it's still streaming—with a soundtrack—You have to know where to look—under the outfits—under the hairdos—under the oldies—We breathe the residues—They coat us—Sometimes encrust us—thicken our minds—clog us—What memory thinks it remembers is a memory being rewritten as it disbands—Each crust of what we call the past dissolves as more past builds up over it—The past is buried—crumbles—decomposes—degenerates into soil—regenerates—does not go to waste—

Beneath the chords of our music, the music we play and that plays us, sounds the continuo—the bass note that doesn't pause—the rumble that's always on the verge of slipping away—never quite gone—lost—found—both—

Our younger selves existed on ground as confusing and solid as our own—just as treacherous, just as uncertain—Our kids say it's worse now—I see why they say that—What would you do differently?—What can *we* do?—

As the glacier of time gouged through the limestone—valleys emerged—gullies—cataracts—We thought we were newly hatched but we were latecomers—Our world emerged from water—and from the elders, who were still alive—or still dead—who were themselves latecomers—Everyone, in the end, is a latecomer—

We saw rivers plunging ahead but they changed course—went underground—broke through the surface—We collected instants—We were deep wells of anguish and hope, we were specks of desire—We longed—met—kissed—loved—said farewell—We were smudges of fear half overcome—straining to make out the music of America the indecipherable—one nation undermined—cruel, unpolished, unfinished—

Straining to start up the music again, to add an nth movement, in a different key—

We flamed up together—in a nation on fire—despite the nation—because of the nation—willful together—confused together—smart together—stupid together—

One of the problems smart people have is they don't know when they're not being smart—

We gambled desire against fear—we improvised—thought ourselves over—rethought—stopped thinking—hallucinated—went for broke—broke—There was never enough time—

So, by fits and starts, we felt, thought, mattered, charged, ripped, broke, and tumbled in time—We passed through—We had energy, mass, dimension, momentum, temperature—We were companions—we rejoiced—we collided—waded to the shores of great oceans of pain—imagined a future where we would be young—

The past is over but nevertheless it moves—

Acknowledgments

THANKS FOR HELPFUL READINGS, AND comments along the way, to Arthur Goldhammer, Carla Guelfenbein, William Hartzog, Wendy Roe Hovey, Paul Levine, Vicki Nerenberg, Sarah Xerar Murphy, and Bob Scanlan; and especially to Paul Auster for a meticulous reading that helped me find my way out of a bulkier, clumsier version.

I am also grateful to the following published works that I consulted and learned from:

Vincent J. Genovese, *The Angel of Ashland: Practicing Compassion and Tempting Fate* (Prometheus Books, 2000)

Martha Prescod Norman Noonan, "Captured by the Movement," in Faith S. Holsaert, et al., eds, *Hands on the Freedom Plow: Personal Accounts by Women in SNCC* (University of Illinois Press, 2010)

Arthur M. Eckstein, *Bad Moon Rising: How the Weather Underground Beat the FBI and Lost the Revolution* (Yale University Press, 2016)

An earlier version of some pages appeared as "Rage Against the Machine" in *Smithsonian Magazine*, January 2018.

About the Author

THE AUTHOR OF SIXTEEN BOOKS including works of social analysis, history, fiction, essays, journalism, and poetry, Todd Gitlin was a leader in the American New Left of the 1960s, and contributed (as activist, commentator, and critic) to subsequent social movements. He was a professor at the University of California, Berkeley; New York University; and Columbia University, where he taught graduate and undergraduate classes in journalism, sociology, American studies, and contemporary civilization, and chaired the interdisciplinary Ph. D. program in communications. He was a visiting professor at Yale University, the University of British Columbia, the University of Toronto, l'École des Hautes Études en Sciences Sociales (Paris), l'Université de Neuchâtel (Switzerland), the American University of Cairo, the Higher Institute of Languages (Tunis), and East China Normal University (Shanghai), and lectured in twenty-seven countries. Todd Gitlin passed away on February 5, 2022, while in the midst of the final edits for this novel.

By the Same Author

Uptown: Poor Whites in Chicago (co-author)

Busy Being Born

The Whole World Is Watching: Mass Media in the Making and Unmaking of the New Left

Inside Prime Time

The Sixties: Years of Hope, Days of Rage

The Murder of Albert Einstein

The Twilight of Common Dreams: Why America Is Wracked by Culture Wars

Sacrifice

Media Unlimited: How the Torrent of Images and Sounds Overwhelms Our Lives

Letters to a Young Activist

The Intellectuals and the Flag

The Bulldozer and the Big Tent: Blind Republicans, Lame Democrats, and the Recovery of American Ideals

The Chosen Peoples: America, Israel, and the Ordeals of Divine Election (co-author)

Undying

Occupy Nation: The Roots, the Spirit, and the Promise of Occupy Wall Street